Lyn Andrews was born and raised in Liverpool. The daughter of a policeman, she also married a policeman and, after becoming the mother of triplets, took some years off from her writing whilst she brought up her family. In 1993 Lyn was shortlisted for the Romantic Novelists' Association Award and has now written sixteen hugely popular Liverpool novels. Lyn Andrews still lives in Merseyside.

Take These Broken Wings

Lyn Andrews

headline

First published in hardback in 2000
by HEADLINE BOOK PUBLISHING

First published in paperback in 2000
by HEADLINE BOOK PUBLISHING

20 19 18 17 16 15 14 13 12 11

ISBN 0 7472 5809 0

Typeset by Avon Dataset Ltd, Bidford-on-Avon, Warks

Printed and bound in Great Britain by
Mackays of Chatham plc, Chatham, Kent

HEADLINE BOOK PUBLISHING
A division of the Hodder Headline Group
338 Euston Road
London NW1 3BH

www.headline.co.uk
www.hodderheadline.com

For the real Hannah Peckham, my four-year-old second cousin. May she never have to experience or endure the fate of her fictional counterpart.

For Richenda Todd, who understands the way I work.

And for the entire staff of my publishers – Headline Book Publishing Ltd – who have worked so hard to make my books so successful and available to bookworms from the Outer Hebrides to Australia. My sincere thanks to you all.

Lyn Andrews,
Southport 1998

Prologue

1916

'Will it die, Da?'

George Peckham squatted down so he was on the same level as his little daughter and picked up the injured, terrified blackbird fluttering feebly in Hannah's cupped hands.

'I've never told you a lie, Hannah, have I?'

The child shook her head while slowly stroking the soft, dark feathers.

'I reckon you're old enough for the truth and sometimes the truth can hurt, luv. I'm afraid it *will* die. Look, its wing is broken and if it can't fly then it can't look for food or be with its friends. The ground isn't a safe place for birds.'

'But couldn't we feed it, Da?' There was a catch in her voice and she gazed at him pleadingly.

George sighed and passed the bird back to her. Hannah was so like her mam. At the age of six she was a beauty, just as Jane had been. Fine-boned and petite, she had Jane's pale complexion that looked like alabaster in some lights. Her hair was very dark brown,

1

as were her eyes that were fringed with long thick lashes which cast a half-moon shadow on her cheeks when she was asleep. You could always tell what kind of a mood Hannah was in by her eyes. Sometimes they were full of mischief and laughter, at others hard with determination and stubbornness, but just now her eyes were luminous with tears that threatened to brim over and trickle down her cheeks.

'There'd be no point, luv. Even I can't mend broken wings. Best leave it by the wall, we've a long way to go.' He didn't say it would be kinder to wring the tiny neck and put an end to its misery. Things were bad enough for her without adding to her confusion and unhappiness.

He stood up, brushed the dust from his uniform and looked down Victoria Terrace. It would be the last he'd see of it for a long time, and his spirits plummeted further.

Once the three-storeyed houses had been the very comfortable homes of the well-off. They were smaller than those in Upper Husskinson Street, Upper Frederick Street, Rodney Street or Faulkner Square, but had been well maintained in earlier years. Now, though, they were a sorry sight. The decorative iron railings that led up to the once-impressive front doors were unsteady, twisted and rusting. The glass fanlights above the doors were broken and fly-speckled; the paint was peeling; the steps were worn and broken and now families crowded every room: the cellar, the attic, the bedrooms and the downstairs reception rooms. But number ten had until today been home for himself and Hannah, and just eighteen months ago it had been home for Jane too. Jane, the pretty, shy, quiet little Welsh girl he'd fallen head over heels in love with. The girl he'd married and who had carried and lost two babies before Hannah had been born and had thrived.

Hannah was still clutching the blackbird. He could see there was no way the determined little girl would simply leave it to its fate. 'Oh, well, take it if you must,' he capitulated. 'Hold it gently but firmly.' He slung his kit bag over one shoulder and pulled the cap bearing the badge of the 20th Kings Liverpool Regiment – the Liverpool 'Pals' – slightly forward to shade his eyes. Then he took her hand. The utter dejection and trepidation he felt at having to leave her weighed heavily on him, as did the fear of what faced him now.

Hannah stared up at her father who was dressed in clothes she'd never seen him wear before. They were stiff and scratchy things too.

'Why do I have to go and live with Cousin Gwyneth, Da? Why can't I stay with Mrs Sweeney? Why do you have to go?'

He had already tried to explain these things to her but she didn't really understand. She knew her mam was in heaven. She remembered her mam and had cried for her to come back, for Mam had never shouted or smacked her. Mam had always seemed to be smiling and she'd sung too, in a language Hannah didn't understand, until she got sick and the angels had come to take her to heaven.

3

Da had told her he had to go to a place far away from Liverpool, across the sea, to help with the war, but she didn't understand about war and battles.

'Hannah, luv, I've told you why. I have to go away and Mrs Sweeney's got her hands full with all her kids and there's no room.'

'But Cousin Gwyneth only has a tiny cottage, you said so.'

George sighed. 'I know, but it's not crowded out like Mrs Sweeney's. It's family you're going to. Your mam's family.' He squeezed her hand trying to reassure her but he himself needed reassuring that he *would* come back for her. The war was going badly.

Hannah liked Mrs Sweeney and the young Sweeneys; there were half a dozen of them but the six-year-old twins, Harry and Lily, were her friends, though often they would only play with each other. Hannah held the bird to her and felt its little heart fluttering with fear.

'I'm going to look after it, Da,' she said firmly. 'I'm going to feed it and keep it warm and make it better, then it'll be *my* friend.'

George nodded. If that's what she wanted then he wasn't going to argue. It would die anyway in a couple of days.

When he'd been conscripted despair had overwhelmed him. He'd folded the papers up, placed them on the overmantel and dropped his head into his hands. How could he leave her? She was just six and her mam had only been dead a year and a half. Of course the neighbours had been great, as they always were in times of trouble. Between them they'd nursed Jane and kept the home going when he wasn't there. When he was out at work they'd taken it in turns to look after Hannah. His wage from the small iron foundry down at the docks had been just enough to keep them; now his army pay would all be sent to Cousin Gwyneth for Hannah's keep, apart from a few shillings for his tobacco and Rizla cigarette papers.

Just whom to leave Hannah with had been a hard decision to make. Everyone in the street was short of money and space, even though all the lads and most of the men were away fighting. Some of the girls and women were now taking the jobs the men had left to put a bit more money into their families' pockets, but there were many who were still living in dire poverty – people with as many as fourteen children to feed and clothe. After sitting for hours deciding who would be able to care for Hannah, he'd written to Jane's relations.

He knew Hannah's choice would be to stay with the Sweeneys, and he knew Ada and Tom and their brood would welcome her, but Ada's idea of cleanliness was far from his and there were always rows and fights going on, mainly due to the fact that Tom was fond of his ale, though there was never any violence. Anyway, Tom would be following him to France in a few weeks.

When he'd told Ada of his plans for Hannah's future she'd folded her arms across her bosom and looked concerned. 'What in God's name do yer want to send 'er there for?' she'd asked.

'They're family, Ada, and you've got your hands more than full with this lot.' He'd gestured around the room with his hand. The twins were under the table, a favourite refuge, while their older brother Arthur was tormenting them, trying to get them to come out. Sam and Gerald were arguing over who should have the cricket ball they'd had the stroke of fortune to find and Kate was chanting a poem she had to learn at the top of her voice, totally oblivious to everything.

'Will youse lot shurrup? I can't 'ear me own voice!' Tom roared.

'Gerrout from under that table the pair of youse or yer'll go ter bed,' Ada commanded the two youngest of her brood.

George looked around the room. It was untidy. It always was. There were old ashes and cinders in the hearth. The range was rusty in parts and hadn't seen a blackleading brush for many a month. The top of the table was covered with old, stained newspapers and dirty dishes. There was no curtain of any kind on the back kitchen window and the panes of glass, some of them with cracks across them, were dirty.

'I know you mean well and I know how much you thought of Jane,' George went on.

Ada nodded. 'I loved the bones of that girl, yer know that, George. God 'elp her, dead an' buried at thirty,' she sniffed. Then her attention was diverted by young Harry.

'Harry Sweeney, gerroff that chair before yer fall an' break yer neck!' she yelled at her youngest son who was balancing on a rickety chair and leaning across the top of the range, trying to extricate something from the clutter on the overmantel.

'I know, Ada,' George replied dejectedly.

'While Hannah is alive, poor Jane won't ever be forgot. Hannah's the dead spit of 'er.'

'I know, but she gets her stubbornness from me.'

'Oh, aye, no one will get the better of 'er without a fight. But she's as cute as a bag of monkeys too,' had been Ada's reply. He prayed his daughter's toughness would stand her in good stead now.

It was a long journey, he'd explained that to her. First there was the tram to the Pier Head, then the ferry boat and then an omnibus to Denbigh which her da had told her would take a long, long time. Finally Cousin Gwyneth would be waiting for them with a pony and trap to take her to the little cottage she shared with her mother a mile from the village of Henllan. But it would be just the place for her black-bird. It was quiet now, covered by the folds of her heavy knitted shawl.

All the way there George tried to keep her spirits up by pointing things out to her: New Brighton, with its old fort and lighthouse, as they'd crossed the choppy waters of the Mersey on the ferry; then the fields and woods and all the animals she'd never seen in their natural habitat before. These were things he too had never seen and he doubted he ever would again. Finally she fell asleep and he lifted her gently on to his lap, her shawl still covering the bird, and encircled her in his arms, wishing he could hold her like this for ever.

It was dark as the omnibus came slowly down the hill to Lenten Pool to stop at the Hand pub that stood at the intersection of the roads out to Henllan and to Groes. He was stiff as he got off and looked around, still carrying a sleeping Hannah and his kit bag. With relief he spotted the pony and trap on the other side of the road outside the church.

'Have you been waiting long, Gwyneth?' he asked Jane's second cousin. Already he was feeling apprehensive. Gwyneth Jones's thin face looked as though it had never been creased in a smile. She was dressed plainly but warmly, for the night air was chilly. Her back was ramrod straight and she looked decidedly annoyed.

'I suppose it was the fault of that contraption,' she said, jerking her head in the direction of the bus.

'I suppose it was, but it's a very long journey.'

Gwyneth tutted. 'I had to wait here. No respectable woman would wait outside there.'

She made the pub sound like hell. The whole family had been very religious, he remembered. They'd come to the wedding and had looked thoroughly shocked the entire day.

'I agree it's not the best place,' he said. Hannah had woken up and was looking around in confusion as George set her down. 'She's slept for the last bit of the way.'

'Then I hope she'll not be awake all night. Mam needs *her* sleep.'

8

George passed the small carpet bag, which contained Hannah's clothes and the rag doll Jane had made, up to the woman. His heart was heavy. He was beginning to feel that he'd made the wrong decision.

'Well, then, lift her in. I've to have the trap back by ten. It belongs to Mr Parry, see.'

Hannah looked up at her father. She was wide awake now and she didn't like the look of Cousin Gwyneth at all. Everything was suddenly strange.

'The money is to come regularly?' the woman asked.

'It will. I've sorted everything out and I know she'll be in good hands. You're family.' He crouched down and drew Hannah into the circle of his arms. He'd do anything not to have to leave her. He just prayed the war would be over soon as he pushed her fringe out of her eyes.

'You'll have to go now with Cousin Gwyneth. I have to wait here until I can get a lift from someone going back to Mold. I'll catch another bus there. You be a good girl, work hard at your lessons and help in the house. I'll write to you and you can write back to me.'

Gwyneth sniffed disapprovingly.

George kissed his daughter on the forehead and stroked her cheek. 'Bye, Hannah, remember your da loves you and always will and your mam is looking down on you from heaven.' He choked but fought to keep his voice steady. 'I'll come back for you one day, if I can.'

As Hannah gazed at him mute misery filled her large brown eyes. Then she put her arms around his neck and buried her face in his tunic. 'Bye, Da. I'll say my prayers every night and I'll be good,' she promised, her voice muffled.

George buried his own face in her hair. Having to leave her was tearing him apart inside. He felt as desolate and heartbroken as the day Jane had died. He'd promised then he'd take the best care he could of their daughter, but neither of them had known that the war would separate him from Hannah. Slowly he disentangled himself from her embrace, stood up and lifted her into the trap.

'Thank you, I really do appreciate this. I know Jane would prefer her to be here than in a crowded city while I'm . . . I'm away.'

The hint of a smile lifted the corners of Gwyneth's mouth. 'It's no bother, there's more than enough to keep her occupied.'

Hannah turned around in her seat, her eyes fixed on her da's face as Gwyneth flicked the reins and whip and the pony moved forward. She still held the bird in the folds of her shawl but with her other hand she waved to him.

George's gaze never left the tiny forlorn figure until the trap was swallowed up in the darkness, then he turned and walked towards the pub. He had a long night ahead of him.

Awkwardly George made his way down the trench; it was still ankle deep in water. The warmer days had made no difference except to the lice and fleas that were more active and added to the dire conditions.

War wasn't 'glorious' at all. It was hell on earth. When he'd first arrived at the front he had not been able to believe what he saw. It was like living on another planet – one whose surface was pitted by deep craters full of water. There wasn't a shrub nor a single flower. There wasn't even a tree, just twisted, blackened trunks that stood like rotting teeth, and line after line of subterranean trenches, also filled with foul-smelling water contaminated by sewage and by the bloated and rotting bodies. When he'd asked why they hadn't been given a decent burial he'd been told that there was hardly anyone left to bury them and finding a decent plot of land to lay them to rest was deemed impossible. The heavy artillery was always blasting the shallow graves of both sides, although not on purpose. Skeletons were tossed into the air and disintegrated, falling as a shower of skulls and bones across trenches and dugouts. There was no pity in this war, George soon found. No peace even after burial. No dignity even in death.

Towards the middle of May reinforcements had arrived and the battalion was taken out of the line. It was with relief that he'd made his way down the communication trenches and then on to Albert and a proper billet. He'd been overjoyed to see Tom Sweeney on his way to the front line for the first time.

Tom already looked pale and drawn. 'God Almighty, George! What the hell have we come to!'

'Just that, Tom, hell is what it looks like and hell is what it is. You get used to it. You have to. Got any fags?'

Tom had passed a packet of Wills Woodbines to him.

'What's the casualty rate?' he'd asked, drawing deeply on his own cigarette.

'Well, it's not what they print in the bloody newspapers.'

'Christ, that's bad enough!'

'We'll both be lucky to come through in one piece, Tom, and so will all the rest of the lads.' He'd held out his hand and Tom had shaken it. 'Good luck, mate,' he'd added. 'Maybe you'll get lucky and catch a bullet in your leg or arm and get invalided home. It's the best anyone can hope for. I even heard a bloke shot himself in the foot, he just couldn't take any more.' And with that he'd slapped Tom on the shoulder and moved away. He hadn't heard anything more about Tom Sweeney.

Now he stood on the fire step, then it would be the scaling ladder, the parapet and then no man's land. The bombardment by the eight-inch Howitzers and six-inch Mark VIIs had gone on for a week, day and night; his ears were ringing, his nerves almost ready to snap. It was something big, they all knew that. The 'big push', and the enemy must know it too. Out there were – he hoped – demolished German trenches and artillery and wide swathes cut in the wire. The dreaded bloody wire. Whenever he managed to get some sleep his dreams were always punctuated by the screams, the sobbing, the pleading that came from wounded men strung out on the wire, unable to help themselves, bleeding to a slow, agonising death. He'd seen Lieutenant Marsden take a rifle one night and slowly and deliberately shoot four men. In all their eyes, it wasn't murder, it was mercy killing, but Marsden had been court martialled and executed. There had been a lot of anger in the battalion about it. The bloody generals didn't have to tolerate the appalling conditions or have their sleep disturbed by pitiful screams.

At last the dawn light filtered through the clouds of smoke and the whistle blew. There was no time now for thinking or even praying. Their objective was the Glatz Redoubt south of the German-held village of Montauban and today was the first of a new month, July. With red-hot shrapnel bursting all around him and the cries of men who had been hit, he began to run. They'd been ordered to walk but he for one didn't obey that order. He managed to get through a gap in the first line of wire and then he felt a burning sensation in his leg and he fell forward as a hail of shrapnel embedded itself in his chest. Splayed out on the wire that the artillery hadn't managed to cut, he fought for his breath but it was hard, so hard and the sounds of battle were fading and it was growing dark. With his last breath and shred of awareness he managed to gasp out one word before the blood that filled his lungs gushed from his mouth. *Hannah!*

Hannah turned on her back and looked up at the ceiling. It wasn't even dark yet. The days were very long in summer. Hannah had a little narrow bed of her own, tucked in the corner of the cottage's single bedroom where the eaves of the roof sloped down. She lay listening to the muffled voices that drifted up the stairwell. She couldn't understand what they were saying as they spoke in Welsh, but over the weeks she'd picked up a few words of her mother's native tongue and she always knew when she was being talked about.

She didn't like either of them. Great-Aunt Margaret, as she'd been told to call her, sat in a rocking chair by the open fire with shawls wrapped around her even when the weather was warm. She frightened Hannah with her wizened face, her white hair pulled back in a knot and her small black beady eyes. She hardly spoke to Hannah but had Cousin Gwyneth dancing attendance on her day and night. Her cousin was always sharp with Hannah and often cross, scolding her for things she knew nothing about. She was a child of the city, not the country, and she found it hard to get used to their strange ways and to the silence and darkness. She'd cried the day her little blackbird had died and she'd wanted to bury it in a small box, but she'd been told not to be so nonsensical. It had only been a bird. She'd felt even more lonely then.

The cottage stood on its own at the far end of a field from which the square bell tower, strangely detached from the church, could be seen above the trees. They never went to church, instead they attended the Chapel, Capel Seion, in the village. Three times on a Sunday she and Cousin Gwyneth walked there and back while Mr Parry took Great-Aunt Margaret in the trap.

When she'd first arrived here there'd been nothing to see, it had been so dark and she'd been so tired that she'd slept until morning. Then when she'd woken she'd remembered that she wasn't in Victoria Terrace any more and her da had gone away. The tiny place, she'd discovered, only had one main room downstairs and a small, dark scullery. The stone walls were thick and a big fireplace took up almost the whole of one wall. There was a sofa, the rocking chair, a stool, a folding table and four straight-backed chairs. There was no gaslight, they relied on oil lamps and candles and the firelight. Whenever she could she would sit on the floor by the fire nursing her doll and looking into the fire, seeing clouds, and castles, and houses, and patterns in the flames. Her daily routine was strict and she was never allowed to play. She rose at sunrise, washed in the bowl on the washstand with water she'd fetched from a nearby stream the previous evening. She made her bed and helped to make the big brass one that Cousin Gwyneth and Great-Aunt Margaret shared after the old lady had gone downstairs. Then it was breakfast, usually an egg and a piece of bread. Then she walked the mile and a half to school. She hated school. Because she couldn't speak their language, and the lessons were mainly in Welsh, the other children mocked and jeered at her. She would tell her da all about it when she wrote to him, which she'd only done once. Cousin Gwyneth said it was extravagant to use more paper, envelopes and stamps. Saturdays were spent in helping to clean the whole house and weeding and hoeing the lines of vegetables that were growing in the plot of land behind the cottage.

She hated Sundays. Apart from going to Chapel she was allowed only to sit still without speaking unless spoken to and read the Bible. There was only one meal, before they went to Chapel for the last time. Oh, how she wished her da would come back soon.

She was startled to see her cousin come into the room in her nightdress with her long hair falling in a plait down her back.

'Is there something wrong?' she asked, timidly sitting up.

'There is. Get up and get dressed, Hannah.'

'Now? It's . . . it's not morning.'

'Of course it's not morning. Do as you're told.'

Hannah got up and hastily dragged on her clothes. Gwyneth looked very cross indeed, her pale face unusually flushed.

When she got downstairs she avoided looking at the old woman and sat down on the edge of the sofa. Something was very wrong, she could tell that from the way the two women looked at each other and then at her.

'Tell her,' the old woman said.

'What . . . what have you got to tell me?' she asked quietly.

Her cousin took a small folded piece of paper from the shelf over the fireplace and bit her lip.

'Tell her, Gwyneth,' the old lady demanded.

'It's from a big office. A place in London, Hannah.

Your da was killed two days ago in a big battle. Mr Roberts from the Post Office brought this telegram.'

Hannah stared at her in disbelief. No! No! He was going to come back for her. He'd said he'd come back. Then she remembered that he'd added 'if he could'. Now they were saying that he'd never come back for her. That she'd never see him again! The tears welled up and brimmed over and she threw herself at Gwyneth, clutching her nightdress, burying her face in the folds of cotton.

'Hush now, hush.' Gwyneth tried to soothe her. The child had been a burden from the time she'd arrived. She had made life even more difficult and she'd had no patience with her at all. Gwyneth had only seen Hannah's father twice. She barely remembered her only meeting with Jane, who with her parents – long dead now – had gone to the city to find work, and Mr Roberts had said that hundreds and hundreds of men – maybe even thousands – had been killed fighting near a river called the Somme. He'd said it was a terrible, terrible tragedy and it would affect every city, town and village in the land. This wasn't the first telegram he'd had to deliver, there had been three more and in a village so small it just showed how bad things were. The child would have to realise she wasn't the only one suffering.

Gwyneth disentangled Hannah's hands from her nightdress. 'Stop that now, Hannah! Dry your eyes and go up and wash your face.'

In a numbed trance Hannah did as she was told and

soon her cousin came up to her and began to get herself dressed. When she'd finished she took Hannah's clothes from the drawer in the chest and put them all in the carpet bag. Hannah was even more confused.

'Come on, Hannah!' Gwyneth said sharply.

'Where . . . where are we going?'

'Into town.'

'To town, now?'

'You can't stay here. I've enough on my hands looking after Mam and this place and besides there'll be no more money.'

'We . . . we're going to . . . to Denbigh?' Everything in her world was topsy-turvy now.

'I just said so. Mr Parry will take us. You'll live in the big place they have there for boys and girls who have no Mam or Da.'

Hannah just stared at her in disbelief. She had no Mam and Da. She wouldn't have a home, except the place they were going to take her to.

'Don't sit there looking like that, Hannah Peckham. It's not my fault you've to go there. I have to do what's best for Mam.'

Slowly Hannah got to her feet. She was frightened to leave this room. Frightened of the world outside, for out there now there was no one who loved her.

PART I

Chapter One

1926

Hannah stood outside the door to Mrs Phillips's office, filled with apprehension. She pushed a few strands of dark hair back under the white old-fashioned mob-cap she wore and rolled down the sleeves of the dark blue dress. What had she done now to bring down on her head the wrath of the matron of the workhouse? She'd stood here so many times before, almost daily when she'd been left here ten years ago by Cousin Gwyneth and a grim-faced, disapproving Mr Parry – a charitable man. It had been so hard for her then. In a matter of weeks her whole world had collapsed and she'd been terrified, not knowing what would happen next. It was no wonder she'd screamed, kicked and bitten half the staff, and after each outburst she'd been beaten and left to sob on the hard bed in the long, cold dormitory. She'd often wet the mattress which resulted in another beating and then she'd had to strip the bed and wash the coarse sheets herself, as young as she'd been, her little arms and shoulders aching with the effort.

She sighed at the memories, knocked gently and

waited to be called in. When the command came she opened the door, entered, and closed the door behind her. This room never changed, although neither had any other one, she thought. The walls were painted dark green as was the door, the window frame and picture rail, although there were no such frivolous things as pictures hanging from it. The walls were all bare. The floor was wood, polished daily by one of the older women, who was destitute like herself. The room was like a cell, she thought, and the metal grille over the window added to the illusion. Matron's desk was a big, solid one that took up most of the space, with its heavy carved legs and feet. Oh, how often had she fixed her gaze on those claw-like feet waiting to hear what her punishment would be this time. There was a clock on the wall which ticked loudly, though maybe it just sounded louder in the silence.

'Unusually, I have summoned you here for a reason other than punishment.' Matron was small, plump, and fresh-cheeked. She looked pleasant enough, until you got to know her, Hannah thought. She'd made that mistake the first time she'd seen her in this very room when her cousin had explained the situation, handed over the telegram and carpet bag and left. She'd started to cry and that's when she'd had her first taste of what the life ahead of her would bring. She'd been shouted at and slapped, which had only made matters worse.

Hannah's eyes remained downcast. She hated this woman almost as much as she hated Cousin Gwyneth.

Matron toyed with the letter in front of her. Hannah

Peckham looked demure and submissive but in reality the woman knew she was neither. In a second her mood could change. Her dark eyes would flash with anger, her cheeks redden with temper and when she'd been younger she would physically attack whichever person in authority had attempted to chastise her. No, she'd never really broken the spirit of the girl who stood before her now. But even she had to admit that, despite the traits of rebelliousness, obstinacy and insolence, Hannah Peckham had grown into a beautiful young woman. Her dark hair was scraped back and plaited but that didn't detract at all from the small even features and almost translucent skin. Thick dark lashes fringed her large brown eyes, as liquid as a deer's. Even the drab shapeless dress the inmates wore couldn't disguise a small waist and gently curving breasts: the very things that needed to be hidden.

'Do you not wish to know why?'

'Yes, ma'am,' Hannah said quietly. From experience she knew it did no good at all to raise your voice or even look Matron straight in the eye.

'I have had a letter from a Captain Beresford, who apparently was Chaplain to your father's battalion.'

Hannah looked up but Matron was concentrating on the letter.

'He says he made a sacred vow to God to make it his duty to find the relatives of every man who died and make sure they are well and have gainful employment, where applicable.' She pursed her lips. She was Chapel and had no time at all for, in her opinion, the misguided and lax tenets of the Anglican religion. The man was also very formal in his wording of the letter: 'where applicable' indeed! 'He has had great trouble finding you and is very distressed to learn that you have spent all this time in a workhouse.'

Hannah's heart began to beat a little faster. Was it really possible that someone cared? Someone cared enough to spend years looking for her?

'So, Peckham, you are to leave us,' Matron said in a brisk, businesslike tone. She paused again. Surely it hadn't been· *that* difficult to find the girl. Someone in the street where she'd lived would have told him she'd gone to live with relatives, mercenary ones as it turned out. She had no time for people like Gwyneth Jones who only cared about that root of all evil – money. As soon as that woman had received the news of Hannah's father's death she'd deduced that there would be no more money forthcoming and had abandoned the child to the Parish, which then had to bear the cost of keeping her. She glanced at the other letter. 'He has found you a position in service in a house in Liverpool. A scullery maid, if you are found suitable. He asks for my opinion on that. Well, you are capable of scrubbing floors. The household is not big. There are few servants. You will live in, but do not expect any luxuries.'

Hannah looked down at the woman in total disbelief. 'I'm to go . . . to have a job . . . and live in?'

'Isn't that just what I've told you? Are you a parrot, girl?'

'No, ma'am, I'm sorry, I'm so . . .' She spread her

hands wide. 'When . . . when do I go, ma'am?'

'When this revolutionary Bolshevik nonsense is over and done with. The country is verging on anarchy. The good Lord alone knows where it will end. A general strike, would you believe! There is Satan's hand in it.'

Hannah knew nothing about this. The women and girls, separated from the men and boys, only rarely left the confines of the workhouse. What was a strike?

'Can I ask who . . . who I'm to work for and where, please, ma'am?'

Matron drew another letter towards her. 'A family going by the name of Hughes. A respectable, God-fearing Welsh family, so I am led to believe. They live in Faulkner Square. Do you know of this place?'

'Yes, ma'am.' Hannah had only a very vague memory of the big houses that surrounded the pleasant squares but she could hardly contain herself. Her pale cheeks were flushed and her eyes sparkled. Matron thought again how lovely she looked – and she knew those looks could be her downfall.

'I should warn you, Peckham, that there are two young men in the household. Should they so demean themselves as to pay any attention to you, I hope you will remember your Christian upbringing in this establishment.'

'I will, ma'am. I really will.' She didn't know what Matron meant but forgot her puzzlement as excitement and relief coursed through her.

'You may go. Continue with your work. I will inform you when you are to leave.'

'Thank you. Thank you so much, ma'am,' Hannah said with a note of pure joy in her voice that did not go unnoticed by the older woman. Well, at least the girl wouldn't be her responsibility for much longer. She hoped this family could keep the girl firmly in her place and not allow any vanity, self-importance or insolence to be tolerated. She herself had had to try to beat such vices from her character for ten years. She wouldn't be sorry to see her leave – for ever.

Hannah went back to work in the laundry, her hands shaking, her eyes bright. She was leaving! She was going back to Liverpool!

She had worked in the laundry ever since she'd come here. Not only the workhouse washing was done there; they took dirty linen from the hospital and the asylum and even private households. The washing room was a gloomy, cavernous place. Around the walls were lines of huge copper boilers from which steam belched all day, sometimes making it hard to see properly, especially on dark winter afternoons. It was hard, back-breaking work feeding the soiled linen into the boilers, stirring the bubbling, steaming water constantly with wooden tongs and then heaving it out and into the long wooden rinsing troughs where it was pummelled and lifted in and out of a constant stream of cold water. She'd been scalded a few times but she had been lucky. There had been some terrible accidents which had resulted in girls being taken screaming in agony to Denbigh Infirmary.

'What did she want you for, Hannah?' little Jessie Williams yelled, struggling with heavy dripping sheets.

Hannah smiled at her. They'd been friends for years. Special friends, and Hannah had always stood up for Jessie when she was in trouble with Annie Pritchard, the inmate who supervised them. Jessie's mousy-brown hair fell in damp strands around her ears and her grey eyes seemed enormous in her thin pallid face.

'I'll tell you later, Jessie,' Hannah shouted back, rolling up her sleeves once more and reaching for the long-handled tongs. Now the work didn't seem hard at all. She couldn't believe it. She had become resigned to the fact that she would probably never leave this place. A few of the girls did go out to work, but only at harvest time to help in the fields. She never had, though; she'd always been considered too rebellious and outspoken. Poor Jessie had not been thought strong enough.

When the fires beneath the boilers had been allowed to die, the day's washing transferred to the drying room, the floor mopped, and the tools put away, the girls filed from the room in silence under the watchful, malevolent eye of Annie Pritchard who disliked both Hannah and Jessie, mainly because of their close friendship. No one liked Annie.

As they washed and tidied their hair, Jessie whispered to Hannah, 'Now will you tell me, Hannah? I'll go mad with waiting, *cariad*!'

'Someone wrote to Matron. A minister, he's been trying to find me.'

Jessie's eyes widened. 'What for?'

'To see if I was being taken care of after my da was killed. Oh, Jessie, I'm so excited! I can't believe it! I can't believe *anyone* would care about me!'

'No talking, Peckham, you know the rules. Will I have to report you – *again*?' Annie called out from further down the room. She had not been informed of the reason for the visit to Matron – which was unusual – but she certainly wasn't going to ask the girl and thereby show her curiosity. Hannah grimaced. Now she would have to wait again until after supper.

Supper, like everything else, was depressing. It was served in the big room called the refectory. Again, all the paintwork was dark green; the windows were small and set high up in the wall. They sat at long trestle tables on hard wooden benches. The inmates served the food on a rota basis. Grace was said and then the plates and bowls were passed out by three of the older women. There was a watery soup, a plate of vegetables with a meagre amount of fatty meat, a slice of bread and a cup of weak tea without sugar. All eaten in silence.

Then came the only part of the day where inmates had what was loosely called Conversation Time, although their hands were never idle. There was always sewing or darning to be done.

'Hannah, what's happened?' Jessie asked. She always sat next to Hannah if possible, but sometimes when Annie was being really spiteful they had to sit at opposite ends of the room.

'I'm leaving here! I'm going back to Liverpool, Jessie! Into service in a big house facing a little square of park, closed in by railings. This man, this minister has found me a job. It's with a family called Hughes. They're Welsh and there are two sons, that's all she'd tell me. Oh, and I'm to be a scullery maid.' Hannah's face was full of animation. 'I must get a day or half a day off, so I'll be able to go back to Victoria Terrace and see everyone there. All the people I knew when I was little, before Mam died and Da was killed! Oh, Jessie, I thought I'd never get out of here!'

Jessie was stricken, and looked at her with something akin to horror. 'Oh, Hannah! What'll I do? *I'll* never get out of here and I'll miss you so much!'

Hannah's excitement died. All afternoon the only thing she'd thought about was herself and leaving this place. She'd forgotten she'd have to leave Jessie behind. She'd forgotten her friend entirely.

'Oh, Jessie, I'm sorry, I am. I never stopped to think. Maybe they'll find you somewhere. Someone might come along, you never know.'

Jessie shook her head sadly. 'No, they won't, Hannah. There is no one, no one at all. I'll be here all my life. No one wants a cripple, see.'

Hannah looked down at her own feet encased in the hard-wearing but heavy boots. Poor Jessie had been born with a deformed foot and limped badly. Some days she said her back hurt too but she'd been told she would just have to put up with it. It was all to do with the way she walked.

Hannah put down her mending and took her friend's hand. 'Oh, Jessie.' They'd been through everything together. 'Look, when I get there I'll ask if there's something for you. Even if there's no job there, there are other rich families around that part of Liverpool. It won't matter about your foot if you're a scullery maid. I'll keep on asking until I find you something.'

Jessie looked at her earnestly. 'Will you, Hannah? Will you really do that for me?'

Hannah nodded firmly.

'But are you sure they won't mind about my foot?'

'You're on your feet all day here, aren't you? And you'll spend a lot of time on your knees, as I will.'

'But they don't mind here, I don't get paid, see.'

'Oh, let's look on the bright side, Jessie. I'm sure *someone* will want you.'

Jessie returned her smile as some of her concern left her. 'When will you go?'

'I don't know. Matron said there's a lot of trouble there. Strikes and revolutionaries. I don't know what they are but I can't go until they are all over.'

Annie had overheard. 'Then you'll be weeks here. Strikes are wicked. Men won't work unless they get more money. They stay at home or go to public houses and get drunk and fight all day. Why should anyone give them more money when they won't work and then waste it like that?' Annie was at her most vindictive.

'How do you know all that?' Hannah challenged. Now that the end of her time here was in sight she couldn't and wouldn't try to hide her feelings any longer. She despised the woman.

'Because Aled Davies told me, see. He's been out working and he heard all about it.'

'And when did you speak to him, Annie? You know it's not allowed. I could go to Matron and tell her.'

Annie's cheeks flushed with anger. 'Never you mind, Hannah Peckham. It'll be good riddance to you.'

'And to you, Annie!' Hannah shot back, glaring at the woman, defying her to take the matter any further. Angrily Annie walked away.

'Oh Hannah, she'll really have it in for me now. Well, for both of us but at least you know you'll not have a long time to wait until you leave.'

Hannah squeezed Jessie's hand. 'I promise you, Jessie, I'll get you out of here. I really mean it!'

She did mean it, she told herself. Poor Jessie's life was bad enough without being left to the mercy of Annie Pritchard and Mrs Phillips with no one to look out for her.

Chapter Two

When Hannah walked out of the gates of the yard that surrounded the workhouse for the last time it was Friday 14 May and the warm sun beat down on her. She lifted her face towards its bright rays and breathed deeply.

The day had come at last. The air around her was no longer permeated by the smells of the workhouse: disinfectant; stale cooking; the rancid stench of dirty, blood-soiled linen; illness; decaying flesh and death. Now she could smell new-mown hay as a heavily laden cart rumbled past, cattle on their way to market, and the pink and white blossom on the hawthorns that lined the lane towards the open countryside.

The waiting had been interminably long. The general strike which had started on 4 May was not ended until the 12th. It had been a long week for everyone, not just Hannah. The army had been brought in and the strike, which had started with the miners but had escalated to include all men and unions within the TUC, had been bitter. In many quarters it had not been viewed with sympathy or even tolerance.

Hannah knew almost nothing of this as she walked on, carrying the old carpet bag which contained so little that it would have been easier to have put her belongings in a parcel. She wore a plain blue cotton dress that came to her ankles. On her head was a cheap straw boater which at least kept the sun off her face. The feeling of excitement and freedom grew as she walked towards town and the omnibus that would take her back to Birkenhead. Then she'd get the ferry and she'd see again the waterfront which was so dear to her heart. It was as if she were an emigrant returning home. She didn't care how dirty, how soot-blackened and crowded Liverpool was. It was home.

Jessie had been in tears the previous evening as they'd said their goodbyes. 'Oh, Hannah, I'm going to miss you so much.' Jessie would be hard at work when Hannah was to leave. She'd not asked if she could have permission to go to see her off. It was useless: it would be denied. Annie would make sure of that.

'And I'll miss you, Jessie,' Hannah had comforted her. 'I'll write, I promise, but don't get upset if you don't get my letters, you know what they're like. They know my handwriting and they'd see the postmark. The best we can hope for is that they'll open them and then give them to you. I *won't* forget you, Jessie, or my promise.' She'd squeezed her friend's hand.

'I know you won't. You're the nicest person in the world, Hannah, never mind just in here. You're the best friend anyone could have.'

'If I find you somewhere and they don't send you, I'll come and fetch you. You're a good worker, you're neat and clean and you deserve something better in your life, Jessie.'

34

She thought of Jessie as she stood outside the Hand in Lenten Pool waiting for the bus to arrive. She'd meant what she'd said to her. She and Jessie were so close. How could she forget her? She still couldn't believe she was out. Really out. Out in the world again without fears of beatings and punishments, humiliation and hurt. She would live in a house. A proper house, with a family, not an institution with inmates. She would have decent food and some of the comforts that had been denied her for so long. Life in the workhouse was so hard, unrelenting and depressing. Oh, she was hot now and her dress was starting to stick to her, but she didn't mind. She would suffer anything, anything at all because she was going home.

When the bus arrived and the passengers alighted, the driver went into the pub to slake his thirst and have something to eat. It would be an hour at least before he would climb back aboard and into the driving seat. Hannah didn't wait sitting on the low wall like the handful of other passengers that had arrived. She got on immediately. Not until the vehicle had moved off, gone up the hill, down the other side and out on to the country road would she really believe her good fortune in leaving this place.

The sun was starting to slip down in the sky when, hot, hungry, thirsty and stiff, she got off and walked towards the ferry terminal. Not far now, she thought. The breeze smelled of salt, a smell so dear that she didn't mind how dirty the waters of the Mersey were. She paid her fare and as soon as the gangway was lowered she was one of the first aboard. She stood on the top deck, clutching the rail tightly, and watched as the familiar trio of buildings drew nearer and nearer. Soon she would set foot in her native city for the first time in ten years. When the ferry eventually tied up, there were tears on her cheeks.

On the tram she looked at every person with interest, noticing the short hair and the short skirts of the girls and young women. Only the middle-aged and older women seemed to have stuck to long skirts and long hair. She felt dowdy and plain. Her hair was still plaited, the blue ankle-length dress was creased and damp under the arms. Her old-fashioned boots were heavy and hideous, she thought as she looked down at them. She particularly envied the pretty shoes the girls wore. They had little heels shaped like an hourglass, pointed toes and a thin strap over the instep, and they were in lovely colours too, not just brown or black. She promised herself that one day she'd have not one, but three or even four pairs of shoes like that.

She had to ask a tram driver the way, as her memory was hazy. After all, she had been only six when she left.

As she walked up Upper Parliament Street she wondered how she would be greeted. With suspicion and coldness? She'd come from a workhouse, after all, and it was only because that minister had asked them that they'd agreed to take her on. She gazed fondly at the little park with its greenery and flowers fenced in by black wrought-iron railings. Only the people who lived in the adjacent houses had keys for the gate. The houses were like those in Victoria Terrace but bigger and, of course, well maintained. The glass in the fanlights gleamed, the paintwork was fresh and glossy, the steps clean; there was even a boot-scraper on the top step. She stood and looked around wondering whether she should go to the front door. There didn't seem to be any side entrances but then she remembered the alleyway at the back. It wasn't like the jiggers in Victoria Terrace. It was wide: wide enough for a horse and carriage or a motor car to be driven down it.

She counted the houses until she came to number ten, then she opened the back gate slowly. She was surprised to see a garden and outbuildings. She'd never known that these houses had gardens. There was a small, well-tended lawn in the centre of which was a small pillar flattened at the top – she was to learn later that it was a bird bath. Variegated shrubs and two laurel bushes grew against the wall and there were flowers in huge pots near to the glass french doors which led on to the garden. She followed a little narrow path bounded by the outbuildings that led to the house. On the wall was the notice 'Tradesmen Only. No Hawkers or Vendors'.

Her weariness had gone. She felt very nervous. She knocked on the back door and waited. What were these people going to be like? *Would* they despise her because she'd come from the workhouse? Would she prove to be satisfactory?

The door was opened by a young woman in her late teens dressed in the black frock with white collar and cuffs that was the dress of maidservants everywhere. She wore a white apron and over her short hair she wore a small stiffened cap.

'I . . . I'm Hannah Peckham. I was told to come to see a Mrs Howard.'

The maid looked her up and down. 'You'd better come in then. I'm Rowan. I'm the tweeny.'

Hannah didn't like to ask just what a 'tweeny' was but she smiled and followed the girl through two small, dark, cool rooms, along a narrow and rather chilly corridor and then into a large cheerful kitchen. It smelled of cakes baking, and of bread, freshly made. There were two other people there, a large, plump but capable-looking woman and a lad she judged to be the same age as herself. She felt so terribly self-conscious in her awful travel-stained dress.

'She's been sent here to see you, Mrs Howard,' Rowan informed them.

Hannah blushed under their scrutiny.

Mrs Howard got up from her chair. 'So, you're my new kitchen maid? I hope you're better than the last one they sent me. That's what comes of getting girls through an agency! I said so at the time but I was ignored. All these new-fangled ideas. I can't be doing with them.'

'Oh, I'll be much better, ma'am! I'm used to hard work.'

'You've come from a workhouse?'

Hannah nodded. 'But I was born and lived in Liverpool until I was six. My mam died and my da was killed at the Somme.' That was a word she'd memorised. 'I went to live with a cousin in Wales.'

'So what happened to her? Did she die?'

'No, ma'am. When we got the news about my da she took me to the workhouse and left me there. There would be no more money from my da, you see.'

All three of them exchanged glances. Those of the cook and the maid were sympathetic.

'Oh, that's very Christian, ain't it?' the lad remarked.

'That's enough from you, Blandford. Mr Thomas wants the motor car out after dinner. He wants it all clean and shining too,' Mrs Howard informed him.

'I'm Bertie Blandford, the sort of odd-job chap. I can turn my hand to most things.'

'Aye, and your tongue will get you hung,' Mrs Howard remarked scathingly. She turned again to Hannah. 'How long is it since you've eaten or had a drink?'

'A long, long time, ma'am. I was given just enough money for my fare.'

The woman tutted and raised her eyebrows. She'd been informed by Miss Siân that the Reverend Beresford had found a girl in desperate straits and so she was to come and live and work here. She'd been sceptical, wondering what type of girl she'd be, but she'd taken an instant liking to Hannah.

'Well, sit down there and I'll give you some cold veal and ham pie and then you, me and Rowan will have a cup of tea.' She silenced the words of complaint on the lad's lips with a quelling look. 'You can have yours later, Blandford, when the car has been cleaned. And the only person in this household that you call "ma'am" is Miss Siân. You call me Mrs Howard and Rowan just that. You'll also be called just "Peckham". Have you got a change of clothes? You look very dusty and grubby.'

'No, Mrs Howard. I've just got a nightdress and some . . . unmentionables in my bag.'

Mrs Howard and Rowan exchanged glances again. It was a long time since either of them had heard of underwear being called 'unmentionables', but that was the workhouses for you. Fifty years behind the times, grim and desperate.

'I'll take you up to your room. You can have a bit of a wash there,' Rowan offered kindly. She didn't have many friends and although she was obviously shy and nervous, Hannah was nearer her own age than Mrs Howard's.

'A room! A room for just me?' Hannah was astounded.

'It's right up in the attic. It's freezing in winter and stifling in summer.' Rowan didn't think it was anything to get excited about. It was the worst room in the house.

'But . . . but it's just for me?'

'God, you sound like a parrot. Come on.'

Hannah was led up the back stairs, across a wide carpeted landing and up another flight of narrow stairs to a door that opened to reveal a small room that reminded her of the bedroom she'd shared in Henllan. It had a skylight window, a single bed, a chest and a washstand with a jug and bowl set. She looked around in pure astonishment. Oh, it was like a dream. She didn't care how small or hot or cold it was. It was *hers*! She could shut the door on the world. There was a lump in her throat and tears in her eyes.

'So you haven't got anything?' the other girl asked.

'No. Just a nightdress, two pairs of drawers and a chemise. Oh, and a pair of stockings.'

The other girl shook her head. 'I'll go and find something for you. That dress is terrible.'

'I know – and I . . . I . . . must smell. It was so hot on the bus.'

'Put your things in the drawers while I fetch an old dress of mine.'

Rowan returned in a few minutes with a short pink and white striped cotton dress. It was faded but Hannah didn't care. It was more like the dresses the young girls wore. Oh, it was such luxury to wash the grime and dust of travel away. She slipped the dress over her head and with some difficulty fastened up the buttons down the back. Then she undid her hair from its plait and combed it out but she had no clips or hair pins so she tied it back loosely with the belt of the blue dress. There was so much she didn't know. So many things she didn't possess.

When she returned to the kitchen it was to find a teapot, milk jug, sugar basin and three plain blue cups and saucers on the table, which was covered by a checked cloth. On a large plate was a slice of cold meat pie with some boiled potatoes and on a side plate a large slice of cake.

'Why, you're a lovely-looking girl,' Mrs Howard said.

Hannah blushed. 'I look and feel better now.'

'You'll have to have that hair pinned up or cut and wear a cap over it. It's not hygienic working in a kitchen.'

'I . . . I haven't got any pins, just a comb. No brush even nor any working clothes.'

'God Almighty! They must be living in the dark ages out there. No brush or pins or work dresses! How do they expect you to manage? Here, sit down and eat this and Rowan and I will sort things out.'

'I think we'll have to go to Miss Siân. Especially about work clothes.'

Mrs Howard nodded. 'Did they tell you how much you were to be paid and about your days off?'

'You mean I'm going to be paid? Have money of my own?'

'Of course you are.'

'I thought . . . I thought being kept was all I should expect. I was just glad of that.'

'Well it's not. Four guineas a month is the wage. You'll have one Sunday a month off – after church. Rowan has Wednesday afternoons off, so you can have your half-day on Thursdays. You'll have to pay for your own work clothes, they'll be provided and you can pay them off at five shillings a month.'

Hannah pressed her hands to her burning cheeks.

42

Four guineas! Four pounds and four shillings all for herself. Oh, what couldn't she buy with all that! The words of gratitude stuck in her throat and tears of happiness and relief trickled down her cheeks. Oh, her mam and da *must* be looking out for her.

'Thank ... thank you,' she managed to get out before breaking down completely.

Rowan put an arm around her shoulders and gave her a handkerchief.

'God, but it must be desperate to be in a workhouse.'

Mrs Howard nodded her agreement. 'We'll have to keep her out of sight of some people in this house,' she said sharply.

Hannah was far too upset to listen or understand.

'Come on, blow your nose and eat your supper. Mrs Howard's pies are the best in the entire city and you'll feel better after that and a good night's sleep.' Rowan smiled. 'Even in that cubby-hole under the eaves.'

Chapter Three

At first Hannah had found the tiny room as stuffy as
Rowan had predicted. There was, however, a glass
skylight in the sloping roof, so she'd dragged the
washstand across the room until it was directly underneath the window, climbed on top of it and, with some
effort, had managed to open it. The cool evening breeze
felt good on her cheeks. She'd washed herself all over,
brushed out her hair, slipped on her nightdress and
lain on top of the bed. There, wide awake, she stared at
the ceiling thinking back to that terrible night when
Cousin Gwyneth had taken her to the workhouse. This
room was so different to that terrible place. 'Thank
you, Da, thank you, Mam, thank you, God,' she said
softly.

She should have been exhausted by the travelling
and the heat, but the events of this momentous day
kept her mind racing and sleep eluded her. She still
couldn't believe just how lucky she was. All this and
money of her own.

She and Rowan had washed up the few dishes and
then laid out the breakfast tray for Miss Siân, who
apparently didn't rise early being of a rather 'frail
disposition, God luv her', so Mrs Howard had explained. Mr Hughes and his two sons breakfasted at

eight a.m. sharp as the two young men had busy days. Mr Thomas worked with his father in the shipping offices of the Union Castle Line of which Mr Hughes senior was a director. Mr Richard had his studies – he was destined to become a doctor then, hopefully, a consultant orthopaedic surgeon. He was a very clever young man, always had been, so Mrs Howard had informed her.

'I'll go and see Miss Siân myself before she goes to bed. You'll have to be sorted out, Peckham.'

So Rowan lent her a hairbrush and pins and helped Hannah to wash the old blue dress. They'd put it through the mangle twice and then hung it out to dry.

'It'll be dry come morning and you can use it as a work dress.'

'Thanks. Everyone is being very kind to me. No one else in my life – well, not since I was six – has ever had much time for me.'

Rowan had shaken her head sadly at that, then they'd both said 'goodnight' to Mrs Howard and had gone to their rooms.

Suddenly Hannah remembered Jessie and some of her euphoria slipped away. Oh, poor Jessie. What was she thinking now, this very minute, as she lay in her bed in that horrible dormitory? Hannah sighed. It was far too soon to ask about Jessie. She'd yet to meet Miss Siân who seemed to be in charge of household affairs. She may not take kindly to taking another girl from a workhouse. She may not be able to afford to take another girl at all, yet there appeared to be no lack of money. Maybe they were just 'careful' and lived 'frugally'. Those had been favourite words of Mrs Phillips. Slowly the thoughts going round in her head faded, her eyelids grew heavy and at last she slipped into a deep, contented sleep.

Mrs Howard had gone upstairs after both the young girls had gone to bed. She'd knocked quietly on the drawing-room door before entering, although she'd been with the family for so many years that she was almost considered to be one of them.

Siân Hughes was sitting by the open french windows looking down the garden where the riot of colour of the flowers and shrubs had faded in the dusk. The perfume of night-scented stocks and roses filled the air. On her knee was her embroidery, something she was almost never without. She turned towards the cook and smiled.

'Isn't it a beautiful evening?'

'It is, and you are the image of your mam, miss. God rest her soul.'

Siân smiled again but with a hint of sadness in her eyes. It was to this woman that she'd turned when her mother had died almost five years ago now. She'd only been sixteen at the time.

Mrs Howard smiled back. She loved Siân Hughes as she would have loved a daughter had she been so blessed. In truth the title 'Mrs' was a courtesy – she had never been married. Siân was a lovely young woman with softly curling chestnut hair, grey-green eyes and a pale skin. She looked delicate and always had been. The fever she'd succumbed to just after her mother's death had left her weak and unable to walk far. She seldom left the house and on the occasions when she did, it was in a Bath chair with a rug draped across her knees.

She would never marry. They all knew that, but she insisted on trying to run the household and be as 'normal' as possible, as she put it.

'She tries so hard to take her mam's place,' Mrs Howard often said, 'I only wish her father would give her credit for it.'

Her father, Ellis Hughes, was a rather dour man who hardly ever showed his feelings, although he loved his daughter deeply and would have given her the world had she asked for it.

'Is everything all right?' Siân queried, for Mrs Howard hardly ever came upstairs at this time of night unless it was important. Rowan came to help her dress and undress if she felt tired, even though the girl wasn't a ladies' maid.

'It's the new girl.'

Siân's forehead creased in a frown. 'Tell me what's wrong. And please could you sit down?'

'You know that isn't proper, miss,' Mrs Howard scolded.

'I do, but I'll get a crick in my neck if you don't, and you know I can't stand for long.' The last words were spoken without self-pity.

Mrs Howard sat.

Siân laid aside her needlework. 'What's the matter with her?'

'It's not the girl herself, she seems pleasant enough and biddable and I think she will prove to be a good worker. It's where she's come from that's the problem.'

'The workhouse, you mean?'

'Aye. It must be desperate in those places. God help the poor souls who end up there.' Mrs Howard shuddered. 'They sent her here with just her fare, the clothes she stood up in and a few underclothes. No work dresses, not even an apron and no hairbrush or pins.'

Siân's expression became serious. 'How on earth did they expect her to cope?'

'I don't know, miss. Rowan's given her one of her old dresses and lent her a brush and pins – she has beautiful hair. Indeed she's quite a beauty, considering.'

'Is she? I'd like to see her.'

Mrs Howard got to her feet. 'I'll go and fetch her.'

'Has she gone to bed?'

Mrs Howard nodded.

'Then leave it until morning. Can you spare Rowan for a few hours? Enough time to go into town and buy the necessities?'

'What about the money, miss? I told her she would have to pay it back out of her wages.'

'That's fair enough, as far as clothes go, but surely hairpins and the like can be provided without cost?'

'They can. Thank you, miss. I knew I could count on your common sense.'

'It's common decency, that's all. You taught me that

and my mother would have done the same thing.'

'Of course she would. God rest her. Now I'll leave you in peace. Will you require Rowan's services tonight, miss?'

Siân looked down at the tray cloth she was halfway through embroidering. 'No. No, thank you. Tonight I don't feel so tired.'

'Then don't be stopping up until all hours of the night.'

Siân smiled. 'You are an irascible tyrant, Edith Howard, do you know that?'

'Indeed I do and your mam knew it too. She would have approved. Someone has to keep an eye on you.'

As she turned to leave the door opened and Siân's face lit up. 'Richard. You're back early.'

Her brother crossed the room and took her hand. 'It was only a two-act play and I was disappointed in it. It certainly didn't live up to the reviews. You look tired, Siân.'

'I'm not! Everyone is always fussing over me.'

'It's for your own good,' Richard Hughes chided gently. He was a tall, slim young man with almost the same colouring as his sister but his hair was a darker brown and his eyes were a deeper shade of green. His face was lightly tanned and more healthy looking than his sister's pale complexion.

'Sit down and tell me all about it. Tom's not home yet and neither is Father. Tom didn't want to go to the dinner. He said it was dull and boring. All those pompous old men.'

Richard sat down on the arm of a Chesterfield. 'He's probably right but if he wants to follow in Father's footsteps and become Chairman of the Board then it's an occupational hazard he'll have to put up with.'

Mrs Howard had her hand on the door knob. 'Will I send Blandford up, sir?'

'No, that won't be necessary, Mrs Howard. I can pour myself a drink if I want one.' He paused. 'Is something wrong? You never come upstairs so late.'

'No, not "wrong". Miss Siân will explain but you won't find it interesting. It's to do with household staff.'

He smiled. 'Then I won't press it.'

The following morning Hannah was given a list of the duties she was required to carry out. She found out that a tweeny was a maid employed to carry out the work of house- and parlourmaid and, in some households, ladies' maid as well, whereas as scullery maid she was to help both Rowan and Mrs Howard when required. She would blacklead the range every morning after raking out the ashes, and build up the fire. She would tidy the kitchen, pantry and larder, scrubbing each floor and every surface. Then she would scrub and peel any vegetables needed for meals that day. Her duties also included seeing to the household linen but not the gentlemen's shirts nor Miss Siân's clothes. The shirts went to a Chinese laundry and Rowan did Miss Siân's things. She had an hour to herself after lunch but she must never be idle. She must read or sew or darn, accomplishments Mrs Howard was relieved to learn she had mastered. After that she would wash all dishes and pans, and help prepare more food. Finally, she would wash up after dinner. She was not allowed to go upstairs for anything unless summoned to.

'I don't mind that. I ... I wouldn't know how to speak to anyone, not properly,' Hannah had replied thankfully. Of course she had to cross the landing but only when she left or returned to her room.

Rowan had been despatched into Liverpool to buy Hannah's clothes. Mrs Howard had given her a list and the money. 'I'll want change from that, Rowan, and don't let them fob you off with some story about not having that size or material or colour so you have to take something else which is always dearer,' had been Mrs Howard's parting advice.

Hannah had been up at five o'clock. She'd slept well and it was the noise of a city waking up that had woken her too. For a few seconds she didn't know where she was, then she remembered and her heart leapt. She was washed, dressed and downstairs blackleading the range when Mrs Howard appeared at six-thirty.

'Well, it's nice to see someone who isn't afraid of hard work. Leave that and put the kettle on.'

'I'm used to being up early and ... and it's a real pleasure here.'

Mrs Howard nodded as she took the tea caddy from the shelf and Hannah passed her the teapot.

Hannah could hardly contain herself all morning so she threw herself into her chores to keep her mind occupied until Rowan returned at eleven o'clock laden with parcels. Hannah got to her feet and wiped her hands on her apron.

'Did you get everything?' Mrs Howard demanded.

Rowan nodded and fumbled in her purse for the change which she laid on the kitchen table. 'I'm spitting feathers! It's really hot out there.'

Hannah was incredulous. 'Is all that for me?'

'There's not all *that* much. It just looks a lot because of the paper bags and parcels.'

Mrs Howard undid the largest parcel and shook out two dresses in a serviceable dark grey material, then two large calico aprons.

'Where's the other one?' she demanded.

'It's in the small parcel,' Rowan replied, pouring herself a much-needed cup of tea.

'Waste. The sheer waste of all this paper! One parcel would have done,' Mrs Howard complained as she undid another one. Inside was a smaller white linen apron and two pairs of white cuffs.

'If for any reason you have to go upstairs, you'll need these.' Mrs Howard placed them down and pulled out a stiffly pleated white cap and added it to the pile.

'There's a hairbrush, pins, black ribbon, stockings, two underskirts and two pairs of drawers, from Marks & Spencer in Church Street. Oh, and I got myself a new blouse and skirt in Blacklers.'

'Oh, did you indeed? Did I send you out on a spree in the Master's time?'

'I didn't really do it all for myself.'

'Then who did you do it for?'

'Peckham. She can have my blue skirt and cream blouse now. I've had them for ages. She can't go around in that old pink striped thing on her days off, can she?'

Mrs Howard raised her eyes to the ceiling. 'As God made them He matched them!'

Hannah was stunned. 'Why . . . why . . . give *me* anything?' she stammered, her eyes fixed on the other girl's face.

'Because you haven't got anything and I like you.'

'What she means is you're near enough the same age, give or take a year or two. Now she'll have someone to jangle with. I can't be doing with jangling on hour after hour about some nonsense or other, not at my age, and she knows it. And you wouldn't get the daylights out of Blandford, never mind something sensible!' Despite her words there was a note of approval in Mrs Howard's voice.

Hannah fingered everything carefully.

'Tie back your hair with the ribbon and wear the cap if you need to go out at all.'

'Have your hair cut, Peckham, it's all the rage.'

Hannah clutched at her long dark locks. 'No! I . . . I couldn't.'

'You can,' Rowan urged.

'You see, she's at it already. Now take those things out of my kitchen, the pair of you, and then come back, it's nearly lunchtime and nothing's even started.'

They went upstairs together.

'Go on, have your hair cut. You'll look great. I wish my hair was as thick as yours and you've got a bit of a natural wave in it. Mine's as straight as an arrow. When I've saved up enough I'm going to have it Marcel waved.'

'What?'

'Oh, it's some complicated way of doing your hair but you end up with it all waved and it lasts for ages if you pin it right each night. Will you just *think* about it? I can make an appointment for you. Go on, you're not in the workhouse now. This is Liverpool! A big city! And it's nineteen twenty six, not eighteen twenty six!'

Hannah's eyes began to dance with excitement. Oh, Rowan was right. She *would* have her hair cut. She was free at last of the constraints of the workhouse.

'All right, I will, as long as no one complains.'

'Who is there to complain? Mrs Howard? She doesn't really mind. Take no notice, her bark is worse than her bite.'

'Miss Siân, then?'

The girl shook her head. 'Miss Siân's lovely. She's really great, it's a crying shame she's been left so frail after that fever. We all thought she was going to die too, like her mam.'

Some of the sparkle left Hannah's dark eyes. 'I know what it's like to lose your mam. I don't remember much about her now, but I can still picture her laughing and hear her singing in Welsh.'

'Did you learn how to speak that?'

'Not really, just a few words here and there and a few little songs, although I don't know what the words mean.'

'Well, Miss Siân will like to know that. They have another house, you know.'

'Another one? What for?'

'For sort of holidays, but they don't do that much these days. They used to go a lot when the kids were young, so Mrs Howard said.'

'Where is it?'

'God, I don't know. In some place that would drive you mad trying to pronounce and the house has got a Welsh name too. "Y-Garn" or something like that.' Rowan raised her eyes. 'We'd better get back down or she'll murder us both. You put on a grey dress and the coarse apron and then come down – and be quick,' Rowan urged over her shoulder.

When Hannah returned to the kitchen Mrs Howard informed her that Miss Siân wished to see her. Hannah panicked. 'Now?'

'Yes, so get back upstairs, change your apron, put on the cuffs and your cap and get a move on.'

Hannah felt very apprehensive as she did as she was told, but she took comfort from Rowan's description of the young woman who had taken up the burden left by her mother of running a house.

Rowan accompanied her and knocked on the drawing-room door.

'There's no need to get all flustered. She's great, I swear she is,' she whispered before opening the door and pushing Hannah inside.

Chapter Four

Hannah felt the same waves of fear and apprehension wash over her as she'd felt whenever summoned to Mrs Phillips's office. It was something instilled in her that would take a long time to obliterate. She took a deep breath and clenched her hands together. She looked down at the floor which was half covered by thick Chinese rugs. The rest of it was polished wood which only added to the illusion that she was once more in Matron's office.

'So, you are our new kitchen maid. It's Peckham, isn't it?'

At the soft, gently encouraging tone, Hannah looked up and her fear lessened as she caught and held the gaze of luminous grey-green eyes. She relaxed a little. They were kind eyes. Rowan had been right, she thought. Miss Siân Hughes looked to be a very pleasant person and not much older than herself. Somehow she'd expected her to be in her thirties at least. An old maid, past her prime. She hadn't given a thought to how her employer would look, but the young woman gazing up at her was pretty in a delicate way. Her hair was cut short and the knitted beige and brown two-piece she wore was very stylish.

'Yes, ma'am. I'm Hannah. Hannah Peckham.'

Siân smiled. Mrs Howard had been right. The girl who stood before her was a beauty, even in the drab garb of a kitchen maid.

'You've come to us from the Denbigh workhouse.'

'Yes, ma'am, but I was born in Liverpool.'

'And had you lived here long?' Siân probed. The girl had no strong nasal accent.

'Until I was six. My father took me to stay with family when he had to go in the army. He was killed.'

Siân shook her head. It was a sad little tale. 'What happened to your mother, Hannah?'

'She died, ma'am. I was only four and a half. She was Welsh.'

'So was my mother. I loved her dearly and miss her . . .' Siân faltered, twisting her hands together.

'I . . . I know how it feels, ma'am,' Hannah interrupted quietly.

'Yes, of course. Yes, you must.' Siân shook herself mentally. 'I hear you were not provided with the necessary items of dress and grooming?'

'No, ma'am, but they have been bought. Rowan went into town this morning.'

'I know. Mrs Howard explained that you will pay for them a little per month?'

'I'd sooner pay it all off at once, out of my first month's wages. I . . . I won't need much money. I've nothing to spend it on. Nowhere to go.'

'Would you not like to go and visit? There must still be people you knew when you lived in . . .?'

'Victoria Terrace,' Hannah supplied. 'Not . . . not

yet, ma'am. When I've been here a bit longer. I really would like to pay off my debts.'

'You are quite sure about that?'

Hannah nodded. 'I'm fed, have decent clothes, a roof over my head, what more could anyone wish for, ma'am?'

Siân smiled. 'You really are a very unusual girl. But I suppose it's your upbringing, which can't have been easy.'

Hannah didn't reply. She had an inkling that Miss Siân had no idea of how hard and unhappy her upbringing had been.

'We do have another house in North Wales. In the Vale of Clwyd. Near Groes. "Y-Garn", the house is called. I was born there. We went quite a lot when we were all much younger, although I did go to school here in Liverpool.'

Hannah didn't speak; Siân Hughes's eyes had a faraway look and Hannah knew her mind was elsewhere, in a place and a house where she'd been happy, secure in the love of caring and wealthy parents. This family had never known hunger, or cold, or lack of comforts of any kind. She guessed that.

But in some ways they were alike. Both their mothers had cared deeply for them, as indeed had their fathers. They were both small and fine-boned. They both cared for other people's plights. Yet in other ways they were so different. Hannah never wanted to set foot in Wales again. She had no fond memories there.

'Do you speak Welsh, Hannah?'

Hannah was surprised by the question. 'Just a few words. I can understand more though and . . .' She hesitated. 'I can sing . . . a bit.'

'You must take after your mother then? My mother had a beautiful voice and I play the piano. What can you sing?'

Hannah's heart dropped. Surely she wasn't going to be asked to sing now?

' "Tyllanod".'

Siân nodded. 'Ah, "The Owls".'

'And "Suo-Gân".'

'A beautiful traditional lullaby.'

Hannah became flustered. 'I don't know what all the words mean, ma'am.'

'You just learned them by repetition?'

Hannah nodded.

'Well, I think we'll get on very well. If there is anything you need, just ask Mrs Howard.'

Hannah inclined her head. Thankfully the interview appeared to be over but the opening of the door made her turn around.

Siân smiled. 'Richard. I didn't expect you back until after lunch.'

'Well, my lectures were over, so I thought I'd come home for lunch. Who is this?'

Hannah was unable to tear her eyes from the tall young man who had come into the room. Her heart had begun to beat very jerkily and she felt the blood singing in her ears. She wondered with panic if she was going to faint. She'd never felt like this before. She'd never seen anyone like him before.

'This is Hannah Peckham, the new kitchen maid.'

Hannah managed to dip a curtsey and drag her eyes from his face.

'Ah, Mrs Howard's "staff problem"?' he queried of his sister, his eyes full of laughter.

'Precisely. But please, Richard, don't interfere.'

He became serious, knowing what she meant. 'I won't, but you will have to extract that promise from someone else too. Perhaps I should speak to Father?'

'No. Leave it to me.'

'Very well. Now then, perhaps you'd be kind enough to ask Mrs Howard just what there is for lunch, Hannah?'

With his use of her Christian name she looked up and knew in that moment that she loved Richard Hughes and would do so all her life. 'I . . . I'm not sure, sir, but I'll ask.' She fled through the open doorway (he having opened the door), her cheeks flushed, her hands shaking.

As she went down the kitchen stairs she clung tightly to the banister rail, trying to compose herself before going any further.

'Where have you been? I didn't expect you to be so long up there!' Mrs Howard demanded, up to her elbows in flour.

'I'm sorry. She, I mean Miss Siân, was asking me about my mam and then . . . then her brother came in.'

Mrs Howard looked concerned. 'Mr Thomas?'

'No. I haven't seen him yet. The . . . the other one.

He asked me to ask you what there is for lunch.'

Mrs Howard could see by the girl's bright eyes and flushed cheeks that something had happened. 'Nothing unless you get on and help Rowan. She can't be in three places at once. She's only just finished laying the table, with that fool Blandford's help.'

Hannah started to take off her cap.

'Leave it on, and your cuffs. Didn't you hear me? Go and help in the dining room. That's upstairs!'

Totally confused, Hannah ran to find Rowan who had just closed the door to the room and was giving young Blandford a clout around the ear.

'You useless, idle little get!' she hissed at him. 'I told you to leave the glasses to me. Well you'll have it deducted from your wages because *I'm* not going to pay for things *you* break.'

'I've come to help,' Hannah said.

'Not before time,' the other girl snapped, glaring at the departing figure of Blandford.

'I couldn't help it, honestly. She kept me talking and then . . .'

'Then what?'

Hannah jerked her head in Blandford's direction.

'Oh, all right, it can wait until we get lunch over.'

'I . . . I don't have to help serve, do I?' Hannah was filled with panic mingled with the hope of seeing him again.

'No. I'll do that. It's times like this when more of us are needed. A butler and a footman and a proper parlourmaid. My head is bursting.'

'Why don't they get more people?'

Rowan dropped her voice. 'It's Scrooge. Tight as a clenched fist, he is. A family of four can easily manage with four servants, is what I believe he said. It wasn't like this before the Mistress died or before the war, so Mrs Howard says.'

'Can't he afford it?'

'Of course he flaming well can. He's mean. Just plain old-fashioned mean. Every time he opens his wallet it gives the moths heart failure!'

Hannah stared at her and Rowan shrugged. Hannah obviously hadn't understood her comments or thought them amusing. Well she'd find out more when they got a minute to themselves.

It was almost mid afternoon before they got a quiet moment. Mrs Howard complained of a headache and went to lie down and Rowan and Hannah went outside and sat in the shade of the laurel bushes, hidden from both the sunlight and the house.

'I've never known it be so warm in May. Mrs Howard made sure she got to her bed before either of us could ask for the privilege of having a headache in peace. My head is thudding.'

'Will I get you something?'

'No. It'll go soon. Give me a few minutes to relax in the shade.'

'What *is* your name? I mean your Christian name.'

'Violet. Vi to my friends, if I had any.'

'You have me.'

The girl opened her eyes. 'It would only confuse things, Hannah.'

'You see, you called me "Hannah". I wouldn't get confused calling you "Vi" in private.'

'You were certainly very confused when you came back at lunchtime.'

Hannah blushed furiously.

'Well? Are you going to tell me what happened, now we're officially friends?'

Hannah bit her lip. 'It will sound . . . stupid.'

'Don't be such a pain, Hannah Peckham. It's too hot to play guessing games. We should have brought a jug of water out with us.'

Hannah pushed a few damp wisps of hair away from her cheeks. 'Well, I was all right with Miss Siân. She *is* lovely and she's not that old either. I expected her to be much older.'

'She's twenty-one next month. There's to be a party. God help us all. He'll have to hire more staff.'

'It was when he . . . he came into the room.'

'Mr Richard?'

'Yes. I . . . I . . .'

Vi Rowan stared hard at Hannah. 'You've gone and fallen in love with him, haven't you?'

Hannah nodded. 'I didn't think anything like . . . this . . . would happen to me. I don't even know him. He's a stranger.'

'And stranger things have happened. But he is nice. He's handsome and kind and funny.'

'Funny?'

'Yes, he'll always stop and have a bit of a joke, like.'

Hannah shook her head. 'He might be all those things but . . . but he'll never love me.'

Vi looked thoughtful. 'You don't know that. There was a parlourmaid in number twenty-four who married the youngest son. They couldn't live around here though. There was murder over it.'

'What did they do?'

'They emigrated. To Australia, I think. And she was no beauty, I can tell you. She couldn't hold a candle to you.'

Hannah was surprised. 'To me? I'm nothing special.'

'Nothing special! Have you looked at yourself? Really looked? You're beautiful. Dressed up in something like Miss Siân wears for special evenings and the fellers would be half killing each other just to dance with you.'

Hannah blushed again. 'Oh, Vi, stop that! I . . . I'm not beautiful. How can I be?'

'You are. The workhouse couldn't take it away from you. I envied you the minute I set eyes on you, even wearing those terrible clothes.'

'I'll have your nice blue skirt and fancy cream blouse for best now. Do you think . . . well . . . do you . . .?'

'He might. He couldn't fail to notice you, Hannah, and . . . who knows? But for God's sake don't say a word of all this to Mrs Howard. She'd be straight to see Miss Siân. She'll already be worried.'

'Why?'

'Mr Thomas hasn't set eyes on you yet. He's the one

to stay well clear of. A real ladies' man. They had trouble keeping maids here at one time. A roving eye and roving hands too if he thinks he can get away with it.'

Hannah began to wish she'd not been so hasty in wanting to pay off her debts so soon. She might have Vi's skirt and blouse but she'd have to wear the ugly boots. Oh, what was the use of even thinking like this? He wouldn't give her a second glance even if she were dressed in silk and satin. She'd still be the kitchen maid. The girl from the Denbigh workhouse. The child born in Victoria Terrace. She had escaped all that, miraculously, and even if she were as beautiful as Vi told her she was, her class and his never mixed socially or any other way. She didn't want to emigrate and she was certain that the thought had never crossed his mind. Why should it? He had every comfort and privilege. No, she'd just have to put him out of her mind completely.

After dinner that night Mrs Howard took Hannah aside.

'Have I done something wrong, Mrs Howard?'

'No, but I wanted a quiet word with you. About Mr Thomas.'

'I see.'

'No, you don't. He had the Mistress demented from the time he came home from boarding school and then university. We couldn't keep staff until the Master had a talk to him and threatened to cut off his allowance, so I heard. He . . . he's very partial to a pretty face,

Peckham. And you are more than "pretty". If he says or does anything to you, anything at all, you must come straight to me.'

'But why would he bother me?'

Mrs Howard raised her eyes to the ceiling. The girl really didn't know how lovely she was but she wasn't going to enlighten her or press the point. 'Haven't I just told you we couldn't keep staff? He's a . . . a bit of a lad with the girls.' She'd nearly called him a woman-iser, a wastrel, which was her own opinion, even though she did like him. He'd always been a pleasant lad, with the ability to charm people if he wanted to, but she knew how much his father disapproved of the way he frittered away his time and money.

'I'll tell you, Mrs Howard, but it's not likely I'll even see him. I'm down here nearly all the time.'

'And that's exactly where I intend to keep you.'

Hannah nodded and wondered if she should change the subject, but at the curt nod of Mrs Howard's head she knew the interview was over.

When they went back into the stifling kitchen Vi and Blandford were both standing by the open door, trying to catch some bit of breeze.

'It's like a furnace in here. Why can't we have a big gas cooker or even an electric one?' Vi asked.

'Because they cost money, that's why, and the range is just as reliable as the day it was put in,' Mrs Howard snapped.

'Well, we'll have our work cut out for Miss Siân's party. Do you know how many are coming?'

'Not exactly, but it will be about twenty-five people.'

'Mainly all the auld ones, friends of the Master's,' Blandford said gloomily.

'That will do from you, meladdo!'

'Surely to God they won't expect us to do it all by ourselves?'

'No. I've already spoken to Miss Siân about that and she says we're to have hired help. She left it all in what she calls my "capable hands". Which means I'll have to sort it all out.'

'Couldn't we have a butler?' Blandford asked.

Mrs Howard looked at him scornfully. 'No self-respecting butler would go near one of those "agencies" but I'll get a couple of lads in to pass the drinks around.'

'When exactly is it?' Hannah ventured.

'Two weeks today and I'm sorry but you'll have to have your Sunday off the week after.'

'Oh, I don't mind,' Hannah answered quietly. She was thinking of Jessie. 'Do you think it would be possible to get another kitchen maid?'

'What for?' Mrs Howard demanded.

'To help. There's a girl in the workhouse, she works very hard, she's quiet, she has no family and she has a twisted foot, but that doesn't stop her working. I promised I'd try and get her something. Something away from the workhouse.'

'Well there's nothing here, permanent, like. There's no use having her here just for the one night.'

Hannah nodded. 'I suppose not. But if you hear of a position, any position, could you tell me and try . . . try and put in a good word for her? She's terribly lonely now I'm not with her and the woman who oversees us is nasty and spiteful.'

Mrs Howard shook her head. 'I'll try. I'll keep my eyes and ears open, that's all I can promise. Now get yourselves to bed.'

Hannah lay on her back staring at the sky through the window in the ceiling. It was like dark blue velvet and the stars were extra bright, twinkling like diamonds in a necklace. It had been a long and emotional day. Every word of the one sentence Richard Hughes had spoken to her was gone over and over in her mind. Tears stung her eyes and rolled down her cheeks. She was just a silly little fool. She *had* to try to quash these ridiculous feelings she had for him but at the back of her mind was the knowledge that she was looking forward to wearing Vi's cast-offs, and having her hair cut, and the hope of seeing him again. Even just a glimpse would do . . .

Chapter Five

After dinner the following evening she tried on the clothes Vi had given her. 'We neither of us have got a decent mirror and it's no good me just telling you how it looks. I know! Miss Siân has a long mirror in her bedroom.'

Hannah protested but then let Vi take her there.

'What if we get caught?' she whispered fearfully. 'I don't want to do anything wrong, I'd be sent back.'

'You wouldn't and anyway she's downstairs discussing the party food with Mrs Howard. Come on.'

Hannah was stunned into silence by the bedroom. It was a large room decorated in cream and a very pale green. The walls were covered in what looked like panels of silk but which in reality was wallpaper. All the paintwork, except for the window frames, was pale green. Heavy pale green velvet curtains hung each side of the huge sash windows. The carpet was cream and went right up to the skirting board. All the furniture was so highly polished you could see your reflection in it and it was inset with mother-of-pearl flowers and leaves.

'Oh, it's like a palace! Just like something in a fairy story.'

'I suppose it is. You get used to it. You stop noticing things. Now come here.'

Hannah stood before the cheval-glass and stared at herself. A stranger looked back at her, a small slim girl with a mass of very dark hair and huge brown eyes. The long cream crêpe de Chine blouse rested on her hips. It had full-length sleeves, a row of tiny buttons down the front and a broad sash. The skirt was royal blue, with a fluted hemline that only reached to her calves.

'I look . . . different.'

'You do. With your hair cut and with a decent pair of shoes – not those great clodhopper boots, you can borrow a pair of my shoes – you'll be turning heads wherever you go.'

Hannah looked apprehensive. 'I don't want any of that.'

'Well, what you want and what you get are two different things. You could of course wear that awful blue thing or maybe a sack,' Vi commented drily.

Hannah smiled. 'No, I'd much sooner have these. You've been so good to me, Vi.'

The girl pursed her lips but Hannah could see she was pleased.

'We'd better get out of here and you go and get those things off. Why don't you give them a sort of "trial run"?'

'What?'

'Wear them when you go out.'

'Out where?'

'Well, to the hairdresser's for a start, and don't you want to go to Victoria Terrace?'

'I hadn't thought of going just yet. I wanted to feel
. . . settled here.'

'Think about it now. Go after you've had your hair
done. That won't take all afternoon. Go on, give the
new Hannah Peckham an airing.'

She felt very nervous as she walked into town on
Thursday afternoon, as though there were a hundred
butterflies in her stomach. Her anxiety must have been
noticeable because she saw people looking at her
surreptitiously.

She almost changed her mind as she sat facing a
mirror while her hair was brushed out. The
hairdresser, a very smart young woman dressed in a
pale blue overall and skirt, had hair that framed her
face like a cap of shining gold. Hannah wouldn't mind
if her hair looked so nice but just what *would* she look
like? Would she love it or loathe it? It might not suit
her at all. She still had time to change her mind. No,
she told herself firmly, remembering how she'd looked
with envy at all the smart young girls. She bit her lip
as the first locks of hair fell to the floor. There was no
turning back now.

An hour later she stepped out into Lord Street.
She felt light-headed. She'd never realised just how
heavy her long hair had been until now. Her hair had
been cut to just below her ears, and the sides flicked
forward to curl on her jawline. She now had a thick
fringe and she'd been given instructions on how to
wash, set and dry it and was reminded that it would

need trimming about every six weeks to keep its shape.

As she walked along Lord Street, heading for Upper Parliament Street and Victoria Terrace, the butterflies once again started their manic dance. Would anyone remember her? Would there still be people she knew or would they have moved away? Would they have been offended that her da had taken her away and she hadn't written to them? At last she reached Victoria Terrace and stood on the corner of the road and a tide of emotions and memories engulfed her. It had hardly changed at all. She remembered everything so vividly but particularly the last time she'd walked up here with her da: a confused, miserable little girl, clutching a half-dead blackbird in the folds of her shawl. There was no need for shawls today, the sun beat down and she wrinkled her nose at the odours that filled the air.

Further down two women stood gossiping and she recognised them immediately. Ada Sweeney and Martha Harper. She smiled and quickened her steps until she was in earshot, then she stopped.

'Mrs Sweeney? Mrs Harper!'

They both turned and stared at her hard, then Ada's face creased in a huge grin. 'God Almighty! It's Hannah! Hannah Peckham. You've grown up! Where've you been all these years?'

Hannah ran the few yards that separated them and flung her arms around Ada. 'Oh, I never thought I'd see any of you again!'

There were tears in all their eyes as Ada led Hannah into the house.

Nothing had changed much in here either, Hannah thought. It was still untidy and cluttered but it had altered in one respect. There was far less furniture in the room than she remembered and all the young Sweeneys would be out at work. Even Lily and Harry.

'How is everyone?'

Ada's expression changed. 'We're coping as best we can. Tom, God rest 'im, was killed the day after your da. And so were Arthur and our Sam, later on, like. Our Sam was only sixteen. He lied about his age. God 'elp them all, it's an 'eavy burden for us all to carry. But I've still got our Gerald, thank God.'

Martha Harper nodded her agreement. 'I lost two sons meself. It was terrible. A shocking waste and look how they treated the fellers that came back. "A Land fit for Heroes." That's a bloody joke! There's no work for anyone, nor will be for those that went on strike. Half the city is living on the Parish, God help them.'

Ada wiped her eyes and passed Hannah a cup of weak tea. 'Still, you look as though you've done well, girl. A proper beauty you are now.'

'I wish everyone would stop saying things like that,' Hannah laughed, trying to dispel the sadness that hung heavily in the air.

'Well you are! Yer mam would be proud of yer and yer look just like her too. I told yer years ago, didn't I, Martha, that Jane would never be forgot around 'ere while Hannah lived.'

'Where are yer living now?' Martha asked.

'In Faulkner Square. I'm in service.'

'You've done well then. Oh aye, there's money in this city for some. Always 'as been, always will be.'

'Who do you work for, Hannah?' Martha asked.

'Mr Ellis Hughes, he's a director of the Union Castle Line but I haven't been there long. Only a week.' She sipped her tea. There was hardly any taste to it. 'I came from the workhouse.'

Ada's mouth dropped open and Martha nearly spilt her tea.

'The *workhouse*! What in God's name were yer doin' in there?'

Hannah told them of her childhood between sips of tea and both women shook their heads and wiped their eyes.

'God luv yer, yer mam must 'ave been spinnin' in her grave, and yer da too. And them supposed to be "family". It's a funny way of treatin' yer family. I told yer da to leave yer 'ere with me. We'd 'ave managed. Yer certainly wouldn't 'ave been shoved into no workhouse. I 'ope that auld bitch rots in 'ell!'

'She did die, Great-Aunt Margaret, I heard that, but Cousin Gwyneth . . .' Hannah shrugged. She supposed she was still alive, she would only be in her late thirties or early forties now.

'I hope she gets shockin' rheumatics, an' she will, livin' in a damp auld cottage in the middle of nowhere. She deserves some punishment for treating yer like that, Hannah, luv.'

76

'Oh, let's talk about something else. I've left all that behind me now. I'm not a child any more.'

'What? Yer're no older than our Lily!' Ada demanded.

'What about your Lily, she's walking out now,' Martha said.

'Is she really?' Hannah exclaimed.

Ada glared at Martha. 'The least said about our Lily an' that feller the better. I don't approve of 'im at all. 'E's a fly-by-night. I know 'is type!'

'Well, there's to be a big party for Miss Siân's twenty-first birthday,' Hannah intervened.

'What kind of a name is that? Siân? I never heard that one before.'

'It's Welsh. Her mother was Welsh too.'

'Well I 'ope they treat yer better than that other lot.'

'Oh, they do. She's lovely, but she's delicate. She never goes out much. She had rheumatic fever after her mam died.'

Both ladies tutted sympathetically. 'So, tell us all about this grand party then, luv, we 'aven't 'ad a good "do" around 'ere since the Armistice.'

Hannah smiled. She felt that she was really home again. This was her city, this was where she belonged, not in some big house with servants, no matter if she herself was a servant. These women had nursed her mam and looked after her. She should have stayed here with them, they were kinder than any relative. From now on, she'd spend her half-day off in Victoria Terrace and she'd help them in any way she could.

* * *

Hannah had settled in well and as she seldom went beyond the confines of the kitchen and yard except on her days off, she didn't see Richard Hughes again. Nor did she see his brother or father. Everyone approved of her new hairstyle and when Blandford saw her 'dressed up' for the first time he said he could easily fancy her himself. He'd been given a clip around the ear for his cheek. 'Hardfaced little sod!' Mrs Howard had called him.

The arrangements for the party were well under way. Mrs Howard spent hours closeted with Miss Siân and she had made out lists and pinned them to the kitchen wall, ticking off each item.

'Well, that's all the food in hand, though I'll be worn out with all the cooking and you'll be sick of the sight of fruit and vegetables, Peckham. The Master is seeing to the drink, but I'll have to watch meladdo like a hawk to make sure he doesn't get at it. He's thick enough when he's sober, never mind drunk! Rowan, what about the flowers?'

'They'll be fresh cut in the morning and arrive in the late afternoon. The florist will arrange them herself.'

'And so she should, the price she's charging. Right. Now that leaves me with trying to get some decent staff. You two will have to wait on. Peckham, you'll have to wear one of Rowan's black dresses and I'll order you a fancy apron and cap.'

Hannah's heart turned over. She would see him again. He might even speak to her. She wished she could wear her best clothes instead of a maid's uniform.

'What about music?' Vi asked.

'I hear that Mr Thomas is engaging some musicians, God help us all! They'll only be able to play this jazz stuff and those awful new-fangled dances, the Charleston and the Black Bottom. I don't approve of either but imagine calling a dance a "black bottom". It's indecent, that's what it is.'

Both girls looked at the floor and Vi decided to change the subject.

'Oh, you should see the dress Miss Siân's got. It's gorgeous! From Cripps in Bold Street.'

'So she finally settled on something from those they sent around for her to see?'

The family had an account at the fashionable shop in Bold Street, the Bond Street of Liverpool. The management fully understood Miss Siân's situation and frequently sent clothes and shoes, hats, gloves and handbags for her perusal.

'Yes, it's pale blue satin under white georgette. The handkerchief hem will cover her legs. The bodice is long too and embroidered with beads and drop pearls. She's got a lovely pair of white satin shoes and she's going to wear her mam's diamond and sapphire necklace and earrings.'

'Oh, it's such a pity she's delicate,' Hannah said. 'She's so beautiful and kind surely someone would like to marry her!'

As the days went by the pace of life became hectic. All the usual daily chores had to be done as well as the thorough cleaning of the downstairs rooms. Furniture was moved; curtains were taken down and sent to be cleaned; 'I want all the rugs taken up, thrown over the line and beaten and every inch of floor polished. All the ornaments are to be washed, carefully. I want the windows to be sparkling, and all the glass light shades too.'

'Even the chandelier in the hall?' Hannah asked.

'Particularly the chandelier. Get Blandford to give you a hand.'

Vi had grimaced behind Mrs Howard's back.

The Saturday morning and afternoon had been manic. A steady stream of people had tramped through the kitchen.

'At this rate the whole house will be in a right state and after we've half killed ourselves flaming well polishing and scrubbing. If that woman with the flowers spills one more drop of water on that floor, I'll kill her!' Vi hissed to Hannah. 'And how we're supposed to find time to get dressed I don't know. I'm to see to Miss Siân so I'll have to be in my best uniform by half past six.'

'Oh, we'll manage. Everything will go like clockwork. Do you think we'll get anything to eat and drink?' Blandford asked, resplendent in his hired uniform.

'At about one o'clock in the morning we might. If we're lucky.'

'Maybe they'll all go home quite early, what with Miss Siân's health.' Hannah tried to sound cheerful.

'And pigs might fly! No, they'll hang on to the bitter end.'

Miraculously, at half past six peace reigned. Everything was done and the hired help were being given their orders and instructions by the elderly, semi-retired butler the agency had miraculously found, much to Mrs Howard's relief. 'Well, at least *someone* seems to know what's expected,' she'd muttered after a brief conversation with the man, during which he'd rattled off the names and addresses of the people he'd worked for over his long years of service and they'd both agreed that savings and the very meagre pensions employers paid were not enough to ensure a comfortable old age, which was why he eked them out by part-time work.

The two girls were told to go and make themselves presentable. Hannah's hands were shaking as she struggled with the buttons of Vi's black dress. She was looking forward to the evening and at the same time she was wishing it were over. Oh, don't be so flaming stupid! Just calm down, she told herself. She was so mixed up that she would drop something or make a fool of herself if she wasn't careful. She tied on the white frilly apron and then set the cap over her hair and held it in place with clips. Vi had given her the shoes she'd borrowed so often. Then she took a deep breath. She wasn't going to make a fool of herself. She *wasn't*. She'd be polite when spoken to, she'd be demure and self-effacing and she'd make sure she stayed well away from Richard Hughes, otherwise she really *would* make a fool of herself.

Chapter Six

They were kept busy for the early part of the evening and once Hannah had got over her initial nervousness she began to take more interest in what was being discussed and noting the beautiful evening dresses all the ladies present wore, and the jewels and hairstyles. She was quite shocked to see some of the younger ones smoking cigarettes in long, elegant holders made of silver, gold and tortoiseshell. She'd never seen a woman smoke before.

'Which one is Mr Hughes and which one is Mr Thomas?' she whispered to Rowan as they re-entered the drawing room with trays bearing more glasses of champagne.

'Mr Hughes is standing by the fireplace. He's the one with the nose like a hawk and a pot belly that would look better on a pig,' Vi answered.

Hannah hid a smile at this irreverent description of their employer.

'Mr Thomas is standing over by the window, chatting to that woman in pink. I've never seen hair *that* colour before! It clashes horribly with her frock. It must be dyed. I wouldn't be surprised if her face is caked in make-up too.'

Hannah looked across the room. She could see what

her friend meant. *She'd* never seen hair that colour red before either.

'Is she a friend of Miss Siân's?'

'God, no! She's probably a floosie Mr Thomas invited. I saw his father give him looks fit to kill when he introduced her. "Daphne" he called her. A real posh name, but I bet it's not the one she was baptised with. Daisy more like.'

Hannah blushed as suddenly her gaze caught and held Thomas Hughes's. Quickly she looked away. Physically he was an older version of his brother but he seemed much more lively, flamboyant and self-possessed. She turned to the group of ladies who were sitting near Miss Siân. She had stood to greet all her guests but she was obviously tired now.

'Would you like another glass, ma'am?' she asked of her mistress who looked very elegant in the pale blue and white dress, with the diamonds and sapphires sparkling in the light. Around her head was a band of the satin to which was attached three white egret feathers. That looked elegant too, Hannah thought.

'No, not just yet, thank you.' Siân turned to a girl of her own age with light brown hair and very blue eyes, their colour enhanced by the royal blue velvet dress she was wearing. Above the elbow of her left arm was a gold bracelet through which a chiffon scarf was threaded.

'Maria, you've hardly had anything all evening, won't you have another glass?'

The girl shook her head. 'No, truly, Siân. It really

doesn't agree with me. I go all light-headed and start giggling about nothing and tonight I don't want to make a fool of myself.' Her gaze swept the room until it fell on Richard Hughes and she smiled.

Hannah's heart dropped. He was coming towards them and there was nothing she could do, apart from snatch away the tray and push her way through the press of people, so she stood still, her eyes fixed on the tray of glasses.

'Maria, I didn't realise you would be here. Forgive me for being such a boor. How are you? You look radiant.'

'I'm very well thank you, Richard, and it's very kind of you to compliment me, although I think "radiant" is a bit too . . .' She paused.

Richard laughed. 'I'm sorry, Maria, if I sounded like my brother. I didn't intend to.'

The girl laughed too and Hannah, glancing sideways, noticed that her cheeks flushed prettily.

'And how is the party going, Hannah? Are we keeping you busy?'

Hannah was startled and looked up. She felt that same surge of emotion as she'd felt the day she'd first seen him. She was mesmerised and blushed herself.

'She's a little shy. She's only been with us a short time,' Siân said kindly.

'Yes . . . yes, sir, it's busy,' Hannah finally managed to reply. Then she tore her gaze away from him and moved away from the group.

All through the buffet supper and the dancing which

followed she felt jittery and on edge.

'What's the matter with you, girl?' Mrs Howard asked tetchily, passing Hannah a tray of canapés which she nearly dropped.

Vi came to her rescue. 'She's nervous, that's all. It's all the excitement going on up there.'

'Well, there's no time for nerves now, you can have a fit of hysterics when they've all gone, if you've any energy left.'

After that Hannah circulated in the drawing room and hall only. All the younger members of the party had moved into the dining room for the dancing. The room had been stripped of all furniture and carpets and a group of three musicians, all in evening dress, sat by the window in the alcove. Miss Siân remained in the drawing room with just two friends; Hannah was glad that the pretty girl called Maria was one of them. Richard and Thomas were both in the dining room.

Mrs Howard had been right in her prediction, Hannah thought. It was after one when the last guests departed and the house fell silent.

Siân sent for Mrs Howard, Vi, Hannah and Blandford. The young woman looked as tired as they were, Hannah thought.

'Mrs Howard, I'd like to thank you for all your hard work that went to make this evening such a success. You have all worked terribly hard and must be very tired, so leave everything until tomorrow morning – or later this morning I should say.' She smiled at them before continuing. 'I certainly won't be wanting breakfast until at least half past nine and I doubt that either of my brothers will be down before ten. It's Sunday, so we'll all go to the late morning service. Goodnight and, once again, thank you. Please convey my thanks to the agency staff, particularly the butler they sent.'

'I will, miss, I don't know what we would have done without him. He took complete charge of all the staff.'

Siân nodded, and then rose stiffly to her feet.

'Can I help, miss?' Vi offered.

'Thank you but no. I'll manage, Rowan. You must be worn out.'

As they filed into the hall, Mrs Howard said approvingly, 'Now that's what I call a real lady. Many would have insisted on us clearing up tonight.'

'Will we have a drink ourselves now?' Vi asked.

'You can make cocoa for us all, Mr Donaldson included.'

Vi's eyebrows rose as she looked at Hannah. Hannah smiled back.

The two girls sat in the kitchen, but Mrs Howard and Mr Donaldson sat apart, deep in conversation.

'They seem to be getting on like a house on fire,' Vi whispered.

'Maybe she'll get married and go off and give us all some peace.'

Vi glared at young Blandford. 'And we might get a real tartar in her place. Keep your mouth shut. *And* you've been drinking.'

'I haven't!'

'You have. I saw you take two glasses off a tray and drink them right down. God knows how many more you've had!'

'It's horrible. I can't see why they make such a fuss over it,' the lad said, unaware that he had condemned himself.

Tired though she was Hannah washed the mugs and started to tidy up. Tidiness had been instilled into her from childhood and besides she'd hate having to come downstairs and face a kitchen that looked as though a bomb had hit it.

'Peckham, leave it,' Mrs Howard said irritably.

'I can't. It's just something I *have* to do.'

Mrs Howard tutted. 'Then Mr Donaldson and myself will go into the butler's pantry to continue our conversation. I hope it's fit to be seen – that room hasn't been used for years, not since we *had* a butler.'

Hannah nodded, then turned and looked around. It was hard to know where to start but she began to stack dishes and glasses on the big draining board. Those she would do later.

An hour later the kitchen looked tidy and she was utterly worn out. She untied the white apron, folded it and placed it on the dresser. She did the same with the cap and then ran her fingers through her hair. Oh, it must be absolute heaven to be able to lie in bed until half past nine or ten o'clock. She'd never known anyone who did that, unless they were very sick.

Halfway across the landing she looked up and saw Thomas Hughes at the top of the staircase. She stopped, unsure of what she should do. She just couldn't ignore him; it would be extremely rude, that much she did know. But should she speak?

'Ah, it's our new little kitchen maid, but promoted I see for the party.' His words were slightly slurred.

Hannah just nodded.

'There's no need to be terrified to open your mouth. I won't bite you, you know.'

'Yes, sir, I mean no, sir.'

He laughed. He'd heard about her looks but had been warned by Siân to leave the girl alone otherwise she would tell Father and this time there would be real trouble. He wasn't a lad any more.

'You *are* lovely. I thought Siân was exaggerating.'

'Thank you. May . . . may I go now, sir? It's very late and I'm so tired. I've been up since five.'

'Of course you may. After I've given you a kiss. I've my terrible reputation to think of. Can't let myself down, but it will be a very chaste kiss. I promise.' He laughed and Hannah could smell the whisky on his breath. She began to back away but he caught her by the wrist, pulled her towards him and tried to kiss her. Her shyness and apprehension suddenly left her, to be replaced by anger. She had a good life now. How dare he think that because she was a scullion she was someone who had no feelings, no self respect. She pulled away and then, with all the strength she could muster, she shoved him hard. He staggered backwards and almost collided with his brother who was standing on the top stair.

The colour drained from Hannah's face. Now she could be in real trouble.

Thomas regained his balance. 'What do you think you're doing, you little bitch?' he shouted. Hannah's reaction had taken him completely by surprise.

'Trying to protect herself from you,' Richard said coldly. Like his furious brother, he too was surprised that she had had the courage to stand up for herself. Most girls from her background wouldn't. You had to admire her, he thought. She looked so different from the painfully shy girl she'd been on the few occasions he'd seen her. Her dark eyes were full of rage and her pale cheeks were flushed.

'Don't you ever learn? Don't you ever listen to Father or Siân?' he demanded of Thomas.

'Oh, don't be so bloody sanctimonious! I meant the girl no harm and if you hadn't have been standing there I'd have fallen down the bloody stairs. She can get out of this house, pack her bags and get to hell out of here. No servant attacks their employer and gets away with it.'

Richard's eyes became hard as he watched Hannah's expression change. She drew in her breath fearfully.

'She's going nowhere. You asked for it. She was defending herself. Father and Siân know you only too well and *I* saw it all.' He turned to Hannah who was visibly trying not to tremble. 'It's all right now, Hannah, you go on up to your room. I'm sorry my brother doesn't act like a gentleman where young servants are concerned.'

'Oh, I see. *You* can call her "Hannah" but *I* can't go near her. So that's the way the wind blows, is it?' Thomas jeered.

Richard lost his temper completely. 'No, it bloody isn't! Not everyone has a mind like yours! She's little more than a child and one who has been badly treated all her life.'

'Oh, my heart bleeds,' was the sarcastic reply.

'I doubt it. Anyway, isn't it about time you found yourself a decent girl and got married? Then you'd *have* to stop harassing young servants.'

'Go to hell, Richard! I'll do *what* I want, *when* I want!'

The brothers glared at each other for a few seconds and then Thomas turned away, entered his bedroom and slammed the door shut behind him.

Hannah was still standing on the bottom stair.

'I'm sorry about all that, Hannah, really I am. He just goes too far, doesn't know where to stop nor care about other people's feelings, but you did right to fend off his advances. No one will blame you for that.'

'Thank you, sir. I just lost my temper. I want to stay here, I'm happier than I've been in my life, and . . . and I've always had to . . . well, to fight for the things I wanted. I am really sorry. I know he's a gentleman and he has had a drop to drink.'

He smiled at her. 'That is the understatement of the year, Hannah, and I'm afraid he is far from being a gentleman when he's like that. Go on up, you must be worn out, it's after two. Is Mrs Howard still up?'

'I . . . I'm not sure, sir.'

'Well, it will wait. I'll see my sister.'

'Oh, no, please don't do that! I'll get the sack and . . . and I can't go back . . . there.' Incipient tears filled her eyes.

She looked so vulnerable, all the anger had left her and he put his arm around her. 'Don't get upset, please, you won't lose your job. It wasn't your fault. You won't be sent back anywhere, I promise.'

She raised her head and looked into his eyes. Oh, she wouldn't have minded *him* kissing her at all. She took the handkerchief he offered and wiped her tears.

'All right now?' he said gently.

All she could do was nod her head.

'Good. Now go and get some sleep. Goodnight, Hannah. Or good morning.'

'Thank you, sir. Goodnight,' she muttered and turned away.

He waited until she climbed the stairs before walking away. She certainly wasn't the usual type of girl who was employed as a kitchen maid. Despite spending almost her entire life in a workhouse she still had spirit and determination and a temper. He admired her for that.

When she finally reached her room she lay down on the bed fully dressed. Oh, she thanked God he'd come along in time. He'd saved her from God alone knew what, he'd put his arm around her, and given her his handkerchief. Maybe . . . just maybe . . . there was a tiny grain of hope. She held the handkerchief tightly against her cheek. She wouldn't give it back. She'd keep it for ever. It would remind her of how kind and caring he'd been.

She awoke to the sound of tapping on her bedroom door and realised she was still fully dressed and that it was daylight.

Vi poked her head around the door. 'For God's sake, Hannah, do you know what time it is?'

'No.'

'Seven o'clock and look at the state of you.'

Hannah scrambled off the bed and began to take off the black dress.

'Throw some water over your face, brush your hair and get down to the kitchen as soon as you can.'

As she did as she had been told she began to remember the events of the night. Oh, what would she do if she saw him again? Would she be called in to see Miss Siân?

Mrs Howard herself had only just got up, Hannah realised as she tied on her coarse apron. Of Blandford there was no sign.

'I've got to say it was a nice surprise to come down to a tidy kitchen, even if the dishes haven't been washed. It will take all morning to do them so you'd better start now, Peckham. Rowan, set Miss Siân's tray but I'll take it up myself.'

Vi looked at Hannah and shrugged. Mrs Howard hardly ever did that.

'Where's Blandford?' Hannah asked, feeling very self-conscious.

'God knows! Probably sleeping off what he drank last night. Oh, he thought he had me fooled but it would take more brains than he's got to get one over on me!' Mrs Howard replied grimly.

When Vi had gone to the linen chest to find a clean tray cloth Mrs Howard came and stood beside Hannah.

'Are you all right, Hannah?'

'Yes. I . . . I'm fine. Tired but fine.'

'That's not what I heard.'

Hannah's eyes widened. 'You saw . . . Mr Richard?'

'I did.'

'It wasn't my fault! Truly it wasn't!'

'All right, don't get all airyated. I know it wasn't your fault. I'll see Miss Siân about it when I take up the tray. It won't happen again, I can assure you of that. You're a good girl, a good worker and I'm not going to lose *another* decent maid.'

Hannah nodded with relief. She wouldn't have to go back to the workhouse. She'd throw herself in the river before she'd do that.

Chapter Seven

Nothing more was said by either family or servants but Ada had plenty to say on the subject when Hannah told her on her next visit. Hannah went to visit every week on her afternoon off, even if sometimes she only stayed an hour.

'Well, the 'ardfaced sod! Just because 'e's gorra pile of money 'e thinks 'e can do anything 'e flamin' well likes!'

'He's caused so much trouble in the past that they have had a hard time keeping girls. Mrs Howard said she used to hate him coming home when he was at university, there were always rows.'

'It's a good job that the other one arrived when 'e did. It's shockin', that's what it is. Martha, luv, shove that kettle on the 'ob,' she instructed her friend and neighbour who now came across whenever Hannah came to call.

'I don't know 'ow yer put up with them at all. The pay in service 'as always been rotten too.'

'Well, it's better than no pay at all. Me an' you know what that's like, Martha.'

To hide the brightness that came into her eyes whenever Richard Hughes was mentioned, Hannah changed the subject.

'I won't get any wages this month, well, hardly any, because I'm paying off what I owe for the things I had to have.'

'Yer shouldn't 'ave ter pay for anything, Hannah! With all their money they certainly wouldn't miss a few pounds. And you coming from the flamin' workhouse with not a penny to bless yerself with an' nothin' but a couple of spare pairs of drawers and a nightdress.'

'At least she *had* a nightie. I've never 'ad one in me life, norra proper one anyway. All I've ever 'ad were threadbare shirts and an auld army overcoat for a dressin' gown.'

Hannah wondered again about the contrasting lives of the rich and poor. Victoria Terrace and Faulkner Square were only a short distance apart, but there could have been an ocean dividing them.

'Well, it's how that lot get their money, isn't it? They hang on to it. They don't go in much for throwing it around except on themselves, but as Ada says, yer shouldn't have had ter pay.'

'Well, I have and I like it that way. It means I owe them nothing. But when I get paid next I'd like to help you both out.'

Ada looked perturbed. 'Help? What do yer mean by that, luv?'

'Well, I won't need all that money and I'd like to give some to you. You were good to me and my mam and now . . .' She shrugged and looked around.

Both women followed her gaze.

'I know we 'aven't got much left, luv, we 'ad to sell

96

the furniture bit by bit ter make ends meet, but we can't take yer money, girl.'

'You *can* and you *will*. I told you I don't need *that* much.'

'God in heaven, just for a second yer looked just like yer da, God rest him.'

Hannah smiled. 'Da could be very stubborn.'

'Never a truer word was spoken. Iffen 'e got somethin' in 'is 'ead, yer couldn't shift 'im,' Ada said sagely.

'I could give you thirty shillings each and still have money over for myself.'

Tempting though the offer was Ada shook her head. 'No, luv, we couldn't take it. Life's hard for the likes of us, Hannah, save as much as yer can. One day yer might well need it. It might be the only thing between you and having to go back into the workhouse.'

'I'd throw myself off the Landing Stage first.'

'Yer see, an' if that 'appened 'ow would Martha and me live with ourselves? Our consciences would drive us mad. It's bad enough now, we was only saying yisterday that we should 'ave made some effort to keep in touch with yer after yer da was killed.'

'How could you? You were suffering too badly yourselves. There was no time to worry about me. I was a stranger, not family, and it was family you lost.'

'You were never a stranger, Hannah, you were born here in this street. Martha an' me helped Ma Wilkinson bring you into the world.'

Hannah smiled at that. The subject of money was never mentioned again. She did however bring something with her on each visit. Sometimes it was a jar of jam begged from Mrs Howard or the leftovers from the previous night's meal; once it was a whole victoria sponge cake that had burned almost to a cinder when Blandford managed to half demolish the back wall getting the carriage out and they'd all run to see what the noise was. The cake had been ruined, Mrs Howard had said angrily, absolutely ruined. 'And meladdo's for the high jump this time, you mark my words,' she'd predicted grimly. But somehow Blandford had managed to talk his way out of being given the sack and Ada and her family had had a slightly crispy, but unexpected treat.

Hannah had settled in so well that she now thought of the house in Faulkner Square as 'home'. With the onset of autumn Vi had persuaded her to buy a good winter coat and hat out of the money she religiously gave to Mrs Howard to keep for her.

'You'll freeze, Hannah, if you don't get one,' Vi had urged.

'I'm used to that. It was always bitterly cold each winter in Wales.'

'It doesn't have to be a new one, Hannah. There's plenty of second-hand shops. You could pick up a decent one for about three pounds.'

So she'd gone along to Franks Quality Garments at Half Price, and bought a navy blue wool coat, a thicker skirt, and two woollen jumpers. She'd also purchased two pairs of thick stockings and a small cloche hat from Blacklers. That at least was new, as were the stockings.

'I've hardly any savings left now at all,' she complained.

'Well, you can't have it and spend it too. It's one or the other, but you did need winter clothes,' Mrs Howard had said.

'I could have got a heavy shawl.'

'Indeed you could not! No one in this house would wear such a thing. It would bring the tone of the whole household down,' Mrs Howard had said indignantly.

There were weeks and weeks when she didn't set eyes on either Richard or his brother. They were in the house, she knew that, and Richard more often than his brother, for there were days when there were no lectures. At times she would cry herself to sleep because it was all so hopeless. She knew she should put him out of her mind completely but that was easier said than done. Even when she was down on her hands and knees scrubbing she thought of him.

Autumn had turned to winter. The trees were bare now, and all the flowers in the little park in the centre of the square were dead. Frequently a heavy hoar frost covered everything so thickly that it could be mistaken for snow. Biting north-easterly winds swept across the Pennines or the Irish Sea, bringing with them sleet and hail. It was bitterly cold in Hannah's little bedroom under the eaves, so at night she was allowed to take a shelf from the oven, wrapped in flannel, to bed with her. 'We can't have you catching cold or freezing to death up there. I'll find you more blankets,' Mrs Howard had promised. But with a heavy linen sheet, a blanket and an old eiderdown there were already more covers on her bed than she'd ever had in the workhouse. She had a discarded dressing gown, too, made out of a grey army blanket, that Vi had given her, and she often wore that in bed. Knowing what she'd lived through for ten years, she never felt as sorry for herself nowadays as other people did.

Hannah still went to see Ada on her free afternoons, and on her Sunday off after church, which all the servants attended, she would sit and read in the warm kitchen, as near as she could pull a chair to the range without scorching herself. She loved reading, it was a form of escape as well as a source of education, and she'd never been allowed to read anything other than the Bible before. She had joined the local library for a penny and was allowed to take two books out per week.

Just before Christmas, she was walking up Upper Parliament Street, her books under her arm, her hat pulled well down and the collar of her coat turned up when she turned the corner and came face to face with Richard Hughes.

'Hannah!'

'Oh, it's you, sir.' She held the books tightly to her and looked down.

He fell into step beside her. 'Where have you been?'

'To the library and to see friends and neighbours

from the street I used to live in.'

He smiled. He saw very little of her but knew she was a quiet girl. She seemed almost painfully shy with any member of his own class that she came into contact with. Out of her uniform she was very pretty with her pale skin and those huge, lovely brown eyes.

'Do you read a lot?'

'Whenever I get the chance, sir. I try to read two books a week. Mrs Howard is always telling me off. She says I stay up too late and that I'm ruining my eyesight.'

He laughed. 'Then by Mrs Howard's reasoning I should be as blind as a bat. The number of books I have to get through is awesome.'

She looked up at him. 'But it's necessary, isn't it, sir? I mean . . . I mean it's going to be your job.'

'It is and I've a lot of work to do yet before they let me loose on the poor hapless souls who come to the hospital.'

'Don't you find it very hard to remember all those long words?' Once she'd found one of his books lying open on the dining-room table when she'd gone to help Vi clear away.

'Sometimes, but as you said, Hannah, it's necessary.'

She hadn't been able to think of anything else to say so they'd walked through the winter dusk in silence the rest of the way.

It was the first real Christmas Hannah had had since she was very young and even those memories were vague.

'It's all right for them up there, it'll be twice the

work for us. I might even ask Miss Siân can we have the services of Mr Donaldson again for a few days, seeing as they will be entertaining. It gives a family more standing to have a butler open the front door to their guests,' Mrs Howard had grumbled.

'Will we really help to put up the tree in the hall?' Hannah asked.

'It's nothing special. It's just another job, Hannah,' Vi said flatly.

'Well, it's one I won't mind doing at all. I can never remember us having a tree even when I lived in Victoria Terrace.'

'Then you can go with Blandford and buy the holly and mistletoe as well. I'll go myself for the goose and the pork. I know they'll be delivered but I like to choose for myself. That way they won't try to palm me off with rubbish.'

'When do we have *our* dinner?'

'When they've finished theirs. Miss Siân always insists on a cold buffet for the evening though, that way we can all enjoy the rest of the day. We all go up to the dining room first thing and Mr Hughes wishes us a Happy Christmas and gives us our Christmas present.'

Hannah was incredulous. '*We* get Christmas presents?'

'We get money. Left to his own devices we'd get nothing off that old skinflint,' Vi said scathingly.

'That'll do from you! You'll speak of the Master with respect or not at all.'

'We all get an extra month's wages, so you'll have eight guineas, Hannah. And you can thank Miss Siân, she's the one who really knows how much we appreciate money, rather than some useless gift,' Mrs Howard had informed her.

Hannah had already started to think what she would do with her money. She'd get something for Vi and then for Ada and Martha. She had some money left and it could be replaced by her Christmas gift. In fact then she'd have more saved up than she'd imagined, it was a small fortune or so it seemed to her.

As a special favour she and Vi were allowed to go to town together for a few hours, as it was decided that it would be best for them to buy the festive greenery. Everywhere was crowded; Hannah had never seen so many people, and they were all so friendly. She was like a child as she stood gazing in wonder at the decorated windows of the shops.

'I never dreamed that shops could be like this! Look at that!' She pointed to one of Lewis's windows that depicted a snowy scene. On a bench was a lifelike figure of Santa Claus that turned its head from side to side and raised one arm up and then put it down.

'What's a "Grotto"? See, it says, "Come and visit our Fairytale Grotto with live people and animals. Sixpence entrance and a toy for every child." '

'It's a sort of show, a fairy story, like . . . oh, *Sleeping Beauty*. It's for kids and no, you can't go in and see it, we don't have time.'

Hannah looked disappointed.

'Cheer up. I've never seen one. Neither have half of the kids in the city.' Vi smiled at her. 'Are you going to

103

get something for your friend Jessie?'

Hannah's excitement was immediately tinged with guilt. She'd forgotten Jessie. Oh, how could she?

'She'd never get it. They would know my writing and confiscate it.'

'Can they do that?' Vi demanded.

Hannah nodded. 'I feel awful, Vi. I'd forgotten my promise to her.'

'Well, I'll keep my ears open. There's always people having rows and giving in their notice at this time of year. We're lucky compared to a lot of people in service. Worked to death for a pittance and no time off over the holiday.'

'Do many leave?'

'Quite a few. God knows we don't get paid all that much, not compared to what you can earn in a factory, but who the hell would want to work in a factory? But we get time off and the money from his nibs. Anyway, you'd have to find board and lodgings and anywhere halfway decent would cost most of your wages. At least we don't have to pay for our keep.'

Hannah nodded her agreement. Vi was right, even though their earnings weren't great, there were so many other benefits.

The tree was in place in the hall and Blandford had brought down the boxes of decorations from the attic. As she'd opened them Hannah had been mesmerised. They were all so pretty and so delicate.

'Hannah, we'll be here all day. You can admire

everything when we've finished,' Vi scolded her.

'At midnight, the way we're going,' young Blandford muttered, but Vi heard him and glared at him.

Two hours later it *was* finished. Blandford had disappeared half an hour ago and Vi had been called down to the kitchen. Hannah stood with the fragile little fairy in her hands. Vi had delegated this final task to herself. She turned it over in her hands. It was so lovely. The whole tree was just beautiful, she thought, gazing at it in awe.

'I never feel as though Christmas is *really* here until I see the tree.'

Hannah turned and blushed. Richard Hughes stood beside her.

'It's the first time I've ever been anywhere where there's been a Christmas tree.'

He smiled down at her. Poor girl, he thought, she'd never had a real Christmas. 'I see you've got the fairy.'

'Yes, sir, Rowan was called away.'

'Right then, up you go, I'll hold the step ladder steady unless you want me to put her up there?'

'No! I mean, it's no trouble at all, sir.' She was begining to tremble and she felt such a fool. What if she fell and broke the ornament? Oh, he'd really think she was just a useless, clumsy scullery maid then.

She managed to quell her feelings until he held out his hand as she came down the last few steps.

'Thank you, sir. I did feel a bit . . . unsteady,' she said, quickly drawing her hand from his before he could feel it trembling.

They both stood back and looked at the tree and Hannah sighed. Richard's gaze was drawn to her face. She was so happy, he thought, that joy radiated from her face, and again he thought how lovely she was.

'This is your first *real* Christmas, isn't it, Hannah?'

'Yes, and I'm going to enjoy *everything.*'

'Good. I'll see you tomorrow morning.'

She looked up at him, puzzlement in her eyes.

'When Father gives you all your gifts.'

'Oh, yes, I'd sort of forgotten.' She smiled as he walked away. She *was* going to enjoy herself and he had reminded her that he'd see her tomorrow. Yes, tomorrow would be a glorious day.

She went up with Vi, Blandford and Mrs Howard on Christmas morning. She shook the hand of her employer as he wished her 'Happy Christmas' and was given an envelope with her name on it. After that her hand was shaken by Mr Thomas whom she studiously avoided looking at, then Richard whose grasp of her hand was warm and firm and made her feel a little dizzy; and at last Miss Siân, who added that she was very pleased that Hannah had settled in so well. She was very diligent and industrious, according to the account Mrs Howard had given of her, and she was looking much better now. She'd put on weight.

'It's all the good food, ma'am,' Hannah said with a smile.

At four o'clock they all sat down in the kitchen to have their dinner, Mrs Howard looking rather flushed.

'It's a fine feast you've cooked for us, Mrs Howard, and we all appreciate it,' said Mr Donaldson. Miss Siân, at Mrs Howard's request, had asked him to come back for the holidays. There were 'thank yous' from everyone else and more praise and Mrs Howard's cheeks glowed.

'Oh, everything would be perfect if only I could find something for poor Jessie,' Hannah said as she passed Vi the gravy boat.

'Who's Jessie?' Mr Donaldson enquired.

'My friend in the workhouse. She's a really good worker and I promised to get her out of there.'

'How good?' Mr Donaldson asked.

'Well, she does everything I do here and did there.'

'What about her foot?' Vi inquired.

'That doesn't bother her, in the way of work I mean.'

'I might be able to help,' the stand-in butler said.

'Could you?'

'We hear all kinds of things at the agency and at the places we're sent to work in. I believe one of the scullery maids at number fifteen Abercromby Square walked out two days ago. A flighty little madam, I hear she was. Wouldn't do a decent day's work and when told off about it, she ups and tells them what they can do with their job.'

Mrs Howard tutted. 'The very idea of it. Cheek!'

Hannah looked from the man to Mrs Howard pleadingly. 'Can anything be done?'

Donaldson was now confident, after a word with Mr Richard, that he would be made permanent, so he took the slightly unusual decision to take this matter up personally.

'I think so. I'll tell their butler about the girl and let you know.'

Hannah beamed at him. Abercromby Square was not too far away and, if they had a butler and more than one scullery maid, the people at number fifteen must have a far grander lifestyle than they had here. Jessie would be frightened to death at first, just as she'd been, but she'd get over it.

Hannah was silent, lost in her thoughts, when Vi's voice penetrated her trance. She was talking about Richard and someone called 'Maria'.

'What about them?' she asked.

'Hannah, you were in a world of your own. I said Mr Richard has been seeing quite a lot of Miss Maria Delahunty – you remember her, she came to Miss Siân's party?'

Hannah remembered. 'Is . . . is it serious? Proper "walking out", I mean?'

'How am I supposed to know that?'

'But you see both him and Miss Siân more often than I do.'

Vi shrugged and Mrs Howard looked thoughtful for a minute. 'Well, I suppose it could be called walking out. Maybe we'll see a wedding in the family in the New Year, but don't go blabbing about that.'

Hannah pushed her plate away. Somehow the goose had begun to taste like sawdust in her mouth.

Chapter Eight

It was Mr Arnold Donaldson who finally got the job for Jessie. He seemed in no hurry to leave Faulkner Square and was very thankful that Mrs Howard protested – on every occasion that Miss Siân or Mr Hughes brought the matter up – that she just didn't know how she would cope without him. She wasn't getting any younger and the place was more 'respectable' with a butler.

'God, she's such a snob! It's only because she's living in the past when everyone who was anyone had hordes of servants,' Vi said scathingly one winter evening as they sat by the kitchen range.

'I don't care, Vi. If he can get poor Jessie out of that place both he and Mrs Howard can walk around with crowns on their heads all day and all night!'

'Well, what's Jessie like then?'

'She's nice, really nice, but she was always getting picked on because she had a limp. I think that's why she was there. She told me one day that she could vaguely remember a man taking her there and saying, "She's no use to me with that leg." '

Vi looked horrified. 'That's terrible! People like that shouldn't be allowed to just dump their kids.'

Hannah nodded. 'I don't know how he got away

109

with it. He must have been her da. At least Cousin Gwyneth was only that, a cousin. I know my da would never have abandoned me like that. He didn't want to go to war, but he had no choice.'

'Thank God I was never in that position,' Vi said with feeling. On her days off she went to visit her elderly parents. Hers was a decent but impoverished family; times were often hard for them because her da had never had good health. She was the youngest. 'So when's Jessie coming?'

'He said the second Sunday in January. She'll only be on approval to start with but I'm sure they'll keep her. I don't see how they could do anything else. I'm to go with him to fetch her. I'm paying my own fare and it's my Sunday off. I don't trust them at all. They could say she was sick or she didn't want to go.'

'I would have thought they'd be glad to see her go. One less mouth to feed. One less to clothe if that's what they can call it – the way they sent you here.'

'I know, but there's a nasty, mean streak in both Annie Pritchard and Mrs Phillips.'

'How come? Is there a Mr Phillips?'

'No, I don't think so. I never heard him mentioned.'

'She's probably a sour old maid then. Takes it out on the girls.' Vi smiled. 'Well, Jessie will be made up to see you.'

'She will. I'll see if I can bring her around here for a bit. I'll write and tell her, even though she probably won't get the letter. They'll open it. They always do.'

Each night as Hannah lay in her bed she thought

about her friend. Had they told her? Probably not, they'd leave it until the very last minute then Jessie would be summoned to Mrs Phillips's office as she herself had been and would think she'd done something wrong and was about to be punished. Oh, she was looking forward to seeing their faces. She'd wear her best clothes, take great care with her hair and she wouldn't be subservient in any way. Then, as always, her thoughts turned to Richard Hughes. She began to imagine him walking down the aisle with her, turning to her, smiling and then kissing her. And she'd look radiant in a white dress and veil and then they'd live together in a nice house and be happy for ever. Everything and everyone was pushed to the back of her mind. She held on to her dream. She knew it was pure fantasy but she couldn't help it. It was the only thing that made life worth living, even though she knew how lucky she was now, being here. He was the most important person in her life, even though he didn't know it.

The appointed Sunday morning dawned at last. Overnight it had snowed and then frozen and the city looked like a scene on the front of a Christmas card. Even the slum areas didn't look so bad, although Hannah knew that the residents of those areas were suffering great hardship. Many would die from cold and starvation.

'It's no good for travelling, isn't this weather,' Arnold Donaldson complained. Both he and Hannah were muffled to the eyebrows; Hannah was glad of all the things she now had to keep out the cold. She had brought the old carpet bag in which there was a knitted scarf, mitts, a hat and thick stockings. She'd gone to Paddy's Market in Great Homer Street and had bought a heavy brown wool coat that was sure to be too big for Jessie but had only cost five shillings. For all she knew it was third or even fourth hand, but when new it would have cost a fair bit. Hundreds of people went to Paddy's Market for clothes. You had to rummage through the piles of them that were dumped on the floor, but the poor of the city had no choice.

It was so cold that the workhouse would be bound to give Jessie a shawl, but she'd remembered Mrs Howard's remarks about shawls and she didn't want Jessie to start off by being improperly dressed.

It was a long journey and one she took very little pleasure in. She did admire the countryside, covered in its blanket of snow, but it made the roads and lanes very difficult for the omnibus, and twice all the passengers had to get out and push as the vehicle got stuck in deep snow drifts.

The pale winter sun was slipping behind clouds of dusky grey that looked like waves breaking on a shore, its last rays lighting with pure gold the duck-egg-blue sky, when at last they reached Denbigh. She clung to Mr Donaldson's arm as they both struggled and slipped their way up the narrow lane that had been so hot when last she'd walked along it.

One of the male inmates was waiting at the gate, shivering and blue with cold.

'You took your time, didn't you?' he said sharply.

'It's the weather and we've come a long way. Now if you'll kindly open the gate we can get on and trouble you no further,' Mr Donaldson answered in an imperious tone.

Jessie was standing just inside the big front door. A huge black shawl covered her head and shoulders, a parcel clasped in hands that were numb with cold.

'Jessie! Oh, Jessie!' Hannah cried and gathered up the girl in her arms.

Tears sprang to Jessie's eyes. 'Oh, Hannah! I can't believe it! It's you, really you.'

'It is. I promised you I wouldn't forget about you.' Hannah noticed with concern how thin Jessie looked and how pale and drawn her face was, even though now her eyes were dancing with happiness.

'This is Mr Donaldson, our . . . butler, I suppose. He heard there was a job going and helped get it for you.'

'Oh, thank you, sir! I'll be grateful all the days of my life, I will. God bless you!'

He coughed, embarrassed by her words and wondering how on earth anyone so small, under-nourished and half-crippled was going to cope with the work. 'On a trial, don't forget that.'

A door opened along the corridor and Mrs Phillips, followed by Annie Pritchard, came towards them. Hannah could see that they hadn't recognised her. She smiled inwardly. She was just dying to see their faces.

'You're rather late but I suppose the inclement

weather has had—' Mrs Phillips stopped. 'Peckham, is that you?'

Hannah smiled at the woman and stepped forward. 'It is. I promised Jessie I'd get her out of this hell-hole and I have.'

Mrs Phillips was stunned; Annie's mouth dropped open. It *was* Hannah Peckham, all dressed up and with short hair and a fashionable hat.

'I've brought her some clothes so she won't be needing this any longer. Give it to Annie.' Hannah whisked the shawl from around Jessie's shoulders and half threw it at Annie. 'Girls in service don't wear shawls.' She opened the bag and passed over what she had brought to a dumbfounded Jessie.

'Er, we would be grateful, madam, if somewhere could be provided for a few minutes while the girl changes her stockings.' The butler looked pointedly down at Jessie's bare legs. The hem of her skirt had come down in places but was short in others, revealing the tops of her boots.

With a very bad grace, Mrs Phillips pointed to a door. She was not used to her position being completely ignored, and Mr Donaldson was showing her no respect at all, indeed his voice was filled with contempt. Mrs Phillips snapped, 'In there. She knows her way. There is no need for *anyone* to accompany her.'

'Madam, I can assure you that I certainly harbour no such intention and I don't suppose Peckham does either. We do not need to be reminded of common decency and privacy.' Mr Donaldson's tone was scathing and Mrs Phillips turned away, her cheeks almost puce. She'd never been spoken to like that before, Hannah thought with grim satisfaction.

When Jessie reappeared she looked even tinier but she was well prepared for the weather. Tears filled her eyes. 'Thank you, Hannah, so much.'

'They're the best I could manage. There's some other things too. A hairbrush, pins, clips, a warm dress and a little tablet of nice soap. That's a present from Vi, the girl I work with.'

'Oh, I've never had anything like this before, see. That's why I'm crying, I'm so happy.'

'You'll be even happier when we get back. You'll have your own bedroom, warm clothes, good food and nice people to work with and talk to. Everything you never had in here.' Hannah's eyes were fixed on Annie's face and suddenly she felt sorry for the woman. It was a terrible life in here with no hope of escape. No wonder she was so spiteful.

'Are we ready to get back now?'

'Yes, we're more than ready, Mr Donaldson.' Hannah took Jessie's arm and together they walked across the snow-covered yard and out through the gates.

There was no time to take Jessie to call in at Faulkner Square, since it was late at night when they finally got back to Liverpool. Hannah hugged her friend and told her she'd see her very soon. Jessie looked up fearfully as Mr Donaldson took her arm.

'You'll be fine, girl.' Adding, not unkindly, 'Don't worry, you've the right temperament and upbringing.'

That night, Hannah lay in her bed thankful of yet another extra blanket Mrs Howard had found for her. Jessie too would now be lying in her own bed in her own room. She'd have had a good supper and, Hannah hoped, would have been made welcome. Jessie had so much to look forward to now. Hannah sighed heavily. It had been a long day for both of them, but she knew Jessie at least wouldn't be eating her heart out for a man she could never have.

At last the winter was over, Hannah thought as she looked out of her attic window and across the rooftops of the city. It was something she did often: Blandford had oiled the catch on the skylight so it opened easily. It was warmer now. The trees in the park were in bud, the ground beneath them covered in daffodils and primulas.

Jessie was doing well. Her two months' trial was over. Everyone was pleased with her work and with the girl herself. She'd gained weight and now had a healthy tinge to her once sallow cheeks. She did find the work hard but she never complained. As she often said to Hannah, 'she'd come to Paradise'. Vi thought that description was a bit far-fetched. All three girls had different days off so once a week they tried to have a few hours together in the evenings, taking it in turns to share the kitchen of the house in Faulkner Square and that in Abercromby Square. Tonight it was the turn of Faulkner Square and Hannah hoped it would be warm enough for them to sit outside, as conversation was rather stilted and limited in the kitchen where other ears were listening.

'I'd put on a coat or something if you intend to sit out, Hannah. You'll catch your death. It goes damp once the light's gone,' Mrs Howard lectured her.

Vi, who was standing behind her, raised her eyes to the ceiling, but Hannah did as she was told and took her coat from the hook behind the door.

When Jessie arrived she too wore a coat over her uniform.

'I'll have no noise from you three. Sounds carry at night and I don't want any complaints from Miss Siân.'

'No, Mrs Howard, we won't make any noise,' Jessie said quietly. She still marvelled at how much her life had changed and, like Hannah, she found no task too hard.

'Can we take a cup of tea out with us, please?' Hannah asked.

'As long as you take mugs not cups and you stay completely out of sight of the windows on the back. A nice sight that would be, three maids sitting sipping tea and gossiping like ladies over afternoon tea!'

'Oh, we'll be careful,' Hannah assured her.

They all clutched mugs and were preparing to go outside when Mr Donaldson, who had been made permanent at the beginning of March, came into the kitchen.

'I can see there's something interesting in the offing, just by the look on your face.'

'There is, Mrs Howard. Indeed there is. The Master has just informed me, and told me to inform the staff, that Mr Richard has become engaged to Miss Maria Delahunty.'

'Oh, that's a turn-up for the book, all right! Fancy, just fancy, a wedding in the offing at last, although I would have thought Mr Thomas would be first. Still, she's a lovely girl. I can't find a single wrong thing to say about her,' Mrs Howard said approvingly.

Jessie smiled and turned to Hannah. 'Oh, isn't that . . .' Her words died as she saw the expression on Hannah's face and the tears that were welling up in her eyes. 'Hannah?'

'She's all right, Jessie. We'll leave Mrs Howard and Mr Donaldson to talk about it. Come on, take Hannah's mug and follow me,' Vi said firmly.

Jessie was very confused for as soon as they were out of earshot and sight Hannah broke down.

'What is it, *cariad*?' Jessie pleaded.

Vi looked at Hannah with pity. 'She loves him, Jessie. She has since the day she set eyes on him.'

'But she said nothing . . .'

'What use was there in talking about it? She's always known she could never have him.' Both girls put an arm around Hannah's shaking shoulders as she cried as though her heart would break.

Vi was right, Hannah thought. She'd always known she could never have him, but there had remained a tiny spark of hope – and she'd had her dreams. Dreams that were now ripped to shreds.

'What will we do, Vi?' Jessie asked, full of concern.

'Get her upstairs to her room. If anyone sees her in this state questions will be asked. Hannah, luv, pull yourself together, just for a few minutes, please, if you can.'

'What will we say?'

'That she's suddenly got a cold. Not very original, I know, but I can't think of anything else.'

'Oh, Hannah, try to stop crying, just for a bit,' Jessie pleaded.

Hannah tried and managed to fight down the terrible sobs and let herself be led inside, across the kitchen, before the avidly curious gazes of the cook and butler, then she shook herself free of Vi's arm.

'It ... it's ... all right. I'll ... just ... go ...'

They stood aside and she ran up the narrow kitchen stairs.

'What's the matter with her?' Mrs Howard demanded.

'A cold. Her nose just suddenly started running.'

'And her eyes began to water, see,' Jessie added. 'Will I go back now?' she whispered to Vi.

'No, you won't. We'll go back outside and have a little chat,' Vi hissed back.

'I feel awful leaving her in such a state, I really do.' Jessie looked near to tears herself, Vi thought.

'Don't you start crying. There's nothing we can do to help now. If we go fussing over her they're all going to notice and start asking questions and we can't add all that to her troubles.'

'I suppose you're right, Vi, but she . . . she's been so good to me, ever since we were little.'

'I know. I've tried to talk sense into her, believe me, but where he's concerned it's hopeless. Still, now she might stop dreaming of the impossible. Oh, I feel some of it's my fault. When she first told me I told her about a girl who *had* married a son in the house she worked in. God! I wish I'd kept my big mouth shut, Jessie, I really do.'

Jessie shook her head and patted Vi's hand. 'Poor Hannah. Poor *cariad*.'

Blinded by her tears Hannah reached the door that led out on to the landing and wrenched it open. Why had she been such a fool? Because that's what she was: a stupid, romantic fool! She knew facing the fact wouldn't help. She couldn't fight off this terrible feeling of rejection and loss.

'Hannah! What's wrong?'

She turned and to her horror through her tears she saw him. She tried to back away but he caught her arm. He could feel her trembling.

'Hannah, you're in a terrible state! What's happened?'

'Nothing! Nothing has happened!'

His voice was full of concern and she wished she were dead or a thousand miles away, or both.

'Something has upset you and upset you badly. Is it Tom?'

'No! No, it's nothing like that!' she gulped between sobs.

'Then what is it?'

He now had both his hands on her shoulders and she couldn't escape. She looked up at him and lost control completely.

'I . . . I . . . didn't know . . . I . . . I . . . love you. I always . . . have,' she choked out.

He looked appalled. 'Oh, Hannah! If I've done anything to make you think I cared for you other than as a sweet young girl, I'm sorry. I'm truly sorry. I'm fond of you, you know that, but . . . but only in a friendly way.'

'I know that! I . . . I know I'm a fool! I'll leave. I'll get another job.'

'Oh, Hannah, no! Not because of me, please?'

'How can I stay now?' she cried.

'Because this is really your home as well as workplace. The first home you've had since you were a child.'

She shook her head; she couldn't speak.

'Oh, I never realised! I'm the one who is a fool! Hannah, I'm sorry, so very sorry.' He meant what he said. She'd mistaken kindness for something else. Surely he'd never encouraged her in any way? Of course, he'd tried to help her, to take an interest in her and how she was settling in. Whenever he saw her, which hadn't really been very often, he'd spoken to her and yes, he did feel some affection for her, but that's all it was. Affection.

Hannah broke free and ran for the attic stairs. He let her go and stood staring after her with concern and regret in his eyes.

Chapter Nine

Richard Hughes stared at the garden through the french windows but he was not admiring the glorious flowers, nor the glossy new leaves on the big laurel bushes, nor the slender sweeping frond-like branches of the willow at the bottom of the lawn that obscured the walls of the outbuildings.

In two months' time he was to be married to Maria. It would be a big event. He was the first of his siblings to be married and Maria's father, a very wealthy self-made man, doted on his only daughter. She was to have the best of everything. The reception was to be held in the Adelphi Hotel where all the well-to-do passengers off the liners stayed, as did visiting dignitaries. He and Maria would stay there too the night before boarding the ship that would take them, eventually, to Italy. When they returned they would take up residence in the house bought by both their parents in Upper Husskinson Street, and he'd work as a houseman in the Royal Infirmary.

He should have been filled with happiness. He *was* happy, he told himself. He *would* be filled with joy . . . if only . . . if only Hannah were not still so upset. He'd only seen her once since that night in the spring. Again they had met on the landing but she'd looked down and gone swiftly up the stairs to her room. She'd looked ill. He had been shocked by the change in her. He wanted to do something . . . anything to help her. Life had been so terrible for her. There was no one he could speak to. His father would be shocked at the very idea of it. He would be told firmly that in no way was he to act like his brother. His brother would be scornful and sarcastic; his sister would be terribly upset. None of them had seen Hannah – fortunately they had no occasion to – but he couldn't let this go on for much longer.

He turned and reached for the bell-pull and tugged it twice. Then he extracted a cigarette from the silver case and lit it. The smoke drifted in a blue mist in the humid air. He tried to compose himself and what he would say.

It was Arnold Donaldson who came in response, knocking quietly before entering. 'Sir?' he enquired politely.

'Donaldson, I . . . I have to speak to someone . . . about . . . well . . . about young Hannah Peckham.' He stubbed the cigarette out in a porcelain ashtray. It was best, he decided, not to beat about the bush. 'I saw her on Sunday night, she was going to bed, and she looked dreadful.'

'She has been a little off colour lately, sir.'

'The thing is, Donaldson . . .' He was fighting to keep his composure. 'She thinks she's . . . in love with me.' He breathed deeply. It was out. He'd actually said the words. He felt easier in his mind already. He marvelled at the man's composure. Not even a muscle twitched; the eyes were expressionless too. He'd been well trained.

'Of course it's just an impressionable young girl's crush. I never gave her any reason at all to think like this. I did enquire about her from time to time, concerned about her happiness and so on. I think you'll agree that she's had a very hard life, and I can only assume that she's taken that interest to be something . . . else, so you can see my predicament.' He paused, waiting for the man in front of him to speak.

Arnold Donaldson was not really very surprised. These things often happened and usually to girls like Hannah.

'I understand, sir. She is impressionable. I had an idea that something was wrong but . . .'

'What am I to do about her?' It *was* just a crush. He wouldn't even admit to himself that there was anything remotely like *love* in the way he felt about her. He'd seen this happen in the hospital. Young doctors seemed to attract the attentions of both nurses and female patients. Richard threw out his hands in the old gesture of appeal.

'Nothing, sir, if you'll take my advice. I understand how you feel, but there is no reason at all for you to be troubled about it. I will personally attend to it.'

'You'll speak to her? Try to make her understand?'

'Yes, I will.'

'Try to be . . . kind to her, please?'

'I will, and may I make a suggestion, sir?'

'Please.'

'Could you avoid using the landing at ten o'clock at night? It would help if she didn't see you, even though it was only by chance that you saw her last time.'

'Yes. Yes, anything if it will help her to get over this.'

'Leave it to me, sir. You have enough on your mind with your own affairs and your wedding. I'll take care of staff matters.'

'Thank you, Donaldson. Thank you.'

When the man had quietly closed the door behind him, Richard lit another cigarette and wandered out into the garden. He should have confided in Donaldson earlier, he thought. It might have been beneficial to Hannah. It might have stopped her making herself ill with misery.

It was dark now, the dew beginning to form on the lawn and flowerbeds whose colours had faded. The air was perfumed with their scent and he breathed in deeply, feeling much better.

Arnold Donaldson went straight to his pantry and sat down. So that's what was behind all this. Mrs Howard, or Edith as she had told him to call her in private, had said she was worried about Hannah. No one seemed to know just what was the matter, but the girl was definitely not herself. He took the welfare of the two girls seriously, as seriously as the welfare of that young hooligan Blandford whom he was gradually knocking into shape. Probably young Vi knew. Would it be best to speak to her or to Hannah direct? He had a little time to spare, so he got out his pipe, poured himself a small port and sat trying to work out what was the best way to tackle the problem.

Jessie and Vi were both worried about Hannah too. They'd tried everything to cheer her up, lighten her mood, bring the smile to her face, the colour to her cheeks. All to no avail.

'I don't know what else to do, Jessie! She'll go into a decline if she carries on like this.'

'Her heart's broken and . . . and people do die of broken hearts.'

'Oh, God in heaven, Jessie, don't start thinking and talking like that! Mrs Howard keeps on at me morning, noon and night and I don't know what to say to her.'

'Should we . . . you . . . see him? Tell him?'

Vi's eyes widened. '*Me* tell *him*! Haven't you learned anything, Jessie? I'd definitely lose my job for something like that.'

'Well, I'd do it, for Hannah.'

'And then you'd lose your job and it would be back to the workhouse for you.'

Jessie bit her lips, torn between loyalty to her friend and her own future.

'I think I'll try once more and then I'm going to go to Mr Donaldson.'

Jessie looked earnestly at her friend. 'Oh, yes! Please try again, Vi. I will too, if you think I should.'

'No, leave it with us, this is where she works. I know

you mean well, Jessie. Don't get upset. And no one would let you go back to Denbigh.'

Vi found Hannah lying on her bed staring at the ceiling. Whenever she had time to spare Hannah came up here. The tiny room was stifling even though the skylight was wide open.

'Hannah, sit up and listen to me, please?'

'Vi, if you've come to talk to me about . . . him, then you're wasting your time.'

'No, I haven't come to talk about *him*, I've come to talk about *you*: Hannah Peckham who will be seventeen next week.'

'I don't care about my birthday.'

'Did I say you should? No, you're seventeen, you're beautiful, you could have any lad but no, you want to go on torturing yourself because you can't have Richard Hughes. There I've said it. You won't even use his name. For God's sake, Hannah, do you want to go into a decline and die?'

Hannah sat up. 'I don't *care*, Vi!'

'Well, *I* do, so does Jessie and so does he. Richard Hughes. There, I've said it again.'

'He doesn't care!'

'He does. Yes, he does. He's a kind, caring person. How do you think he must feel, knowing how much suffering he's unintentionally caused you?'

'He doesn't know the way I still feel. How upset I still am.'

'Oh, yes he does.'

'How . . . how do you know that?'

'Because I asked Mr Donaldson to tell him, tactfully, like,' she lied.

Hannah wiped away a tear. 'And . . .'

'Mr Donaldson said to tell you that Richard is very sorry to hear you are still so upset. He saw you one night and he knew something was very wrong.' Now there was a faint gleam of interest in Hannah's dark eyes.

Hannah shook her head. She'd never thought that he might be upset about her. That he was still upset. She'd just dragged herself through each miserable, pointless day until it was time to try to sleep. Only in sleep could she forget about him and the pain and rejection.

Vi seized on this spark of interest. 'You don't want him to be all worried and upset, do you?'

'No. No, that's the last thing I'd want.'

'Then give him a chance, Hannah. Pull yourself together, start eating again and I mean properly. Mrs Howard's got me half demented over you and your meals, or lack of them. Start going out again. You haven't been to Victoria Terrace for weeks. They'll all wonder what's wrong. They'll think you've stopped caring about them, or that you've gone off somewhere without telling them. Come with me tomorrow night to Jessie's. We'll all have a walk in the park. It'll be nice and cool in the evening. *Please*, Hannah? Stop thinking of yourself and think of him, that's if you *really* do love him.'

Hannah stared down at her worn coverlet. Vi was

right, she thought. All she'd done was think of herself, not him. She'd caused so many people so much worry. Oh, how selfish she'd been.

Seeing the new light in Hannah's eyes Vi put her arm around her. Thank God it had worked.

'Come on, Hannah, get up, wash your face and go down and ask Mrs Howard for something to eat.'

'I'll do that.'

'Good. Now I've got to go down too.'

The following afternoon Hannah put on her straw hat and went to see Ada. She was filled with remorse. What would they think of her? Oh, she was so glad Vi had made her see sense. She'd eaten her supper last night and her breakfast this morning and noted the looks of relief that passed between Vi, Mrs Howard and Mr Donaldson. Blandford never seemed to notice anything.

The afternoon sun was scorching. A haze of heat shimmered over the cobbles and perspiration ran down the back of her neck. Ada's front door was wide open, as was everyone's in the street. They usually were, but now all the doors and windows were open to catch any breath of air. The houses were cold and damp in winter and like ovens in summer.

'Well, Lord luv a duck! Hannah! We thought yer'd upped and gone again. We've missed yer. What's 'appened to yer, girl? Yer look terrible. 'Ave yer been sick? Sit down there, it's like a flamin' greenhouse in 'ere. I've the back door open an' all the winders but

I'm 'alf suffocated. What we need now is a good storm.'

Hannah sat down on a kitchen chair with a rickety leg. 'I'm sorry. I should have come, I should at least have sent word. Vi said you'd think I'd left again.'

'Then what's been up with yer, luv?'

'I've been really stupid. I've not been sick at all. I've been "love sick".'

'Love sick?'

Hannah nodded, trying to find the words and stay calm enough to speak them. She struggled for a few seconds. 'I . . . thought I loved someone.'

'Who? One of those young fellers you work for?'

Hannah nodded.

'Oh, God, not the one who tried to take liberties with yer?'

'No. Not him. The . . . the other one.'

Ada shook her head, she had a good idea of what was coming next.

'Did yer tell him, like? An' what did 'e say?'

Again Hannah nodded. This was so hard, so very hard, but she knew she had to tell Ada and then maybe she'd feel better, feel like her normal self again. No, never that. She'd never be the same girl again, the experience had changed her. 'When Mr Donaldson told us all that he'd got engaged, I . . . I just broke down. Jessie and Vi have been so good, but I met him . . . on the landing . . . and he said . . .' She swallowed hard. Every word he'd said to her that night was burned in her brain. 'He said he was sorry, that . . . that he hoped I . . . and I just broke down and told him.'

'An' that's it? You 'aven't seen 'im again?'

'Once, but I didn't speak or even look at him and he didn't speak to me either.'

Well, thank God he was a gentleman and hadn't taken advantage of the poor girl, Ada thought. The other one would have, she was sure.

'It's for the best, Hannah, luv. The likes of us don't marry the likes of them.'

Hannah lost control. She flung herself into Ada's arms and sobbed.

'That's it, luv, you 'ave a good cry. Gerrit out of yer system.'

'Why him though? Why him? Oh, I miss my mam and my da! I miss them so much! Why did they have to die? Why? Why did they have to leave me? Everyone I love leaves me. I'm jinxed!'

Ada shook her. 'Now that's enough of that! Yer're not jinxed. It wasn't your fault yer mam and da died. It was the filthy houses caused yer mam's fever and it was a bloody war that killed yer da and my Tom an' me lads. As fer this feller, yer just *couldn't* marry 'im, Hannah, an' that's not your fault either. Now I'm 'avin' no more talk of jinxes. Wipe yer eyes while I put the kettle on. I'll not ask Martha over terday. Do yer want 'er to know at all?'

'She might as well, you're both like aunties to me.'

Ada smiled. 'That's better, luv, an' yer know yer can always come ter us fer 'elp.'

Hannah managed a watery smile. She did feel better. She had a cup of tea with Ada and another little weep, then Martha came over of her own accord and, with a few more tears, the story was told once more. But by the time she set off for home Hannah did feel more resolute, promising to eat, take care of herself and visit regularly.

She got to the bottom of the street when the first rumble of thunder rent the air and the first huge drops of rain fell. In seconds it was lashing down and she started to run. She'd be soaked through if she couldn't find shelter. She'd have to try to get to one of the shops and stand in the doorway until it passed over. She almost fell into the doorway of Lockhead's Newsagents and into the arms of a young man.

'Here, get in behind me. I'll keep most of it off you. It's warm so I don't mind – and I certainly don't mind for a girl like you.' He grinned down at her.

She pushed a few strands of damp hair back under her hat. 'I'm sorry, I wasn't looking where I was going. I just wanted to find some shelter.'

'That's all right. Are you very wet?'

'No. Not too bad. I think my hat is ruined though.'

'It looks great to me. What's your name? I haven't seen you around here before, have I?'

'It's Hannah. Hannah Peckham. I don't live here, I'm in service in Faulkner Square and I seem to have a terrible habit of charging into people.'

'I'm not complaining about that either, Hannah Peckham.' He laughed. 'Nor living with the gentry. It beats breaking your back all day. I'm Alfie Duggan, by the way.'

Hannah grimaced. 'It's not as soft as people think. Look.' She held out her red work-roughened hands.

He took them in his own and turned them over. 'Washing soda?'

She nodded.

'And hands like these weren't made for scrubbing floors.'

'Oh, stop it! You're a stranger and I don't—' The words turned to a scream of fear as a thunderclap exploded above them and the blue lightning lit up the sky. She clung to him, terrified.

He looked down at her. She was a real beauty, even soaking wet. Wouldn't the lads at the George be green with jealousy if he turned up with her on his arm?

'You can look up again now, Hannah.'

She blushed as she realised her predicament. Nice girls didn't hurl themselves into the arms of strange lads.

'Oh, I'm sorry. I don't know what you must think of me. I was terrified. I hate thunder and lightning.'

He laughed. 'There's no need to be sorry and my mam hides under the table she's that terrified of it. My da's usually beside her but he's not frightened, just paralytic drunk most of the time.'

She still felt shaky and confused.

'Look, I'll see you home. Do you live in?'

'Yes, but really there's no need . . .'

'What happens if it kicks off again?'

She hesitated. He looked nice enough. In fact he was quite handsome and he'd made her smile and protected her. She would feel safe with him.

'All right. Thanks, Mr Duggan.'

'Oh, you can tell you're in service. Mr Duggan! Call me Alfie, everyone else does.'

'Then call me Hannah,' she replied as she stepped out of the doorway.

Chapter Ten

She was depressed as she boarded the tram the
following Thursday afternoon on the way to visit Ada.
Although they all tried to skirt around the subject, for
her sake, the arrangements for the wedding seemed
to have taken over the whole household, even though
there were weeks to go yet before the actual day
arrived.

'Are you going to be all right now, Hannah?' Vi
questioned her, looking worriedly at her friend.

Hannah nodded. 'I think so. Oh, I know it's
impossible for me to try to pretend that life is . . .
normal again. That there's not going to be a wedding,
but I can't ask you and Mrs Howard and even Jessie to
avoid talking about it. It's not fair on all of you. It's
going to be such a great occasion.'

Vi sighed. 'I know. That's the worst part of it. If it
was going to be a quiet "do" it would be better. And I
know how much everyone upstairs is looking forward
to it. Miss Siân's worn me out trying on outfits. Most
of the stock of Cripps seems to be piled into her
bedroom. What she'll choose in the end God knows.
Oh, there I go again. I'm sorry, Hannah.'

'Vi, you don't have to go apologising all the time. It
would be far worse if it were Miss Siân that was getting

married.' She paused. 'I mean there would be more fuss.'

'If it was Miss Siân, then the situation wouldn't arise at all, would it?'

'No, you're right. I'm just so confused.'

'Try to ignore it, Hannah, and I'll do my best to try to remember not to go blabbing about it.'

Hannah had nodded, knowing full well that she couldn't ignore it. She'd have to lock herself in the cellar if she wasn't going to hear *any* talk about it. Blandford commented on it each time she saw him: mainly complaints of how he had to polish that car to within an inch of its life. It was to be used to take the family to the church and after that to the reception.

'All that standing around waiting until they decide it's time to go to the Adelphi, then I've to come back here and then go back for them at half past eleven. I'll be worn out.'

Mrs Howard glared at him. 'You, worn out! That'll be the day.' Vi also glared at him and he'd shrugged, not knowing what they were all so sharp for.

Hannah knew she'd have to shake herself out of this mood before she got to Ada's.

To her surprise, as she alighted from the tram Alfie Duggan was standing waiting for her.

'Don't you ever do any work? How did you know I would come today?'

He grinned. 'I work shifts and it was pretty clear that Thursday is your afternoon off. It was last Thursday when you were here, any fool could have worked that out.' He pushed his cap to the back of his head.

She couldn't help but smile at him.

'So, I've been waiting here for about half an hour. Shall I walk down with you?'

'If you like, but it's not far.'

'I know that. So, what's been going on in your life, Hannah Peckham?'

'All the usual things and . . . and there's to be a wedding the first week in October and already everyone is fussing.'

'Who's tying the knot then?'

'One of the sons.'

'I can't see what all the bother is over then, if it's only one of the lads. I know there's no end of carrying on if it happens to be a girl. Mam was halfway round the bend by the day our Maureen's wedding arrived. She's still paying for it and me da's no help to her, always boozing.' He looked thoughtful. 'I don't suppose any of us are much use to her, never have been and probably never will.'

'It's . . . it's different in a wealthy family.' She didn't want to talk about this at all. 'How many of you are there?'

'Six, but two are married. Do you get a full day off at all?'

Glad of the change of topic Hannah's mood lightened. 'Yes. One Sunday a month.'

'God, they don't hurt themselves, do they?'

'It's the usual thing.'

'When's your next Sunday off?'

'In a fortnight.'

'Well, will you come out with me, Hannah?'

'Out?' She was surprised. She'd not really given him much thought over the last week. She'd been depressed still and there were nights when she'd been unable to sleep, tossing and turning, her mind turning things over endlessly.

'Yes, out. We'll go for a ride to Otterspool or get the ferry over the water. Anything you'd like to do.'

She looked up at him, unsure of how to answer him. 'I only met you last week.'

'I know that, but, well . . . it's not actually "walking out" is it? Just an afternoon and evening, like.'

Hannah hesitated, filled with uncertainty. There didn't seem to be any harm in it. He did look and act in a respectable way. It wasn't anything serious and maybe it would take her mind off other things.

'All right. Thanks.'

'So where do you want to go?'

She shrugged. 'I don't know.'

'We'll go to New Brighton then, unless there's a thunderstorm,' he joked.

She smiled. 'I was such a fool, wasn't I?'

'Don't be so daft. There's plenty of people who are afraid of them. Fellers too, but they won't admit it. We'll go across on the ferry, go on the fair, sit on the beach – you can even paddle if you like – then have fish and chips, and if you're not worn out, we can go to the Tower Ballroom. Except I can't dance.'

'Neither can I, so can we leave that out?'

'Sure. We can have a bit of a flutter, if you want to. It's not legal, like, but there's plenty of fellers who are "runners" and, who knows, you might be lucky.'

Hannah frowned. 'I didn't think there were any races on a Sunday.'

'Granted there's not a lot, but you can still find one or two.'

'Gambling's illegal off the racecourse.'

'I know. Bloody miserable stupid law. A working feller doesn't have many pleasures in life and those he does have they'd make illegal if they could. The price of ale and fags is already too high. Have you ever played "Pitch and Toss"?'

She shook her head. She had no intention of putting any of her hard-earned money on a horse or a dog or a game of chance. That was illegal too, or so Blandford had told her one day.

'I'll show you, on your Sunday off,' he laughed.

'If you're trying to "lure me away from the paths of righteousness" you've no chance.' She smiled.

'What's with all this "luring and righteousness" stuff?'

'It's what they teach you in ... in the workhouse.'

'Bloody hell, Hannah! Oh, sorry. You were in a workhouse?'

She nodded and then told him her life story.

When she'd finished he looked at her in a different light. 'I'd never have believed it, not in a million years.'

'Well, it's true.'

'You deserve to enjoy yourself then.'

'Thanks.'

'We didn't have much when I was growing up, we lived from hand to mouth, sometimes we still do, but things never got so bad that we had to go in the workhouse.'

They had reached Ada's house.

'I'd better go in.'

He nodded. 'So, I'll see you a week on Sunday then? What time and where?'

'About half past eleven. We all go to church on Sundays.'

He looked at her askance. 'All of you? Do you have to, like?'

'Yes, we do, but I'll meet you at the Pier Head, under the Liver Clock.'

'Which one? There's two.'

'The one that faces the river. In fact I'll stand on the steps at the main entrance.'

'I'll see you then, Hannah.' He smiled and walked away. She was one in a million, he thought. She had a good steady job. Probably the pay wasn't much but then she got her keep. She had no relatives to object to him taking her out, and he liked her. He liked her a lot. More than any other girl he'd been out with and there'd been quite a lot of them over the years.

'Who was that feller you were talking to?' Ada asked as Hannah walked into the house in Victoria Terrace. 'I was in the lobby but I couldn't see 'im properly, the lamppost was in the way.'

'A lad I met last week. I got caught in that storm. I was terrified and he saw me home. He's nice.'

'Well, I hope so. Iffen I hadn't been so flamin' frightened meself I'd have run out after yer. I 'ate flamin' storms. So does Matty Harper. Martha says 'e starts shakin' all over an' she can't do nothin' with him until it's passed an' 'e's calmed down. He says it's like 'earin' all the 'eavy guns they used in the war. Day an' night that went on. 'E shakes all over. Anyway, 'as 'e got a job, this feller?'

'Yes, he works shifts. It's permanent but I don't know where it is or its name.'

'So that's why he's strolling around on a weekday afternoon. At least it's steady, an' there's not many jobs like that in this city nowadays. But you be careful just the same.'

'I will. He's taking me to New Brighton for the day on my next Sunday off.'

'That's nice. 'E sounds decent enough. Many a feller would 'ave let yer gerrome by yerself even if yer were terrified. I wish to God our Lily would find someone else.'

'Why don't you like this lad of hers?'

'Because 'e's no good and 'e'll come to a sticky end, that's why. The whole flamin' family are no good. Idle, useless drunks and gamblers – an' other things too. The girls and women are as bad, but will she listen? She will not. Sticks 'er nose in the air and says, "I'm not listenin', Mam. I'm not listenin' to anythin' you say

about Jack." I wish to God 'er da was here. 'E'd sort
her out all right, and 'im too. I don't know what'll
become of 'er – but yer 'aven't come ter listen ter me
moanin'. Now sit down and tell me what kind of a
week yer've 'ad.'

Hannah sat. 'Not too bad.'

'What's that supposed to mean?'

'Well, they're all trying not to mention the . . . the
wedding in front of me, but it's hard for them and me.'

'Hannah, yer'll get over 'im. Yer'll meet someone
else, from yer own class. Maybe it's this lad who's
takin' yer out. They're not all 'ooligans around 'ere.
Who knows when "Mr Right" will turn up? Yer're much
better than you were last week, aren't yer?'

'I am, but . . . but . . .'

'Now put all that out of your mind,' Ada instructed
firmly. 'In fact you'll be much better when this flamin'
wedding is over.'

'I know that.'

'It's just a pity it isn't sooner.'

'Apparently it's very early, so Mrs Howard said.
They've only been engaged a short time. It's usually a
year, maybe two.'

'Well they can both afford it, can't they? They don't
need ter save up for a decent frock an' veil an' then
furniture an' things like we 'as ter do. Or start off in
someone's front room, sharin' a house with God knows
'ow many others. Never a chance ter be on yer own,
like. No privacy at all. God, I was mortified when we
lived with Ma Sweeney until I got used ter it. Still, 'e is

only the groom, there's not so much fuss. Mother of the bride usually 'as all the worry an' expense but I've told our Lily that iffen she weds that feller I'll not lift a finger and I'm not scrimpin' and savin' and doin' without. *That* lot always seem to have money for booze and bettin', they can foot the bill.'

'You really don't like them, do you?'

'No, I bloody 'ate 'em! And I'm not on me own.'

Ada looked at Hannah. When she replied Hannah realised just how upset she was, for she never normally swore.

When Hannah got back she found the kitchen in turmoil. There were dishes – dirty and clean – all over the table and work surfaces. The big teapot stood in the middle of the table surrounded by crumbs of cake and bread. The rack that hung above the range airing clothes had been lowered and was in everyone's way.

'What's happened, Vi? Where's Mrs Howard?'

'Well might you ask! I've been left to do the flaming supper. Says she can't cope.'

'Cope with what?' Hannah automatically began to stack dishes.

'They've only brought the flaming wedding forward because the ship's not now going to the places they particularly want to go to. So they've booked with another shipping line and Miss Siân is going to have a party, just for the women, two days before!'

Hannah sat down. Another party! She didn't think she could cope either. She'd have to see Maria

Delahunty and listen to all the plans, the hopes, the dreams. How was she going to deal with that? She didn't even want to set eyes on Richard's bride-to-be. She wasn't over him. She had only just begun to feel better and now it was going to be dragged out and paraded before her eyes. Every detail of the dress, the church, the reception, the . . . the honeymoon.

'When will that be, Vi?'

'In a flaming fortnight! Oh, Hannah, I'm so sorry. I shouldn't have told you like that.'

'It doesn't matter, Vi. I think the sooner it's all over and done with the better. He'll have gone and they . . . they have their own house to come back to and . . .'

'And what?' Vi demanded, thankful that Hannah had taken the news so well.

'Well, I've agreed to go to New Brighton on my Sunday off with that lad, Alfie. He was waiting for me when I got to Victoria Terrace. He works shifts,' she added in case she had to explain yet again why he wasn't at work.

'Well, thank God something good has happened today. You go, Hannah. Go and enjoy yourself. Forget all about this lot here.'

'Do you want me to help with supper?'

'Oh please. I know it's only a cold collation. If I'd had to cook anything I'd have given in my notice and gone! Sometimes she's the living end with her flaming headaches.'

'She's not been too bad since Mr Donaldson came permanent, like.'

'No, she hasn't, but he backed her up today, saying she had every right to be upset. That they were being very unfair but that he'd try and help as much as he could.'

'So where is he now?'

'Sitting in his flaming pantry with a bottle of the Master's port. He doesn't think anyone knows and he's not fool enough to go mad with it. He'll only show his face to see if everything is ready to be served. I've sent Blandford up to set the table but you know what he's like. Would you nip up and see that he's not breaking everything before him, then come and see to this salad stuff?'

Hannah smiled at Vi. 'Shall I run around and see if Jessie's got a minute? There are enough of them in that house, they wouldn't even miss her.'

'Go on then, but be quick, Hannah! This lot has to be on the serving buffet in half an hour but I'm getting to the stage where I don't care if it's flaming well late. And if Miss Siân says anything I'll tell her the reason.'

'Oh, Vi, you wouldn't? Mrs Howard's not so young any more.'

'I would and if she can't cope with the job she should flaming well retire because I'm not going to be put upon like this again.'

Hannah fled towards the back door.

Chapter Eleven

As the month drew to its close the oppressive heat seemed to be over. The mornings were much fresher. The sunlight was sharper, no haze surrounded the sun and a westerly wind seemed to chase the cumulus clouds slowly across the sky. The evenings too were cooler; darkness descended much earlier and dew began to form on the lawn and flowers as dusk approached. Almost everyone was thankful for the change in the weather, yet they knew that autumn was approaching fast. Already the leaves were beginning to turn yellow.

Hannah had enjoyed her Sunday out with Alfie Duggan. On the ferry trip they'd stood on the top deck and a stiff breeze had blown her hat off. She'd cried out as it was her only hat and laughingly he'd run and caught it.

'Why don't you leave it off?' he asked, passing it back to her.

She examined it closely for damage. 'Because it's not "proper" to go out without a hat, if you've got one.'

'Well, hang on to it hard because I'm not spending my time chasing after it.'

She'd looked quickly up at him but there was no sign of annoyance in his face; he was smiling, rather cynically, she thought, and it made her uncomfortable.

'Why are you looking at me like that? I didn't mean it. I was joking, Hannah.'

She'd smiled. Trust her to get the wrong end of the stick. But for the rest of the journey she went hatless. She'd put it back on once they got off the ferry.

'What shall we do first?' he'd asked as they'd gone ashore.

She looked at the crowds of people, all eagerly looking forward to some form of entertainment for the day. New Brighton, with its sandy beach, promenade, tower, fun fair, numerous cafés and kiosks, zoo and lighthouse was a popular place for day trippers and holidaymakers. 'I don't know. You choose.'

'No, it's your day out.'

'Oh, I just don't know. I've never been before.'

'Let's go to the fun fair then. Someone told me they've got this new ride and it's dead exciting. That must be it over there.' He pointed and her eyes followed his index finger. Her heart sank. It seemed to consist of small carriages on rails that went up and down at very steep angles. She bit her lip.

'I . . . don't know, Alfie, it looks a bit dangerous.'

'Well, that's half the fun, Hannah. Oh, come on, don't worry, I'll hold you safe. It's a good bit of excitement and none of my mates have been on it yet.'

She followed him to the little kiosk where he paid for them both, then stepped into a small and, as she thought, unsteady box-like carriage. After that she didn't really remember much more. They went at a terrifying speed, up and down and he held her around the waist tightly as she screamed with fright. When they got off she clung to his arm.

'Oh, oh, please can we go somewhere where I can sit down and have a drink? That was terrible. I was scared to death! I thought any minute the carriage would come off the rails and we'd all be killed.'

He laughed and tucked her arm in his. 'All right, no more "terrifying" rides. Not even the Ferris wheel, but we could try the bobbey horses,' he suggested as they skirted the carousel.

'Maybe later,' she replied, glancing at the painted and gilded wooden horses. She still felt decidedly shaky.

He found a table at an open-air café and bought her a glass of lemonade.

'Are you sure you wouldn't sooner have something stronger?' He himself clutched a pint of beer.

'No, this is fine.'

He sat down beside her and emptied his glass in one go. 'That was good. It's thirsty work, enjoying yourself. I'll just have another quick one and then we'll go and find some fish and chips. We can eat them walking along the promenade to the zoo.'

She didn't say what she thought Mrs Howard would say about that, instead she sipped her lemonade. She really was enjoying it. There were so many new things to see and do.

At six o'clock they boarded the ferry that was packed with day trippers going home. She was tired but it had been a great day. They'd found a chippy that had a few little tables where you could eat your meal and have some bread and butter and a pot of tea too. Neither of them had felt like the tea but he showed her how to make sandwiches with the chips.

'You mean you don't know how to make a chip butty? Call yourself a Scouser? Everyone knows how to make chip butties. We invented them. Look, you take one piece of bread, put as many chips as you can on it, and put another piece on top. Dead easy. You can put more salt and vinegar on if you want.'

'It's just that we never had anything like that in Denbigh and Mrs Howard always calls them "sandwiches". I think she'd go mad if I called them "butties" *and* if she could see me now.'

'The trouble with you, Hannah, is that you've been brought up too strict. It isn't your fault, but I saw you frown when I had another pint. It's warm, I was hot and thirsty so I had another drink.'

'Alfie, did I say I didn't like you having more beer?'

'No, but I could see it in your eyes.'

She sighed. 'Maybe you're right. I've always had to live by rules and regulations – and punishments too.'

'Well, have you enjoyed yourself today?'

'Of course I have. It's been really great.' Visits to the tower, the side shows, the lighthouse and the old fort at Perch Rock had followed the trip around the zoo. She'd taken off her shoes and stockings and, holding her skirt up, she'd paddled in the warm sluggish water. She meant what she said and she'd not thought of Richard Hughes all day.

When they got off the tram, he walked her to the back door.

'I'm on the afternoon shift next week so I won't be able to see you. What about the week after?'

Hannah was thoughtful. She didn't want to neglect Ada. 'I always visit on Thursdays, but I could leave early. We could go for a walk in the park.'

He nodded. A walk in the park cost nothing. Today had cost him a fair bit, almost all what he called his 'drinking money'.

'Then I'll meet you at the top of Victoria Terrace at, say, three o'clock?'

'Won't you come and call for me at Mrs Sweeney's?'

'No. It would waste time. You know what the auld ones are like. You can't get away from them and all they ever talk about is how great "the auld days" were when everyone knows they were really terrible. Much worse than they are now and times are far from good these days.'

Hannah smiled at him. 'I'll meet you at the top then.'

He leaned forward. 'Don't I get a kiss?'

She looked down. He had spent a lot of money making her day pleasant and she felt obliged to him. What was one kiss anyway? 'All right, just a quick one.'

She was surprised by the pressure of his mouth on hers. She'd expected just a peck but when she drew away she felt strangely pleased, something she thought she would never be. She'd thought that only Richard's kisses would have made her feel any kind of emotion.

'Goodnight, Alfie, and thanks. It's been a really great day.'

'I'll see you a week on Thursday then?'

She nodded before disappearing into the back garden, closing the gate behind her.

As the day of the wedding drew nearer the more busy things became and the more Vi and Jessie worried about Hannah.

'Do you really think she'll be all right?' Jessie asked earnestly as they sat in a corner of the kitchen at Abercromby Square. Hannah had had to stay behind for a few minutes to help Mrs Howard get the baking started for the cakes and pies for the 'buffet' Miss Siân was holding. They'd scrubbed the big table clean and, when Vi left, Hannah had been in the larder sorting out the various tins of ingredients Mrs Howard would need.

'I don't know, Jessie, and that's the gospel truth.'

'Well, she seems a bit better since she started seeing Alfie. Have you met him?'

'No. She met him on the corner of the road last week but she's going out for the day with him on Sunday: Miss Siân's given us all a day off. She said there won't be much to do after the wedding and they can manage with something cold and she'll make the tea herself.'

'*She'll* make the *tea*!' Jessie's eyes were wide.

'I know, Jessie. It took me back a bit I can tell you and Mrs Howard got all airyated about it saying she wasn't to come into the kitchen at all. What would people think? Miss Siân said "people" wouldn't know and she didn't care what they would think if they got to know. She just wants a couple of trays set out. She'll come down to boil a kettle. Oh, there was quite a battle of wills over *that*. Mrs Howard was saying she wasn't having no day off but in the end she agreed. She's going to see her sister in Aintree. She's some sort of housekeeper there. I shall go and see my parents and Hannah's seeing Alfie.' Vi hoped this Alfie Duggan was just the person Hannah needed to be able to put Richard Hughes out of her mind for good.

On the evening of the buffet party everyone was busy running up and down from the kitchen to the drawing room.

'Thank God there's only a dozen of them!' Vi muttered to Hannah as they passed on the stairs. 'Are you all right?'

'Yes. I'm fine,' Hannah replied, but it was a lie. The bride-to-be looked so very pretty that she was filled with jealousy. Maria Delahunty's eyes were sparkling with excitement and happiness, her skin positively glowed and she wore a beautiful dress of salmon pink crêpe de Chine that had intricate tucks and folds and which seemed just to float around her calves, above the silk stockings and cream leather shoes with a T-strap fastening.

'Peckham, could you bring my future sister-in-law a glass of lemonade or fruit cordial?' Siân was being very formal this evening whenever she spoke to the staff.

'Of course, ma'am,' Hannah muttered, her eyes downcast.

'You see, Peckham, I have to keep a clear head for tomorrow morning. I'm going for the final fitting of my wedding dress. It's been such a rush to get it finished in time!' Maria confided.

Oh, you couldn't help but like her, Hannah thought miserably. And strangely, what she had always felt for Richard Hughes had begun to change since she'd started seeing Alfie. Those feelings hadn't diminished, they were just different, she supposed. Mind you, she didn't like being called 'Peckham' by the girl. She'd never thought twice about Siân's use of her surname, but it grated on her nerves when used by Maria.

'I . . . I hope it will be . . . satisfactory, miss,' she managed to reply, refusing to look at the girl.

'Peckham, are you quite all right? You look flushed and your eyes are very bright.'

'No, ma'am, I mean yes, ma'am, I'm fine. Maybe it's just all the . . . excitement.'

Siân nodded and turned to Maria again and Hannah left the room quickly.

She reached the top of the kitchen stairs before the tears overwhelmed her. She leaned her aching head against the wall. Oh, she felt terrible. The feelings she'd tried so hard to fight down over the past weeks broke free. She just wished it was all over and that she would never have to see Maria again or hear a single detail about the wedding. Thank God she was going out on

Sunday. She'd get through Saturday as best she could. It would be so hard; at least after they'd gone to the church the house would be empty until they returned late at night. But they would be without Richard. This thought only made her shake with the effort of controlling her sobs.

'Hannah!'

She turned, her eyes swimming with tears. No! No! He was supposed to be out. She couldn't bear this. Why now of all times? *Why* did she have to meet *him*? She hadn't seen him for weeks. It was fate playing cruel tricks. Oh, she should have gone straight down to the kitchen. She wouldn't have minded Mrs Howard or Mr Donaldson, even Blandford, seeing her in such a state. But seeing *him* was just too much.

He placed his hands on her shoulders, genuinely concerned for her. She looked so miserable and dejected.

'Hannah, please don't cry. Please don't upset yourself over, well . . . me.'

'I . . . I . . . never meant to get upset. I can't help it.' She was trembling again at his touch.

She looked so fragile, so helpless and yet so lovely, he thought. How could he be easy in his mind now knowing he'd upset her again? He wished he could have told Siân to give her the evening off. But how on earth would he have explained *that* request away? He didn't know what to do but he couldn't leave her in this state. Gently he raised her chin with his forefinger and looked into the eyes that were the colour of autumn leaves reflected in a puddle after a shower of rain. He was mesmerised and did what he would always call the most idiotic and selfish act in his life. He bent and kissed her gently on the lips. Lips that opened beneath his before he tore himself away.

'Oh, God! Oh, Hannah! I'm sorry. I never meant to do that! Forgive me?'

'There's nothing to forgive. I ... I love you, remember?'

'No, Hannah! It's just infatuation, not love, and I should never, never have laid a finger on you. God, I'll never forgive myself and ... Maria ...!' He turned quickly and almost ran across the hall, wrenched open the front door and was gone, swallowed up in the darkness.

She leaned back against the wall, drained of all energy. Even though he'd never meant to do so, he'd kissed her. She raised her fingers and gently touched her lips. He'd *kissed* her. He must have *some* feelings for her in his heart, no matter how deeply hidden. She felt exalted at the knowledge, then she was plunged again into despair. He was getting married in two days' time and it was to Miss Maria Delahunty, not to her.

'Hannah! For God's sake what's the matter now? Mrs Howard is screaming in there because she's waiting for you to take up the—'

'Oh, Vi! Vi! Vi, he kissed me!'

Vi was horrified. 'Oh, God, not Mr Richard?'

Hannah nodded.

Vi exploded. 'I could kill him! I could just *kill* him!

How *dare* he! He's getting married on Saturday and his fiancée is sitting in there! And after all you've been through, after what we've all been through! God, men are selfish, even the best of them! Did he say anything?'

'He said he was sorry, that he never meant to do it and that I . . . I don't love him at all, it's just in – in – a word I didn't understand. But he *must* love me, even if it's just a little bit.'

'Wait there until I come back,' Vi commanded.

Hannah closed her eyes. She didn't care what anyone said. She *knew* she was right.

Vi looked flustered when she came back.

'Get down those stairs now or we'll both be murdered.'

'Oh, so the pair of you have decided to do some work, have you?'

'I'm sorry, Mrs Howard but I . . . we got delayed.'

'How "delayed"?'

'Mr Richard delayed Hannah by talking to her in the hall. She couldn't get away.'

'Really? Well, the pair of you get back up those stairs and take these "fancies" up with you. You can explain or have hysterics later when they've all gone home,' she said, looking hard at Hannah and then catching a glance from Vi. He was supposed to have gone out hours ago. Now he'd gone and upset Hannah again. He was acting more like Mr Thomas than himself, Mrs Howard thought. As her sister always said, 'Thoughtless the lot of them in one degree or another!' and she agreed wholeheartedly with that sentiment.

You only had to look at Hannah to see that there would, indeed, be hysterics later on.

Chapter Twelve

She was proved right. At half past midnight when all the guests had left Hannah came down into the kitchen with a tray laden with dirty glasses and dishes. She set it down on the table and burst into tears. She couldn't pretend any longer.

'Blandford, go and make sure the garage is secure and that the back gate is bolted,' Mr Donaldson instructed the mystified lad.

'Rowan, I think this calls for a small glass of brandy. She's distraught. Go up to the Master's study, he's long since retired to bed. "Can't be doing with all those girls and young women twittering like a flock of swallows," I believe were his words. Pour a small – and I mean small – amount from the decanter. Take a glass up with you. We can't be using the best crystal.'

Vi did as she was told. Oh, why couldn't Mr Richard flaming well leave Hannah alone?

'Peckham, go along to my pantry, I want to have a few words with Mrs Howard.'

Hannah too did as he bade her. She felt as though she was walking through a mist, that everything was unreal, beyond her grasp or understanding.

When they'd both gone Mr Donaldson turned to Mrs Howard. 'Edith, I'm going to have to do something about that girl. This can't go on.'

'You don't mean you're going to sack her?'

'No. Most of this is not her fault. I've yet to learn what upset her again tonight, but it's connected with Mr Richard and Miss Maria.'

When Vi came back with the brandy the butler turned to her. 'Now, what has brought this on, Rowan?'

'Mr Richard.'

'Mr Richard?' Mrs Howard echoed, looking worriedly at Mr Donaldson.

'Yes. She was having a hard time coping having to listen to all the descriptions and fuss and arrangements, but she was managing – until she met him in the hall and . . . well . . .'

' "Well" what?' Mrs Howard demanded.

'He kissed her.'

Mrs Howard was scandalised. 'He did *what*?'

'She was crying and he was talking to her, telling her not to get upset and then . . . well, then he kissed her.' Vi's lips were compressed in a thin line of disapproval as she waited for their response.

'Well, I would never have dreamed that he could do such a thing.'

'And only two days before he gets married and to that lovely girl,' Mrs Howard added. 'It's a disgrace. What on earth's got into him? He was never like this!'

'Until Hannah came,' Vi muttered under her breath. In her opinion Richard Hughes *was* like his brother in some ways. He just wanted to have his cake and eat it too.

162

'Shall I have a word with Miss Siân, do you think?' Mr Donaldson queried of Mrs Howard. It was a shameful way for any gentleman to behave and he was equally appalled.

'All that will do is upset her and then she'll go to the Master who will demand an explanation from Mr Richard and the whole thing will be blown up and cause ructions. No, best not to. Leave it with me. Give me that glass, Rowan.'

Vi handed over the glass to Mrs Howard, wishing it was herself and not the cook who was going to try to calm Hannah down.

Hannah was still standing, gazing unseeingly out of the small window that overlooked the kitchen garden, now in darkness.

'Hannah, sit down and sip this,' Mrs Howard instructed gently. The girl looked awful. At least he would be out of their lives after Saturday and good riddance too if this was the way he was disrupting the household.

Hannah sat down and took a sip, then shivered and gasped as the fiery liquid burned her throat and made her catch her breath. 'Drink it slowly. In sips. It'll do you good. Now, Hannah, we have to get this sorted out once and for all. We . . . you . . . will probably never see Mr Richard again after Saturday. Put him out of your mind. I've said this before. Young hearts mend quickly.'

Hannah shook her head. 'No. No, mine won't.'

'It will. How he behaved tonight was scandalous,

163

scandalous. I would never have believed he could act like that.'

'He . . . he kissed me, so he must . . . love me.'

'He doesn't. If he did then why would he be getting married? Hannah, have you no pride? No self-esteem? He's made your life a misery of late. *He's* not been suffering. Oh, no. He's been going around choosing houses and fancy honeymoons that cost more than we all earn in a year. Do you think he really cares about you? He doesn't. It was a moment of weakness. On Saturday he'll leave this house and start a new life and he won't be thinking of you. Far from it. Forget him, Hannah. I do know how you feel,' she said more kindly, patting Hannah's shoulder. 'I know from experience how you feel now but you will get over him. It just takes time. That's all – time. Get yourself something to occupy your free hours. That's what I did. That's how I learned to cook. I started off like you – a kitchen maid – but I watched and learned and remembered.'

Hannah looked up into the older woman's face and saw that Mrs Howard's eyes had misted over. She must have loved and lost someone too.

'Finish that up now and then go straight to bed. Never mind the dishes or anything else. You are upset and exhausted, but think about what I've said, Hannah. Think of yourself, think of your pride.'

Hannah tried to take some comfort, find some hope in Mrs Howard's words, but it was so hard. She had sobbed into her pillow, then fallen into an uneasy sleep.

She woke early and went over it all in her head: all her feelings, her experiences and what Mrs Howard had said about pride and self-esteem, and she made up her mind. Mrs Howard was right. She'd never see him again after Saturday and she'd made a spectacle of herself. She knew that Miss Siân knew something was wrong and she didn't want anyone else to realise what it was. It was bad enough that all the staff – with the exception of Blandford – already knew.

Her resolve was strengthened by her friends. Now, she felt such a fool. She'd behaved like a stupid child, crying for the moon. Why did she always have to end up being the one who got hurt? The one who seemed to be 'used'. The one not 'fitting' enough to do *anything*?

'Probably because you've been treated so badly all your life. You think you don't amount to much but you're wrong, Hannah. Dead wrong. Show them . . . him . . . everyone that you don't care any more. That you *have* got your pride,' Vi had encouraged her.

She'd nodded. Vi was right. All she could do was forget him, no matter how hard it would be. She *did* have her pride.

How she got through Saturday she didn't know. She stayed in the kitchen scouring pans when every other member of the staff went up into the hall to wish Richard Hughes happiness in the future. Hannah's absence was put down as 'an indisposition' by Mr Donaldson when Siân asked about her. Richard had looked away embarrassed by the look in Vi's eyes. She couldn't disguise her contempt for him and he saw it.

It was useless now to try to attempt an explanation. He couldn't find one himself. He'd tried. He'd drunk half a bottle of whisky just 'trying'. Next morning, he was still none the wiser and had a terrible headache.

That night Hannah hadn't slept well but she got up on Sunday feeling much better, knowing she would be going out for the day. Alfie always made her laugh and she certainly needed someone to cheer her up, to make her see that it wasn't the end of everything just because Richard was now married and finally beyond her reach. Alfie wasn't, though, and she *was* fond of him. But would he ask her to marry him, giving her a valid reason for leaving the house in Faulkner Square? She had always had to fight for the things she'd wanted – she'd told Richard that once – but she *couldn't* fight for him anymore. She *could* for Alfie, if she wanted to.

After what seemed like an eternity she had made her decision. She wanted Alfie. She wanted to be Mrs Alfred Duggan. She knew it was a very bold and forward thing to do, but she was determined. Far more determined than she'd been for months. Somehow, it felt good.

They set out early for they were going across the river to Thurstaton Common. Hannah had said she would take a picnic and Mrs Howard had packed a basket for her.

Neither of them spoke much on the tram or the ferry until Hannah began to wonder why he was so silent. Up till now she'd thought he was being considerate, letting her tell him in her own time about yesterday.

As they walked towards the omnibus that would take them out into the countryside, she turned and looked at him.

'Is there something wrong, Alfie? You don't look well and you've been very quiet.'

'I thought that's what you wanted me to be. You nearly bit my head off when I asked you did you have any small change for the tram.'

'I'm sorry, Alfie. I was probably sharp...'

'Sharp? You were like a bloody carving knife.'

She was taken aback. He'd never sworn before.

'Are you feeling sick?'

'Yes, I am. I feel terrible. I thought I was going to *be* sick on that ferry.'

She looked concerned. 'You should have told me. We could have gone back, I wouldn't have minded. I'd have got through the day ... somehow. I could have gone out with Vi, she's going to see her mam and dad.'

He turned and looked down at her and managed a smile. 'I'm sorry, Hannah. I'd forgotten it was yesterday and I feel so terrible because I had one bevvy too many last night. It's a hangover I've got but it's not fair to take it out on you. It's my own fault. I should have had more sense.' He didn't tell her that he'd had a win on the horses yesterday and had spent the lot on drink with his mates.

'Look, let's not drag all the way out there. You'll be jolted and bumped all the way. That won't do your headache any good and you *will* be sick and besides, we all do stupid things at some time in our lives.'

'I'd forgotten just how caring you are, Hannah.'

'Where shall we go then? It's not too late to do something else. Let's walk along the front by the river and see where we end up.'

'New Brighton is where we'll end up and it's too cold to be on the beach today.'

Hannah didn't know what to suggest next, so they settled for the much shorter journey to Bidston Hill. 'It'll be nice there. I've never been before but I've heard it's pretty. All the leaves on the trees will be falling and the colours will be great.'

'Well, I'm not climbing up to the top. The Observatory and Windmill will wait for another day.'

He looked so awful when they got off the bus that she led him to a bench under a tree whose branches were low and sweeping.

'Sit there until you feel better. Will some ginger beer help at all?'

He grimaced. It wasn't beer at all, it was a type of fizzy drink made from God knows what but with ginger added. 'I'll be fine soon, Hannah, honestly. I've been rotten to you so far, but I'm determined that you'll enjoy the rest of the day. In fact I think I'll go and get a "hair of the dog" in that pub over there. Do you want to come with me?'

She shook her head. She didn't understand him. He said he had a hangover yet now he was going to have an alcoholic drink. 'I'll sit here and wait for you.'

'I won't be long, I promise. Five minutes at the most.'

She managed a smile. She realised she had been too strictly brought up. She must seem like a real kill-joy to him. All prim and prissy.

He was as good as his word. He was back before the five minutes were up.

'Ah, that's better. Now let's enjoy the day. I'm a real misery guts with a hangover.'

She smiled at the comic face he pulled. 'Isn't every man?'

'I suppose so and that goes for women too.'

'I've never known a woman who drank – well, apart from Miss Siân and her friends.'

'Then you've lived a very sheltered life, Hannah Peckham.' He tucked her arm through his. 'Were you all right yesterday? I mean, how did it all go?'

'Once they'd left, it was fine. Very quiet. I went to give Jessie a hand. The other kitchen maids left and poor Jessie has to do all the work until they get someone else.'

'I'll never understand why you girls keep working in these houses. You're being exploited.'

'What?'

'Made use of.'

'Where did you learn a word like that?'

'The Union. We're trying to get pay and conditions bettered. Look at you. You work all the hours God sends for your keep and a pittance and you can be sacked for nothing if your face doesn't fit or if you do something terrible, like breaking a posh vase.'

'Oh, Alfie, it's not *that* bad really! It's much better than the workhouse.'

'Aye, I suppose *anything* is better than that. Well, let's not ruin the day by arguing or me getting on my soap box,' he conceded.

'Have you been in a union long?' Hannah asked.

'Oh, a couple of months. My brothers joined so I thought I might as well go along too.'

'Did you go on strike? I had to wait until it was all over before they'd let me come back here.'

'Yes, but that general strike was a waste of time. They gave in too easily. And we didn't get a penny while we were off, nor a penny when we went back. It's not improved what we earn, or the conditions we have to put up with, so it was a waste of time and money.'

He looked at her. Politics didn't interest her and they certainly didn't interest him. He'd only gone along with his brothers to see if any excitement might arise, and they'd all been in the forefront when that bit of rioting and looting had gone on, until the flaming army had arrived and someone had been shot. They didn't mess around, the bloody soldiers.

'I'm not really interested in politics.'

'Neither am I, after that fiasco. It was like a flaming circus.'

Hannah glanced at him from beneath her eyelashes. She'd made up her mind last night but now she was going to have to try to get him in the same frame of mind as herself and it wasn't going to be easy. Well, she'd have to make an effort.

'I'm not interested in politics,' she repeated, 'I don't understand them. I'm more interested in you. We . . . we get on well together, Alfie. I've never met anyone like you.'

He looked at her quizzically. 'Well, I've certainly never met anyone like you.'

'I don't want to stay in service for ever, Alfie, I . . . I want to get married, have my own place – no matter how small – and . . . and children too. Eventually. But . . . but it doesn't have to be . . . eventually, Alfie. It could be . . .'

'What do you mean, Hannah: "It could be . . ."?'

'It could be . . . soon and I think . . . I think I'd like to have a baby quite . . . quite early too.'

He was lost for words. He'd never felt like this about any other girl, but married? He'd be able to get away from his grasping, complaining mam and all the others for a start. Hannah was in service so she'd keep a place clean, and cook well too. His mam's cooking was diabolical and very unpredictable: if she didn't want to cook, she didn't. They went to the chippy or to one of the 'cannies' or canteens where women sold hot meals from their doorsteps. And, of course, Hannah was a real 'cracker' to look at and would be even more so without her clothes, lying beside him in bed. He made up his mind and found his voice.

'I knew you were the girl for me as soon as I met you, even though you were sopping wet. I'd like to marry you, Hannah! I know we've only been out a few times, but . . . but, well . . . I do love you. I'll be good to you, Hannah, I swear I will. You'll never want for anything.'

She looked down at her hands resting in her lap. She liked him a lot and he loved her. He was quite handsome; he made her laugh; he had a job; he'd treat her well; he was of her own class. True, she hadn't known him very long but . . . it would stop her thoughts from straying to Upper Husskinson Street. And she'd made her decision last night. She *had* to leave the house in Faulkner Square and all its memories if she were going to try to forget Richard. There was nobody's permission she had to ask.

He put his arm around her and drew her to him. 'So, will you marry me, Hannah?'

'Yes, Alfie, I will and we *will* be happy, I know it.'

His forehead creased in a frown. 'I haven't got any money to buy you an engagement ring.'

'I don't *want* one, Alfie. Hardly anyone, people like us, have engagement rings. Just . . . just a wedding ring will do.'

He was relieved. 'When do you want it to be?'

She didn't stop to think about this either, she'd worked it out last night. 'As soon as possible, if that's all right with you?'

'It's great. Come here.' He kissed her passionately until she drew away, breathless.

'Alfie, people are looking at us.'

'Let them. They're probably dead jealous.'

He kissed her again and held her close to him. She felt breathless, swept along on a tide of emotions she didn't understand.

'We'll make it soon. I'll find out. I think there's some sort of special licence I can get, unless you want to get married in a church.'

'No. No, I don't want all the fuss. Brougham Terrace will do, as long as you're standing beside me.'

'You can be certain of that, Hannah.'

Chapter Thirteen

As Hannah walked up Upper Parliament Street, she pondered her situation. Was she mad? Was she completely crazy to marry someone she didn't know very well? Oh, she'd just have to push all the doubts away. It was too late now and she was determined to carry out her plan.

When she got back Vi had returned but there was no sign of either Mrs Howard or Mr Donaldson.

'I'm sure he went with her,' Vi said. 'Do you think there's anything going on between them? Do you want some tea? I came home early, I'd had enough of my lot for one week. The moans and complaints and . . . What's the matter with you? You look about to explode!'

'I am. Oh, Vi, I'm . . . I'm getting married!'

Vi was so shocked that she kept the teapot at an angle so tea overflowed from the completely filled cup into the saucer and then on to the tablecloth.

'Vi! The tea!' Hannah cried.

'Oh, damn! Get a dishcloth and a tea towel, Hannah! She'll have my life!'

'Get the tablecloth into the wash now, or it will be permanently stained and then she *will* have your life.'

'Oh, never mind the flaming tablecloth! Did I hear you say you're going to get married?' Vi was still aghast.

'You did. Alfie proposed to me and I accepted.'

Vi sat down at the table, the stained cloth wrapped up in a bundle in her arms.

'Hannah, you hardly know him! He's the first lad you've ever been out with. Oh, you can't be serious!'

'I am and that doesn't matter. He . . . he said he'd take care of me, get somewhere decent to live and—'

'You do realise that you'll have to give notice and leave here?'

'Of course I do, but maybe that will be for the best.'

Vi dumped the cloth on the table, stood up, took Hannah's hand and looked at her closely.

'Hannah, you're just marrying him on the rebound. You don't love him.'

'I do, in a way,' Hannah protested.

'That's not good enough for a marriage. You've got the rest of your lives together and if you don't really love him when the "worse" bit of the promise comes – and it will – you'll fall to bits.'

'It *is* enough, for me, Vi. He *does* love me and he's going to get a special licence, so it will be soon. I know I'll have to leave here. I'll probably have to get factory work as his wage won't keep us.'

Vi threw up her hands in horror. 'You're mad! You are stark raving mad, Hannah Peckham! You could have your pick of fellers.'

'I can't.'

'You mean you don't want to. Because you can't have Richard, you aren't even trying to build a life, find someone decent you *do* love. No, you have to go and accept the first proposal you get. Oh, I despair of you! I really do.'

'Why do you despair of her? Now what have the pair of you been up to while I've been out? I can't leave you alone for a few hours.' Mrs Howard unbuttoned her coat and took off her hat. Mr Donaldson was doing likewise.

'Ask her. I'm just lost for words. Maybe she'll listen to you.'

'Well, Hannah?' Mrs Howard asked.

'I'm getting married.'

'What? Who to, in God's name?' Mrs Howard was visibly shaken.

'To that Alfie Duggan she's been seeing. She hardly knows him,' Vi informed them, scooping up the table-cloth.

Mr Donaldson and Mrs Howard looked at each other conspiratorially, then Mrs Howard nodded. 'Hannah, come with me,' she said briskly.

Hannah followed the older woman to Mr Donaldson's pantry which Mrs Howard shared with him now as a sort of small sitting room.

'Hannah, you know that everyone in this house cares about your welfare, even Miss Siân.'

'Mr Richard didn't,' Hannah said quietly.

'He did, in a way that a friend would care. I thought all that was over and done with but obviously I was wrong, you're still carrying a torch for him. Hannah, don't marry on the rebound. "Marry in haste, repent at leisure." I remember how it feels, I've told you that.

Don't do this, girl, you will regret it and then you'll be tied to a man you don't love for the rest of your life. It's a big decision to make, Hannah. Who is he, where does he live, what does he do for a job? Do you even know any of the answers?'

'I know he works in Foster's, the iron foundry. He comes from a big family; Duggan is his surname. He lives in Byles Street but I've not been there yet.'

Mrs Howard shook her head. 'So you've not even met any of his family yet?'

'No, but I will soon.'

'Oh, Hannah, what are we going to do with you? You'll only be swapping one skivvy's job for another, looking after him and for the rest of your life, without wages of your own when you've got kids. Is that *really* what you want?'

'Yes,' Hannah said firmly. 'I won't mind looking after him and I want babies. I want a real home. I've never had one.'

'I thought that you looked on this as your "home" but obviously you don't. And how are you going to manage – moneywise?'

'I'll find work and I've some money saved up, you know that.'

'That won't last long, Hannah, not when you come to buy furniture and bedding and all the other things you'll need. I don't suppose he's got any money saved coming from a big family and all. He probably gives his mam money for his keep and what's left has to cover things like fares and clothes.'

'I don't care if he hasn't got a penny. I'm going to marry him. I don't have to ask permission. I have nobody to ask.'

'Hannah, please? Think again?'

Hannah shook her head. Her mind was made up.

They all tried to talk her out of it. Mrs Howard, Vi and Jessie and Ada, whom she informed on her next visit. Her announcement met the same shock as it had been received with by everyone else.

'Well, at least she can make up her own mind. She doesn't 'ave ter ask permission,' Lily Sweeney said, breaking the silence. She had taken the afternoon off, saying she wasn't well, something her mother disapproved of as she obviously was not *that* bad and she'd lose half a day's pay. 'Well, good luck to yer, Hannah,' the girl went on, eyeing her mother with open hostility.

'Hannah, why does it 'ave ter be so soon? Why can't yer wait, save up a bit?'

'No. I want to get married quickly. You understand that, Lily, don't you?'

'Oh, I understand all right. Anyone with any sense would understand,' Lily shot back.

'Lily Sweeney, if I 'ave any more cheek out of you, I'll belt yer, big as yer are! Now shurrup! 'Ave yer met 'is mam yet, Hannah?'

'No, but I will soon.'

'I can understand yer wantin' to gerrout of that place but I can't understand why so soon. Anyway, where does he live, this Alfie?'

'In Byles Street.'

Lily caught her breath and Ada looked worried. 'What's 'is name? 'Is surname?' she demanded.

'Duggan. Alfie Duggan.'

Lily gave a cry of disbelief and Ada got to her feet. 'Oh, holy God! He's one of *that* lot! Hannah, his brother is that Jack Duggan that *she's* goin' out with! They're a terrible common family. Terrible altogether! I've told yer they're always drinkin' and gamblin'. Oh, 'e'll lead yer a merry dance, I can tell yer that, girl. I'm fed up tellin' milady 'ere the same thing. 'E'll 'ave every penny offen yer. Yer mam and da would be tearin' their 'air out. Hannah, 'e's not for you, luv.'

'I . . . I didn't know about his family, but he's not like that when he's with me.'

'Neither is Jack. But she won't even give 'im a chance. I'd be marryin' *him* not 'is flaming family,' Lily added scathingly.

Ada glared at her. 'I'll see ter yer later, yer 'ardfaced madam,' she snapped back before renewing her entreaties to Hannah. 'You don't know 'im, Hannah, luv.'

'I know him well enough to want to marry him.'

'No, you flamin' well don't! It's on the rebound.'

'It's not.'

'It is and you'll 'ave ter leave that posh house an' there's yer job gone out of the winder.'

'I don't care about that.'

'Oh, you will in time when you're stuck in one room in some auld fallin'-down 'ouse with a couple of kids 'angin' on to yer skirt an' 'im down the boozer an' gamblin' 'is wages away, that's if he bothers to go to work at all. His da's an idle, drunken sod, an' so are 'is brothers. She used ter *try* but she gave up. "If yer can't beat 'em, join 'em", is *her* motto. The only one ter finish up halfway decent was their Maureen an' she cleared off as soon as she got 'er hands on a feller soft enough ter marry 'er. Hannah, I thought you 'ad more sense.'

'He loves me. He will be good to me, he *promised*.'

'Why didn't 'e tell yer about our Lily an' that Jack? 'E knows 'ow I feel. 'E knew I'd give yer a good talkin' to, ter change yer mind, that's why.'

'I love him,' Hannah answered resolutely.

'Well, *I'd* not believe the daylights out of 'im. A leopard can't change its spots. But yer've got yer da's stubbornness.' Ada shook her head in despair. 'Yer'll finish up back where you started, Hannah. In the workhouse.'

'No! Even if I have to beg in the streets I'd never go back!'

'Take no notice of 'er, Hannah, she just hates the lot of them because 'is mam likes a drink,' Lily said.

'Likes a drink! That's a bloody joke! She's in the pub morning, noon and bloody night. She's let all them kids run wild, no wonder they're all bloody 'ooligans.'

'Mam, you believe everything you hear. You don't know, you don't *really* know,' Lily exclaimed, adding her support.

'Well, I'm going to marry him. I don't suppose you'll come . . .'

181

'She won't but I will. Hopefully, one day, I might just get to be your sister-in-law.'

'Over my dead body you will, Lily Sweeney!' Ada retorted with conviction.

Since she insisted on ignoring their advice, everyone except young Blandford treated Hannah coldly. She bore it with fortitude and determination, although she was hurt. But when she saw Alfie on her afternoon off she felt better.

'I got a licence. Just the usual one. I didn't think you'd want to be married in two days' time?'

'No I don't, Alfie, but in other ways I wouldn't have minded.'

'Have they all been getting at you?'

She nodded. 'I expected it. Vi, Mrs Howard, Jessie, Mrs Sweeney.'

'Take no notice of that auld one. She hates our family. She won't let their Lily marry our Jack until she's twenty-one an' needs no consent.'

Hannah didn't want to dwell on that subject.

'So, when is it for?'

'Saturday the twelfth of October. That leaves us a few weeks to find somewhere to live and get a few bits and pieces. I'll get a suit from the thirty-shilling tailors.'

'And I'll get some kind of a dress. It won't be a long white one though.' She smiled a little sadly. She'd decided on every detail of the dress she'd dreamed of wearing to marry Richard Hughes – in her fantasies.

The dress wouldn't have been too fancy. It would have had a short train, long lace sleeves and bodice and she'd have had a short veil held in place with fancy combs. But all that too had just been a dream.

'You've had a rotten time with them, haven't you?'

She nodded and he put his arm around her.

'I love you, Hannah. Take no notice of then. We'll be dead happy.'

'I know, it's just that it's so hard to cope.'

But cope she did. They found a couple of rooms in a house in Rankin Street. They bought all the necessities and some 'luxuries', a lot of them second-hand from pawnshops, but she didn't care. It was a new life, a new beginning.

'Jessie, will you stand for me?' she asked of her friend after Vi had made yet another attempt to change her mind.

'Be a sort of bridesmaid?' Jessie asked shyly. She was still very timid.

'Yes, but you won't need a special frock or anything. I'm just having a suit. I saw a really nice one in Sturla's and a hat to match.'

'You'll have to have some sort of bouquet,' Vi put in, seeing at last that nothing was going to deter Hannah now and giving up the struggle. 'I'll buy it for you. I'll get it from that lot who did the decorations for Miss Siân's birthday party.'

'Thanks, Vi. It will be lovely, but you don't have to get it from them. Something cheaper will do.'

'Is there going to be any sort of a "do" afterwards?'

'No. Just a drink for Jessie and Jack and you if you will come?'

'No thanks, and I'm not being awkward, Hannah. It's just that you'll have left and it will be a bit hectic here until we find someone else to replace you.'

'They've given me a couple of hours off, Hannah, will that be enough?' Jessie asked.

'That's fine, Jessie, and we'll still be friends, won't we?'

Jessie hugged her. 'We'll *always* be friends, Hannah. I'd still be stuck in that terrible place but for you.'

Hannah looked thoughtful. 'Vi, could you suggest to Mrs Howard that she takes someone else from a workhouse to replace me?'

Vi nodded, but didn't think Mrs Howard would do that. Hannah and Jessie had both proved to be good and willing workers but that wasn't always the case, and the cook had already confided in her, saying she'd pick a girl herself this time.

That evening Miss Siân sent for Hannah. She was apprehensive, hoping Miss Siân wasn't going to try to talk her out of it too. That would be terrible. She might even be swayed and say she'd stay and give up Alfie.

'Ah, Peckham. Come in,' Siân Hughes indicated, smiling.

'Thank you, ma'am.'

'I hear you are leaving us to get married?'

'Yes, ma'am. But I . . . Everyone has been so kind to me that it's hard to . . . to . . . leave.'

Siân nodded. 'You must be very happy though?'

'Oh, I am, ma'am.'

'Well, here is your reference, should you need it in the future, and this is for you, a wedding present.' She handed an envelope over to Hannah.

'Oh, thank you. You've been so good to me.' There were tears in her eyes and she saw Miss Siân blink rapidly and put the piece of white lawn and lace that was a handkerchief to her nose.

'Please remember, Peckham, if you ever need my help in any way, all you have to do is ask.'

'Thank you. That's very . . . kind of you. I'll miss working here. I'll miss everyone but I'll never forget that it was you who took me in. You who got me out of the workhouse. All my life I'll be grateful for that.' She choked a little.

'Then may I wish you every happiness?'

Hannah nodded her thanks, unable to trust herself to try and speak.

When she got back into the hall she looked around. She *would* miss working here. Mrs Howard was right. She'd come to look on this house as her home. She opened the envelope. There were two white five-pound notes inside and a little card. Ten pounds! She uttered a prayer for Siân Hughes that maybe one day someone would love her. She deserved it, she was so generous and good.

A week later, on a beautiful autumn morning, Hannah left the house in Faulkner Square for ever. She was wearing the royal blue skirt and jacket, with a white blouse underneath, that she'd bought especially for today. Her newly washed hair was covered by a small close-fitting hat of the same blue, trimmed with a large bow of white satin ribbon on the side. Jessie was with her, wearing her best sage-green coat over a dress of the same colour trimmed with cream braid. Her hat was cream and she'd borrowed gloves and a bag from Vi. They went on the tram to West Derby Road to the soot-covered building where marriages took place and where births and deaths were registered. Jessie didn't think it was good luck to have an obviously bereaved family standing in the hallway as they went in but she said nothing.

Alfie and his brother Jack were waiting, both looking very smart in new suits, white shirts with winged collars, ties and with caps clasped in their hands.

'Well, he's certainly picked himself a stunner!' Jack said with a grin.

Hannah smiled. He didn't look *that* bad, she thought, wondering why Ada disliked him so much. But then she remembered that it was his family Ada couldn't stand.

'Are you nervous, Hannah?' Jessie asked in a whisper as they all trooped into the dismal, austere room that had a table at one end and some chairs placed in rows. There wasn't a single flower in sight. Poor Hannah, she thought, why hadn't she waited for a church wedding? It would have been worth it.

When they stood before the solemn-faced registrar

and Hannah made her wedding vows some of her nervousness had passed. It had all happened too quickly and there had been no time to think or dwell on things. Before she knew it she was Mrs Alfred Duggan and Jessie was kissing and hugging her.

'Well, now that's out of the way, let's go over the road to Gregson's Well, I'm spitting feathers!' Jack laughed and, taking Jessie's arm, he guided both her and the newlyweds across the busy main road to the pub. They'd all have a glass of something to toast Hannah and Alfie before going their separate ways.

As they sat in the snug, side by side, while Jack and Alfie carried in the beer and two glasses of port and lemonade, Jessie looked at her friend closely. Hannah looked happy enough, she thought, but was she happy inside, where it *really* mattered?

PART II

PART II

Chapter Fourteen

1929

Hannah watched Jessie as she came up the road. The sash window with the half-rotten frame, but clean shiny panes, was wide open. The hot July sun beat down on the small and slightly stooping figure. Poor Jessie, Hannah thought with pity. Her bad leg was causing her a lot of pain now and was making her stoop. Her shoulders were becoming more and more rounded, her spine was increasingly bent. She still worked in Abercromby Square but it was obvious to everyone that the work was too heavy for her. At the end of the day Jessie would almost crawl to her bed, exhausted. All she'd had for the pain until recently was aspirin, which she bought from the dispensary. Vi had given up trying to get her to see a doctor, she'd told Hannah.

'It would only be a waste of money, Vi. There's nothing he can do. I was born like this, see.'

'There must be *something* he can do, Jessie,' Vi had urged.

'No there isn't!' Jessie had replied.

Hannah knew that Vi, who was very fond of Jessie,

had even spoken to Miss Siân; Siân had been so concerned that she'd asked Richard to see Jessie. He too had been kindness itself, Jessie had told Vi. He'd said there was an operation that could be performed on her foot which might ease the pressure on her back, but she wouldn't be able to work for three months. That was out of the question for how could she support herself? she'd asked. He was sorry for her predicament and arranged for the dispensary to supply her with stronger painkillers, the bill to be paid by him. Hannah prayed that Jessie's employers would be kind and keep her on in another position, maybe as a parlourmaid or tweeny.

It was so hot that Hannah dabbed at the beads of perspiration on her forehead with a piece of cloth as she went to the open door to greet Jessie.

'Hannah, why aren't you resting?' Jessie said with concern.

'I've enough time for that. You look worn out, Jessie. Come and sit down and I'll make us both a cup of tea.'

'It's just the heat, Hannah, it drains me, see. I'll be all right when the cooler weather comes.'

'I know this heat is affecting everyone. Mrs Ahearn down the road is in bed with a fever and some are saying it's typhoid, and everyone is terrified they'll catch it. It's the conditions, Jessie. The privies stink and food goes off and then gets thrown out and goes rotten, and everywhere there're swarms of flies. I've got everything covered with butter muslin.'

Hannah set the kettle on the fire. It wasn't a range

but a proper fireplace. The house only had one range and that was in the kitchen. Hannah and Alfie rented the front room and the upstairs front bedroom. She had no other form of heating in winter and needed a fire in summer to cook on, no matter how hot it was. She placed her hands in the small of her back and grimaced with weariness.

'Hannah, you've only got a fortnight or so to your confinement, it'll be all over and you'll be your old self again. So sit down.'

Hannah smiled at her. She too would be glad when her baby was born. She and Alfie had been married for twenty-one months and she'd changed from the girl who had left the house in Faulkner Square. She felt she had at last grown up. She was no longer a girl, with girlish dreams and fantasies. She was a woman now. A wife, and soon she'd be a mother.

The money she'd saved and Miss Siân's wedding present had all gone into making these two rooms clean and comfortable. Alfie, his brothers and his mates had limewashed all the walls except one in the bedroom; they'd had so much beer whilst doing it that they'd been too drunk to finish it so she'd done the last bit herself. There was new lino on the floors and rag rugs. Net curtains hung in the windows and heavy draw curtains too, which helped keep out the draughts in winter. She had a table and four chairs, a dresser, a sofa and two rocking chairs, plus a mesh-fronted food press in the downstairs room. All her washing, including the dishes, was done in the tiny, cramped scullery downstairs that she shared with her neighbour. In the bedroom was a big brass bed with a feather mattress and plenty of blankets and quilts for the cold winter nights. She'd also bought a wardrobe and two chests of drawers. She had a mirror on the wall and a china dressing table set that had chips and a few cracks. Downstairs on the mantel she had two matching vases and a clock and a nice picture of a rural scene on one wall.

She'd managed to get a job at Barker and Dobson's sweet factory which was a lot better than the tobacco companies or other factory jobs. It was hard work keeping house and going out to work, but she'd had to do it until she started with the baby. At least it had been clean work and the pay had been better than she'd received whilst in service. And she'd needed it for Alfie liked his beer and his betting. She'd stopped complaining about that after the row they'd had the first time he came home the worse for drink and with no money.

'Don't be such a bloody misery, Hannah! You're not used to working fellers. You were kept apart from all men in the workhouse and you didn't have much to do with those toffs you worked for. I work bloody hard all week, so I deserve a bit of a treat. I've told you time and again, Hannah, you've led too sheltered a life.'

She'd been incensed. 'I work hard too, Alfie! I work in the factory all day and I wear myself out keeping this place decent. What treats do I get?'

'Well, it was you who was in such a hurry to get

married, don't come moaning to me now,' he'd shouted before going up to bed leaving her angry, hurt and disillusioned – and his meal ruined.

She was finding out gradually that what Mrs Howard had said about marrying in haste and repenting at leisure was true. It hadn't been too bad at first, in fact it had been great in some ways. He was always laughing and joking and they went out a lot: only cheap outings, but he'd taken her to the Gaumont Cinema for her birthday and had bought her a little silver cross and chain. She was fingering it now.

'Hannah, are you . . . are you happy?' Jessie asked. She knew her friend too well not to notice that there was something troubling her other than the heat and her pregnancy.

Hannah frowned. 'You never miss anything, Jessie, do you?'

'No, I don't. What is it, *cariad*?'

Hannah eased herself down in a chair. 'Oh, it's a lot of things, small things but . . . well I think Alfie is spending too much money in the pub and on betting and he's had what he calls "a run of bad luck" lately. We should be saving up, Jessie. There'll be three of us soon and it's surprising how much a baby needs and I want mine to have more than I did. I've tried to tell him all that, but he won't listen and then he gets angry and starts shouting and I wish . . . Oh, Jessie I wish I had more people to talk to.'

Jessie nodded. Hannah didn't see much of Vi these days, as Vi was courting the son of one of her mam's neighbours. Ada Sweeney didn't visit, nor did Hannah go to Victoria Terrace after Ada had taken it on herself to go to see Alfie's mam, Vera Duggan.

'That poor girl's got no mam to look out for her, nor da either. It's my duty to go and see that flamin' auld trollop and tell her that if 'e treats Hannah badly, 'e'll answer to me. Hannah's 'ad enough to put up with all 'er life. I wish she'd stayed put with the Hugheses.' When she'd said this to Martha Harper, her friend had agreed wholeheartedly and offered to go with her, but Ada said she'd manage on her own.

The visit had ended up in a yelling match with abuse being hurled from one end of Byles Street to the other and Ada swearing she'd have nothing more to do with any of them and if Lily persisted in her intention to marry Jack Duggan when she was twenty-one, then she could go to hell and never cross her doorstep again.

It was a situation that upset Hannah for she was very fond of Ada, but she supposed Ada had her pride too and she had been publicly humiliated by Vera Duggan and two of her daughters.

'What about Mrs Ross?' Jessie inquired about the other woman living in the house.

'No. She swears, she drinks, she leaves those kids on their own, or sitting on the pub doorstep, for hours and I wish you could see the state of her place. She's always sending one of the kids down to borrow something – tea, sugar, milk – after spending the housekeeping in the pub. I don't want her here.'

Jessie nodded. No, Maggie Ross would be no

company for someone like Hannah. 'Well, you'll be able to get out and about soon. You'll be able to walk in the park and talk to people. Other girls who take their babies out for walks in the fresh air. Have you got a pram yet?'

'Alfie's supposed to be picking it up tonight on his way home. We got it from an advertisement in the newspaper; it's second-hand, so it was cheap. I'll probably have to scrub it out but I won't mind that.'

'I bet Alfie will change, Hannah, when he becomes a da.'

Hannah smiled. 'Oh, he's not bad, Jessie, really. I moan about him too much. He's very generous some-times.'

Jessie noticed the look of sadness in Hannah's face. Hannah was smiling but the smile never reached her eyes. She doubted that Hannah would ever get over Richard Hughes. She couldn't tell her friend of the latest news, gleaned by Vi, that Maria was pregnant and everyone was delighted, Richard most of all. It was a happy marriage and he was climbing the ladder of success in his career.

'I brought you these.' Jessie fumbled in her bag and passed two knitted white matinée coats to Hannah.

Hannah's expression changed. 'Oh, Jessie, they're lovely. Where did you get them?'

'One of Vi's sisters-in-law had a baby but he's grown out of these, so she gave them to me for you. She said there'll be other things too as he grows and Vi said he's the last. She's got four already. Vi's sister-in-law said to

Vi that he could tie a knot in . . . "it", now he's finally got the son he wanted.'

Hannah smiled. She didn't care whether she had a boy or a girl, and the clothes would be very welcome. She knew Alfie wanted a son, but she herself didn't mind. They'd be a family and she'd always longed for a family of her own.

Jessie chatted on about the Hughes household. That the cook and the butler seemed to be getting closer. That there had been a huge row between Mr Thomas and his father over the girl called Daphne, so bad that Miss Siân had had to go to bed, she was so upset. That Blandford had tried to hide the fact that he'd eaten a whole pie from Mrs Howard but had been sick and she'd said it served him right. But she never mentioned Richard and Maria. She finally got slowly to her feet.

'I'd best get back now, Hannah, but I'll come next week and maybe Vi will come with me then.'

'I'd like to see her. I really would.'

Hannah stood leaning against the door-jamb, watching Jessie walking down the street. At least Jessie did come and see her, she thought, and her friend could have stayed at home and rested.

As she reached the bottom of the road Jessie stopped, turned and waved. It was something she always did. Hannah waved back and turned away. She hadn't even started to gather up the teacups when she heard a commotion. She ran to the door and saw a small crowd gathered at the junction of the crossroads. Instinctively she raised her hand to her throat. Jessie!

Oh, it can't be Jessie! She began to run but after a few steps she had to slow down, fighting for breath. The nearer she got she could see a car, a policeman and another man arguing. With her heart in her mouth she pushed through the crowd.

'Let me through, please? Please, I must get through. Who is it?'

'A girl by the sound of it. That feller with the car knocked 'er down. 'Ere, are yer all right, girl?' the man asked, noting her condition and the stricken look in her eyes.

'Yes, but please let me through!'

He took her arm and elbowed his way forward. 'Let 'er through,' he continued to shout until they got to the front of the crowd and she went straight to the policeman, her heart thumping. She could not bear to look beyond him to what lay in the road.

'Oh, please, sir! What's happened? Who is hurt?'

The constable was about to turn her away but changed his mind at the look on her face.

'A young girl, small, light brown hair, this fool ran her down.'

'I resent that, Constable, I did not knock her down. She stepped out in front of me and I am not a fool. Your superiors will hear more of this.'

'Oh, they will indeed, sir,' the policeman said grimly.

A young lad tugged at the policeman's sleeve. 'I saw 'im! I saw that feller come dashin' round the corner. 'E run straight into 'er.'

'I did no such thing and that young urchin is lying!'

199

'Well, the girl's dead and in my book that's man-slaughter and I think you'll find it's the judge's verdict too.'

Hannah cried out and pushed past the policeman to reach the figure huddled on the ground as the loud clanging of an ambulance bell became clearer. She dropped to her knees and tried to lift Jessie but her bulky figure made it awkward.

'Oh, Jessie! Jessie! You can't be dead! You can't leave me, Jessie! You're like my sister! You can't be dead!' she cried as the full realisation began to dawn on her. Oh, no, she loved Jessie so much! They'd shared all life's hardships together and the good times too. No, Jessie couldn't be dead, surely she was just unconscious?

Two more policemen had arrived plus the ambulance and crew.

'Come on, luv, let me help you up. There's nothing you can do for her now,' one said, holding her arm gently but firmly as she got to her feet.

Hannah gazed up at him, the tears coursing down her cheeks. It couldn't be true. Only a few minutes ago she'd been talking to her friend and now . . .

The crowd was dispersing. A sergeant was remonstrating with the car driver, the other policeman was writing down what the young lad was saying.

'Did she have any family, luv?' the first policeman asked.

Hannah shook her head. 'No. No one. She . . . she came from a workhouse . . .' She dissolved again into tears.

'All right, luv, calm down.' He led her to the car and eased her down on to a seat. 'That's better. Now, where did she work?'

'She was in service at number fifteen, Abercromby Square. Jessie Williams, that's her name.'

'And your name?'

'Mrs Hannah Duggan.'

She was too distracted to notice the look that passed between the constable and the sergeant. A look that said, 'She's one of *that* lot.'

'Well, there's nothing anyone can do for her now.' He signalled for the ambulance driver to approach.

A pain tore through Hannah's stomach and she screamed and hung on to the constable's sleeve.

'Here, mate, I think you'd better take a look at her.'

Hannah screamed again.

'It's all right, luv. Don't panic. We'll take you to Oxford Street in the ambulance. Hang on to me.'

'As one light goes out, another is lit. I'll get another ambulance for the poor girl lyin' there. And for God's sake show some decency, cover her face up. Sod regulations, put your tunic over her,' the ambulance driver said as he helped Hannah into the ambulance.

'Can't do that, it's more than my job's worth. We don't wear a shirt underneath. Haven't you got something?'

'Jesus Christ Almighty, damn you and your bloody bosses. Hey, Jack! Bring us a blanket, will you? This lot are useless! Just remember it's the property of the Royal Southern Hospital and not the Liverpool City

Police! I want it back!' he said scathingly, glaring at the constable.

For the next five long and tortuous hours Hannah strained and sweated and thrashed about in agony as the contractions became more frequent and all the time she cried out one name: 'Jessie!'

When Alfie finally arrived at the hospital, having been informed by Maggie Ross who'd been in the crowd and had seen everything, Hannah was half asleep, her baby daughter wrapped up tightly and held in the crook of her arm.

'Oh, Alfie! Alfie! It's all been so terrible and yet . . .'

'I heard about poor Jessie. That feller should be strung up. Thinks because he's got money he can do what he likes, tearing round the city at that speed. Well, it's put a stop to his capers – they're going to do him for manslaughter. He'll go down and he won't like that. Jail's no picnic. The others inside won't take kindly to him either, not for killing a girl, and with the money he's got. He'll get a hard time.'

Hannah tried hard *not* to listen. 'Alfie . . . look.' She held the baby out to him but he made no attempt to take her from Hannah's arms.

'Alfie, she's yours . . . ours.'

'She . . . ?'

Hannah nodded.

'God, I'd be terrified to touch her. I'd drop her or do something terrible. She's awfully small.'

Hannah smiled tiredly. 'I know but she's come early

... They said she's quite healthy and she'll grow, and fast too. What shall we call her?'

Alfie shrugged. It really didn't matter what they called her. He'd wanted a boy so he'd only thought of boys' names and now his feelings of disappointment were beginning to surface.

'Oh, you choose something, Hannah.'

Hannah wiped away a tear from her cheek. It had been a terrible day. Her friend was dead, and it would take a long time to get over that, but it had ended so wonderfully. Jessie was beyond pain and worry now and she had had her baby.

'Jessica, after poor Jessie,' she said, stroking the baby's face gently.

'That's a bit fancy, isn't it? Why not call her just Jessie?'

'No. In my mind and heart there will only ever be one "Jessie" and ... and they'll be burying ... her soon. No, Jessica is what she'll be called, always,' she finished firmly.

Alfie looked decidedly put out. A girl and a flaming fancy name too. Well, at least it was a good excuse to go down to the George and get bevvied. It's not every day a feller becomes a da, he thought. Even if he's got a girl and not a lad.

Chapter Fifteen

The sun was beating down again the following week when Jessie was buried. It was too nice a day for a funeral. There should have been grey skies, a cold wind and maybe even rain, Hannah thought. Her heart was so heavy. Her eyes were red-rimmed with crying and the dark circles beneath her eyes were evidence of sleepless nights. Even the cost of the funeral had been a painful issue – it had seemed even in death no one had wanted to take responsibility for poor Jessie. Of course everyone in the house in Faulkner Square had been shocked and very upset when they heard the news. Hannah had begged Alfie to let them know what had happened to Jessie. She'd written a note for him to just pass in before he went to wet the baby's head with his brothers and mates.

'I can't believe it! I can't believe I'll never see her again. Oh, I should have gone with her. She asked me to,' Vi cried, wiping her eyes.

'Now it's no use talking like that,' Mrs Howard said. 'I'm a firm believer that when your time comes you'll go. The poor girl was in terrible pain and it would only have got worse. She wouldn't have been able to work and then what would have happened to her?' Mrs Howard had been fond of Jessie too. She went on, 'Vi, get down to the hospital and see Hannah because she'll be terribly upset and that useless husband of hers won't be of much help from what *I've* heard about him. I met that woman from Victoria Terrace – quite by chance, she recognised me from Hannah's description – and she was telling me what a terrible family they are. An absolute disgrace to the neighbourhood, she said. She just can't understand Hannah. She begged her not to marry him, said that it would all end in tears, but apparently Hannah has a very stubborn streak which I know full well.'

So Vi had gone and Hannah had clung to her and her tears for her friend mingled with those of Vi.

'Look at it the way Mrs Howard does. She's out of pain now, there's no need for us to worry over her. She'd only have ended up in desperate straits because she wouldn't be able to cope in, say, five years' time.'

'I know, Vi, but . . . but there's another worry.'

'What?'

'Who's going to pay for her funeral?'

'I hadn't thought of that, Hannah.'

'I have and it's so important that she has a decent one, not a pauper's burial. She had nothing for so many years, Vi. We both used to feel terrible when one of the inmates died and was carted off in a plain box to be buried God knows where and without a minister even. I wouldn't want that for her, Vi, and I've nothing saved up or I'd pay myself.'

'Neither have I. But don't you worry about it,

Hannah, I'll speak to Mrs Howard when I get back. Now, let me look at the little one. Is Alfie made up with her?'

'Yes and no really. Yes because he seems to be a bit stunned that she's his own flesh and blood . . .'

'And no because what?' Vi demanded.

'Because she's not a boy.'

'Oh, honestly, men are so thick! All they ever worry about is themselves and their pride. They want to be able to say, "My son this, and my son that". Take no notice. He'll probably be blind drunk for days just the same and he'll get used to it. Maybe next time he'll get a son.'

Hannah nodded wearily. Alfie had been in to see her and the baby just once. He was certainly overdoing the celebrations: she wondered where he was getting the money from.

Vi had conveyed Hannah's wishes about Jessie's funeral and Mr Donaldson had gone to make enquiries at Abercromby Square. He'd come back with a grim expression on his face and disgust in his eyes.

'So, what did they say?' Mrs Howard demanded.

'They said it's not their responsibility. She only worked for them, the family must pay.'

'There is no family! Did you tell them that?' Mrs Howard retorted angrily.

'I did and the reply to that was, "Then the Parish must see to it and bear the cost." ' He took his bowler hat off and smoothed it carefully before putting it on the hat stand.

'Well, I've never heard of anything so disgraceful. They refused to pay and with the money they've got!' Mrs Howard was incensed, so incensed that when she went upstairs with Miss Siân's supper tray, something Vi usually did, she'd told her mistress. Siân Hughes had been as shocked as the cook and sat down and wrote a note to Jessie's employers. Blandford had taken it up there and then and after a while a note had been delivered addressed to Miss Siân Hughes. Mrs Howard was then informed that Jessie's funeral would be paid for by the household in Abercromby Square.

'And I should think so too, Edith,' Mr Donaldson had said thankfully as Mrs Howard had sat opposite him in his pantry with a small glass of sherry in her hand. For her nerves, she'd said when it had been offered.

'And thank God that we have employers who have the common decency to care. It's a comfort to know that should any of us find ourselves in such a state we'll be treated with respect. Miss Siân told me so herself. I've never liked any of that lot, out and out snobs they are. You should see the carry on of their parlourmaids. You'd think they had thousands in the bank and were titled ladies!'

Hannah had been taken to the church by Mrs Howard. She had to go. She just *had* to, she'd replied to Mrs Howard's horrified question as to why she was signing herself out of hospital when she had at least another week to go before they'd let her home with the baby. Two weeks in bed was the usual time a new mother had to rest.

'Just sit there,' Mrs Howard had said as she'd pushed Hannah and the baby into a pew. All the staff had turned out, which Hannah thought was wonderful. Even Blandford looked well in a dark-coloured jacket and trousers, white shirt and black tie and with a black armband on the sleeve of his jacket. She was very taken aback to see Siân Hughes, dressed entirely in black and with Vi at her side. She'd never in a million years have expected her to come. It wasn't 'done' – but then Siân Hughes had little time or patience with conventions. Hannah thought again how unfortunate it was that Siân hadn't found a nice young man who wanted to marry her. For all her money and luxury, Siân had known grief, ill-health and, Hannah suspected, unfulfilled hopes and dreams.

When the service and the burial were over, Mrs Howard took Hannah's arm and Siân came over to her.

'Mrs Duggan, Hannah, I'm so sorry, it's so tragic.'

'It is, miss, but at least she had a decent burial and it was very, very kind of you to come.'

'I know that both you and Rowan were very fond of her, as indeed were Mrs Howard and Mr Donaldson. It's a sad loss.'

'It is, miss, and she was so young and had really only just started to enjoy her life.'

Siân nodded. She and Hannah had both suffered

from bereavement. Then she smiled. 'May I have a look at your daughter?'

Hannah smiled back and pulled the thin shawl from around the baby's head. 'She's only a week old, miss.'

'She's beautiful, Hannah. Her eyes are like big copper pennies. But you shouldn't be standing around here. You should be in bed.'

'We told her that, Miss Siân, but she insisted,' Mrs Howard said shaking her head.

'Well, I'd best get back. She'll need feeding soon.'

'I'll walk with you to the tram stop,' Mrs Howard offered.

Hannah nodded her thanks and turned away, just in time to see Alfie and his brother Jack hanging on to the church gate for support and grinning drunkenly. Her heart turned over. Oh, no! Why? Why had they come? Why in that state too and with Miss Siân here?

'It's my husband and his brother,' she informed Mrs Howard.

'So what do you two want?' Mrs Howard snapped at both of them, knowing how humiliated Hannah must feel.

'Come to pay our re—respects,' Alfie said, his speech very slurred.

'Well, you've been now so get off, the pair of you,' Vi hissed.

'Alfie, go on home now. I'm coming with Jessica in a minute.'

'What . . . what's the matter with you coming with us? Are we too common for your fancy friends?' he replied loudly. 'This is nice, Jack, isn't it? They don't want us here.'

'Alfie, go home, please,' Hannah said, anger starting to rise up in her even though she was feeling weak and the strong sun wasn't doing the baby any good either.

'No. Jack and me are going to see Mam. We'll get a drink an' a laugh with her.'

Hannah's patience snapped. 'Then get out of my sight, the pair of you, now! The state you're in is a disgrace. You *are* a pair of common drunks.'

Alfie's expression changed. 'Who are you calling common? I wasn't common when you wanted to marry me. Oh no, I was just what you wanted and you were all meek and mild then,' he jibed.

Mrs Howard drew herself up. 'I've heard all about you two and the rest of your family. Get out of here, both of you, before Mr Donaldson calls the police and has you removed! You're right. We *don't* want you here and Hannah's upset enough without having a slanging match with you to contend with. Clear off.'

Alfie and Jack turned away, to Hannah's infinite relief. Thank God Miss Siân had remained behind, talking to the vicar.

'Do you want me to come home with you, Hannah?' Vi offered, for Hannah's face was very pale and her eyes were full of anger.

'No, really, Vi, I'm fine. I can manage him.'

'Are you sure?' Mrs Howard asked. 'I didn't like the look of the older one.'

Hannah nodded. She was burning up with fury and shame.

'All right then, but I'll be down to see you soon,' Vi promised.

'You just make sure you rest or you'll be back in hospital,' Mrs Howard said firmly.

When Hannah finally got home she was exhausted with both the heat and the effort. The place was a mess but she didn't care. She felt awful. Why in God's name had he turned up in that state? Didn't he realise how upset and weak she was? That she really shouldn't have left hospital? Didn't he have *any* sensitivity? And where had he been all week? With his brothers and his mam? She'd only met her mother-in-law once. She'd come to inspect their 'new home' as she'd called it, with heavy sarcasm, and Hannah could tell she'd been drinking. Now Hannah only had enough energy to make herself a cup of tea before she sat down and began to feed Jessica.

She had managed to tidy up a bit before she heard Alfie's footsteps in the lobby and she frowned. She wondered if she had enough patience left to cope with him. She'd just have to try to get him upstairs to bed.

He almost fell through the door: he was very drunk. She'd never seen him like this before.

'Alfie!'

'What are you doing . . . here?'

'It's my . . . our home, remember, and don't shout. You'll wake Jessica.'

'I'll shout my head off if I bloody well want to!' he yelled.

Hannah frowned as a fretful wail came from the crib in the corner that was in reality a drawer lined with cheap cotton. 'Now see what you've done.'

'She's always bloody crying.'

'How would you know that? We've been in hospital – not that you'd remember, you only came in once. I've not been home, and this mess you've made of the place shows.'

'This is *my* house! *My* bloody house. I pay the rent, not you!' he shouted. He kicked out at a chair and sent it crashing over. The noise made the baby cry in earnest.

Hannah was furious. 'Get to bed! You're drunk and useless and . . . disgusting.'

He laughed cuttingly. 'A posh word from your posh friends!'

'Oh, get to bed, Alfie!'

She wasn't expecting it so the blow across her face that sent her sprawling on the floor made her scream.

'Don't speak to me like that again!' he bawled.

Hannah was on her feet, her eyes blazing. She snatched up the nearest object, a pan, and hit him with it with all the strength she could muster.

He staggered back, swearing.

'Touch me once more and I'll belt you again.'

He lunged forward and she raised the pan again but he was too quick for her and grasped her wrist so tightly that she released her grip and let it fall. Another blow sent her flying back against the wall and she could taste the saltiness of blood on her mouth.

'Get out! Get out of here!' she screamed. She was shaking with fear and exhaustion. To her surprise and thankfulness he did. He staggered into the lobby and slammed the door so hard that Jessica began to scream.

Hannah took the wailing baby out of her crib and sat down, still shaking, tears of fright, shock and pain filling her eyes as she held Jessica tightly to her. Oh, God, things had never been this bad. He'd never raised a finger to her before. She touched her face gingerly. It felt as though it were on fire. Her lip was already swelling, she could feel it, and her shoulder was aching too. It was the shock that was the worst thing. He had turned into a menacing drunk and that frightened her. Was this the way he was going to act in future? Was it *her* fault? Was it because she came from the workhouse that he felt he was justified in treating her like this? Did he despise her so much? Was it because he'd wanted a son? Was he everything Ada said he was? She was just too exhausted to think it through or do anything more than fall asleep in the chair, the baby in her arms.

When she woke the sunlight was streaming in through the window; the curtains hadn't been drawn. She was stiff and her whole body seemed to ache. She had difficulty opening one eye and her lips were swollen to twice their normal size. She dragged herself up and placed the baby in her crib. The act of bending sent pain shooting to her head and she thought it was about to explode. Slowly she straightened up. She was still dazed, but she'd better wash her face and try to make a start on cleaning up. She only hoped that he was suffering with a terrible hangover so he'd know how bad she felt.

She'd stacked all the dishes – she'd take them down to the scullery later – and swept the hearth and the floor; she'd picked up and folded all the clothes she found lying around, most of which needed washing (though that would have to wait); she'd washed and dressed Jessica and was sitting feeding her when the door opened. Automatically she froze in the chair. He looked terrible.

'God, Hannah, I've got the worst head I've ever had in my life and my tongue feels as if it's got a fur coat on.'

'So have I,' she answered coldly.

He looked at her. 'Hannah, what happened to you? Your face is all bruised, and you've got a black eye.'

'Don't you remember, Alfie?'

'Remember what? I was as bevvied as the landlord's cat.'

'You did it. You hit me, twice. You sent me crashing into the wall.'

He looked at her with astonishment. 'Me? I did that? I . . . belted you?'

'You did. Who else is there?'

'Oh, God, Hannah, I don't remember. I swear I don't! Oh, look at the state of your poor face. I'm sorry, luv, so sorry.' He was nearly in tears and her heart softened.

'I never thought you'd do anything like that.'

'Hannah, I'm sorry. I didn't mean it. I love you!'

'Oh, Alfie, you hurt me so much and I was so tired what with the funeral, the heat, the baby . . .'

He put his arm around her shoulder, drawing her close. 'I'm sorry. I'm truly sorry. I'll never, ever touch you again, I swear it!'

'Then will you stop drinking, *please*? It's the drink that makes you like that. You've been getting worse and worse lately.'

'Oh, Hannah, of course I will. Just one pint after work, luv, I swear. God, I feel terrible.'

She managed a lopsided smile then grimaced in pain.

'You sit there, luv, I'll go and get something for my head from her at the back, then I'll go and get something for your face. I'll stay off today to look after you both.'

She lifted her face to be kissed. She believed him. He had been so drunk that she knew he was telling the truth: that he hadn't meant to hurt her. And now he'd promised to cut his drinking down to one pint and she couldn't begrudge him that. He did work hard. She felt infinitely relieved as she stroked her daughter's soft, dark hair.

Chapter Sixteen

As the summer wore on and then faded into autumn Jessica thrived. To Hannah's great relief, Alfie kept to his promise. He had never laid a finger on her since that terrible night. But the memory of it made her go cold and often invaded her dreams.

Each morning she got up early to light the fire, boil a large pan of water for tea, washing and Alfie's shave. The room was always tidy and warm, the table was set and the porridge ready to serve when he came down. After Alfie had gone to work, which was now a more regular daytime shift, she cleaned up, washed the dishes and did the washing, ironing, shopping and baking. All the chores were done on a different specified day and were on top of the everyday routine running of a home.

Each afternoon she put the baby in the pram and walked, usually to Princes Park which had a lake.

When she was tired she would often sit on a bench in the shade of a tree just watching people go past while Jessica slept. The baby looked like Alfie. She now had his light brown hair, her skin was pale but her eyes were brown like Hannah's, and she had a smile that would break any heart other than one of stone, so Vi often said.

They were walking in the park one glorious golden

October afternoon on Vi's half-day. The air was warm, the smell of dying leaves faintly pungent. Occasionally one would fall gently to the ground to join those that already lay in a layer on top of the grass. At one point, near the lake, a man with a rake was gathering them up in piles.

Vi could see something was troubling her friend. There had been a couple of weeks back in July after Jessie's funeral when Hannah had pleaded illness and tiredness when Vi had suggested coming to visit her. Perhaps she was feeling ill again?

'Hannah, what's the matter?' Vi finally asked.

'Nothing.'

'There is.'

Hannah shrugged. 'Oh, it's only a stupid niggling thing.'

'Let me be the judge of that, Hannah.'

'It's Alfie,' Hannah sighed.

'He's not out boozing every night, is he?'

'No.'

'Then what's he done now?' Vi demanded.

'It's Jessica. He doesn't seem very interested in her. He hardly ever picks her up and when she cries he gets irritable, as though she's getting on his nerves.'

'She probably is. I've told you before, Hannah, men are selfish pigs. I don't suppose he does anything for her. You can't honestly say you want him to wheel her out in the pram or anything like that? Men go mad if you ask them to help, no matter how much they love their kids. They'd be skitted soft by their mates.'

Hannah smiled. 'Does Georgie fall in the same class as a "selfish pig" too?'

'Oh, he's not too bad, as fellows go.'

Hannah laughed. 'You see.'

'It's him I wanted to talk about today.'

For the first time that afternoon Hannah looked closely at Vi. Her friend seemed full of barely suppressed excitement. 'I can see you're just dying to tell me something. Go on, what is it?'

'Georgie and me are getting married,' Vi answered, blushing.

'Oh, Vi! That's great news. I'm so happy for you. When's it to be?'

'After Christmas. In January to be exact. We're saving up but . . .'

'But what?'

Vi looked apprehensive. 'But we won't be living here, Hannah.'

'Not in Liverpool?'

'Not in this country at all, that's the hard bit. We're emigrating to Canada. Georgie's got relatives out there, not far from Toronto, St Catherine's, it's called. He'll get a good job, what with working on the railway here, and I'll get something, although I don't think it will be in service. I don't think people have servants over there, not like we do here anyway. I think only the very, very rich people have them, but there's plenty of other jobs. Anyway, I'm sick of being at everyone's beck and call.'

Hannah was stunned. 'But, Vi, it's an awfully long way. It's the other side of the world with an ocean in between. What if you don't like it? What if you can't settle?'

'I've got to try, Hannah. Georgie says his cousin's letters are full of things to do. There's so much space, you see. It's not like here with everyone all crowded together. It won't be like the streets here, with the terrible courts off them where you can hardly see daylight and only one privy and standpipe between everyone. People like us can even buy their own houses. Can you believe that? Me owning my own house . . . well, us owning our own house. And a house with a big garden or "yard" as they call them. And there's so many things to do. It's *different* to here.'

'I'm happy for you, Vi, really I am, but I'll miss you terribly. Have you told anyone else yet?'

Vi shook her head. 'No, I'll need my wages. Mam's agreed to let me keep them all to help out, like. You know I always took money home. I'll give my notice in next month. It wouldn't be fair to give them just a few weeks. They've all been so good to me and it's not easy finding servants these days.'

'Yes, I know, Vi. They were good to me too, especially Miss Siân. Is there anyone special in her life yet?'

Vi shook her head. 'No, it's mainly only Mr Thomas's friends who come to the house now and she doesn't like them and I can't say I blame her. There's always rows between him and the Master too.'

Hannah tried to shake off the mood of depression that had fallen over her. 'Is it to be a proper wedding?' she asked, thinking of her own austere wedding day.

'If by "proper" you mean church and a white dress, then yes. There won't be a big do afterwards as we're going to sail the same day. But you will come, Hannah?'

'Oh, Vi, wild horses wouldn't keep me away. What date is it?'

'Saturday the seventh of January. We're sailing on the *Empress of France*.' Vi laughed. 'All those Canadian Pacific Empresses are painted white, they'll match my dress.'

'Are you going to keep your dress on?'

'I might as well get my money's worth out of it. It won't be worn again although Mam says I should cut it short and have it dyed. Maybe I will when I get there.'

'Will it be all right if I bring Jessica? There's no one I'd trust to mind her for so long.'

'What about Mrs Sweeney?'

Hannah shook her head sadly. 'No, I couldn't ask her. I haven't been to see her since before I married Alfie. How could I go, the way she was humiliated and the way he was carrying on? She'd say "I told you so" and I couldn't stand that.'

'Well it won't be for all that long. It's ten o'clock at the church and then we board at twelve noon. Just enough time for something to eat, a bit of a chat, a drink and . . . Oh, Hannah, I'm scared.'

Hannah put her arm around her. 'What of, Vi? Going over there?'

'Not really, well, just a bit, but it's being married and . . . and well . . . you know.'

Hannah smiled at her. 'Vi, stop thinking like that.

You love him and he loves you and it's . . . it's not as bad as everyone says it is. In fact you might surprise yourself. You might like it.'

'But how will I know?'

'You won't. Unless you have a trial run.'

Vi was horrified. 'Oh, Hannah! I couldn't do that!'

'No, you couldn't, so stop worrying. Now tell me all your plans.'

When Hannah returned home she looked around and felt a little envious of Vi. She had a wonderful future ahead; Hannah would miss her. Vi and Jessie had been her only friends; now Jessie was dead and Vi was leaving and she'd never see her again.

Her gaze settled on the mantelshelf over the fireplace and for a few minutes she wondered what was so odd about it, then it dawned on her. Her matching vases had gone and so had the clock. She left Jessica in her pram and sat down. A feeling of dread washed over her. He'd obviously sold or pawned them. But why did he need the money? He had money for his drink each night. She made his wages stretch by skimping and saving. She was a good manager. She only ever had a very small portion of whatever it was they were having for tea, saying she'd had something earlier and wasn't too hungry. It was hard but she did it so neither he nor Jessica ever had to go without.

She had the table laid and his meal ready when he came in at half past six. Jessica had been fed and washed and was drowsily drooping her head on

Hannah's shoulder. Hannah put her finger to her lips as she gently put the baby in her crib.

'That smells good, luv,' Alfie said quietly. He found it easier on everyone if he kept his voice down. It was far better than having to put up with a whinging kid. He had enough to put up with with Maggie Ross's kids always bawling and yelling and screeching.

'It's just a bit of haddock and some mashed potatoes. I had mine earlier.' She sat down at the table and looked at him. He looked away and flushed slightly.

'Why did you pawn the things off the mantelpiece, Alfie?' she asked quietly.

He flung his knife and fork down. 'You don't miss a bloody thing, do you, Hannah?'

'No, I don't, but seeing as I dust them every day I would notice that they were gone. I'm not stupid, Alfie.'

'Oh, you're not that all right. You've eyes like a bloody hawk.'

'Alfie, I don't want an argument. Just an explanation. I loved those things. It's things like them that make a home look, well, cosier.'

'I pawned them because I needed the money, OK? Now can I have my tea in peace?'

'But why did you need the money?' she pressed him.

He got up, the legs of the chair scraping noisily on the lino. 'Why? Why? I don't have to tell you why.'

'No, you don't, but seeing as I bought them with the money Miss Siân gave us for a wedding present I think I deserve some kind of an answer.'

'I put all the money I had on a horse. A sure thing, our Jack said. It's still bloody running, they're probably out now with torches looking for the bloody animal!' he replied sarcastically.

'So there's no money for the housekeeping?'

'Not much. I have to have my fares and my pint. You'll just have to manage, Hannah.'

She stared up at him, anger in her eyes.

He glared back. 'If you're going to sit there giving me daggers all night, then I'm off out. Keep the bloody tea.' He pushed the plate across the table.

She got to her feet. 'Yes, go on, spend the rest of the money and then we'll all starve and you'll have to walk to work,' she yelled after him as he banged out.

She sat down and dropped her head in her hands. Oh, why were things always going wrong? What was the matter with him? And she had no one to confide in. Soon she'd be waving Vi off to a new country, a new life. She felt so lonely and so bereft that she laid her arms on the table, bent her head and cried.

When he came in he didn't speak to her, and she continued to darn the heel of his sock, not raising her head. Later, he got into bed, turned his back on her and went to sleep; she could smell the beer on him. How was she going to manage now? There would be no money for a week; he'd just been paid. They couldn't starve and she'd need money for coal and gas for the lighting. She tossed and turned beside him until at last she came to the decision that she herself would have to pawn some items, but she felt as though she was just beginning down the slippery slope of debt and worry and hardship.

Again the following day he said nothing to her when he came in from work at lunchtime. He finished early on Saturdays. As usual the table was laid and the air was permeated with the smell of scouse. Hannah herself was cutting thick slices of bread with the carving knife.

'I thought you had no money? Have you been holding out on me, Hannah? Have you got some saved?'

His attitude infuriated her. She'd promised herself she'd be calm and reasonable but she wasn't standing for this. She spun round towards him, the ladle still in her hand.

'No, I've no savings of any kind. I took the picture and most of the crockery down to Goldring's. We have to eat and pay for the roof over our heads even if it is half falling down.' She ladled the stew from the pan into two bowls and she filled her own up to the brim too. 'It's blind scouse. It's all I could manage if I'm to pay the bills and buy food until you get paid next.' She sat down opposite him.

The meal was eaten in silence and when they'd finished, she gathered the dishes together on a tin tray.

'I'm taking these down to wash. Will you keep an eye on your daughter, please?' How she hated this coldness between them. Why did he never laugh and joke the way he used to do? Why was he so chilly towards her? She was doing her best for him, for them all. All she'd ever wanted was a proper family life.

When she returned she was determined to make an effort. She put the dishes away and went and sat on the arm of the chair he was sitting in, reading the *Echo*.

'Alfie, why do we always seem to be arguing and fighting these days?' She put her arm around his shoulder. 'I try so hard. I really do.'

He let the paper slip on to his knees. 'I don't know why. You seem to want too much.'

'Too much of what?'

'Of everything. None of my sisters or sisters-in-law carry on like you do if I have a drink or a bet. Just because it wasn't allowed in the workhouse . . .'

She sighed. It was the old excuse. The one he always used against her. 'Alfie, I'm different now. I've grown up and away from my past.'

'Well, it doesn't look like it to me,' he said sulkily.

She decided that this topic of conversation could end only one way. In a row. So she tried to change the subject.

'Vi's getting married to Georgie in January and guess what?'

'What?'

'They're emigrating.'

'What the hell for? He's got a good job. It's a job for life on the railways and a bit of a pension at the end of it.'

'She said he thinks things are better there.'

'Where?'

'In Canada.'

'God Almighty! Isn't he satisfied with what he's got?'

'Vi said that people like us, working class, can own their own houses there, if you work and save hard. Imagine that, Alfie. It's . . . it's amazing.'

'Why the hell would anyone want to own their house? You'd have all the repair jobs to do for a start.'

'The landlord doesn't do much about repairing this place. He hasn't spent a single farthing on it and it's half falling down.'

'Well it sounds bloody daft to me, going all that way when he's got a great job. It's not like just moving to another town.'

'She's invited us, all of us, to the wedding. She's going that very same day. They board at twelve o'clock. She's going in her wedding dress.'

'She's going round the bloody bend if you ask me, Hannah!'

'Well, I said we'd love to go, so . . .'

'So what?'

'Well, I'd like to buy her something, Alfie, to remind her of . . . us, and I'd like something new to wear, if it's possible. I haven't had anything since we got married.'

'Where the hell do you think all this money's going to come from? Bloody Father Christmas?'

'Alfie, please don't swear.'

'There you go again, nag, nag, nag.'

'I don't mean to. I was thinking . . . thinking of getting a job.'

'What kind of job? Who's going to see to her?' He jerked his head in the direction of the crib.

'Probably factory work. I'll have to find a baby minder.' The thought of leaving her baby with someone strange filled her with anxiety. 'Just for a short time, Alfie, until we're on our feet again.'

'Oh, do as you please, Hannah, just give me some peace. I told our Jack I'd meet him in the Grapes at half past two.' Hannah said nothing. She wished with all her heart that Jack Duggan – in fact the whole family – would go to Australia. Even that wouldn't be far enough away. They were all a bad influence on Alfie.

Hannah had been lucky. She'd been taken on in a shop, a greengrocer's on the corner of Rankin Street. It was getting nearer and nearer to Christmas and everyone was getting busier. The pay wasn't much and it was cold in the shop – there was no form of heating and the door was permanently open – but it was better than work in a factory. She was paying Evvie Taylor who lived further down the street to take care of Jessica. The woman was obviously very capable as she looked after five other children, nearly all of them under twelve months old. Hannah saved her wages but sometimes she had to supplement the housekeeping Alfie gave her with her own money.

She'd seen a very nice table lamp that she wanted to buy for Vi. Its base was a gold-coloured figure of a lady with raised arms, and the glass shade was made up of pieces of coloured glass. It was electric; she'd been a bit worried about that until the man told her that in a big modern country like Canada they were bound to have electricity laid on.

'There's women flying them aeroplanes across the Atlantic these days. A sign of the times, is that. So they're bound to have electricity,' he'd told her. She was paying it off each week. It would be paid for by the date of the wedding.

She'd bought Jessica a dress, a matinée coat and matching bonnet. They weren't new but they'd been well cared for. For herself she'd only been able to get a hat, but at least it was new and it matched her brown and cream checked coat. She was often exhausted when she picked her daughter up from Mrs Taylor but Jessica seemed to be tired out too, something she really appreciated.

One evening the week before the wedding Vi came to see her. It was bitterly cold and the north-easterly wind found its way under doors and in through warped window frames.

'I suppose I'm going to have to get used to the cold. Georgie says they get terrible winters. All snow and ice and heavy frost, but the summers are great.'

'Oh, Vi, I'm going to miss you.'

'I'm going to miss a lot of people.'

'Then why go?' Alfie asked from over the top of his newspaper.

'I wouldn't expect you to understand, Alfie,' Vi retorted.

Hannah bit her lip and Alfie folded the paper and got to his feet.

'Well, I can see that the pair of you will be nattering away all night. I think I'll go and see my mam.' He wound the white muffler around his neck and shrugged on his jacket.

'Alfie, put that overcoat on. The old army one you use for work,' Hannah urged.

'No, I'll be all right. That thing is filthy.'

'It's a wonder he notices, coming from that pig sty,' Vi muttered under her breath. Hannah said nothing.

'You are still coming?' Vi questioned her.

'Of course we are. Look, I'll show you what I've bought for Jessica.' She went to the dresser and opened a drawer, then spread the items of clothing out on the table.

'They're lovely, Hannah. It's a pity she's not older, she could have been a bridesmaid.'

'Maybe one day she will. Alfie's eldest brother's son is nearly fifteen.'

'But would you want her to be bridesmaid to one of that lot?'

'Oh, Vi, please don't start,' Hannah begged.

'I'm sorry. I just never think. *You* can call your husband an idle, useless, drunken sod, but, according to Mam, let anyone else do it and that's overstepping the bounds of friendship. I suppose she's right. What have you got for yourself?'

'A new hat – and it *is* new.'

'What about meladdo?'

'Oh, I'll sponge and press his suit. He can look very smart when he wants to be, but we don't get out much these days.'

'How are you finding that Mrs Taylor?'

'Oh, she's great. Jessica is washed and in her nightie and already half asleep when I pick her up. She sleeps all night, she's so good.'

'Too good? Shouldn't she be teething by now? Mam told me she hated it when we were all teething. She got no sleep day or night.'

'I think Mrs Taylor would tell me if she was crying, but I'll ask. Oh, tell me all about everything.'

'Well, I'm not telling you about my dress. That's a secret. But our Rose and Millie are having wine-coloured dresses. Our Rose said they'll freeze and they'll look all drab and miserable, but I don't care. Mam said it's my day. We're all going to go to Ye Crack in Rice Street. It's small but it's handy for the Pier Head. Oh, Hannah, I'm looking forward to it so much. Not just the wedding, but the ship bit as well. Georgie says it'll be like a cruise. There's always a band on the stage to see you off and paper streamers—'

'Even in winter?'

'Even in winter,' Vi replied firmly.

'I can't think of a better thing to do on your wedding day. And don't worry about your wedding night.'

'I'll probably be sea-sick. Da says the weather's always terrible in winter once you cross the Mersey Bar.'

'You won't, Vi! You'll be too excited anyway.'

Vi clasped her friend's hand. 'Oh, Hannah, I wish you were coming too.'

'How can I? Alfie thinks you're mad as it is. I'm

afraid I'm stuck with Liverpool.'

She gave her a squeeze. 'That's not so bad, Hannah.'

Looking back to her childhood Hannah agreed. There was no way she would ever live anywhere else – or so she hoped.

The morning of Vi's wedding dawned clear, bright and frosty.

'At least she's got a decent enough day for it,' Hannah remarked to Alfie as she dressed Jessica, hoping the little girl wouldn't be sick or make a mess of her 'new' clothes.

'We'll all freeze, especially her. At least we can wear coats,' he replied, struggling into his one good white shirt which Hannah had starched and ironed the night before. 'Where was he having his stag night?'

'I've no idea.'

'I notice *I* wasn't asked.'

'He doesn't know you. He's only met you once. It was for family and close mates.'

'I suppose you're right. Are you ready?'

'Almost.'

Jessica started to cry and Hannah picked her up. She'd asked Mrs Taylor if Jessica was any trouble. Did she cry a lot during the day? 'No, Hannah, she's a lovely baby. A real sunny smile she's got. Always gurgling, she is,' had been the reply and she'd been relieved.

'What's the matter with her? She never cries these days, thank God.'

'It's probably her teeth coming. Vi's mam said three of her kids cut their teeth with bronchitis.'

'Oh, God help us all! That's all I need. No flaming sleep.'

Hannah was gently feeling the baby's gums. 'Oh, Alfie, she's got one, no, she's got two, I can feel them. Look!'

Alfie peered into his daughter's mouth. 'I can't see any teeth and I'm not poking my finger in her mouth to feel either.'

Some of Hannah's elation disappeared. He still didn't take much notice of his daughter. She wondered why Mrs Taylor had not mentioned the fact that Jessica had cut two teeth. It must have been painful for her, her little gums were red and swollen. She'd ask her again on Monday.

Despite the cold and the thinness of her dress, Vi looked beautiful, Hannah thought as she stood with Alfie at the back of the church. Jessica was very cross this morning, she thought as she rocked the baby in her arms. If she didn't stop crying Hannah would have to take her out. Already the vicar had paused and looked pointedly at her. She remembered her own wedding day with some sadness. Vi had flowers, candles, an organist and bells. She'd had none of that. Vi's dress was of white satin, very plain but with a row of small pearl buttons down the front of the bodice. She had a short veil and just a satin-covered Alice band. More suitable for boarding a ship, so her mam had advised, than yards of net that would probably be stepped on, or get twisted around something or torn on bits of sharp metal. Her sisters looked rather chilly, Hannah thought, but the dresses were nice and they carried small bouquets.

Halfway through the service Hannah was finally forced to take Jessica out. She walked up and down in the churchyard trying to soothe her daughter. She was worried. Should she take her to the dispensary doctor? What if it wasn't just teeth? What if it was a fever? She was very hot. She'd see after the wedding was over and Vi and Georgie had sailed down the Mersey.

By the time the wedding was finished the baby had cried herself to sleep and Hannah was distraught. Alfie was no help. He was swigging beer with Georgie, his brothers, friends and both the da's. Jessica definitely had a high temperature. Hannah had managed to have a few words with Vi's mam who had told her if Jessica was still burning up when she got home, then the best thing would be for her to see a doctor, even though it cost money. It would be money well spent, Hannah thought.

She tried to concentrate fully on the newly-weds' departure. The ship's rails were crowded with people, mainly emigrants, and Alfie was shouting and cheering with everyone else. To Hannah the band seemed very loud and it was a terrible crush. The air was rent with the shouts and cheering as the for'ard hawsers were let go. The band played on. All the other ships in the river, at anchor in the Sloyne and tied up to the Prince's Landing Stage were blasting their steam whistles, and the Master of the *Empress of France* answered with three long deep blasts. You could hardly think clearly, Hannah thought. Any other day she'd have been enjoying the spectacle and cheering like everyone else. The paper streamers, the last tangible links with departing loved ones, finally broke as the tugs pulled the *Empress* out into the river.

Hannah couldn't wait for the crowd to disperse. She was going straight to see Doctor Mills.

Chapter Seventeen

Hannah took Jessica to the doctor's house immediately. She had two shillings in her purse and she hoped it wouldn't cost more. Alfie had stayed with the men from the wedding group who had all decided to carry on the celebrations after the ship was under way down the estuary. They'd gone to the Style House at the Pier Head and heaven alone knew when or if they'd get home. Hannah was so worried that she didn't really care. Alfie could look after himself, Jessica couldn't.

The woman who answered the door in response to Hannah's persistent knocking did not look at all pleased. She was some kind of maid, Hannah deduced.

'I'm sorry but the doctor is entitled to his time off, like everyone else. He's working himself to death. He gets no peace as it is, without people hammering on the door.'

'Oh, please, this is a real emergency,' Hannah pleaded.

'Then take her to hospital,' was the terse reply.

'No! No, I'd have to leave her there and I couldn't do that. Please, could you just ask him? I've got the money. She's so hot, just feel her poor little forehead!'

The woman declined. 'You'll have to wait until the other doctor arrives. He stands in at weekends and a couple of nights so Doctor Mills can get some rest.'

'I'll wait then. How long will he be? Oh, you don't know how worried I am about her. She's the only one I've got and I can't take a risk of her . . . dying . . . and you know how many do.'

The woman sighed heavily and held open the door.

'Go and sit in there and wait.' She pointed to a door that had the words 'Waiting Room' painted on it.

Hannah didn't sit down, neither did she notice how sparsely it was furnished or how spotlessly clean it was. 'Oh, please God let him agree to see us,' she prayed. She had a very real fear that her baby would die.

She was startled when Dr Mills opened the door and came into the room.

'I'm waiting for the other doctor. She said it was your day off.'

'It is, but when she told me it was a baby I decided to come down.' Dr Mills was a kindly man and seeing Hannah's distress he was moved.

'Now Mrs . . .?'

'Duggan,' Hannah supplied.

'Mrs Duggan, what's wrong?'

Before Hannah could tell him the door opened and Hannah gasped out loud. It was Richard Hughes.

'Ah, Doctor Hughes. We have a bit of an emergency so I thought I'd take a look.'

'Hannah!' Richard exclaimed.

'You know Mrs Duggan?'

'Very well. Before her marriage she worked for my family.'

Hannah felt relief surge through her. Richard would know what was wrong. She would trust him implicitly.

Richard was taken aback at seeing her again – and at the way she looked. She was thin and poorly dressed. Lines of anxiety were etched on her forehead and her dark eyes were filled with fear.

Richard took the baby from her and held her gently. 'What's the matter, Hannah?'

'She's got a fever, she's terribly hot. I know she's cutting teeth but surely . . .' Her eyes pleaded with him.

'Let me have a look at her too,' Dr Mills said.

Jessica was fractious as, with Richard's help, Hannah removed the bonnet, knitted coat, dress, underskirt and vest. The older man felt the baby's head and shook his own. Hannah felt fear gnaw at her insides.

'Richard, hold her as still as you can while I listen to her chest.'

Hannah watched Dr Mills sound the baby's chest, front and back. Worried though she was she noticed how easily and how gently Richard held her child.

'Run your finger over her gums, Richard.'

He did so. 'She must have had a bad time cutting those teeth. Has she had you walking the floor with her of a night, Hannah?' She was obviously very tired and there were dark circles under her eyes.

'No, she hasn't. She's my first so I don't know too much about teething or fevers. But it's very strange. People have told me about all kinds of things that can affect babies, but she sleeps all night, there's never any problem with that. It . . . it's just that today I've had her out, we were at a wedding and she was getting into such a state that I had to come out of church with her.'

'Did she sleep last night?'

'Yes. Not a murmur out of her.'

He shook his head, looking puzzled. 'Well, she's got a high temperature but her chest is clear. I'll give you something to lower the temperature and sponge her down with tepid water, that will help too. If there's no improvement bring her back or call me or Dr Hughes out.'

'Oh, thank you. I'm so relieved.'

Richard looked puzzled.

'Is there something bothering you?' Dr Mills asked his young locum.

Richard nodded. He'd heard or read of something similar occurring. 'There is. If it's all right with you, I'll walk Mrs Duggan home. I won't be long and there is something I want to discuss with you.'

'I've no objections unless you intend to be gone for the rest of the afternoon and evening.'

Richard laughed and opened the door for Hannah.

'Where do you live, Hannah?' he asked when they were outside.

'In Rankin Street.' She was much calmer now. She'd got over her fright and the shock of seeing him here. 'I thought you worked in the hospital.'

'I did. But, now I'm a junior partner to a consultant in Rodney Street, I find the time to help out around here too.'

She nodded slowly. That was so like him, to give up

his free time to help people who couldn't afford Rodney Street prices or indeed any price at all.

'What does your husband do, has he got a job?'

'Yes. He works in Foster's iron foundry. It's not much money but it's steady.'

'You look different, Hannah.'

'Do I? I suppose I've grown up.'

He didn't miss the note of regret in her voice. Or was it unhappiness? He knew that everyone thought she had married in haste.

'I know it's none of my business but . . . are times hard for you? You look very tired.'

Hannah nodded, but she couldn't bring herself to tell him the truth about Alfie.

'And do you work, too?'

'I do. As I just said Alfie's job doesn't pay much and I need things for Jessica.'

'So, who looks after her while you're at work?'

'I pay a woman down the street, Mrs Taylor, to look after her, She's very good, she minds other babies too.'

His thoughts turned again to the baby. 'And she says she's had no trouble with your baby during the day?'

'No, she says Jessica is very good. That she's always smiling and gurgling.'

He looked thoughtful. 'Will you be taking her there on Monday?'

'I don't think so. I can't leave her while she's like this.'

'She should be much better by then. Once the teeth

break through the gum there's not as much pain.'

'You seem to know a lot about it.'

'I've learned a lot about many things since I've been working with Dr Mills.' That was true, he thought bitterly. The conditions people lived in often filled him with such anger.

When they reached the house he wasn't surprised by its condition but he was upset to see how she lived now, compared to the comforts she'd had when she'd worked for them.

Hannah stopped in the lobby and began to search for her key. She didn't want him to see what she'd been reduced to. Her cheeks burned with embarrassment.

'Let me hold her, Hannah, while you find your key.'

She passed Jessica over and delved into her bag, found the key and opened the door. It would be the height of bad manners not to ask him in but oh, she was so mortified.

'Will you have a cup of tea?' she asked, taking the baby from him.

'No, thank you, Hannah. You heard Dr Mills. I can't stay. Besides you'll want to get her to sleep and then get some rest yourself.'

'I wish I could,' she replied, thinking of what state Alfie would arrive home in. A thought flashed through her brain, making her cringe. What if he came home now, blind drunk? Oh, she would die of shame!

Surreptitiously Richard looked around the room. It was clean and tidy enough, but she had so little. There were few comforts, that much was obvious. His heart went out to her.

'Hannah, are you happy?' It was a question he had no right to ask but he needed to know.

She hesitated. What could she say? That she was as miserable as sin? That she was regretting ever leaving Faulkner Square? That she still loved him – for she did. As they'd walked from the surgery she had realised it. Not with the girlish, breathless, giddy kind of love she'd felt since the day she'd first set eyes on him, this was far deeper. It was a woman's love not that of an impressionable girl.

'Yes, I am,' she forced herself to say. 'I know it's not a palace and there are so many things we can't afford, but we are a family, that's all I ever wanted from life. A real family of my own.'

'I'm glad, Hannah.'

She looked at him steadily. She wouldn't ask him about his own life and if *he* was happy or not, or if he had any children. That knowledge would haunt her, she knew it would, just as the events of today were something she would always remember. The day Vi got married and had left for Canada. The day when she realised that she really did love Richard Hughes.

He shrugged off the strange feeling that had overtaken him. A feeling of protectiveness, possessiveness. A feeling he had no right to harbour at all.

'Hannah, I'm asking you to take her, as usual, to this Mrs Taylor. Leave her there for about two hours and then go for Dr Mills. Unfortunately I won't be able to come myself. Monday morning's appointment book is full. I can't even take an hour to come here.'

Hannah was totally confused. 'Why?'

'There's something not quite right here and I want to find out what it is.'

'But . . . but will she be well enough by then?'

'I should think so.' He opened the black leather bag he'd brought with him. 'Take these powders. They should do the trick. I'm not saying they won't stop her from crying, but they will get the fever down and help to quieten her. You could also rub a little oil of cloves on her gums. It may help. Will you do as I ask, Hannah, even though you don't understand my reasons and I can't explain them to you yet?'

'Yes, yes I will. But only because it's you. I trust you. You know that.'

He nodded, his eyes downcast. He hated to see her in this place but what could he do? She was a wife and mother now.

'I'll get some oil of cloves, give her a powder and sponge her down.'

'Good, but take her to this woman on Monday. I don't think we'll really need to see her again before then.'

'How much do I owe you, or Dr Mills?'

'Nothing, Hannah.'

She shook her head determinedly. 'I don't want special treatment. I've got the money.'

He admired her for her pride. 'I'm sure you have

but I work with Dr Mills for that very reason. I don't charge for my services. Like Dr Mills it infuriates me to see how people have to live, through no fault of their own.' He couldn't keep the note of anger from his voice. 'But, regarding your child, I have my suspicions and if they're right, it will be me who should be paying you. I'd better get back now. Take care of yourself, Hannah, she needs you.'

She sat in the armchair, nursing Jessica. She'd given the baby one of the powders in a little milk and it seemed to have done the trick. She'd also sponged her down, but there was nowhere open for her to buy the oil of cloves and Mrs Ross didn't have any. Jessica was much cooler and far less fractious now. Her eyelids were drooping as Hannah sang 'Suo-Gân' to her. She probably wouldn't see Richard Hughes again, unless Jessica took a turn for the worse and she didn't want that to happen. But why did he want her to take Jessica to Mrs Taylor as usual and then go for him? She tried to puzzle it out until her deliberations were interrupted by the sound of singing. Oh, God! she thought. It was Alfie and by the sound of it he'd brought Jack with him, or maybe it was the other way around. Fear and apprehension rose in her as her mind went back instantly to the night he'd beaten her. She'd just have to stay as silent as she could.

They were both drunk, but Jack Duggan wasn't as bad as his brother.

'Sorry, Hannah, girl. I found him hanging on to a

lamppost at the bottom of our street, legless, so I brought him home, like.'

'Thanks, Jack. I . . . I . . . had to leave him with the wedding party, Jessica was sick.'

'They always are, bloody kids,' Alfie said, slurring his words badly.

Hannah said nothing.

'Well, I've brung him home safely, I'll gerroff now. I'm meeting Lily.'

God help Lily, Hannah thought for a moment. But then she thought that Lily Sweeney must already be aware that Jack was a heavy drinker and gambler, something she herself hadn't known about Alfie, until it was too late.

'Well, don't I get a kiss or nothin'?' Alfie said belligerently, hanging on to the edge of the table.

'Alfie, not now, please? I had to take her to Doctor Mills. I was so worried about her.' She wasn't going to tell him that Richard Hughes had been here . . .

'It's a pity you don't worry about me like that. And how much did that feller charge?'

'I had two shillings, but he wouldn't accept it. He was very good and kind.'

'What's his game then? What's he up to? They don't usually refuse money.'

'He was kind and concerned, Alfie. He didn't have a "game". He gave me some powders for her too.'

'Load of bloody rubbish. They're probably flour or baking powder. My mam says you can't trust any of them doctors. They rob you blind after they've got you all confused with their fancy words.'

'Well, he wouldn't take any money and I gave her one and it's worked.'

'Then put her down and come and give me a kiss. I'm your husband, remember?' He cackled. 'I'll bet that Vi and Georgie are bang at it by now.'

She cringed at the coarse expression. 'Oh, Alfie, please, not now. Have something to eat and some tea and . . .' She didn't finish, the last thing she wanted now was for him to be demanding his 'rights'. She was exhausted. All she wanted to do was crawl into bed and sleep. She always took the crib upstairs.

He glared at her malevolently. 'You're a cold bitch, Hannah. You got what *you* wanted out of *me*. Now I want you.'

Oh, had he no consideration, or feelings at all? she thought, getting up and putting the now sleeping baby into the crib. She had no intention at all of letting him anywhere near her tonight.

'Well you can't have me. I'm worn out with worry and you're drunk, again.' She hadn't meant it to sound like that. So hard and mocking.

He stared at her, cursed under his breath and then turned and staggered out of the room.

She breathed a heavy sigh of relief as she heard his slow footsteps going up the stairs. 'Oh, thank God!' she said and she meant it. She'd give him half an hour and then she'd carry the crib upstairs.

He said nothing at all to her the following morning. In

silence he ate the salt fish that was the traditional Sunday breakfast in Liverpool. Then he put on his jacket and muffler, reached over to the dresser and picked up his cap.

'Alfie, where are you going?' she asked tentatively.

'Out.'

'I can see that. But where?'

'Bloody anywhere! Somewhere far away from you and her! She's all you ever think of. You have to go and ruin a decent "do" by taking her home – sorry, to a bloody doctor – and for no good reason.'

Hannah's temper flared up. 'There *was* a good reason. A very good reason, Alfie! She had a fever and she's only six months old. Babies of that age die around here, you know that. What was I supposed to do, Alfie? Sit and watch her die?'

The fretful wail of a baby in pain broke the silence between them and Hannah immediately got up.

'Oh, that's just about all I can stand. *Her* bloody yelling all day. It's Sunday, a day of rest, but I'll get no bloody rest here,' he said, slamming out of the room. Why the hell did she always put the baby before him? He was the one who'd married her. He'd done her a favour getting her out of that drudgery in Faulkner Square. And this was the thanks he'd got. Well, she could go to hell from now on. He'd keep back most of what he earned – let her manage. He'd have his pleasures and he'd find another girl to give him what she'd been denying him for months now!

* * *

That night, Hannah went to bed knowing what kind of a mood he would be in when he got back, if he got back. All day she had been worrying about him, her baby and the future. He was becoming a hardened drinker and gambler. What would she do if he got worse? And then she'd pushed those thoughts out of her mind and begun to worry about her visit to Mrs Taylor's in the morning. At ten o'clock, he still hadn't come home and so she'd gone to bed. She tossed and turned for a while, anxious about everything, but at last she fell into a deep sleep.

Next morning, as always, his breakfast was on the table when he came down, silent and bleary-eyed, and neither of them spoke. She was relieved when he left for work. She'd have to think up an excuse for missing her own work this morning, she thought as she took Jessica down the street reluctantly. She'd given her another powder last night but she'd kept the other one. She wasn't at all happy as she passed her baby over to the woman.

'Back at work, Hannah?' Evvie Taylor asked.

'Yes, unfortunately. She's not been very well over the weekend, Mrs Taylor.'

'Poor little thing. Well, we'll make sure you're well looked after today, won't we?' She took Jessica from Hannah's arms and closed the door.

Hannah went back home and busied herself with the daily chores until the two hours were nearly up and then she went along to see Dr Mills.

The same woman greeted her. 'Oh, it's you. He's left instructions for you to wait. He has two more patients to see to first.'

Reluctantly Hannah entered the waiting room and sat down on the edge of a wooden bench. She hoped he wouldn't be long. She was very uneasy and doctors' waiting rooms seemed to be the ideal place to catch things. Only sick people went there after all.

It seemed an eternity before he finally came through, wearing a heavy overcoat and with a trilby hat on his head. He also carried his black leather Gladstone bag.

'I took her to Mrs Taylor like you said, sir.'

'And how has she been?'

'Much better, but her gums are still red and sore. I couldn't get any oil of cloves.'

'More teeth on the way, but no fever?'

'No, sir. I told Mrs Taylor she hadn't been well and she said she'd make sure she was well looked after today.'

He nodded and for the rest of the way he was silent.

Hannah reached up and banged hard on the door knocker while Dr Mills looked up and down the street. Something should be done about the housing and sanitation around here, he thought grimly. No wonder there was so much disease and illness and high infant mortality. He did not agree with the still widely held Victorian edict that the poor actually wanted to be poor, that if they didn't want to live the way they did then they would make every effort to drag themselves out of the gutters, courts and alleyways. It was a ridiculous fallacy. There *was* no steady work or decent wages for the majority of them. They fought a constant battle with the appalling slum housing and lack of basic sanitation. If they were dressed in rags and were dirty then it wasn't their fault. Education, housing, employment were what most of them wanted. Not hypothetical platitudes.

Evvie Taylor opened the door. 'Hannah! I . . . I didn't expect to see you until tonight. Have you forgotten something?'

'No, Mrs Taylor.'

Dr Mills stepped forward and said firmly, 'Mrs Duggan would like to see her child, Mrs Taylor.'

The woman's gaze went quickly from Hannah's face to his. 'Well . . . it's not . . . convenient. I've just got them all settled . . .'

'Settled or not, she would like to see her child,' he persisted.

Mrs Taylor's expression changed. 'I can't be expected to be doing things like this. I have a routine and I have to keep it otherwise it affects . . . everyone. Come back later, say dinnertime.'

'Madam, you will let Mrs Duggan see her baby and *I* would like to see her too.'

The woman backed away. 'Who are you?'

'Dr Mills. Lead the way, if you please,' he commanded.

The room was tidy, Hannah thought, but six small cots had been crammed into it as there had only been two when she'd first come to see Mrs Taylor and 'look the place over' as the woman had said.

'They're all asleep,' Hannah said.

'Didn't I tell you I'd just got them all settled. Are you satisfied now?'

Dr Mills looked around and then asked Hannah to take Jessica out of the cot. She did so, watched by the baby minder, whose gaze darted around the room as if looking for a means of escape. He took the sleeping child from Hannah, bent over her and sniffed.

'I thought so. Laudanum. She's been drugged. I had my suspicions, but now I have the proof. I assume that they are all drugged?' He turned to a now ashen-faced Mrs Taylor. 'It makes it very easy for you, doesn't it? Take the money and keep them quiet all day.' He turned to Hannah. 'Mrs Duggan, take Jessica home. I'll deal with matters from now on. The first thing I'm going to do is call the police,' he said grimly.

'I was only doing it to . . . help. It helped me and all their mothers. Who else could they leave them with? At least it's clean here.' Evvie Taylor wrung her hands.

'Tell all that to the judge, madam,' was the cold reply.

Hannah waited for the doctor to come to the house. She'd seen him leave and go to the corner where attached to a telegraph pole was the blue wooden box that held a police telephone for use in emergencies. Then he returned and shortly afterwards she'd seen a police car arrive and two officers get out. She was surprised to see that one of them was a woman, but then who would have looked after the babies when they took Mrs Taylor away?

'Mrs Duggan, through your instincts and very real concern, a wicked woman has been apprehended. It would only have been a matter of time before she gave one too much and the poor little thing would have died.'

'What will happen to her?'

'She'll go to jail. The law is very strict. We in Liverpool were fortunate enough to have the very first Children's Society, long before the N.S.P.C.C. was formed.'

Hannah nodded thankfully.

'I'm afraid you'll have to find someone else to look after her, but make sure it's someone you know or has been recommended to you.' He extended his hand and she nervously took it. Professional people overawed her as they did everyone in the slum areas.

'Thank you, sir,' she said quietly.

'No, thank you, Mrs Duggan,' he said, smiling, before he turned away.

Hannah sat down and held her baby to her. Oh, she'd had a lucky escape, but she would find it almost impossible to get someone of the ilk he'd suggested. No, she'd have to give her job up, that was all. It would mean that she had to rely totally on Alfie and that was a sobering thought.

Jessica was still asleep when Alfie came home, looking sulky and disgruntled.

'You didn't go to work then?' he queried.

'No. They arrested that Mrs Taylor. Dr Mills came

with me and, Alfie, they were all drugged. Six little babies all still and quiet and packed into one room. They could have died. He said it was only a matter of time. She's a wicked woman.'

'Sticking your nose in again, Hannah. Causing more trouble.'

She felt her cheeks redden with anger and she turned on him.

'Is that all you can say? *I'm* causing trouble! Never mind that that woman could have killed Jessica and we were actually paying her! Don't you care at all for your daughter, Alfie?'

'No, I bloody don't, although you do! You care for her more than you care for me.'

'I don't! At least I didn't, until lately! You're a drunk! You're a gambler, and you don't care a fig about anyone other than yourself, Alfie Duggan!' she yelled at him, her fury causing her to shake.

'Don't you bloody yell at me, you bitch!'

'Or what? You'll belt me again? But this time you can't plead drink.' She was so furious that she didn't care if she goaded him.

'I'll do what I like! You're a hard-hearted bitch. You used me to get you out of that house and away from that bloody feller! Well, you can just put up with things. If you won't work then you can go begging in the bloody streets to keep her and you! I've spent enough on the pair of you! From now on I'll do what I like with *my* money!'

She stood quivering with rage. There was nothing

left of the cheerful, joking lad she'd married. He hadn't hit her but she knew that from now on things were going to get very bad. She couldn't leave her child so she couldn't find work. She thought of Richard Hughes. She fervently hoped that Maria Delahunty appreciated her husband. She would have given anything, she'd have sold her soul to the Devil, to change places with her.

Chapter Eighteen

Things indeed got very bad. Alfie hardly ever came straight home from work, and when he did he was drunk. Hannah never spoke to him unless it was absolutely necessary. His temper these days was volatile and she didn't want to provoke him. She wondered how he managed to get up the following morning, obviously with a hangover, and go to work. But if he didn't work he'd have no money for drink. She knew he often went to his mam's to cadge something to eat, or the money for chips or a pie, since his mam wasn't renowned for her cooking. She'd wondered where the woman got the money from in the first place until she'd heard rumours that his father was high up on the police's list of habitual drunkards and suspected fences!

She had had no money from Alfie for nearly four weeks. The coal had long since run out and now she had to rely on orange boxes and penny bundles of 'chips', as firewood was called. She'd pawned or sold everything that he hadn't managed to get to first to pay for his gambling, which seemed now to be as much a habit as drink. They were down to the bare necessities and she knew in time that even they would have to go: they'd be sitting on orange boxes and sleeping on the floor.

It was bitterly cold but that morning she'd taken the quilt from their bed and most of her clothes to Goldring's. She wouldn't borrow money from the moneylenders, their reputation was too terrifying.

She'd asked Emily Stanley, one of her neighbours, to look after Jessica one evening while she went to clean offices. Emily was not much older than herself and yet she had three children and was pregnant again. When she'd gone to collect her the baby was crying and she'd taken her straight home. She was wet through and there were bite marks on her legs. Hannah was horrified for she knew what had caused them. Rats. The old houses were plagued with them. Alfie had nailed up all the holes in the skirting boards of both their rooms and the lobby. She never left food out, it was always locked in the mesh-fronted press and they had put poison down and traps. She'd never been bitten, nor had Jessica or Alfie. She'd been too vigilant.

She was freezing cold as she sat as near as she could to the spluttering fire, a heavy woollen shawl wrapped around both herself and the baby. She was hungry. She'd never been this hungry in her entire life before. Even in the workhouse they'd had three meals of sorts a day. She hadn't eaten for two days. All she'd had were cups of weak tea without sugar. She remembered Ada's words when she'd offered to give both Ada and Martha money each month. She *couldn't* go back there. Everyone, but particularly Ada and Martha, would say 'I told you so'. Oh, she wished she'd taken notice of them. She *had* saved some money but she had nothing to fall back on now. When everything was gone she'd just have to go on the Parish. But would she get any help from them? Her husband had work, steady work, and that was something that was really becoming harder and harder to find. There were so many men and lads out of work now. They stood around in groups on the corners, sharing a single cigarette. They had no money now for drink. She'd heard soup kitchens had been discussed and she prayed they would become a reality and soon, for she wasn't the only woman in the city who was hungry, cold and half-demented about how to keep body and soul together and a roof over her head.

The fire had died and she got to her feet stiffly. It was so cold that already there was ice forming on the inside of the windows. She'd sleep in all her clothes tonight and she'd bring Jessica into the bed too to keep her warm and safe.

She picked up the stub of a candle that was the only form of light she could afford and which she used sparingly. Then she froze as she heard footsteps on the bare boards of the lobby. She'd hoped to be in bed before Alfie came in.

Oh, no, not again, she thought despairingly as he stood swaying in the doorway.

'I was just going up to bed. It's so cold in here there's ice already on the windows.'

'Bloody ice out there too, plenty of it.' He laughed derisively.

'Alfie, for God's sake, will you give me some money,

please? I . . . I can't go on like this. We'll be flung out in the street soon, we've nothing much left to pawn or sell. There's been no rent paid for three weeks now. I'm desperate.'

He grinned maliciously. 'Oh, the boot's on the other foot now. *You're* desperate.'

'Alfie, please?' she begged.

He took off his cap and glared at her. 'I haven't got any money.'

'You must have something, just a few pence. I could get us something to eat.'

'I'm not hungry.' His unfairness and selfishness brought the colour to her cheeks.

'No, you've been to your mam's, haven't you?'

His eyes narrowed. 'So what if I have? There's more bloody comfort round there.'

'There's more of everything round there,' she snapped, her patience completely gone. She thought with mounting anger of how he'd left her to cope in a house where there was no heat or light or food, while he'd been enjoying himself. 'Oh, everyone knows where she gets the money from. And your sisters too. They all might as well go to Lime Street, just like the rest of them,' she blurted out, past caring now.

'Don't you bloody call my mam a tart nor our Doreen and Betty either!'

'They're not much better.'

He lunged forward and lashed out. Hannah screamed and fell but, shaking her head to clear it, got quickly to her feet, knowing if she stayed on the floor he would kick out at her. 'I hate you! I hate you, Alfie Duggan!' she screamed.

He hit her again and again and she covered her head with her arms in an attempt to protect herself. If he continued, he'd kill her and then what would happen to her baby? The thought gave her courage and she lashed out and raked his face with her nails. He bellowed with pain and caught her by her hair; she screamed, twisting around in agony until he released her, leaving him with a clump of hair in his fist. She immediately turned to her baby who was crying, but he was quicker and she watched in horror as he picked the child up by one arm.

Blind fury filled her. No! No! She wasn't going to stand by and let him hurt her baby.

'Leave her alone! Put her down or I'll kill you! Do you hear me, Alfie Duggan, I'll kill you!' she screamed. She kicked out at him, catching him on the shin. He yelled, dropped Jessica and turned on her again.

She was no match for him but she fought until, dizzy with the pain, her strength failed.

She clasped the crying baby to her as she crouched against the wall, her back to him. He'd have to kill her before she'd let him touch her child again.

She waited for the blows and the kicks but they never came. He staggered back into the lobby and then there was silence. Slowly she dragged herself upright. Her head was spinning, her eyes were half closed and every bone in her body was broken, or so she thought. With trembling fingers, the nails of which were broken and bleeding, she gently felt around Jessica's head and face. No, she wasn't hurt. But what if he came back? Where was he? She hadn't heard the front door slam shut. She hoped to God he'd gone to bed, but she hadn't heard his footsteps on the stairs either.

Slowly and with great difficulty she felt her way around the room, her back to the walls for support. The front door stood wide open but there was no sign of him. Again, groaning with each step she took, she managed to get down the lobby. Then she saw him. He had passed out on the doorstep. One foot was still inside the lobby. She just stared down at him. Why had she ever married him? She was at her wits' end. She could hardly move. She held Jessica to her as tightly as she could. The baby was still crying. He had been going to hurt her baby. He would have killed her. She moved his foot and slowly closed the front door. It was freezing out there but she didn't care. He had almost killed her and would, she was certain, have killed her child. She didn't care any longer what happened to him.

She was cold, shaking and in great pain and she knew that if she stayed here both she and Jessica would also freeze to death. She had to get away. Get out of here. But where to? She tried to think clearly. Ada! That's where she would go. She had no pride left now. She was desperate. But it was a long way to Victoria Terrace, the shape she was in. Yesterday it would only have been a short walk, tonight it would take for ever, but she *had* to go. There was nowhere else.

She held Jessica close to her, wrapping the shawl around them both and, half stooping, half limping, she made her way down the lobby and opened the front door. She couldn't look at his face. Unsteadily she skirted around him. I *must* keep going! I *must* keep going! she said to herself. Already the frost was heavy on his clothes.

It seemed to take hours to walk the short distance and with every step she took, agony enveloped her. She barely knew where she was going. A blackness descended on her from time to time but somehow she fought it off.

'Are you all right, luv?'

The voice seemed to come from heaven so she raised her head and squinted up. It was a policeman. The collar of his cape was turned up, his helmet was pulled low down over his forehead.

'I . . . I . . .' Darkness was descending again.

'Jesus, Mary and Joseph! You're in a terrible state. Who did this to you?'

'I . . . I don't know.' She couldn't tell him the truth, that much registered in her mind.

He didn't press her. Judging by the state of her face she was badly beaten. 'Where are you going?'

'Victoria Terrace. To . . . to . . . Mrs Sweeney.'

'What number?'

She tried hard to remember. It was such a simple thing and yet it eluded her.

'Never mind, let's get there first.' Gently he lifted her.

'My . . . Mind my . . . baby.'

It was the first time he'd noticed that she was carrying a baby. God, if he got his hands on the feller who'd done this he'd give him more than a dose of his own medicine.

He wrapped them both in the voluminous folds of his cape and carried them to Victoria Terrace. Hannah leaned her head against the heavy serge of his tunic.

'You just point out the house, luv,' he said. She pointed to Ada's front door. The street was empty, the houses in darkness, only the spluttering gas streetlamp gave any sign of life. Gently he set her down and knocked loudly on the door. When there was no answer he used his truncheon. Hannah leaned against the wall, her eyes closed. She was safe. She was back where she belonged.

Ada opened the door, an old overcoat around her.

'What the 'ell are yer doin' knockin' me door down at this time of—' She caught sight of Hannah. 'Oh, my God!'

'I found her staggering along. She won't tell me who did this to her, she was trying to get to you.'

'Hannah! Oh dear God, Hannah!'

Hannah broke down competely and Ada put her arms around her and drew her inside. The policeman closed the front door. It was almost as cold inside the house as it was in the street.

'I think she should go to hospital.'

'No!' Hannah's voice was rasping and hoarse.

'Well, I can't make you go.'

'She'll be all right now. I . . . We'll take care of her. Would you do me a favour and go and knock on the door of number sixteen and tell Martha Harper to come over?'

'Give her some sweet tea and try and warm her up.'

'I've got tea but I've no sugar.'

He nodded, his gaze having swept the room. 'I'll ask this Martha if she's got some.' He dug into his pocket and pulled out two half-crowns and put them on the table. That would pay for a bit of comfort in the way of heat and a warm drink.

Ada fussed around her. 'Hannah, luv, did 'e do this to yer?'

'Yes. He . . . he . . . was going to kill . . . her.'

'The fiend! The bloody fiend! When that scuffer comes back, you tell him to get round to your house and bloody arrest him! He's half killed you.'

'I . . . I . . . can't do that,' Hannah gasped as she moved.

'Why not?' Ada demanded.

'I left him on the step. He'll freeze to death. He . . . he had passed out. I . . . I did it on purpose.'

Ada thought for a moment. She couldn't care less about Alfie Duggan. After what he'd done to her, Hannah wouldn't have had the strength to get him inside the house anyway and besides she was distraught. But if she told the police where he was they'd go round, arrest him and cart him off to the nick. For a few seconds Ada struggled with her own conscience. This was a very grave step but the world would be a better place without Alfie Duggan in it. He could have killed both Hannah and Jessica and he'd probably do so in future, in a drunken rage.

'We'll tell him nothin', Hannah. They'll not be able to prove anythin'. And, God forgive me, but that vicious *bastard* won't be no loss to anyone.' The word summed up Ada's feelings. She'd never call anyone a 'bastard'. It was a terrible, terrible thing to be illegitimate. Society shunned you altogether for the whole of your life. You were an outcast.

Hannah could only nod her head slowly for the pain was excruciating.

Ada had stirred up the fire and put the kettle on the hob when the policeman came back with Martha.

'Oh, God, Ada! Did he do that?'

'I don't know for certain who did it,' Ada replied, glaring at Martha who instantly understood.

The constable squatted down to be on a level with Hannah. 'So, luv, just who *did* do this?'

Hannah gazed mutely at the two older women.

They both shook their heads.

There was total silence in the room. Eventually the constable got up. He'd get no answers from any of them but he knew that the perpetrator would pay. They didn't call in the police, they doled out rough and summary justice themselves. Her husband, because that's who he was certain had done this, would probably be beaten to within an inch of his life by half the men in this street.

'Well, I can't force you to tell me, but can I be

certain that she'll be looked after – and the baby as well?'

'You can, officer, you can be very certain of that,' Ada replied firmly.

'Well, I'll be off then.' He picked up his thick white woollen gloves and the money he'd left on the table. He replaced it with a ten-shilling note. 'Get some coal, that baby will freeze to death otherwise.'

Ada nodded her thanks and showed him out.

'He knew it were your husband, Hannah, but he doesn't know his name. Rest easy now, luv. Martha and me will take care of you and the little one.' She picked up the ten-shilling note. 'Well, at least some of 'em 'ave an 'eart. Right, luv, let's get you on the sofa and see what we can do about your face.'

Hannah started to cry with relief but it hurt so much that she had to bite back the tears.

'Martha, I've a bit of medicine, we'll give her that. It'll 'elp her to settle easy.'

Martha nodded, not knowing Ada would be giving Hannah laudanum, the drug that had been used on Jessica and which had been instrumental in bringing this plight down on Hannah.

Chapter Nineteen

For two days Hannah had lain on the sofa in Ada's kitchen, drifting in and out of sleep. Sometimes she remembered what had happened, usually when she heard Jessica crying, and sometimes she didn't.

Ada and Martha had sat up all night with her after the policeman had left.

'I could kill 'im with me own two 'ands!' Martha had said angrily.

'Yer won't need to, Martha, that's all been taken care of.'

'By who?'

'By Hannah. The swine was so paralytic 'e fell out of the 'ouse and she shut the door and left 'im. Not that she could 'ave lifted 'im after what 'e'd done. That's why she wouldn't tell that scuffer who did it. 'E'll be dead come morning and I hope 'e roasts in 'ell for ever!'

Martha had nodded, agreeing totally with her neighbour. 'Do yer think we should get a doctor ter see her, like? That scuffer left more than enough money.'

'We'll see how she is later on. You wouldn't get one of them fellers out 'ere at this time of night. Not ter the likes of us. Oh, the 'igh an' mighty, yes, but not us.' Martha had nodded her agreement.

When morning came the family stirred. Ada had sent Martha home at half past six and had dozed in the chair.

'Mam, what's going on?' Lily demanded, confused by the scene that met her eyes.

'It's Hannah and the little one. That swine 'as beaten 'er badly. I'm goin' ter send for a doctor.'

Lily looked at Hannah's face and was horrified. 'Oh, Mam, what did he do that for?'

'How the 'ell do I know? Anyway, 'e probably didn't need no reason. I suppose 'e was blind drunk. She said 'e'd gone for the baby too. Now, milady, perhaps yer'll see sense! It was the brother of that no mark Jack Duggan what did this to 'er. Oh, yes, yer might well pull a face. They're all the same in that family. Bad through an' through, an' that Jack'll do the same ter you if yer're daft enough to marry him! I warned Hannah, God knows I did, but she wouldn't listen ter me an' for a while, I thought maybe I was judgin' 'im too harshly. Well, I wasn't,' she finished grimly.

Lily had said nothing more. She'd got ready for work, had something to eat and left the house, her mood very serious as for the first time she considered the fact that her mam might just be right.

Martha had gone for Dr Stanhope and he arrived just after eleven o'clock. Ada didn't have much time for him as his attitude was condescending and his manner, to say the least, brusque.

'I want yer ter look at 'er, sir, I've got the money,' she said firmly.

He nodded curtly and knelt down on the floor beside Hannah, examining her face, her arms and then the rest of her body. He tutted and shook his head.

'What's up? Is there somethin' real bad, sir?'

'No. Not that I can tell. She's probably got some cracked ribs, she really should go to hospital.'

'Not while I've got breath in me body she won't! Them places do more 'arm than good, an' she'd 'ate it. It would remind 'er of the workhouse where she was brung up. She's not goin' ter no 'ospital.'

'Who was responsible?' he demanded.

'Her 'usband.'

'Did you call the police?'

'No. You should know, doctor, that we 'aven't much time for the police around here.'

'Then there is nothing further to be done, if you won't help yourselves. Is this a regular occurrence?'

Ada's forehead creased in a frown. 'A what?'

'Does it happen often?'

'No, it's the first time.' And the bloody last, she added under her breath.

'All she can do is rest. Bind up those ribs and I'll give you something to ease the pain. Make sure she's kept warm and comfortable and that she eats.'

'Will yer have a look at the baby an' all while yer 'ere, please?'

The doctor looked shocked. 'He surely didn't beat a baby?'

'Not exactly, that's why she's in that state, she fought for her baby, like any decent woman would.'

In silence he examined Jessica.

'There's nothing wrong here, thank God. If there had been I would have reported it to the police and then something would have been done. Good day. Send word to me if she worsens.'

Ada nodded and handed him a half-crown which he took and pocketed.

'Not a flamin' charitable bone in 'is body, that feller. He did nothin' an' 'e still took the money!'

'And saying make sure she's kept warm and comfortable. The likes of him don't know the kind of lives we have, an' he doesn't want to either!' Martha was just as incensed.

'Well, we'll do our best. God 'elp us we've not much ter keep body an' soul tergether ter start with,' Ada replied.

All evening, Lily was subdued. Ada was thankful that she made no attempt to go and see Jack Duggan, she even helped Ada to spoon some broth between Hannah's swollen lips. Harry and Gerald were grim-faced and tight-lipped, their anger suppressed.

'Dear God, the mess he's made of her face. I just hope it's not as bad when the swelling and the bruises go. She was a real beauty.'

Hannah was more worried about Jessica than herself.

'Look, Hannah, luv, I've told yer the doctor looked at 'er and there's nothin' wrong with 'er. Just teething and we all know 'ow ter cope with that. We've 'ad a lot of practice, 'aven't we, Martha?'

'Oh, we have.'

'What will I do? I can't stay with you for ever.'

'Will yer stop worryin' about things like that? Just get yerself better and then we'll sort somethin' out. Now take a few sips of tea. Yer to rest, that stuck-up feller said, and rest yer will or me and Martha will want to know why.'

But Hannah did worry. She was starting to feel better. The aches and pains were becoming just mere discomforts. The swelling of her mouth and eyes had almost disappeared but her face was black and blue, as was the rest of her body. She was worried about Alfie's family for they were notorious for their drunken fights.

'I can't let them come around here,' she said to Ada.

'They won't come 'ere.'

'But what if they do?'

'Even the women in this street are a match for that lot. They're bullies, always 'ave been. Can't win a fight on their own. Oh, no, they 'ave to be mob-handed. Cowards the lot of 'em. Stop worrying, Hannah.'

But she couldn't help it. As she lay staring into the flickering flames of the fire in the range, the gift of the caring police constable, she tried to work out what was best for them all. Herself and Jessica. Ada and her family. Martha and her family too. Maybe Ada was right. Maybe there would be no repercussions. She could go to work and Ada would mind Jessica. She'd get factory work, she'd take any kind of work to pay for their keep. The decision comforted her. It took away some of the terrible guilt that she was now beginning to feel over Alfie. She didn't know what had happened to him. If Ada knew, and she probably did, then she wasn't saying anything. Lily surely must have told her mam *something*. Each time she mentioned Alfie to Ada, when they were alone of course, Ada would bolster up her spirits and resolve by saying she had just been defending herself and Jessica too in a way. What would have happened if she'd stayed? He *would* have killed them both in time. Anyway, he couldn't get himself up the stairs and he'd fallen down the step – 'just remember that, Hannah. If yer hadn't gone ter see where 'e was, 'adn't decided to come 'ere, then the end result would have been the same. 'E'd still have frozen to death.'

That night Lily came home almost in tears.

'Now what's up with yer?' Ada demanded.

'Oh, Mam! I . . . I've lost me job.'

'Lost it? How did yer lose it? 'Ave they given yer the push? What did yer do?'

'Nothin', Mam, honest! We've all been laid off. There's no orders, they can't pay us. Oh, Mam, it's the same everywhere. I'll never get another job.'

Ada was genuinely concerned. The state the city, aye the country, was getting in was becoming desperate. She'd always relied on the money her kids had worked for. She'd lost her husband and two sons, all of whom would have contributed to the upkeep of the home. Now there was only Harry's and Gerald's wages coming in. Kate was married and had her own worries, and the same bills had to be faced.

'Oh, Lily, I'm so sorry,' Hannah said with genuine regret and worry too. If it was true then how on earth would she get work? Again the shadow of the work-house seemed to loom over both herself and Jessica. No! No! She'd go on the streets to support herself and her child rather than go into that institution again and subject her child to all the misery she'd suffered.

'Yer'll 'ave ter keep tryin', Lily, an' I'll 'ave ter try all the offices, mornin' and night, like, for cleanin'.'

'Mam, would they take me on too? Cleanin', like?'

'Well, I suppose they would, it's just that it's always been married women desperate for money that's gone cleanin'.'

'Well, if I don't get another job, *we'll* be desperate.'

Ada had nodded. The three women stared at each other, tired, anxious and dejected.

To make matters worse, Jack Duggan arrived on Ada's doorstep the following night.

'What the 'ell do yer want?'

'Where's Lily? She hasn't been near our house for days.'

'She's finally got some sense! She realised at last just what the whole flamin' lot of youse are like!'

'You know, don't you, you old bitch? You know that our Alfie is dead. That snotty-nosed wife of his left him out to die of cold. He was as stiff as a board when that neighbour, that Ross feller, fell over him in the morning.'

'Well I'm bloody glad of it! He got what was comin', an' iffen youse lot go to the scuffers then I'll tell them a thing or two about yer and yer family. I know what comes in through yer back door. Stuff that's always fallen off a lorry or some other tale – all bloody lies. Stuff from burgled 'ouses too. There's not one of yer that's any good, yer're a bad lot and Hannah's well rid of all of youse!'

Jack's face had gone bright red. 'She's here, isn't she? That's why your Lily hasn't been to see me. She's living with you. No one has seen her for days, so the neighbours round there told us. How could she be when she was here with you?'

Ada stepped forward, wagging a finger in his face. 'Now listen ter me, yer yellow-bellied, thievin' little toerag! You an' all yer effin' family can just stay away from this street or yer'll wish yer'd never set eyes on Hannah! There's fellers in this street that'd knock yer from one side of this street ter the other iffen I told them what *'e'd* done ter Hannah and more importantly ter that baby! No one around here takes kindly ter wife bashin', let alone baby bashin'. Just remember that.'

'You listen to me, you evil old cow! The fellers in this bloody street aren't known for their guts. There's a few wife bashers down here and all! So don't come that with me. Me and the rest of us will be round ter see that bloody Hannah. She's a bloody murderer, that's what she is, an' I'll see she bloody hangs for it an' all!'

276

He turned away leaving a quivering Ada on her doorstep.

Lily appeared behind her. 'Oh, God, Mam! He means it! You know what they're like! *I* know what they're like.'

'Well, thank God for that at least!'

'But, Mam, what'll we do? Go to the scuffers?'

'How the 'ell can we do that, Lily?' Ada snapped. 'She stepped over 'im. Left 'im dying there. They can't prove it, but they'll have a damned good try!'

To Ada's horror she caught sight of Hannah standing in the kitchen doorway, her hand to her throat.

'Hannah, luv, yer're not to worry about anythin'. Go back in where it's warm.'

'I can't stay here. I can't let you suffer because . . . because of me. I'll have to leave.'

'Yer can't leave, Hannah! What will yer do? A woman alone with a baby and no money and not able to get any either! Hannah, I can't – *won't* let yer go back into a workhouse!'

Hannah sat down; her legs were about to give out on her. 'I'll think of something.'

'Like what, luv?' Ada sat beside her and took her hand.

'I'm trying to think. Just wait a minute . . . I remember now that Miss Siân said if I was ever in need of help I should go to her. That's what I'll do, I'll go to her.'

'You'll tell *'er* everythin'?'

Hannah nodded. 'She'll understand. She'll think of something, she will!'

'When will you go, like?' Lily was still fearful.

'Tonight, if someone will come with me.'

'Hannah, at least wait until termorrer!' Ada begged.

'No, it might be too late tomorrow.'

Ada sighed and told Lily to get her coat on. She'd stay and mind Jessica. She was afraid that Jack Duggan would come back and Lily would be no match at all for any of them. If they did come and it was absolutely necessary she'd send for the police, because despite what she'd said to Jack she was well aware that there were a few men in the street who would sympathise with the Duggans.

It was very uncomfortable for Hannah to walk so Lily paid for them to go by tram even though it was only a short distance.

'You can't walk that far, Hannah. You'll be ready to drop by the time we get there,' Lily had insisted.

Hannah had been so thankful although each jolt of the tram sent pains shooting though her and she had to wrap her arms around herself to try and protect the broken ribs. By the time they reached Faulkner Square her face was white and drawn and she was leaning heavily on Lily for support.

'What will you say, Hannah?'

'I don't know yet, Lily, but it'll be all right. We'll go in the back way.'

As they went up the pathway, Lily was very apprehensive. She was in awe of people who lived in houses like these.

The back door was opened eventually by a strange

young woman wearing the uniform of a maid. She was clearly the new tweeny who had taken Vi's old job.

'Yes?' she demanded sharply.

'I . . . I'm . . . Hannah, I used to work here. I'd like to see Miss Siân, please. It's urgent. I need help.'

The girl looked at both of them with suspicion. They both wore shawls and one of their faces was a mass of bruises.

'She means it. Can't you see she's telling the truth?' Lily demanded.

'Miss Siân's not here but I'll go and see Mr Donaldson. What name was it?'

Her heart had sunk like a stone when the girl had mentioned Miss Siân's absence. 'Hannah. Hannah Peckham.' In her dazed condition she didn't even think to use her married name.

'Can't we come in and wait? It's freezing out here,' Lily asked.

'I suppose so,' the girl said with a very bad grace.

'Hannah, what'll you do now? You heard her. Miss what's her name isn't here.'

'Don't worry, Lily, Mr Donaldson knows me and he's a kind . . . man.'

Lily could see she was in terrible pain. 'Well I hope to God he hurries up.'

When he saw her face Arnold Donaldson was appalled. 'Hannah! Hannah! Come into the kitchen! You look dreadful.'

'Oh, she is, sir. She's in a real bad way,' Lily said.

When Hannah at last sat in a comfortable chair and

looked around the familiar kitchen, the tears welled up in her eyes.

'What has brought you to this state, Hannah?'

Between gulping, painful sobs she explained.

He looked sombre. 'Miss Siân's in Wales. She's gone there with Mrs Howard and Blandford. Things here haven't been too . . . too good and she was getting very depressed. The Master and Mr Thomas, you understand?'

Hannah nodded.

'Are you well enough to travel, Hannah?'

'Travel?'

'To Y-Garn. That's where she is. You'll be welcomed there. She was very fond of you and Violet. It will be good for your baby too. Fresh country air, good food.'

To go back? She'd sworn she'd never go back. But that was then. Now things were so bad that she had no choice.

'Yes. Yes, I'm well enough to travel.'

'Good. I'll arrange everything. You must stay here. Stephenson can go back with this young lady, bring your things back and your child. You'll be safer and more comfortable and Mrs Sweeney will be less anxious too. You must tell her, that if there's even a hint of trouble, she's to go straight to the police.'

Hannah sank back in the chair and covered her face with her hands. It was all so daunting, but it was the best thing for all of them.

Chapter Twenty

It was Ada herself who arrived with the baby and a small bundle of things that she'd hastily put together: things she could hardly spare but that Hannah would need.

Stephenson followed, an openly mutinous look on her face. She had had to go to that terrible house in that awful area. It had smelled too. Trips such as this were definitely not what she was paid for.

'Mrs Sweeney, it was good of you to come yourself.'

'Well, I couldn't trust a slip of a thing like this one to bring a baby here safely.' She passed Jessica over to Hannah. 'Hannah, I'm sorry, luv, but there's nothin' much for 'er in the way of clothes. I've done me best for yer and our Lily's sent yer a few clothes too, for yerself, like.'

Hannah nodded thankfully. She had nothing except what she was wearing: she'd left what few things she owned behind in Rankin Street. She'd not even brought anything for Jessica. They'd cut up an old sheet to make nappies for her.

'Mrs Sweeney, will you rest and have a cup of tea? It's bitterly cold out there.'

'Oh, I will, thank you, sir. Yer're right, it's bitter.'

'Stephenson, put the kettle on and set the dishes

out, then you can make up a bed.'

The girl nodded curtly. 'Here we go again,' she muttered under her breath. It wasn't the usual practice for a maid to be waiting on people like Mrs Sweeney.

Ada caught the look and stared hard and coldly at the girl. It was a good thing Hannah seemed to trust this Donaldson feller, *that* one would do nothing out of kindness. A stuck-up little madam if ever she saw one. She sipped the tea carefully from the porcelain cup that was handed to her with a bad grace. She'd have felt more comfortable with a mug, not this flimsy cup and saucer.

''Ow will she get there, sir? This place in Wales, I mean?' she asked tentatively. Arnold Donaldson's formal manner and the grandeur of the house made her feel very uncomfortable. When questioned, Lily had told her it was very posh and, though she'd only seen the kitchen that was enough to go by, Lily had been right.

'First she'll go to the Pier Head, then on the ferry, then an omnibus. It's a long journey.'

'Hannah, yer can't go all that way on yer own, luv, yer're not fit, not fit at all.'

'I'll be fine, truly I will. When I've had a night's sleep I'll be just fine.'

'Let me come as far as the omnibus with yer at least?' Ada begged.

'I think Mrs Sweeney's right. You really shouldn't be travelling on your own, but of course I'll get a Hackney cab to take you down to the ferry.'

Ada looked even more uncomfortable. People like herself didn't ride in Hackney cabs.

'Is there something wrong with that?' Arnold Donaldson asked. The woman was obviously of the poor working class, yet she'd taken Hannah in and defended her.

'No . . . No, nothin', sir.'

'Good. I'll telephone Miss Siân in the morning and tell her to expect you tomorrow evening. The Exchange is bad enough during the day, but at night it's hopeless, especially in such rural areas. In fact I doubt many people have telephones in the country so I suspect that the Exchange is shut down for the night.'

Ada shifted uncomfortably in her chair, balancing the now empty tea cup and wondering what she should do with it. They had a telephone in the house, and another one in the country house too. Hardly anyone had one telephone, let alone two. Reluctantly she got to her feet, glanced at the cup and saucer and then at Stephenson. The maid took it from her.

'Well, I'd best be off then. I don't want ter leave our Lily on her own for too long, like.'

'Mrs Sweeney, if anyone threatens you, you must go straight to the police. From what Hannah has told me there was little she could do. An unconscious man is a dead weight and there's hardly a pick on her.'

Ada nodded. Oh, he'd been a 'dead' weight all right. He'd been a millstone around Hannah's neck. Now if the Duggans turned up on her doorstep, she would call in the police. This feller would back up her story and the police would be bound to believe him rather than the likes of Alfie Duggan's family who were always under suspicion and had been for years. And Hannah would be safe. Safe and well out of it in this house in Wales that she'd learned from Hannah must be even bigger than the one in whose kitchen she now stood.

Hannah leaned back in the chair, Jessica now asleep. She was so relieved yet little things worried her still.

'Mr Donaldson, I . . . I can manage with the things Mrs Sweeney brought for me, but I've hardly anything for Jessica, particularly in the way of clean nappies.' She caught the hostile look the maid gave her. 'I don't expect anyone to wash them but me, but can I . . . well, will you mind if I dry them in front of the fire? This is a kitchen after all.'

'Certainly not, and Stephenson can find a bucket, fill it with cold water and let them soak. In the meantime, Stephenson, would you go up and make up a spare bed? We have quite a lot of them these days.'

The maid left in high dudgeon and Hannah didn't blame her. She knew what Vi's reaction to such a request would have been. Oh, she wished Vi were still in Liverpool.

Twenty minutes later she lay in the warm comfortable bed with Jessica asleep in the crook of her arm. She remembered how she'd always looked at the sky from the window in her attic room on the floor above this. She *was* doing the right thing, she told herself. It was better for everyone. Ada, Lily, Jessica and herself. She wasn't looking forward to the journey, but that couldn't be helped. This time she wasn't going to an institution that was grim and without compassion. She was going to a comfortable house that had always been full of happiness, or so she'd heard. She understood how all the bitter arguments and the somewhat solitary life Siân Hughes led here had made her return to a place where she'd always been happy. It was a luxury she'd never had. Her eyelids were becoming heavy. The feather mattress was soft and comfortable, the crisp white sheet, blankets and coverlet were another luxury. She felt warm and for the first time in months she could sleep without fear of what hardships tomorrow might bring.

The following morning Hannah was washed, dressed and feeding Jessica when Ada arrived, in the quite obviously borrowed brown coat and hat, stockings and shoes. She was blue with the cold.

'It's bitter enough for two pair of bootlaces out there.'

'There's tea in the pot, Stephenson made it fresh about ten minutes ago. Mr Donaldson usually takes his meals in his pantry.'

As soon as she'd come downstairs that morning she'd settled Jessica on the armchair that was Mrs Howard's favourite. She had touched the new maid on the shoulder.

The girl had turned and looked at her with apprehension.

'I know it must be hard for you to understand all this: looking after me and my baby isn't what you're paid for. I was a kitchen maid here and Mr Donaldson and Mrs Howard always treated me kindly. I knew they would help me now I'm in trouble. I've been very foolish, I've made a real mess of my life, but that's not your concern either. I'll be gone out of your way in a couple of hours, but I wouldn't like us to part with bad feelings. What's your name, your christian name?'

'Elinore.' The girl had replied grudgingly. At least this girl spoke well, she thought, unlike the one called Lily. She had good manners and quite obviously understood that all the extra and menial tasks Elinore had had to carry out were not part of a tweeny's job, but she was grateful just the same. It took a certain degree of humility to admit that.

'Can I call you Elinore?' Hannah had asked.

'Yes, as long as—'

'Mr Donaldson doesn't hear me,' Hannah finished for her.

The girl had smiled.

Now Elinore willingly poured a cup and passed it to Ada who sat as near as she could to the fire in the range.

'At least the ferry ride will be calm. Thank God fer that. If it'd been blowin' a gale, yer'd 'ave been thrown all over the place and that wouldn't do yer any good at all with them ribs. Hannah, will yer stay for at least another day? Yer're worn out and them ribs is still sore an' it's a terrible long journey especially in one of them

286

omnibus things. An' then there's the baby. 'Ow will yer manage with nappies, like?'

'I'll find some way, somewhere to change her, and we'll both be fine, truly we will.'

'My mam used to take us out a lot when we were babies and she had a bag made of oilcloth – you know, like the stuff they use for tablecloths,' the maid interrupted.

''Ow did she manage ter make a bag of that?' Ada demanded.

'She folded it so the shiny side, the waterproof side, was facing inwards and then she sewed it up the sides with a darning needle.'

'It's a good idea, Elinore, but—'

'But where are we goin' ter get somethin' like that, an' what's more, 'ow do we sew it?'

'I was just trying to be helpful.'

'I know and it's a really good idea, Elinore. If we had more time I could make one myself.'

'Then why not stay and make one this morning?' Ada saw an opportunity to try to change Hannah's mind.

'No, really, I'll manage. Miss Siân will be expecting me.'

'Perhaps I could get Mam to make one and we could send it on to you.'

'Thanks, but I don't think she intends to be travelling backward and forward,' Ada said with a note of sarcasm in her voice.

Arnold Donaldson appeared in that quiet way he

had, appearing as if from nowhere.

'Are you both ready? The cab will be here any minute.'

'Yes, thank you, Mr Donaldson. Thank you so much for everything. You could have turned me away. After all, I had left and I was only ever a kitchen maid.'

'And can I say thanks too, sir. Yer've put me mind at rest. I love the bones of this girl, just like I loved her poor mam, and I'll be easier in meself too.'

'Perhaps one day you can go and visit,' Elinore said, studiously ignoring the look of censure on the butler's face.

'Thanks, girl,' Ada replied. 'But we don't go in much fer outin's, not that far anyway.'

'Here, I made these sandwiches for you to take with you.'

Hannah took the packet which was wrapped in greaseproof paper. 'That's really good of you, Elinore, thank you.'

'Come along now, the cab's arrived. I'll see you both into it.'

Ada looked very sheepish as she and Hannah sat in the hooded, horse-drawn cab with the apron pulled up around them. Mr Donaldson spoke to the driver and then stepped down and leaned towards them.

'Have a safe journey, Hannah. Someone will meet you. And this is for your fare back, Mrs Sweeney.' He handed some coins over to Ada and then they were off.

'I feel like Queen Mary herself ridin' in this. It's a good job I borrowed this coat an' 'at. I nearly came in

288

me shawl. Martha said, "Yer can't go up there lookin' like a shawlie," so she went up and down the street until she'd got this stuff.'

Hannah managed a smile. 'You'll be the envy of the neighbourhood.'

'I already am! Didn't Martha tell them all why I needed decent things? She's gorra mouth on 'er like a parish oven at times.'

Hannah smiled. 'Then why not go back in one?'

'Wouldn't that be something, but no, I couldn't waste money like that. What he's given me will stretch fer a few groceries. I can't waste it on vanity.'

Hannah was thankful that the river was calm. All the way in the cab she'd been in agony as it jolted over the cobbled streets. Ada helped her down and bought the tickets and then took her arm as they boarded the ferry.

'I'm glad you came with me.'

'So am I. At least I can see yer on to this 'bus thing. Make sure yer're settled, like. I might even 'ave a word with the driver, tell 'im ter go easy, yer've 'ad enough knocks fer one day.'

'I don't think he'd take much notice. No, I'll just have to bite my lip and bear it.'

'Well, at least it will be better for the little one out there. Good fresh air, fresh food an' milk. A city's not the ideal place to bring up kids but we 'ad no choice. You do, Hannah. Make the best of it.'

Ada saw her safely settled on the bus and had a word with the driver who looked at her with bemused tolerance.

Hannah took her hand and squeezed it.

'I'll be fine now and I'll write. Lily can read the letters to you. I'll never be so stupid and wilful again. You warned me, you all warned me, but I thought I knew better. Once I get sorted out I'll make some plans for the future. Plans for myself and for her of course.' She stroked the soft little cheek and her baby looked up at her and gurgled. 'See, she's fine.'

'Well, I'd better go back now, luv. You write ter us. Both me an' Martha will be worrying, like.'

Hannah managed to wave before Ada's stout figure turned the corner and was lost to view.

As they travelled across the Wirral Peninsula Hannah remembered the last time she'd made this journey. It had been with Mr Donaldson to bring poor Jessie to Liverpool. It had been just as cold that day too, and there had been snow. This morning there was no snow and she was thankful for it. There was no way she could get off and help to push if the vehicle got stuck.

As she passed the fields and hedgerows sparkling with frost, she continued to think of that last journey. Then she'd known she would be returning that same day; today was different. She was going back to a country that held only bitter memories for her but she'd have to make the most of it. It was for Jessica's future as much as for her own.

Denbigh hadn't changed she thought as at last and in the early dusk of the winter evening, they came to a halt outside the Hand. She was so stiff and sore that one of the other passengers helped her down and it was with heartfelt relief that she caught sight of Blandford, muffled to the eyes, waiting with a pony and trap.

'Hannah! Hannah, over here! I'm perished with the cold and so are you by the look of it.'

She smiled. 'I am and I'm stiff, but it's great to see you, Blandford. It really is.'

'Let me help you up and then we'll get going. There'll be a roaring fire, a pot of tea and some of Mrs Howard's pies waiting.'

Hannah laughed for the first time in weeks. 'And we all know just how much you like her pies!'

'Carry on like that and I'll get a cob on!' he replied but there was laughter in his eyes.

'Is it far?'

'Not really.'

'You hold her while I get up.'

The lad looked horrified. 'Me! Hold her? I'll drop her!'

'Oh, all right, but you really will have to give me a hand. How is Miss Siân?' she asked when she was finally installed in the trap.

'Better than she was back there.' Blandford rolled his eyes expressively. 'It was shocking. The rows! The carry on out of Mr Thomas! Morning, noon and night! Well, let's go. Mrs Howard is looking forward to seeing you and the baby.' He paused. 'Was it . . . was it very bad, Hannah?'

She nodded. 'I was such a fool, Blandford.'

'Well, we all make mistakes,' he replied solemnly, and for the rest of the journey he was silent.

Daylight had almost gone. The winter dusk was falling rapidly over the fields and hedgerows. The stone boundary walls that lined the lane were thrown into sharp relief against a haze of blue- and lilac-tinged mist. Blandford at last turned the pony and trap into a wide gateway whose five-bar, white-painted iron gate bore a plaque of Welsh slate. Cut out and edged in gold was the name 'Y-Garn'. The long driveway ran between fields in the middle of which stood three solitary oak trees, their trunks gnarled and twisted with age, their branches etched sharply like a mass of woven threads against the skyline. The pony suddenly swung to the left and the house became visible, surrounded by trees and gardens.

Hannah almost gasped aloud. It was far bigger than she'd imagined. Far bigger than the house in Faulkner Square. It was almost a mansion.

'Is . . . is that it?'

'Yeah. You've never been here before?'

'No. I thought the house in Liverpool was big.'

'Well, it's big but it's not as . . . posh, if you understand.'

'No.'

'Well, things are sort of old, the furniture and stuff. Everything looks used. Oh, you'll see for yourself. Mind, I like it better. It's got more of a "family" air about it.'

Hannah's gaze went slowly over the façade. The grey slate roof looked dull in the evening light. The walls were painted white and all the windows were of the long sash variety. The front door was similar to the house in Liverpool but above it was a portico supported by two columns and the steps were wider and flatter. Two of the windows showed lights, mellow light, Hannah thought, like the light from candles or oil lamps or even gas. There wasn't the harshness that electric light shed, which often made a room look stark and too bright. The curtains were not drawn across the windows – who was there to peer curiously in? She knew just what Blandford meant when he said it was big but not 'posh'. It was a family house, a big one, but it was more welcoming than any grand Georgian mansion.

Blandford drove on and round a corner bounded by a wide lawn and the darkening shapes of evergreen shrubs. The noise of the wheels on the gravel and then the flags of the yard sounded very loud in the stillness. Hannah's mind instantly went back to the day she'd first seen Cousin Gwyneth's cottage, and the darkness that had enveloped everything and the unbroken silence and stillness. She shook herself mentally. This was different. Miss Siân was nothing like her cousin. She'd be welcome here and she was determined not to be a burden or an encumbrance as she'd been in her cousin's home. This house would be very far removed from the cottage in Henllan. Maybe she'd go back there, just to see if the place had changed, if her cousin still lived there.

She smiled as she saw a figure standing on the kitchen doorstep, an oil lamp with a fancy glass mantle in her hand. It was Mrs Howard and as the cook came down the steps and across to the trap Hannah felt a lump in her throat and her eyes misted with tears. She'd missed Mrs Howard so much, more than she'd even realised until this moment. Her time here would be very different to the short time she'd spent with Cousin Gwyneth and the long, bleak miserable years she'd spent in the Denbigh workhouse.

Chapter Twenty-One

'Come inside, it's freezing. Mr Donaldson telephoned this morning.' Mrs Howard fussed over her, her brow furrowed in a frown as she scrutinised Hannah's bruised face. 'Oh, Hannah, girl, you poor, poor little thing. We know all about it, how he treated you.'

'Miss Siân knows too? All of it?' Hannah asked anxiously.

'She doesn't know about you walking out and leaving him lying there, although Arnold . . . er, Mr Donaldson told me that bit. There wasn't a single thing you could do to help him, not after the state he left you in, so I heard – but never mind all that, come into the kitchen before that poor baby freezes,' she added, noting the fact that the shawl the child was wrapped in was much too thin for winter.

The kitchen was bigger and more old-fashioned than that of the house in Liverpool, but it had a sense of peace and tranquillity. And like the other kitchen it smelled of bread and pastry, a smell that flooded Hannah with a sense of relief.

'How is Miss Siân?' she asked.

'Give Jessica over to me while you take off your things. Your poor hands are blue. Sit down in that rocking chair by the range.' Mrs Howard settled all three of them down comfortably then went on. 'Miss Siân's so, so much better in herself since we moved here permanently. I used to worry myself half to death when she was younger, aye and up to a few months ago what with the carryings on in Liverpool. She's really blossomed. I put it down to good fresh food grown locally. You know, all the meat has been fattened up and then slaughtered locally too and the butter and milk here are so much better. Then there's the clean air, the peace and quiet, no traffic and people aren't always racing about. She's grown much stronger, there's colour in her cheeks too and she goes to the parish fêtes and other events. Only as a guest of course, but she really enjoys them.'

'I'm so glad, she's so lovely.' Hannah sat and watched Mrs Howard draw the shawl away from Jessica's face.

'Oh, she's a little beauty, Hannah,' she purred.

'I know and she's very placid, except when she's hungry. Then we know she's got a healthy pair of lungs.'

'Aye, like someone else I know.' Mrs Howard said looking at Blandford. She'd not forgotten the episode of the fruit pie. She passed the baby back to Hannah and busied herself making tea and cutting slices of meat, bread and fruit pies.

'Put her on the other chair while you have your tea.'

Hannah rose with a grimace as a pain shot through her, but she bent, biting her lip to stop herself from crying out, and placed Jessica on the upholstered armchair.

Mrs Howard had missed nothing as she sat down

opposite Hannah with her own cup of tea.

'What happened, Hannah? Why did he beat you? You're a good girl, you're quiet and well mannered. Oh, I wish to God you'd never married him.'

'So do I. Everyone tried to stop me but I wouldn't listen to reason. He wasn't any good. The whole family is no good but I refused even to think about them. He drank and he gambled. It wasn't too bad at first, until I had Jessica. He . . . he resented her. He didn't care a fig for her. He was always complaining when she cried. Then his drinking and gambling got worse. We had nothing in the end.' She warmed her hands on the sides of the cup and sighed. 'I even had to pawn the quilt from the bed and the clothes off my back. And we'd had a nice home. Oh, it was nothing like this. It was only two rooms but I kept them clean and we had nice things. I couldn't work, there was no one decent that I could trust to look after her. So all I had was whatever he gave me. Often it was nothing at all. Not a farthing. Then he got violent. He beat me and the last time he went for Jessica and I wouldn't stand by and watch him hurt my baby. I . . . I fought as hard as I could, but he was too big and too strong for me and I honestly thought he was going to kill us both. That's why I . . . left him. I had no one to turn to, except Ada. Ada Sweeney. She did what she could but his brother threatened her and her family. Her husband and two of her sons were killed in the war, she has no one to protect her so I couldn't stay there.' Her shoulders started to shake as the sobs made any further conversation impossible.

Mrs Howard got up and put her arm gently around Hannah's shoulder. 'Hannah, you did right coming here. It's best for everyone. Hush now, calm yourself, it's all over. Put it all out of your mind. I'll go and tell Miss Siân you've arrived, although she would have heard the wheels of the trap on the gravel.'

Hannah was so tired and so relieved that she leaned her head back and closed her eyes. She thanked God for Siân Hughes's charity and goodness. Before she drifted into sleep a young girl appeared.

'Hello, I'm Winifred and I'm the hired help, or at least one of them,' she said in a lilting voice that reminded Hannah of Jessie.

'I'm Hannah, I used to work for the family in Liverpool. That's my baby, Jessica. We . . . we've come back, sort of. To work.'

The girl nodded. 'I'm used to babbies, my mam's got four beside me. I'm the oldest, that's why I come here to work, to help out, see. My da works on the land and there's not much money in that. It would be different if he had his own farm or some land even, but we live in a tithe cottage and Mam is always worrying about Da getting older or getting sick so he can't work.'

'Why?'

'Because the house goes with the job. Lose your job and you lose your home, see.'

'And what happens then?'

'We get chucked out.'

Hannah thought sadly that poverty wasn't confined

to towns or cities, it was present here in the countryside too, just of a different kind.

Mrs Howard came back into the kitchen. 'Oh, I see you've arrived then, Win. Well, get started on those dishes, girl. Hannah, she wants to see you, and she asked particularly to see the baby.'

Hannah looked at her questioningly. 'Is everything all right?'

'Of course it is. Get along with you, it's up the stairs, into the hall and then the door to the left.'

Hannah felt very apprehensive. The hall seemed huge and shadowy. There was an old-fashioned hallstand in one corner and a brass umbrella stand in another. The staircase wall was covered in portraits of grim-looking men and women. The Indian carpet was a little threadbare by the doorway and the brass doorknob looked tarnished. She knocked quietly and went in when summoned.

Siân was sitting close to the fire in a Victorian armchair covered in rose-pink velvet that had obviously had a lot of use, as had the two big sofas covered with a pink and green chintz, and the rug that covered most of the floor. There were ornaments everywhere and flowers too, even though it was in the depths of winter. But she remembered how Siân loved flowers and how the house had been so full of them the day of Siân's party for Maria. She did look well, Hannah thought.

'Ma'am, it's very good of you to take us in. You didn't *have* to,' she said quietly.

'You were a very diligent and industrious worker,

Peckham. Oh, I'm so sorry, what is your married name?'

'Duggan, ma'am. But I'd left, and you were kindness itself, even giving me a wedding present. I know Mrs Howard has told you what . . . what happened. I've made such a mess of my life.'

'Yes, Mrs Howard told me and I'm so sorry that things didn't turn out well for you. Please sit down. At times like this I shall call you Hannah. We are not as formal in the country. I know it's not the "done" thing for you to sit but you must be worn out.'

'If you insist, ma'am.' Hannah was thankful for Jessica was heavy and she was sore and aching.

Siân smiled. 'I do insist and please call me Miss Siân. Ma'am makes me sound like a dowager duchess who's nearing eighty.' She laughed and Hannah thought how pretty she was when she did so. She sat down on the edge of one of the sofas and waited.

'Hannah, no one could fail to be moved by your plight. You've experienced such terrible things. You must stay here, both of you.'

'But I couldn't do that! I *must* find work.'

Siân looked surprised. 'You have work. You will be helping Mrs Howard and acting as a tweeny, just as Rowan was. I'll inform Father. This house is far bigger than the one in Liverpool. We *need* more staff,' she said determinedly.

'What about Jessica? Who will look after her?'

'The local girls who come in daily. Supervised by Mrs Howard and yourself.'

Hannah couldn't believe her good fortune. 'Oh, I'll do my best, miss! I really will! I'll do anything at all, no matter how hard or menial. My keep and Jessica's is all I'd need.'

'No, you will be paid as a tweeny, which will be five shillings a month more than you were paid when you worked in the house in Faulkner Square. It's only fair.'

Hannah was on the verge of tears. She'd never expected to be given a job here. She'd intended to try to find work and save up for somewhere to rent. She'd certainly not expected to be paid by Siân Hughes. 'Oh, *thank you*, miss.'

Siân smiled. 'Will you let me see the baby? Perhaps I could hold her?'

Hannah passed the baby over and Siân held her as though she were made of glass. 'Hannah, she's beautiful.'

Hannah smiled. Siân had made no mention that Jessica didn't resemble her a great deal.

Siân stroked the soft little cheek and Jessica waved her fists in the air and gurgled happily. Siân's heart missed a beat. One day, one day maybe she too would be able to hold a baby of her own like this.

Hannah bent down. 'I think I'd best take her back, she's not like this all the time. She can cry very loudly on occasions. And it's getting late: I think I'd better get myself sorted out. Thank you, thank you so much, miss, for every single thing. I don't know where I would have ended up without you.' She paused. 'Well, I do know. I'd be back where I came from. The workhouse.

I'll never, ever be able to repay you, miss.'

'Hannah, I don't expect payment. Now off you go and find your way around the house. It's a bit rambling but you'll get used to it.'

As Hannah turned to leave Blandford entered, his expression very serious, his manner very formal. He was followed by a young man in clerical garb.

'The Reverend Henry Proctor to see you, miss,' Blandford announced in deep and respectful tones that any undertaker would approve of. Before Hannah closed the door she saw Siân rise to greet the young man, her eyes sparkling and her cheeks tinged with pink. Hannah smiled to herself. At last! At last Siân seemed to have fallen in love. Hannah had only the briefest glimpse, but the Reverend looked pleasant. How Hannah hoped that he returned Siân's affection.

Hannah's physical and mental scars gradually healed as the weeks passed. The work wasn't hard as quite a lot of rooms were closed off, with the curtains drawn and the furniture draped in dust sheets. There was plenty of help if they needed it. The sons and daughters of the farm labourers were only too willing to turn their hands to anything that would earn them a couple of shillings. She came to love Y-Garn. Blandford was right, everything in the house showed signs of wear and tear, but she loved to polish up the legs of the chairs and tables, take the rugs outside and give them a good beating, aided by Win and her friends. She enjoyed cleaning the windows and taking down and washing the long curtains. She'd carefully dust all the ornaments and pictures, until Siân commented on how lovely everything now looked.

'You are a breath of fresh air,' she said to Hannah as she gave her her wages. 'And you've more than earned this.'

Hannah relayed this to Mrs Howard, who agreed, 'You certainly have, this house hasn't been so well cared for since the Mistress, God rest her, was alive. You're a good worker, Hannah, but get a couple of those big strapping girls to help you next time you take it into your head to spring clean the entire house.'

'I've never been afraid of hard work and I like it here. I never thought I would, but I do.'

'And so does Jessica. Look at the rosy cheeks on her. Before long she'll be into everything. We'll have to have eyes in the back of our heads.'

'I'll watch her,' Win offered. She came in on Mondays to help with the washing.

'Thanks. I'd appreciate it, Win. At least I know you won't be filling her full of laudanum.'

'Shocking that was, Hannah! Shocking,' Mrs Howard said, shaking her head. Hannah had told her all about Evvie Taylor.

Mrs Howard taught her how to cook. It was simple but wholesome and nourishing food, for there was very little entertaining at Y-Garn and Siân preferred simple meals to lavish dinners and buffets.

'The secret in pastry making is to have your hands,

utensils and rolling-out board as cold as possible. Run your hands under the cold tap if necessary and have a marble surface if you can.'

Under her guidance, Hannah became a proficient cook. On the quiet Blandford told her that her pies were as good as Mrs Howard's and her sponge and fairy cakes were better.

'Much lighter – but for God's sake don't tell her I said so! She'll kill me!'

'And so she should! Now get out of this pantry!' Hannah laughed, but she felt very proud of herself just the same.

She was shown how to make sugar icing, fondant icing and royal icing; butter cream, blancmange, jelly, even butter and cheese.

'It might stand you in good stead some day, Hannah. Learn all you can.'

She thanked Mrs Howard profusely, little knowing that her words were to come true.

With her wages she bought clothes for Jessica and the bare necessities for herself, mainly dress material for Rhian Jones's mother to make up. She was a seamstress. Rhian was yet another local girl who helped out.

'You've a knack for it, Mrs Duggan,' Mrs Jones had remarked, and so for a quarter of what they would cost in a shop, Hannah had a few decent outfits.

She'd also bought a pram, second hand but it was far better than the one she'd left behind in Rankin Street. It gave her more freedom and each afternoon, providing it wasn't raining, she walked for miles along the country lanes with Jessica looking around and clapping her little hands when anyone or anything passed by. Sometimes she slept, but not often. Hannah was so proud of her.

March was unseasonably warm and there were signs of spring all around her. The bulbs were beginning to push their way upwards; aconites grew in profusion beneath the trees that were already starting to come into bud. She often came back from her walks with bunches of catkins, aconites and daffodils, knowing how much Siân loved flowers – even wild ones which somehow seemed more appropriate in the house than exotic bought flowers. She loved to hear the songbirds and the rasping cries of magpies and rooks and others who were all building nests. She thought how nice it would be if Miss Siân were to get married soon, in springtime. Hannah had soon discovered that the Reverend Henry Proctor was indeed in love with Siân. It was obvious to everyone in the household that one day very soon, Siân would agree to become his wife and move to the large grey stone Rectory that was the house next door, so to speak, as Mrs Howard explained it, although there were acres of fields and hedges between it and Y-Garn.

'But what will happen to this house and to us?' Hannah had asked, a little concerned.

'We'll move with her. A clergyman doesn't earn a fortune, but she has enough for them both. I don't know exactly what will happen to this place though.'

'Will it be sold? That would be a shame.'

'I don't know and neither does anyone else for the moment. Go out and fetch the post, Blandford, save the poor man trudging all the way around the back.'

As the lad did as he was told Hannah remained silent and thoughtful. She just prayed that when Siân was married, Richard and Maria wouldn't move in here. She couldn't stand that. She couldn't go through all that pain and anguish again.

'There's one for you, Hannah, from Vi by the look of it – all them foreign stamps. And two for Miss Siân. One is from Mr Richard; I recognise his writing.'

Mrs Howard glared at him. 'You just give those letters to me, meladdo! You've no business speculating on who they're from. You're getting too big for your boots by far. In fact the way you're carrying on I'm thinking of sending you back to Mr Donaldson. One of the village lads could do most of the things you do and would be thankful too. There'd be no cheek and impudence from them.'

Blandford pulled a face and left the kitchen.

'Is it from Violet, Hannah?'

Hannah smiled. 'It is. It's been forwarded on, twice. My neighbour must have sent it to Ada. Ada knows this address.'

'You'd better write back to Violet and tell her you are living here now. How are things going with her out there?'

Hannah scanned the lines of neat writing. 'She says she's settled in now. Things are very different. Even some words are different, they have different meanings. But Georgie has a good job with Canadian Pacific Railways and she works in a factory that puts fruit into cans. Apparently they live near a fruit-growing area. They're saving up hard for their own place. It will only be small, she says, but it will be *theirs*. It's hard work, but she says she's happy and it's better than being stuck in Liverpool. They've had a lot of snow. She says she's never seen anything like it. Six feet deep in places where it's drifted. They have something she calls "ice rain" too.'

'What's that?'

'Apparently it's rain but as soon as it touches anything it turns to ice. It's really very dangerous.'

'Well you can keep that! Winter is bad enough here and I'm always glad to see the back of it. One of the others *is* from Mr Richard; I'll take it up. That lad's tongue will get him hung one day!'

Hannah waited for her return. Very little had been said about Richard and Maria during the time she'd been here and as far as she knew this was the first letter that had arrived. Sometimes Mr Hughes telephoned but the line was so bad that it wasn't very often.

'Hannah, are you going out this afternoon?' Mrs Howard asked when she returned to the kitchen.

'I was hoping to.'

'Then would you go with Blandford this morning for the monthly order? I'm getting very low on sultanas and flour. You'll have to go to Denbigh and I just can't trust that young fool with a list. He'd lose it and he's always trying to sneak into one of the pubs and him still two years under age.'

'Yes, of course I will.' The grocer's would of course deliver, and be only too pleased to do so, but Hannah loved to drive to the little market town that nestled at the foot of the hill that was crowned by the ruined castle. 'It's a nice day, we'll go in the trap. Jessica loves to look around.'

'Aye, she's very bright. Bright as a button. Make sure she's well wrapped up, you can't trust March weather.'

Hannah got her coat, hat, scarf and gloves and dressed Jessica in her warm outdoor things Rhian Jones's mother had made. Then she got out the sheepskin rug to cover all their legs and feet. When she was dressed they went out into the yard where Blandford was waiting.

'I'll drive, Blandford.'

'Only after we get to the crossroads or I'll be killed. Someone will see and then I'd be in trouble. Mrs Howard says she doesn't trust "that bad tempered, obstinate little mule"! If I let you drive she'll haul me over the coals. She might even send me back to old misery guts in Liverpool. I keep telling her it's a pony not a mule but she never listens.'

'And you're taking too much notice of these lovely country girls to mind what the "mule" is doing!' Hannah laughed.

Once at the crossroads she sat the baby beside her,

wedged in between herself and Blandford, and told Blandford to keep tight hold of her, then she took up the reins. She liked driving and the pony was never obstinate with her. She marvelled that a city girl as she always thought herself to be could be so at home in the country. In some ways it was like Vi's life, especially as they were both now surrounded by open spaces.

Her thoughts turned to the idea that had grown in her mind for weeks. She refused to admit to herself that it was becoming an obsession. No, it was just something she *had* to do. Something to get out of her system and, once voiced, she could stop looking back and start looking at the future. It was her own personal demon that had to be exorcised and the sooner she got it over and done with the better.

'Blandford, on the way back can we go via Henllan? I lived there years ago, just for a while.'

'It's just like Groes. It's a village. What is there to see?'

'I know it's just a village, but I have a relative, a cousin who lives there. At least I think she still does.'

'You mean the one who dumped you in the work-house? You never talk about her but I can't say I blame you for that.'

'I'm curious about her.'

'We should have brought the car. That'd give her something to think about. Hard-hearted old bitch.'

'Bertie!'

'Sorry, Hannah.'

She looked sternly at him. 'You know we can't take

the car, it's for Miss Siân's use only, we'd both get the sack.'

'Mr Donaldson's not here, who else is there to give us the push?'

'Mrs Howard for a start. She's always saying you'll end up in Walton Jail.'

He grinned. 'It's a long way to Walton and I'm not *that* bad!'

'So, we'll go today?'

He sighed. 'If we have to.'

Hannah smiled grimly and flicked the long carriage whip and the pony broke into a trot. It would be interesting to see the expression on Gwyneth's face – if she still lived there.

They'd bought all the groceries Mrs Howard had asked for and Blandford packed them on the shelf under the seat.

'Do you want to go on driving?' Blandford asked.

'Yes, I'll arrive with a bit of style.' She turned the trap around and they headed for the crossroads at Lenten Pool and the road out to the small village. Nothing had changed, she thought. The fine house that Mr Roberts, the local builder and undertaker, had built for himself and his young family stood at the intersection of the main street of the village and the lane that skirted two of the outlying farms. The small school was still exactly the same. But her memories of the time she had spent there were vague. They passed E. B. Jones's Provisions and the Post Office, went down the hill towards the church and then they turned off to the right and took the lane that was really little more than a cart track.

Hannah tightened the reins and the pony stopped. She just sat there and looked at the cottage. It was even smaller than she remembered, as was the garden and vegetable patch.

'It's not much to look at, is it? I mean it's not like the country cottages you see on railway posters or postcards.'

'No, it isn't at all like them. But there's smoke coming from the chimney so someone still lives there.'

'Will I wait here with Jessica?' Blandford offered. He had no real wish to linger here, it was downright depressing. There didn't even seem to be any curtains on the downstairs window. Just a plant in some kind of pot stuck on the window ledge.

Hannah felt a little nervous as she knocked on the door and stood back and waited, patting the bow on the side of her hat. She was well dressed owing to the position she held. Her dark blue coat was fashionable, as was her hat, she wore stockings and neat black shoes that were fastened with a T-strap. Her dark hair was well cut and shone with good health. What are you nervous of? she asked herself.

She didn't have to wait long before the door was opened by a middle-aged woman with greying hair snatched back in a bun. She wore old-fashioned clothes that had seen better days, but she hadn't really changed that much. She'd just grown older.

'Hello, Gwyneth,' Hannah said quietly.

The woman stared hard at her, screwing up her eyes. It was obvious that she needed spectacles.

'Who are you and what do you want?' she asked, her voice full of suspicion.

Hannah stared back. 'Don't you remember me? I'm Hannah, Hannah Peckham. You dumped me in the workhouse after my da was killed.'

Gwyneth took a step backwards, astonishment and slowly dawning guilt in her eyes.

'Thanks to you, Gwyneth, I had a very miserable childhood until the chaplain from da's regiment found me. I went back to Liverpool but now I live and work at Y-Garn, Mr Ellis Hughes's country house near Groes. You probably know of it. I made something out of myself despite you. I don't suppose you've even given me a thought since you left me in Matron's office all those years ago.'

The woman's hand went to her throat as she fought to control herself. 'How was I . . . to know? I had Mam to see to, life wasn't . . . easy. I didn't know what else I could do. It was Mam, see.'

'Yes, I do "see". But don't bother your head about me now, Gwyneth. I'm doing fine. Far better than you by the looks of things.'

The woman gained control of herself. 'That's nice to know,' she said sarcastically.

'Yes it is, isn't it?' Hannah replied, a hard edge to her voice. 'I earn more money in a month than you do in a year. I've known poverty too but that wasn't my fault. That's Blandford, sitting in the trap, he's the odd-job lad and that's my daughter he's holding. My husband's dead. I'm a widow, but I'd rather go on the streets than have her suffer the way I did. For all your running to Chapel three times on Sundays, you're not a good person. You're a hypocrite, Gwyneth. Do you think God hears your prayers? "Love thy neighbour" is one of the Commandments, isn't it? And didn't Christ say "suffer little children to come unto me"? I was only a child, six years old, and I was confused and unhappy, but you didn't think of showing me any of the kindness that's mentioned in the Gospels. But I managed well enough without you. I have a good life. I've known what it's like to be wanted by a man. I have Jessica and I'm happy. I doubt that you are or ever will be, Gwyneth.' And she turned on her heel and walked away.

Gwyneth watched her get into the trap, take the child from Blandford, kiss and settle her down, then take up the reins. She could feel the bile rise bitterly in her throat. Hannah, this spectre from her past returned to haunt her, was right, she had virtually nothing and nothing to look forward to except loneliness and old age. She had no money put by and when she was too old or infirm she'd finish up in the workhouse where once she'd left Hannah.

'She didn't look very happy,' Blandford said.

'She isn't and I don't care.' Hannah sighed, relieved to have unburdened so much anger. 'I used to hate her, now I pity her.' And maybe now, one day, she could forget the woman who had done so much to damage her life.

Chapter Twenty-Two

It had been a glorious afternoon for a walk and Hannah had thought with amazement how quickly the time had passed. She'd been here over a year and she'd been happy.

When Hannah returned from her stroll in the afternoon Mrs Howard told her that they were all wanted upstairs.

'What for?' Hannah asked, hanging up her coat.

'Can't you guess?'

'You mean Miss Siân and the Reverend Proctor?'

'Something like that.'

When Mrs Howard, herself and Blandford trooped into the drawing room it was to see a radiant Siân Hughes sitting on the window seat with the young clergyman standing close to her, holding her hand.

'You wanted to see us, miss,' Mrs Howard stated.

'I do. I have some news, wonderful news.' Siân gazed up into Henry Proctor's face. 'Henry and I are engaged.' Siân held out her left hand for them to see the ring.

'Oh, congratulations! We're all so happy for you – for you both,' Mrs Howard exclaimed.

'Yes we are, miss. We're thrilled,' Hannah added. Blandford nodded his agreement. The Reverend Henry

Proctor looked flushed and very pleased with himself.

'Can I ask, miss, have you set a date yet, for the wedding I mean?'

Siân smiled at her fiancé. 'We haven't set an actual date, but it will be in September.'

'Will it be here or in Liverpool?' Mrs Howard asked. Her position with the family allowed her to ask questions the other members of the staff wouldn't dare to mention.

'It will be in Liverpool. The Archbishop of Liverpool will probably officiate, with Henry being a minister himself.'

'Then it'll be a grand do?'

Siân shook her head. 'No, just family and a few close friends.'

Mrs Howard was disappointed. 'No white wedding gown then?'

'Oh, yes, I'll definitely have that. Richard and Thomas will be ushers and Maria will be my matron of honour, if she's fit, of course.'

Hannah looked sideways at Mrs Howard. Just what did Siân mean by 'if she's fit'?

'I'll do something special for dinner tonight as a bit of a celebratory meal. I take it your reverence will be staying?'

Henry nodded.

'That would be lovely. Thank you, and thank you for your good wishes,' Siân gushed.

Mrs Howard nodded. They were all dismissed. When they got back into the kitchen, Hannah took Mrs

Howard aside as both Win and Rhian were there, working.

'What did she mean about Maria being "fit"?'

Mrs Howard looked at her. She couldn't keep up the pretence. 'She's expecting a baby,' she said quietly; she glanced at the young girls and was thankful that they were talking together in Welsh.

Hannah sat down in the rocking chair. Why did she feel like this? Shocked, hurt and envious? Just lately she hadn't thought about Richard too much, she'd thought she was over him, but she wasn't. All the emotions came flooding back, particularly how she'd felt that evening he'd kissed her.

'I'm sorry, Hannah. I should have told you.'

'No, it's all right. I'm just . . . surprised, that's all. I suppose it is only natural for them . . . for her . . . to be a mother.' She just wished she could believe her own words but inside a voice was crying, No! No, it wasn't natural! It was the proof of their love for each other. She felt so excluded, so betrayed. Oh, she was being such a fool. But they would all be going back to Liverpool for Siân's wedding and there would be no way of avoiding either Maria or Richard.

'When is it due?'

'Oh, it's only early days yet. Don't you be fretting about things like that.'

Hannah nodded. How could she not 'fret' about it?

The days that followed were quite hectic. Mrs Howard was going back to Liverpool, as was Blandford; they would be needed there as Siân would be spending time in Faulkner Square, organising things. Hannah was to stay on to cook and be in charge of the hired help, for Mrs Howard had said Miss Siân would be returning as often as possible to be near to her fiancé and away from all the rows going on in the house in Liverpool. Arnold Donaldson kept her well informed.

'I can't understand the Master at all,' she said to Hannah one evening as they sat in the kitchen. 'If Mr Thomas wants to go to perdition, then let him go. Let him earn a living, find digs, pay for everything out of his salary. Oh, he'd soon appreciate the life he's got and stay away from those places he frequents with girls like that Daphne. If it was me. I'd kick him out and let him fend for himself. No wonder Miss Siân wants to spend time here. It's a happy time, she doesn't want it all spoiled by the carry on of her brother. A cad, is what he is. I know it's an old-fashioned word, but it just sums him up.'

Hannah had spoken to Win and Rhian Jones who'd been very pleased that they were to be given steady work as kitchen maid and parlourmaid respectively. Young Arwell Jones, Rhian's brother, was to take Blandford's place. Hannah was effectively running the household and sometimes the responsibility of it all made her stop and think how far up in the world she'd come.

Siân had returned for a long weekend in mid April and when Hannah asked about Mrs Howard Siân had sighed. 'I'm afraid my father is intent on keeping her there. Apparently there has been quite a succession of

318

temporary cooks that have not pleased him at all – he is fond of his food. But you cook very well and I'm not a fussy eater as you know. Neither is Henry. Perhaps you would consider cooking for us after we're married? Your lifestyle wouldn't change very drastically and I know how you feel about Jessica. Fresh air, good food, things like that.'

Hannah had been taken completely by surprise.

'Oh, miss, are you sure? I mean . . . I mean I'm not up to Mrs Howard's standards.'

'That won't matter and I'm sure you'll manage very well.'

She felt very grateful. She hadn't wanted to go back to the house in Liverpool where there was every chance she would see Richard Hughes frequently.

She was showing Rhian how to mash potatoes so that they wouldn't be full of lumps when the post arrived. She glanced at it. One from Vi, the others were for Miss Siân. She tucked Vi's letter into the pocket of her dress; she'd read it later on. She wiped her hands and changed her apron. 'Rhian, go on mashing them. I won't be long.'

She knocked at the drawing-room door and entered at Siân's response.

'The post, miss.'

'Oh, thank you.' Siân sifted quickly through them. 'One from Richard,' she said eagerly, tearing the envelope and scanning the lines. Then she cried out and let the letter fall to the floor.

Hannah had been on her way out but she turned.

'Oh, miss, what's wrong?' She hoped there was nothing wrong with him.

'It . . . it's Maria. Oh, poor Maria. She lost the baby again. This is the second time.'

'I am sorry, miss. I really am.' She did feel sorry for Maria, it must be awful. She thanked God for Jessica.

Siân nodded. 'I must telephone her or at least Richard, he must be heartbroken too. I think it might do her good, when she's recovered of course, to come and stay here for a while. It's peaceful here and there are no memories to upset her. She's never been here.'

Hannah's heart felt like a stone. Much as she pitied her, she didn't want Maria here. She didn't want to cook for her and have to try to console her, but there was nothing she could do about it.

That afternoon, after her walk with Jessica, Hannah was told by Rhian that Miss Siân had been looking for her. As she took off her coat, then Jessica's, she instructed the young girl to prepare afternoon tea and keep an eye on Jessica.

'You have been looking for me, miss? I'm sorry to inconvenience you. I had Jessica out in the pram.'

'That's all right, you know it is. I telephoned and I have extracted a promise from Richard that as soon as she's able to travel, he will bring Maria here to stay for a while.'

'That's . . . that's good news,' Hannah replied. He was coming. He was coming too, if only for a very short time. How would she cope with that? What if he decided to stay longer? She pulled herself together. He couldn't stay, he had his work and it was important. He'd probably drive Maria here, stay overnight and return to Liverpool. All she could hope for was that that was what he would do. If he stayed she knew she would feel the way she had done before she'd married Alfie.

They arrived a week later. She'd had to prepare one of the bedrooms for them and her eyes had misted with tears as she'd done so. Here in this room they would sleep side by side; he would lie with his wife in his arms to comfort and console her. With all her heart she wished it could have been herself who would lie beside him. Each day her feelings were becoming stronger and stronger, no matter how much she tried to fight them and dismiss him from her mind. She would have to see them at some time, even though she had tried to work out the times when she could send Rhian in her place.

Siân had asked her to put fresh flowers in the bedroom. 'Always so lovely, they make such a difference,' Siân had said. But Hannah hadn't picked them herself as she often did for Siân, she'd ordered them from the florist's shop in Denbigh.

She was on edge all morning, even snapping at Win who looked surprised and hurt. As she heard the wheels of the car on the gravel every muscle in her body tensed. She knew that in keeping with the informal atmosphere at Y-Garn Siân and Henry would greet them on the front steps and Rhian would serve lunch. Before that, however, she would have to show them to their room, that little piece of etiquette was part of her job. When the bell in the kitchen jangled loudly she bit her lip so hard it hurt. She would just have to get on with it.

She was outwardly poised as she entered the drawing room but inside she felt sick with nerves. She tried to keep her gaze fixed on Miss Siân and Maria Hughes but at last she was forced to look at him. He smiled and her heart started to beat jerkily and she clenched her hands to stop them shaking. She would never, never stop loving him no matter how long they both lived. No, this wasn't a girlish infatuation any more. She'd been through so much since she'd first seen him that day in Liverpool, and still he had this effect on her.

'You are looking very well, Hannah.'

She took a deep breath. 'Thank you, sir. I enjoy living here.'

'And the country life obviously suits you.'

'It does. It suits us both.'

He held her gaze. 'Of course, that must be important to you; given that you're a mother.'

'And a widow.'

'Yes, I'm sorry.'

She tore her gaze away from his and prayed her voice wouldn't betray her feelings. 'If you would like to follow me I'll show you to your room. Your luggage has been taken up by Arwell and I'll unpack for you while Rhian serves you with lunch. I should mention that it's pointless to call them both by their surnames, they are brother and sister and their name is Jones.'

'Then "point" taken, if you'll pardon the pun,' Richard said, but Hannah had turned away. She opened the door and led them into the hall. All the way up the stairs she could feel his eyes on her, or was it just imagination?

Hannah opened the bedroom door and stood back to let Maria enter.

'Flowers, such a lovely thought,' Maria said quietly, smiling at her. Hannah noticed how pale she looked. Pale but still pretty.

'They were Miss Siân's idea, Mrs Hughes.' She hoped her voice was steady. 'I'll leave you now, but if there is anything you need, please ring.'

Richard watched her as she left the room. She was a beautiful young woman now, there was no disputing that, and she was more poised and self-confident. Far more mature, but that was only to be expected. He had heard that her late husband hadn't been much good but that's as much as he knew about the marriage. She had a child, something he didn't. Maria's miscarriages had upset him more deeply than he'd have believed possible. How old was Hannah's child? He thought hard, she must be nearly two years old by now. Siân sometimes mentioned her. He searched his memory for her name. It was something pretty, something unusual. Jessica, that was it. He turned to his wife who was looking very tired.

'Do you feel well enough for lunch? You could have

a rest and just have dinner later, I know Siân won't mind. Or would you like something up here?'

She smiled at him. He was always so thoughtful. 'I'll just have a wash and then come down. It's so long since I've seen Siân, apart from the flying visits when she comes to Liverpool. She's always been so contented living here.'

'I have the feeling that we are going to have quite a few "flying" visits in the future. My future Reverend brother-in-law seems nice enough. A bit quiet, subdued I thought, but as long as she's happy, that's all that matters, and Father will approve of him. Mind you, had he not been a clergyman he would be suspicious. He'd think Henry Proctor was just marrying Siân for her money.' He laughed but underneath he was thinking about his frail sister. He hoped she wouldn't go through the kind of pain in her marriage that he and Maria had gone through.

Chapter Twenty-Three

Richard left the next morning and Hannah let out a sigh of relief as she watched the car go down the driveway and turn the corner. Perhaps now she wouldn't be so tense; her nerves had been strung out like piano wires. The whole weekend had been desperate for her as the emotions she had thought were buried deep inside her came surging upwards again.

On Saturday afternoon when she'd unpacked Maria's clothes she had felt so uncomfortable, especially with the underclothes. They were so delicate; she wished they were hers: all the crêpe de Chine and silk camiknickers, the nightdresses and wraps embroidered and edged with lace. They were such intimate things. She'd held a pale ice-blue nightdress against her. It was so delicately frilled around the hem that it would look as though whoever was wearing it were standing on clouds. If only she could wear it and see the look in his eyes. Her hands were shaking as she'd carefully folded it and laid it on top of the pillow. There was no way at all that she could have opened the small crocodile case that belonged to Richard. She'd run her fingers over the raised crinkly surface, knowing that it would have cost far more than she would earn in six months. No, he'd have to unpack it himself, indeed he probably would. He would know very well that the duties of a ladies' maid didn't extend to include waiting on any gentleman. If need be young Arwell could do it.

Somehow she'd got through the rest of the afternoon and evening, although later on when she'd gone and sat on the bench in the garden, needing the freshness of the evening air after the stifling heat of the kitchen, she'd felt certain he was watching her from somewhere.

At half past eleven Siân rang for her.

'Yes, miss?' she enquired.

'Hannah, my sister-in-law's stay may be a prolonged one. She has said how much she likes it here, but should she wish to return to Liverpool then arrangements, particularly regarding her clothes, would have to be made quite quickly.'

'I understand, miss. I'll make sure that the washing and ironing is kept up to date.'

'Thank you, Hannah. I know Maria appreciates your help, as I do. You work hard and run the household very well, considering your age. How old are you now?'

'I'll be twenty-one later this year, miss.'

Siân smiled. 'You'll have reached your majority. We must do something to celebrate it.'

'Thank you, miss.'

'It seems like only yesterday since the party I had when I was twenty-one. Do you remember it, Hannah?'

'I do, miss. I remember it very well.' It was the truth, she thought. It was the night Richard had saved her from the unwanted attentions of his older brother. 'Will that be all, miss?'

'Yes thank you, Hannah. Oh, my fiancé will be here for supper. I forgot to mention it.'

'That's all right, miss, it's always a pleasure to cook for him.'

She went back to the kitchen where the two girls were laughing at the antics of Jessica who was covered in honey. 'Oh, look at the state of you!'

'It's my fault, Hannah, I gave her a crust with honey on it. Mam says honey's good for you.'

'It is, but not to get yourself covered in it. Jessica, give Mam that crust, I'll have to put a clean dress on you.'

'I'll see to her, Hannah,' Rhian offered.

She looked gratefully at the girl. 'Thanks, I can see we're heading for a tantrum.'

'Will Mrs Hughes be staying long, Hannah?' Win asked.

'I don't know, Win, that's the truth. Miss Siân thinks it may be quite a while, but she told me to keep up to date with her washing, and that she'll inform us when she knows exactly when.'

'Will Miss Siân be here then?'

'I suppose so. Why do you ask?'

The girl flushed and looked down.

'Win, what's the matter?'

'Well, I . . . I heard that she was going back to Liverpool on Friday, to try on dresses.'

'Who told you that?' Hannah demanded. She knew

of no such plans and Siân hadn't mentioned it.

Win looked very uncomfortable. 'It was only a bit of gossip, see.'

'No, I don't *see*.'

'Rhian heard Miss Siân and the other lady talking at breakfast. We thought you might have known. I'm sorry for speaking out of turn.'

Hannah was annoyed. 'And so you should be. I will not tolerate such gossip and tittle-tattle.'

The girl nodded, her cheeks bright red now, and she made an excuse and left the room.

Hannah gripped hold of the back of a chair. Siân was going to Liverpool, leaving her to attend to Maria. Of course Siân didn't know about Richard and herself – what was there to know anyway? That once he'd been so concerned for her that in a fit of madness he had kissed her? But she felt unhappy at being left alone with Maria and annoyed by the fact that Siân hadn't informed her. She decided to go and ask if it were true.

When she entered the drawing room, Siân smiled apologetically. 'Oh, Hannah, I forgot to tell you that I'm going to Liverpool on Friday, a fitting for my wedding dress. I should have told you earlier. It just slipped my mind. I'm sorry. I have so much to think about lately that I'm beginning to have lapses of memory. I'm thankful that I'm having a quiet wedding. If it was a big one I think I'd have a serious attack of nerves.'

'Will Mrs Hughes be going too?' Hannah asked, hoping Maria had changed her mind. After all, she was to stand for Siân just as Jessie had done for her.

'Good heavens, no. She's here to rest. In fact she was telling me half an hour ago that she thinks she might well stay here until the wedding. She says it's so peaceful. None of the noise there is in a big city and the weather is so beautiful.'

Hannah swallowed hard. So, she *was* going to stay that long.

'Of course Richard will come when he can, probably at weekends, and there will be times when he will have to come and fetch Maria for fittings for her matron of honour's dress, but he won't stay long and put any extra pressure on you.'

'Oh, that's all right, miss,' Hannah managed to reply. He'd be here for the weekends and she would have to wait on his wife for God alone knew how many weeks. Her spirits plummeted. Her position was becoming unbearable.

After lunch she put Jessica in the pram and walked down the drive. She'd glimpsed Maria and Siân sitting on a bench in the shelter of the blackthorn hedge. It was a lovely spring day; soon they would be into May and then summer and she'd heard that many of the farmers, for a variety of reasons, thought it was going to be a hot one. Maybe that would encourage Maria to stay even longer and she would expect to see her husband every weekend and that would only make matters worse for herself. She couldn't help but bump into him and that would be so hard. As she walked she found herself thinking more and more about leaving the Hughes's service and going back to Liverpool to live and work. She certainly didn't want to go. She, too, loved it here. It was far healthier for Jessica, she had a position that was envied and respected by the local women and girls. But if Maria stayed she would have to think more deeply about it. She would just have to see how things progressed, she thought sadly.

Things progressed at a rate she certainly was not happy with. As the weeks passed Siân was away more often and Richard drove down each Friday night and returned late on Sunday evenings. Even though it was a big house she couldn't avoid him completely although she did everything in her power to do just that by leaving Rhian to see to as much as the girl was able. She had trained Rhian so well that Siân had remarked upon the fact.

'She's a very willing and capable girl, miss,' she'd said when Siân had finished praising them both.

Each time she saw him, she longed to be able to hold a conversation with him. She longed for him to put his arm around her waist as she'd seen him do once to Maria, and to feel his lips on hers as she'd done once before. That was a precious memory she cherished. She lay awake for hours knowing that their bedroom was only one floor above her large bedroom at the back of the house on the ground floor. She knew she was losing weight because these days she hardly ate enough to keep a bird alive, but she always managed to stay calm and collected before the young girls. She wanted no gossip, not even a hint of it.

Each day that passed she viewed the prospect of her return to Liverpool in a more favourable light. She could find no fault in Maria's behaviour. She was a thoroughly kind and considerate young woman who made no unreasonable demands on the staff and who clearly loved her husband dearly.

Now that the days were hot and the evenings warm and long, Maria and Siân spent a lot of time in the gardens and of course Henry Proctor was a daily visitor. Some evenings they took supper in the garden with a young couple who lived a few miles away. Charles Tate was a member of the family who owned Tate & Lyle's Sugar Refinery in Liverpool. On these occasions Hannah asked Rhian to bring two of her friends to help wait on them and when the guests had gone and the two young women went back into the house, the girls would bring the dishes, cutlery, linen and the furniture back into the house.

Jessica was growing fast. She was a chubby toddler whose curiosity was insatiable and therefore no one could take their eyes off her while she was awake. She could also speak very well for her age and sometimes she threw tantrums, not unlike the ones Hannah herself had indulged in in the workhouse. But that had been different, she told herself. She'd been confused and frightened. Jessica's were always because she wanted her own way.

'She'll be a right handful as she gets bigger, Hannah,' Rhian had commented.

'As I was myself, but I was a lot older than she is. Now, Mam will smack you if you do that again,' she warned the little girl whose eyes were the same colour as her own, but were full of stubborn determination.

'You shan't have your lovely cake with the candles on if you're a naughty girl. Come on to me, *cariad*,' Win coaxed.

There was to be a little party for Jessica's birthday. Just three other small children and Hannah, Rhian, Win and Rhian's mother who had made Jessica a beautiful dress for her party. Hannah sighed. It really *was* a beautiful dress with its hand-smocked bodice and frilled skirt, and she'd bought her a pair of white ankle socks and white buckskin shoes. Jessica was bound to spill something down her dress. She'd have to wear a bib and that in itself would be a battle. Jessica hated bibs.

Siân and Maria had both expressed a wish to come to the party. 'Just for a few minutes, Hannah. She's such a little beauty,' Siân had said.

'But one with a temper, miss.'

'I would never have believed it,' Maria had added, her voice full of longing. Jessica was such a beautiful child and she so wanted a baby of her own.

Hannah knew this and, despite her better nature, she couldn't wish that that would soon come about.

Everything had gone very well. There had been no tantrums from Jessica. She'd submitted calmly to wearing a bib and hadn't ruined her lovely dress. The other children had been well behaved too. Siân and Maria had come to help them blow out the candles and laughed like everyone else at the delight and wonderment on the child's face and the sparkling joy in her big brown eyes. After everything had been tidied away and supper was over, Hannah carried a rosy-cheeked, completely tired out two-year-old to the little bed in her own bedroom.

'There now, you've had a lovely day, be a good girl for Mam and go to sleep.' Hannah kissed her cheek, laid her down and pulled the sheet over her. The night was far too warm for blankets or quilts. For a few seconds Hannah stood looking down at her sleeping daughter. Jessica was the only good thing that had come out of her disastrous marriage to Alfie. She sighed and turned and then stood mesmerised as she caught sight of Richard in the doorway.

'I didn't hear you arrive,' she said in a very low voice.

'I'm sorry, Hannah, I was looking for Maria and Siân.'

'They've gone to the Rectory for a few hours. It was rather noisy earlier on and the Reverend invited them over. It's Jessica's birthday and we had a little party for her.'

He stepped into the room and looked down at the sleeping toddler.

'Oh, Hannah, she's lovely. She's like a Botticelli angel. You must love her very much.' His voice was filled with yearning and envy.

'I do, sir.' His presence seemed to fill the whole room and Hannah was holding herself firmly in check.

'Please don't call me "sir".'

'I . . . can't call you anything else.'

'Not even "Mr Richard"?'

She shook her head; she didn't trust herself to speak. He was so close that she could reach out and touch him.

'I wish you would, Hannah.'

Again she shook her head and refused to meet his eyes.

'I thought we were friends?'

He sounded hurt and she looked up. 'We can never be . . . I can't be . . .' She couldn't go on.

'I'm sorry, Hannah. Don't worry, there is no chance of me taking advantage of you as I did once before.'

'I was just a bit of a girl . . . then. I've grown up.'

'I can see that and there will always be a place in my heart for you. I can still see you standing in the drawing room, dressed in the awful clothes they'd sent you in. You were pretty then, Hannah. Now you are beautiful, truly beautiful.' He turned and was gone before she had time to say a word. She pressed her hands to her burning cheeks. He *did* feel something for her! What had he said? 'There will always be a place in my heart for you.' Oh, how could there be? It was obvious to everyone that he loved his wife dearly. Perhaps he only meant it to sound as though he considered her to be a close friend? But he remembered the way she'd looked the day she'd arrived at the house in Faulkner Square.

334

Oh, there was no choice now. She would have to leave because if he ever found her alone again she knew she would throw her arms around his neck and she suspected that he wouldn't be able to resist, despite the fact that he loved Maria. But he could never be hers so the best thing would be for her to go.

She gave her notice in to Siân at the end of August.

'Hannah! Hannah, what has upset you?' Siân was very concerned.

'Nothing, miss, I swear it.'

'But I thought you loved it here, the countryside, your position.'

'I do, it's just that, well, I want to be independent, miss. I've been thinking about this for a long time. But may I say how much I appreciate every single thing you've done for me? I won't go until after the wedding.'

Siân was upset. 'But, Hannah, what plans do you have to support yourself?'

'I'm going to open a canteen.'

'A what?'

'I'm going to make and sell pies from my own doorstep. There are so many people who would go hungry but for the canteens or "cannies" as they call them in Liverpool. And now with the way things are – no jobs for the men – they'll be a godsend to the poor. I'll only charge a penny. I know it will be hard to make ends meet at first but I've saved some money.'

'Well, if you're set on it, Hannah.'

'I am, miss. I hope to do well and be able to provide

Jessica with all the things I didn't have.'

'Where will you go? Where will you live until you find suitable premises?'

'With Mrs Sweeney. I know it'll be cramped but it won't be for long. I really *do* intend it to be a success.'

Siân smiled a little sadly. 'I'm sure you will, Hannah, but I'm so sorry to lose you. I know we are of very different classes but I've always looked on you as something other than just a servant.'

'Thank you, miss. You've always been good to me.'

'But you will stay to see me in my wedding gown?'

Hannah smiled. 'I wouldn't miss that for the world. You'll look so beautiful.'

Chapter Twenty-Four

True to her word Hannah stayed on. Maria was particularly upset that Hannah was leaving and taking Jessica with her. She had started to find excuses to see her and always made a fuss of the child. It was sad to see how much she longed for a baby of her own, Hannah thought. Richard said nothing, nor did he join his wife and sister in their requests that Hannah stay on. He was aware of feeling more than a little fond of Hannah and looked upon her departure as a sensible thing for both of them. After the wedding Y-Garn was to be shut up until such time as Mr Ellis Hughes decided what to do with it.

The week after Hannah's announcement, they all moved back to Faulkner Square. It was just like the old days, Mrs Howard remarked.

'Hannah, do you really know what you are doing this time?' the older woman asked one evening.

'I do,' she replied firmly. 'You know why I can't stay on and I *do* want to be independent and make a success of this venture. There's no one else involved this time and I'm older and wiser.'

'And older and wiser people than you have opened businesses that have failed and have lost their money.'

'I have to try. And I'll be able to have Jessica with

me, when I find the right property.'

'And you know as well as I do that the "right" property is going to be in somewhere like Victoria Terrace. Is that a decent place to bring up a child? It most certainly is not. Have you even told them in Victoria Terrace that you're back in Liverpool?'

'No, not yet.'

'Because you're afraid they'll tell you you're a fool to give up such a good job and that you'd be far better staying on with Miss Siân.'

'Oh, don't think I haven't thought of all that. I've spent hours agonising over it.'

'Then go back with them after the honeymoon.'

She shook her head. 'No, I'm set on this.'

'And, God knows, when you are "set in your mind" nothing or no one will make you change it. Did you write and tell Mrs Sweeney you were coming back?'

'No, I wanted to surprise her.'

'Oh, you'll do that all right, but you'd better go around and visit her before someone sees you and tells her. Victoria Terrace isn't all that far away and you don't want to ruin the "surprise".'

So, the day before the wedding, she wheeled Jessica in the pram to Victoria Terrace. It looked even more dilapidated, dirty and run-down than ever, she thought. Was she mad to bring Jessica back to this? Mrs Howard had been right about the exact area to open a cannie.

When they reached Ada's house she put the brake on the pram and lifted Jessica out. As ever the door was open, even though there was a chill in the air now, and she walked straight into the kitchen.

Ada looked up from peeling potatoes. 'Hannah! Hannah, is it really you?' she cried, knife, potato and peelings all dropped.

'Of course it's really me! I've come home for good.'

Ada was taken aback and was silent for a few minutes, wiping her hands on her apron.

'Shall I put the kettle on?' Hannah asked. Nothing had changed much here, she thought, except for a few more pieces of shabby furniture.

Ada sat down. 'Oh, give me a minute ter gerrover the shock.'

'Here then, hold Madam.' Hannah sat Jessica on Ada's knee and the child instantly began to struggle to get down.

'Now, just stop that. Mam wants you to be a good girl and sit on Aunty Ada's knee. If you behave I'll give you a sweetie.'

'Lord above, Hannah, 'asn't she grown? I know yer said in yer letters that she was gettin' big but it's not until yer actually see 'er that yer realise just 'ow big.' She struggled with the wriggling child. 'Yer'll 'ave ter take 'er, she's like a little eel. I'll make the tea.'

Hannah lifted Jessica on to her own knee and gave her a sweet.

'Now what did yer say ter me just then? Somethin' about comin' back?' Ada asked as she pushed the kettle on to the hob and got out the old Fry's cocoa tin that served as a tea caddy.

'Yes. I am. Miss Siân's getting married tomorrow.

They've closed up the house in Wales.'

'So is she going ter live 'ere then?'

'No. They will live in the Rectory, it's just across from the church. I told you he was the vicar there.'

'Oh, aye, our Lily read it out to me. I remember now. Then will you be living round there in Faulkner Square?'

'No.'

'Then where the 'ell are yer goin' ter live?'

'Can I stay here with you? It'll only be for a short time. I want to get a place of my own.'

'Are yer mad, Hannah? What do yer want ter go an' give up a job like that for? An' what will yer do for a livin', like?'

'Can I stay?'

'Of course yer can, yer know that. We've 'ad no trouble with them Duggans since I reported them ter the scuffers.'

'Thanks. I'm going to open a cannie. I've got some savings.'

Ada shook her head. 'It's norra good time ter open anythin'. There's no work for anyone. I even 'eard they are goin' ter dig a tunnel under the river ter take cars an' buses and trams. 'Ave yer ever 'eard the like? If it gets an 'ole in it it'll flood the whole flamin' city. But it's supposed ter give some of the fellers a bit of work.'

Hannah's expression became serious. 'I've seen the men and lads standing on the street corners; there seem to be more of them than when I was last home.'

'There are, so yer see it's norra good time ter do anythin'.'

'I think it is. I'm going to bake pies. I'm a good cook; Mrs Howard taught me. Then I'll sell them for a penny.'

Ada was astounded. 'For a penny? 'Ow the 'ell are yer goin' ter make any money ter keep yerself an' milady there?'

'I've got some money saved up. It will be enough to keep us until I start to make a profit.'

'Hannah, luv, yer don't understand. Things is desperate. People can't buy 'ardly any food, even though yer will be undercuttin' the shops. Yer'll 'ave ter buy the makin's first an' yer'll 'ave ter live.'

'I know. But I'm certain I'll do well. What I sell will be real value for money.'

Ada looked closely at her. 'That's not the whole reason, is it, Hannah? There's somethin' else, I know you.'

Hannah grimaced ruefully. 'You certainly do know me. No, it's not the main reason. I had to get away. I was seeing far too much of . . . him.'

'Oh, God Almighty, Hannah, yer're not still carryin' a torch fer 'im, are yer?'

'I'll always love him. I know I'll never be able to have him, but that won't stop me loving him and if I had stayed I'd be as miserable as sin, even though they have been very, very good to me.'

'They 'ave. There's not many like that Miss Siân an' Mrs Howard. God bless them both.'

'So, I'll bring my things down on Sunday, if that's all right? On my way back I'll go into Kennedy's and buy some second-hand furniture and have it brought down. Will that suit you?'

Ada nodded. 'I'll get our Lily ter 'elp me give the room the once-over ternight.'

'Then on Monday I'll go and see if I can find some sort of decent house to rent.'

'An' just where were yer thinkin' of settin' up this cannie?'

'By the docks somewhere.'

Ada rolled her eyes. ''Ave yer seen the 'ouses down there? 'Alf of them are worse than this an' this is no palace.'

'There must be one somewhere that I can clean up a bit.'

'An' what about the little one? Do yer think the dock road is the place fer kids? I thought *you'd* know better, Hannah.'

'Well at least I'll be able to keep my eye on her myself, not like last time.'

'They should 'ave thrown the key away on that Taylor woman! Well, I can see yer've made up yer mind. Yer're just like yer da. Yer're quite 'appy with the front room? There's 'ardly anythin' in it, like.'

'It'll be fine. I'll get what we'll need.'

Ada suddenly cried out, 'Hannah! She's after the teapot!'

Hannah was just in time to snatch Jessica's fingers away from the brown glazed teapot.

'Yer'll 'ave ter 'ave eyes like an 'awk with 'er. Perhaps she'd better stay with me, until yer get goin', like.'

'Perhaps she should, but she can be a little madam at times. She throws tantrums.'

'Just like someone else I know! She's a dead spit of you across the eyes, but that's all – she looks like *him* an' the rest of *that* lot. God 'elp 'er.'

As Hannah walked back to Faulkner Square she felt happier. She was sure her plans would work and although they would be living in the same city, if she had a home near the docks there was very little likelihood of her seeing Richard Hughes again and she would have other things to occupy her.

'Well, what did she say?' Mrs Howard asked.

'More or less the same as you, but I'll be moving my things there on Sunday and I'll start looking for a place on Monday. Ada's going to look after Jessica for me.'

'I wish you'd change your mind, Hannah.'

'I *have* to do this,' she replied quietly.

The older woman sighed. 'She wants to see us all tonight.'

'What for?'

'So she can say her goodbyes, I suppose. There's not going to be much time in the morning.'

'Oh, I was really looking forward to seeing her in her dress.'

'You will. We all will. The Master's told us to be in the hall at nine o'clock sharp to see her off. Thank goodness Mr Richard will have already gone, as will Mr Thomas.'

Hannah nodded, knowing what Mrs Howard was telling her.

After supper they all trooped upstairs: Mr Donaldson, Mrs Howard, Elinore Stephenson, Blandford and herself.

Siân was standing in the hall waiting for them, her father beside her looking very pleased with himself.

'I'd just like to thank all of you for everything you've ever done for me, especially you, Mrs Howard, and I'd like to give you all something to remind you of me.'

'You're not going to die, Siân, you're just going to live in Wales,' Mr Hughes said with a little snort of a laugh. It was the first time Mrs Howard had ever heard him laugh. He must be pleased, she thought. Perhaps Mr Thomas had promised to settle down at last.

'Yes, well, I don't want to be too formal so here, would you like to distribute these, Mr Donaldson, please? Just a small gift.'

Arnold Donaldson took his position very seriously and made a brief and very formal reply before giving everyone a small bag with a name tag attached to it which obviously contained money.

'The only one with any common sense in this family,' Mrs Howard muttered under her breath.

No one opened their bags until they were back in the kitchen.

'It's gold sovereigns!' Elinore cried. 'I've got two! I'll never, ever spend them. Oh, isn't she kind!'

'I've got four!' Blandford informed them.

Neither the butler nor the cook had opened theirs, feeling the coins and judging – accurately – that there were more than two or three. Hannah let her gold coins slip from their bag on to her hand. There were seven of them. Enough to fall back on if times became lean, but like Elinore she hoped she would never have to spend them.

Elinore could hardly contain herself the following morning. 'Oh, I know she's going to look like a princess!' she said excitedly.

'She will but if you don't finish your chores soon you won't be going up to see her,' Mrs Howard reprimanded her, although she was full of suppressed excitement herself. She felt that in a way it would be like seeing a daughter in her bridal gown – she had known and loved Siân like the child she had never had.

Blandford suddenly burst in on them. 'Quick! Quick! The carriage has arrived. It's an open landau and it's full of flowers!'

'Oh, we haven't been sent for!' Elinore wailed.

'Someone's forgotten to tell us! Come along, up into the hall now,' Mr Donaldson instructed.

They arrived in time to see Siân descending the staircase, her father following in his morning suit with Maria dressed in lilac silk. Both Siân's brothers had already gone to the church, something Hannah was glad of. But Siân looked beautiful. Hannah heard Mrs Howard sniff and Elinore already had a handkerchief in her hand.

'How do I look?' Siân asked of Mrs Howard.

'You look like a . . . a princess! Oh, your mam would have been so proud of you.'

Siân smiled wistfully. 'She would. She *will*, I firmly believe that she can see me.'

'And she'd approve of his reverence,' Mrs Howard added.

A lump had come into Hannah's throat. Siân looked radiant. The dress was exquisite. It was white satin but the whole of the skirt and the long train was covered in beadwork and pearls. On her head Siân wore a small tiara of drop pearls and diamonds – obviously a family heirloom – and her full-length veil was of white guipure lace. The bouquet she carried was of white madonna lilies, roses and trailing smilax. Oh, she deserved to be happy and she *would* be, Hannah thought. Siân was the most generous, thoughtful and caring person she'd ever known. How could anyone do otherwise than wish her every blessing and happiness?

Chapter Twenty-Five

On the Monday morning Hannah set out to look for a suitable house, but the closer she got to the streets that bordered the dock estate the more her spirits plummeted. She hadn't thought that housing could get any worse after a night spent in Ada's front room. But it had. She'd spent so long in the country she'd forgotten just how dirty and depressed this area was. In a city like this, with such a wealth of beautiful public buildings, there shouldn't be such terrible slums. Everywhere, standing on street corners or outside pubs were groups of men and boys in threadbare, shiny jackets, moleskin trousers, white mufflers and cloth caps – the uniform of the poor – and they all looked gaunt, hungry and desperate. What they needed was work and there was none.

She felt very conspicuous, her clothes being far better than those of any of the women and girls she saw on the streets, and, a little uneasy, she clutched her bag tightly to her. She left the main road as she got to the bottom of Parliament Street and walked along Chaloner Street opposite which was the Queens Dock. There was very little work going on although the two branches and the graving dock were full of ships, their masts and rigging like a forest of branches. Here and there was the funnel of a steamship. This would be a very good area but oh, the poverty was appalling.

When she returned home, cold, tired and hungry, Ada asked about her day's wanderings.

'I'd forgotten, I really had. You were right, it's terrible down there.' She shook her head sadly.

'So, yer didn't see nothin'?' Ada asked.

'No, but it's the right area.'

'So what'll yer do now?'

'Keep looking.'

'Hannah, why don't yer change yer mind an' go back with Miss Siân?' Ada pleaded. Hannah was used to much better things now.

Hannah shook her head. It was so tempting, especially after today, but she *had* to make a new life for herself.

'Well, I'll come with yer termorrer. Two 'eads are better than one.'

'Would you? I felt overdressed and positively ashamed to be so, there's women down there with no shoes or stockings, just bare feet under their long skirts and old shawls to keep them warm.'

'God 'elp 'em all with winter comin' on. It's a disgrace, the flamin' Government should do somethin' about it. It's always been bad for the dockers but now it's even worse. 'Alf the city's got no work an' they've got families to keep. There's many who'll go hungry, aye and starve ter death this winter.'

'Well, I can't think of a better time to open a cannie. At least I'll feel as though I'm doing something to help.'

'Aye, well, the Lord 'elps those who 'elp themselves,' Ada said sagely. 'But 'ow can yer 'elp yerself if yer can't gerra job?'

The following day it was raining. Peering up through the kitchen window at the grey, leaden sky, Ada shook her head. 'It's in fer the day, is that, and none of us are goin' ter traipse around lookin' fer 'ouses. We'll be soaked ter the skin after an hour.' Hannah had to agree that she was right, so instead she and Ada, Martha and Lily, who was herself out of a job, worked out just how much she would need to spend and just how much money she would make.

'I 'ave ter admit that it won't cost that much fer flour an' fat and fillin's, but I can't see yer making anything at all charging just a penny.'

'The biggest expense will be rent an' coal an' light. Yer'll 'ave ter 'ave an 'ouse that's gorra biggish range in the kitchen fer all the bakin' yer're goin' ter do, Hannah,' Martha added.

'And you'll need some help or you'll half kill yourself looking after Jessica and the housework and everything if you're going to spend so much time baking,' Lily added.

'I know. I'm not afraid of hard work, it's just getting into a routine, but I'd be really grateful if someone could mind Jessica for me.'

'Yer know I will, Hannah,' Ada offered.

Hannah was glad it wasn't raining as she looked out of the kitchen window a day later. It was just a grey miserable day but she was determined that she wasn't coming back until she had found somewhere.

Jessica had been left in Martha's care as Ada and Lily accompanied her.

'God Almighty, I've never seen things so bad. There's enough ships in the docks but there's nothin' much movin'. There's sailors with this lot.' Ada nodded towards the groups of men. 'An' it's not often yer see one of them out of work unless they're bone idle or are caught pinchin' things.'

'I told you there wasn't. How in God's name are these men going to feed their families, Ada?'

'With your help, Hannah, an' I don't mean just with food.'

Hannah looked at her quizzically.

'When we find somewhere half decent yer can bet yer life the flamin' landlord won't do no repairs.'

Hannah nodded. Cleaning and furnishing she could do herself, but repairs to the building would have to be done by workmen.

They were halfway down Norfolk Street, which was off Simpson Street, and were being watched by all the women who lived there either from their doorsteps or through curtainless windows, when Hannah stopped.

'What's up with yer?' Ada demanded.

'That one looks empty. The one over there. It doesn't look too bad either.'

'Maybe they just can't afford any curtains an' that's why it looks so empty. Every other house in the street is packed to overflowin'. An' all that lot should be at school.' She indicated a group of children sitting on the kerb, their bare feet in the gutter, their clothes torn, dirty and ragged. 'But yer can't send 'em lookin' like that. I know 'ow it feels ter 'ave ter keep 'em away because they've nothin' decent to wear, an' then yer get the flamin' fellers from the School Board knockin' on yer door and wantin' ter know why.'

'Well, we can at least ask, Mam,' Lily said impatiently.

Hannah crossed the road and approached the house next door to number fourteen. The door was slightly ajar so she knocked hard upon it.

A child answered it, a girl of about six wearing only a faded print dress that was much too short for her. Her legs and feet were bare and her hair was a tangled mop.

'Is your mam in?' she asked, bending down.

The child nodded.

'Then can I talk to her?'

'She said iffen yer were from the rent feller I've ter tell yer we 'asn't got no money. Me da's got no work.'

'No, I'm not from anywhere like that, honestly,' Hannah said encouragingly.

'Go an' get 'er an' don't 'ave us standin' on the doorstep,' Ada commanded.

The child left the door open and they all had a closer view of the lobby. There were large patches of damp on the walls and some of the floorboards were missing.

Ada sadly shook her head. 'There'll be nothing left

of that floor cum Christmas an' then they'll 'ave ter start on other rooms.'

Hannah nodded her understanding. Things were really desperate when even the floorboards had to be burned for fuel and wood certainly didn't last as long as coal.

The woman finally came down the lobby. She looked old and bowed down with worry. She clutched a shapeless old woollen cardigan tightly to her, her long dark skirt hid bare legs and her feet too were bare and dirty.

'I wonder, could you tell me, is the house next door empty?'

'What do yer want ter know fer?'

'Because iffen it is, she wants ter rent it,' Ada said firmly.

'It is. They was turfed out last Friday by the bailiffs. Some people 'ave no pity. "Only doin' our job, missus!" Bloody bloodsuckers! Bloody leeches!'

'So who is the landlord?' Hannah asked.

'Feller called Josh Redfern is the agent, no one knows who the hell owns the fallin'-down lousy auld houses.'

'And where can I find him?' Hannah persisted.

'At this time of day in the bar of the Alexandra.'

Hannah and Lily began to turn away but Ada hadn't finished.

'What sort of a state is it in?' she asked the woman. 'Are the floorboards missin', like? Though I'm not sayin' iffen they are it weren't necessary. An' I suppose it's damp?'

The woman shrugged. 'Aren't they all? There's hardly any boards upstairs and the lobby's just like this 'ere. Yer've gorra try an' keep warm and cook, like, 'aven't yer?'

'Yer 'ave, luv, thanks. I'll be seein' yer.'

'So, it's off to the Alexandra,' Lily said, stating the obvious.

'It is,' Hannah agreed.

'I can't say I like it. A pub is no place fer a decent woman unless there's a snug, an' even then money's too 'ard cum by ter be linin' the landlord's pockets.'

They picked out Josh Redfern quite quickly from the small group of men at the bar. He was the one who was better dressed and had a full pint glass on the bar in front of him. They all turned around and stared with hostility at the women.

''Ere, youse, we want a word with yer,' Ada demanded loudly, ignoring the annoyed stares.

'Mam!' Lily hissed.

'What's up with yer, Lily?'

'Everyone's looking at us, Mam.'

Before Ada had time to reply to Lily or address the men again, Hannah approached the group.

'I was told that you, Mr Redfern, are the agent for number fourteen Norfolk Street?'

'An' what if I am?' he asked.

'Don't be so flamin' 'ardfaced. She can buy an' sell youse lot,' Ada growled.

He looked Hannah up and down. This one wasn't short of a few bob. 'Why do you want to know?'

'Because if it's in a decent enough condition and the rent is a fair one, I'd like to rent it.'

'Seven and six, to you.'

'I'll give you five shillings and that's not negotiable.'

Ada rolled her eyes. God knows where Hannah got these big words from, it must be mixing with the high and mighty Hugheses.

'Seven and six,' he persisted.

'What a shame you can't see beyond your nose. I was prepared to make it habitable, which would have been a good investment for your employer, whoever he is. But not at seven and six a week. There will be other landlords only too willing to rent property to me and have it improved.'

He stared at her hard. This one was no fool and she'd been well educated. He certainly didn't know what 'negotiable' or 'investment' meant. 'All right, five bob a week.'

'Good. Then perhaps you can give me the key so I can go and see what I'm getting for five shillings. If I think it's in too bad a state of repair, then I'll bring you back the key.'

'I want to see some money first before I hand over any key.'

'I want never gets,' Ada quipped sarcastically.

'Two shillings, returnable if it's not what I want.' Hannah handed over two silver shillings.

'What the 'ell does someone like 'er want ter live in bloody Norfolk Street for?' the landlord asked, but all he got in the way of an answer was a shrug of Josh Redfern's shoulders.

'Yer found 'im then?' the woman next door said. She was now leaning on the door-frame, her arms folded across her chest.

'I did and I told him I wasn't taking it if I don't think it's in too good a state.'

Hannah's heart dropped as she pushed open the front door and walked down the lobby, carefully avoiding the gaps in the floorboards.

''E's gorra nerve askin' five flamin' shillin's fer this, Hannah. Would yer just look at the muck in there?' Ada pointed to the floor of the front room whose door was missing.

'I'll go up the stairs, Mam,' Lily offered.

'Just be careful, Lily.'

Hannah was viewing the kitchen and more importantly the range. It was in a terrible state but it was quite big enough to bake a fair number of pies as it had two ovens.

'What do you think?' she asked of Ada who was looking around the dismal, dirty room.

'It needs a flamin' good clean and them walls need a coat of limewash an' yer'll 'ave ter take a wire brush ter that range, look at the rust on it.'

Hannah was trying to open the door of the top oven. 'This will need a bit of oil on it.'

'Just shows how long it is since it's been used, God 'elp 'em.'

Lily came back downstairs. 'You'll have to be careful, them stairs is wobbly and the banister rail has gone.'

'So, what sort of a state is it in up there?' Hannah asked.

'The back bedroom isn't too bad. It's got all the floorboards and there's no damp, but the other one is shocking.'

'So, do you think I should give Mr Redfern the other three shillings?'

'I wouldn't give that feller the time of day, let alone five flamin' shillin's. Tell him yer'll give 'im four an' that's yer last offer.'

It was with a very bad grace that Josh Redfern took Hannah's offer.

'I'm going to need someone who can fix the stairs and put back all the wood that's missing. I'll need someone to make sure the gas is safe as well,' she said to Ada as they walked home.

'By the time yer've got furniture and stuff, it won't leave yer with much, Hannah.'

'I've some "reserve money" but I don't want to use it unless it's absolutely necessary.'

'Then leave me ter sort out the workmen, they'd be robbin' yer blind, and don't give 'em no wages until the job's finished or yer'll not see 'em again. Just give 'em enough fer materials. Me an' Martha an' a couple of others will cum an' give yer an 'and ter make the place look presentable. The state it's in now yer couldn't cook an' sell anything, yer'd have the 'Ealth an' Sanitary lot down on yer.'

'And they'd be right, too, and yet they expect families to *live* in conditions like that.'

'We'll call in ter Kennedy's on our way 'ome an' gerrall the cleanin' stuff from 'er who 'as the shop on the corner of Lonsdale Street.'

It was seven days later when Hannah moved into number fourteen Norfolk Street. It certainly looked far better now, although there were only the bare essentials in the way of furniture. They'd all worked like demons, scrubbing floors and washing windows and paintwork. The two men she'd hired had made a good job of the repairs: it hadn't cost her a fortune and they'd painted every piece of wood. It had taken a full day's work to get the rust off the range and blacklead it. As a precaution, she'd had the chimney swept, although Ada had said and the sweep had concurred that it was probably only the soot that was keeping the chimney from falling down. So she'd had the outside painted and had had new guttering put up. She had cotton gingham curtains on all the windows because gingham was cheap but always looked fresh and clean. Looking at the yard at the back, 'It's filthy! Yer'll catch somethin' 'orrible from it,' had been Ada's prediction. So she had enlisted two of the neighbours to clean it up and scrub out the privy with soda and Jeyes Fluid.

'So, when are yer going ter start sellin' stuff?' Ada asked next, looking around with admiration.

'I'll start by baking all day tomorrow, then I'll have a stock that will just need to be warmed up in the bottom oven.'

'Will I help you, Hannah?' Lily asked eagerly.

'Thanks, Lily, even if it's just minding Jessica.'

'So 'ow are yer going ter advertise?' Ada asked.

'I'll put a sign up on the window: "Hot Pies a Penny", and just wait until people have tasted them and told their friends and neighbours. Word of mouth is always the best way.'

'Well, I'd start with the neighbours, luv. An' it wouldn't do no 'arm ter give 'er next door a couple free, ter test, like. She's probably gorra a mouth like the flamin' tunnel they're buildin'.'

At the end of the week Hannah knew it was going to be a success. She'd had to stay up half the night baking and Ada had helped her. She'd given Mrs Kelly next door five pies just to 'taste' and within an hour she had half the street standing in a queue outside her front door.

'God, Hannah, you'll have to borrow someone's oven if this keeps up,' Lily remarked as they sat counting the pile of pennies. Ada was on her way with Jessica.

'Well, there's your mam and Martha and I suppose Mrs Kelly would help out in return for coal and a few pies.'

'Hannah, don't start giving them away. It'll get round that you're a soft touch.'

'Maybe I am, Lily, I can't help it.'

'Well, they're getting good value for money as it is. I heard Mrs Doran from down our street say she'd never tasted anything like them. The pastry just melted in your mouth. She'd come down here just to see, like.'

Hannah smiled. 'I had a very good teacher,' she replied, thinking of Mrs Howard.

The weather was getting much colder and wetter now, Hannah thought as she prepared to open up. October had been wet and very windy and now November was here and with it came the dense, choking yellow fogs that chilled you to the bone. The house was warm even though the front door was open, as the range was in use day and night and the doors to the two downstairs rooms were fully closed. It was Lily who helped her most while Ada came down to see to Jessica who was rapidly picking up the thick nasal Liverpool accent. But Hannah was so busy and so tired that she hardly had time to think of anything or anyone, let alone Richard Hughes.

She jammed the piece of wide flat wood that served as a counter between the two sides of the door-frame and covered it with a white cloth. She had a pile of old newspaper cut into squares in which she wrapped the pies if requested. Most people just crammed them into their mouths, they were so cold and hungry. She'd heard that soup kitchens were now being discussed in earnest and she was glad. Her heart went out to the women who didn't have the necessary penny looking despairingly at the line of people who always seemed to be waiting at her door. These women were desperate to feed their families, going without themselves to do so. If anyone was still waiting around at the end of the day, she always gave them something.

'Lily, will you bring the first tray through now,' she called, tying on her apron that had a large pocket in which she put the money.

'Coming, Hannah,' Lily replied. Hannah was now paying her a few shillings for her help. Lily was glad of it, and working for Hannah meant none of them ever went hungry either.

No sooner had she set down the tray than people began to jostle each other.

'We're not selling anything until you settle down,' Lily said briskly, then she took a step backwards, her hand to her throat. 'Oh, God!'

'What? What's the matter?' Hannah asked.

'It's . . . it's . . .'

A man had shouldered his way to the front. 'Aye, it's me, Lily. Jack Duggan. I suppose you thought you'd seen the last of me, didn't you, Hannah?'

'What do you want?' Hannah demanded coldly.

'Well, it's not just a bloody pie! I heard you'd moved down here an' that you're doing well. You must have a few bob now.'

Hannah just glared at him. 'Well, if you think you're going to get some of it you're mistaken.'

'You killed our Alfie!'

'I didn't! I couldn't have moved him if I'd tried, not the state he left me in, and if you want to make something out of it then I'll get Mr Donaldson's sworn statement.'

'Who the hell's he?'

'The butler for the Hugheses.'

'I don't care how many statements you get, you still killed our Alfie an' now me Mam wants something off you. You can afford it.'

'You, your mam and the rest of your family can go to hell!' Hannah yelled at him.

People were pushing and crowding him.

'Get out of here, these people are hungry,' Hannah said sharply.

'Aye, go to hell, Jack Duggan! Thank God I found out about you,' Lily added.

He lunged towards Hannah and caught her by the shoulder. 'Then I'll have to take it out of your face!'

Before anyone could do anything he hit her hard across her face and she cried out in pain.

Lily screamed, 'Go for the scuffers! Go on, quick, or you'll get nothing today or tomorrow!'

The two women who had been standing behind him disappeared.

Hannah had now managed to twist out of his grip.

'You lay another finger on me, Jack Duggan, and you'll regret it!' Her cheek felt as if it were on fire and all the memories of that terrible night came flooding back to her.

'It's not me who's going to do the "regretting", Hannah!' He smirked maliciously before grabbing and hitting her again. She reeled backwards against the wall, holding her cheek.

Then he was grabbed from behind and yanked away from the doorway by the collar of his jacket.

'Oh, it's one of *you* lot, I might have known!'

Hannah had never been so glad to see a policeman in her life.

'He . . . he belted her, I saw him and so did all these people,' Lily cried.

'You'll get no help out of this lot!' Jack jeered, knowing no one would back Hannah up except Lily.

He yelped in pain as his arm was twisted up his back.

'Is that so, well, we'll just see. Tell me the whole story, miss.'

'He . . . he's my brother-in-law, or he was. He came here today just to make trouble and then he hit me.'

'That's right, that's what he did,' Lily added.

'I'm sure he did. Hasn't got the guts to take on a feller. Now, anyone else see this?'

There was silence and a shuffling of boots.

'If you don't help her you'll get no more pies, at least not for a penny! He's one of them Duggans!' Lily appealed to the group.

Jack was still struggling.

'If you don't pack that in, I'll have you for resisting arrest and with your record that's enough to send you down for a year.'

'I . . . well, I saw him,' one of the women who had gone to find the policeman said tentatively.

'An' so did I. We were all waiting for 'er to open, like, and 'e pushed 'is way in and then belted 'er.'

'Yer bloody liar. Yer bloody nark!' Jack yelled. He got a cuff around the ear.

'No swearing and no insulting women! Behave! Do you want to press charges, missus?'

Hannah could feel her lip beginning to swell. 'Yes. Yes, I most certainly do.'

'Right, could you get your coat and come with me?'

'Go on, Hannah, I'll manage here,' Lily said.

'Assault, causing grievous bodily harm and resisting arrest. You'll be spending quite a long time in Walton and you won't be missed around here! One less of you lot for us to worry about. Move! Ladies, will you come along too?'

'Not before I've 'ad me pies. I was first in the queue an' the kids an' 'im are all starvin'.'

'Here,' Lily sorted out four pies and wrapped them. 'Take them home and then get down to the police station.'

'Is they free?'

'Yes, go on, I haven't got all day, I'm on me own.'

The woman grabbed the parcels and ran quickly across the road. Lily smiled with satisfaction. They'd have nothing to fear from Jack Duggan or his family again. She'd despaired of anyone, apart from herself, backing up Hannah's story. This was the first time she'd ever heard of anyone voluntarily helping the police, but hunger made people do strange things.

Chapter Twenty-Six

Jack Duggan was sent to Walton Jail for five years hard labour. Hannah had been very relieved but it was with great difficulty that she, Lily and Martha had managed to restrain Ada from going to do battle with Vera Duggan. Ada had not forgotten her humiliation at the hands of Vera and her daughter.

Hannah's business thrived as the Depression deepened. Over the sixteen months since she'd opened her cannie, her profits had increased week by week. She'd had to use the ovens of nearly everyone she knew and as payment she bought the coal for their ranges and allowed them to keep three or four pies per day. She was also very grateful for Ada's help in looking after Jessica who seemed to be growing at an alarming rate. In July Jessica would be four and soon Hannah would have to think about sending her to school. It had been a chance remark by Lily that had stirred up an old memory and given her a new idea.

'You wouldn't get so many people going to a real café. For one thing they'd have to pay more and for another they couldn't be snatching and fighting,' Lily had said after she'd heard a derogatory remark from one of the women waiting in the queue.

Hannah's mind had gone back to the first time she'd

been out with Alfie, when they'd gone to New Brighton and had sat in a café.

'Lily, I think you've just given me an idea.'

Lily was intrigued. 'What did I say?'

'I went to New Brighton for the day once.'

'So?'

'So I think I'll turn the front room into a bit of a café.'

'What for? This lot won't be needing no café.' She couldn't believe that Hannah was serious.

'Not a proper café, Lily, just somewhere they can get a warm drink and eat their pies. Just some benches in a room really, but one with a roaring fire.'

'You'd never get them out. They'd be there all day.'

'Not if I charged, oh, say a farthing more and limited it to fifteen minutes.'

Lily had shaken her head. She couldn't see the point and she doubted that there would be many who would be willing to pay the extra, even though it was so small a charge. So she'd sounded out her customers, particularly the older more careworn ones.

'I'd give me eyesight ter 'ave a few minutes peace an' quiet in a warm room. We've 'ad no fire for months!' had been the one reply she'd been looking for.

'Well, I agree with our Lily. Yer'll never be shot of 'em. Put two or three of 'em in a warm room an' yer'll never shift 'em. I'd certainly charge more than a farthin'. Make it an 'alfpenny.'

'Sometimes they haven't even got the penny, let alone a halfpenny extra.'

'Well, it's up ter you. That's just my opinion,' Ada had stated, but Hannah had gone ahead with her idea just the same.

On a particularly damp, dark March day she looked around the room with some satisfaction. It didn't look bad at all. There was lino on the floor, she'd set wooden benches in rows and a fire burned brightly in the fireplace. The room was warm and cheerful, even though there were no ornaments. That had been the one thing Ada had insisted on after Hannah had tried to talk her round.

'Leave anythin' in there that can be pinched an' they'll pinch it. It'll be a few bob in their pockets after they've pawned or sold it. I think yer're mad, Hannah, I really do. 'Aven't yer gorr enough work without this?'

'It'll only take a few minutes to clean. Mrs Kelly will do it for me. Just a quick mop over the floor, tidy up any bits of paper, wipe down the windowsill and clear out the ashes.'

'Yer too good ter that woman.'

'Maybe, but at least her kids don't go hungry.'

Lily was also admiring their handiwork and the new notice that advertised the 'Pies for a Penny', and the fact that for a farthing more you could eat them in comfort and warmth.

Ada arrived and took off her coat, hat and the muffler that covered her nose and mouth. 'Hannah, there's a letter cum ter our 'ouse fer yer,' she said, handing it over.

'Oh, it's from Vi! See the stamps?' She'd told Ada all

about her friend Vi's new life in Canada.

She scanned the lines and her eyes lit up. 'Oh, she' coming home!'

'What for?' Lily asked.

Some of Hannah's euphoria disappeared. 'Her man is very ill and so is her da. Her elder sister Alice wrote and told her and asked that if it was at all possible, she should come home.'

'She must 'ave a few bob ter be comin' 'ome.'

'She says it will take a big chunk out of their savings but that Georgie doesn't mind if she really wants to come. She's worked as hard as he has.'

' 'E sounds like a decent feller,' Ada said approvingly

'He is.'

'So when does she get 'ome then?'

'In a week, providing the weather's not too rough She says we should look in the *Journal of Commerce* and that will give us more of an idea of the exact time.'

'Why in there? What's this "commerce" to do with when she'll arrive?' Ada couldn't understand it.

'Because it gives the movements of all shipping in and out of Liverpool.'

'Well, there's not much of that these days.'

'God, I couldn't go on one of them ships, it's so far and I'd be terrified in a storm.'

'Well I wouldn't trust March weather one bit. It's bad enough on dry land,' Ada said ominously.

Hannah had no time to write to Vi but she sent a telegram at what Ada said was a ruinously expensive rate, telling her she'd go and meet her when she docked.

'Will you keep the place going for me, please?' Hannah asked of Ada and Lily, thinking she'd take Jessica with her.

'Hannah, yer should know by now that yer needn't bother ter ask questions like that.'

'I do but I won't take either of you for granted. You've been too good to me.'

'Yer like one of the family now, luv,' Ada had replied.

Hannah hugged her, touched by the words. She'd always longed for a family of her own, and her attempt at creating one had ended in disaster. Being considered part of the Sweeney clan was some consolation.

It was a cold blustery March morning. The wind was whipping up white-crested waves on the surface of the choppy grey river and howled between the buildings of the waterfront when Hannah and Jessica got off the tram at the Pier Head. Hannah was full of excitement; she'd thought she'd never see Vi again. Jessica was dressed in her best coat and hat and she had white doeskin gaiters that fastened with a row of tiny buttons up the side, over white knitted leggings and leather shoes. Hannah was so proud of her, she was beautiful and very bright. She'd do well at whichever school Hannah chose to send her to.

'Come on, take Mam's hand and hold on tightly,' she instructed. 'Can you see the big ship? The one painted all white but with the three yellow funnels?'

The child nodded. 'Will she like me, Mam?'

Hannah laughed. 'Of course she will! She's lovely and so are you!'

The passengers hadn't begun to disembark but the landing stage was crowded with friends and families waiting for them. There were cars and cabs awaiting the wealthier passengers and porters too to carry luggage to the boat train in the Riverside Station.

Hannah scanned the decks crowded with people that rose high above them until she caught sight of a girl waving and shouting. She picked Jessica up. 'Look! Look up there, there's your Aunty Vi! Wave to her.'

The child did and so did Hannah and she called to Vi too, but the wind was too strong and too many other people were shouting for Vi to hear anything.

When Vi finally came down the gangway with her case Hannah struggled forward through the crowd. 'Vi! Vi! Over here!'

Vi grinned and pushed her way through. 'Hannah! Oh, Hannah, it's great to see you! God, is this Jessica? I can't believe it, she was only a baby!' Vi hugged them both.

'She'll be four in July. Vi, I can't believe it's actually *you*!'

'Well, it is and I was never more glad to see the mucky Mersey in my entire life. God, what a crossing. We were chucked around all over the place and was I ever sick! I thought my last moments had come, but here we are.'

They walked towards the trams at the terminus, arms linked, Vi carrying her case and Hannah carrying

Jessica. The little girl wanted to walk, but Hannah said no. 'You'll get your lovely shoes and gaiters all dirty. Let Mam carry you until we get on a tram.'

'No! I want to get down, Mam!'

'Well, you can't so don't start to be a naughty girl.'

'Oh, you can see who she takes after all right,' Vi laughed. ' 'Er grandma was just the same!'

'Will you come home with me first or do you want to go straight on?'

'I'd think it would be best if I went straight home, Hannah. I'll come tonight.'

Hannah nodded. 'How are they both?'

'I don't really know. I've had our Alice's letter for nearly three weeks but I think someone would have sent me a telegram or been there to meet me if . . . if . . . well, you know.'

'I do, Vi. But, think about it, at least you had them for all your life.'

Vi nodded, thinking how awful it must have been for Hannah to lose her mam and then her da while she was so young.

'I'll come down tonight, Hannah. I'll see you too, Jessica, and I've got something nice for you.'

'Oh, Vi, you shouldn't have. It must have been expensive to come back.'

'It's nothing much, Hannah, really it isn't.'

'What is it, Aunty Vi?'

'It's a secret so you'll have to wait until I come to your house, and you'd better be a good girl for your mam too.'

Jessica looked at her new 'aunty' solemnly.

'God, Hannah, she looks just like you even though she's got his hair and skin colour.'

'She's got my temper and stubbornness unfortunately. I'll see you tonight.' They embraced before Vi got on board her tram and Hannah walked the short distance to hers.

'Can we meet her?' Lily asked when she got back and there was a lull in business which they knew from experience wouldn't last long.

'Of course, if you want to.'

'Did she say what it was like living over there?'

'No, she didn't really have time. She wanted to get straight home. She said the crossing was terrible though.'

'I told yer it would be,' Ada said with some satisfaction. 'Did she say 'ow 'er mam an' da are?'

'No, but there'd been no telegram so she took that as a good sign. And nobody came to meet her.'

'Well, that's very nice, isn't it? The girl comes halfway across the flamin' world, at God knows what cost, an' nobody even goes ter meet 'er. Oh, very thoughtful, that is,' Ada said scathingly.

'Do you think you could get those things off Jessica before they're filthy? I have the feeling that if I try there will be tears. She knows she can't get away with murder with you. She plays me up.'

'That's because yer're too soft with 'er an' she knows it. I know yer're proud of 'er, Hannah, an' that yer love 'er, but sometimes they needs a firm 'and.'

* * *

They'd finished work for the day. The lobby floor had been swept and mopped, the board 'counter' had been scrubbed, the cloth put in to soak. Mrs Kelly had cleaned out the front room and had gone home to a warm house with some brisket and kidney, the remnants of the fillings that really couldn't be kept overnight.

Jessica was ready for bed but was allowed to wait up for Vi. Ada said she was worn out and that once they'd met Vi, both she and Lily would go home.

'Eh, Mam, I want to ask her loads of questions!' Lily protested.

'Well, they'll have ter wait. Give 'em some time ter 'ave a good jangle, they 'aven't seen each other fer ages. Yer'll come 'ome with me,' Ada stated firmly.

Lily raised her eyes to the ceiling and pursed her lips.

'An' it's no good pullin' faces an' sulkin', Lily!' Ada reprimanded her daughter sharply.

Vi arrived at a quarter past seven.

'God, I'd forgotten how flaming damp it is here. We get snow and ice but it's a sort of "dry" cold, not dampness that gets into your bones.'

She handed her coat and hat to Hannah who hung them up.

' 'Ow is yer mam and da, luv? I'm Ada Sweeney an' this is our Lily.'

Vi nodded. 'I know, Hannah's mentioned you lots of times. Da's not too bad. It's his chest, he finds it hard to breathe. It's all those years working on and off on that coal cart. But Mam . . . well, I don't think she'll last much longer,' she finished with a catch in her voice.

'Oh, Vi, I'm so sorry, I really am.'

'That's all right, Hannah. I know that you for one really understand and I don't want her to go on suffering the way she is. So I might be here for longer than I intended. But never mind my troubles, let's talk about something else. Have you been a good girl for your mam, Jessica?'

Jessica nodded.

'She's been as good as gold all afternoon,' Ada confirmed.

Vi drew a brown paper bag out of the bag she was carrying. 'Then she can have this.'

The child tore the bag open impatiently. Inside was a small doll, dressed like a sailor, complete with navy blue velvet bellbottoms and tight tunic with the white collar. On its head was a white hat bearing the words 'S.S. *Empress of Scotland*' in gold embroidered letters.

'Oh, Vi, it's much too good! It must have cost a small fortune!'

'Not as much as you'd think, Hannah. It's just something a bit different.'

'Give Aunty Vi a big kiss and say thank you,' Hannah instructed her daughter.

Jessica did so and Vi caught her and held her closely, releasing her with reluctance.

'Now then, Lily will take 'er to bed and then we'll

gerroff 'ome, Hannah, luv. Let yer 'ave some time tergether. I'll send our Harry down early in the mornin' with my batch of stuff.'

'Thanks,' Hannah said with a smile.

She put the kettle on and made a pot of tea after Lily and Ada had gone.

'Oh, it's great to get a decent cup of tea. That was the first thing I asked our Alice for. I couldn't even keep a cup of tea down on the ship. That's one of the "down" things about home. You can't get a proper cup of tea anywhere. Our Alice sometimes sends me a packet of tea, though you're not supposed to send stuff like that in the post.' Vi sipped her tea with relish. 'Heaven!' she declared.

'So, tell me all about *everything*. I saw you hang on to Jessica. Does that perhaps mean . . .?'

'Yes, oh, yes it does, Hannah. I'm having a baby. I haven't told Georgie yet or he'd never have let me come over.'

Hannah grinned. 'You should have told him but maybe just before you went up the gangway – he couldn't have done much about it then. Oh, I'm so happy for you, Vi, I really am. You seem to be doing well too,' she added, having taken in the good warm winter coat, the fashionable hat and the blue and cream suit Vi was wearing.

'We have. It's been hard work, Hannah, for us both, but we've saved like mad and it's not as expensive to live over there as it is here, although that might not last. I don't understand all the ins and outs that have caused the Depression but it seems to be bad here and in America, so the newspapers say.'

'It is, but have you enough saved for your house? Imagine – "*your* house".'

'Well, we will have to save a bit more now but yes, and we've seen just what we want. It's only small but it has a porch, a big kitchen and a living room, three bedrooms and a bathroom with a toilet, a tub and a hand washbasin. Then there's the basement. There's plenty of room for washing and storing things. Some people use it as another bedroom or sitting room or just for the kids to play in in winter. And, best of all, it's got a biggish yard out back.'

'A garden?'

'Yes. Oh, Hannah, it's so different from here. It's so clean, there's so much space, and the orchards are huge and in spring the blossom is just gorgeous. Georgie and I went to Toronto on a special outing last Christmas. It was really something to see, Hannah. And the lake! It's not like a lake is here, just a few miles of water. It's huge, it's like a sea. They have big ships sailing on it.'

'You sound as though you really love it.'

'I do. We both do. There's no traffic noise, things don't get covered in soot in a matter of months, the air is fresh and there isn't any fog. Well, hardly any. It's not like it is here where you can't see or breathe, it's just a mist. You should come – you'd love it.'

'Maybe one day for a holiday, Vi, but not now.'

'You're doing well, Hannah, why don't you expand?'

'Expand?'

'Yes, get a couple of other places, say over in the Scotland Road, Netherfield Road area.'

'I'd never thought of that. I'm having difficulty keeping up with the demand as it is.'

'Pay someone to run them for you. Sell tea and soup and bread as well or instead of pies, for . . . I don't know, a halfpenny?'

'Vi, you don't know just how desperate things are here. This city is on its knees.'

'Then help it out. Help people, Hannah, even if they haven't got much money. You could even open your own bakery. It would be a big decision but it would be cheaper in the long run. Just something small with a handful of workers. Think about that!'

'I would *really* have to think about that, Vi.'

Vi nodded and sipped her tea.

'Do you ever think of "him", Hannah?' she asked uncertainly.

'Not often these days. I *had* to come back to Ada's, I wrote and told you why.'

'But you still love him. I can tell.'

'I'll always love him, but I can never have him and after Alfie . . . well . . .'

'Once bitten twice shy. But someone will come along, one day, Hannah.'

Hannah shook her head. 'No. No, I can never love another man. Richard is . . . always will be the only one.'

Vi nodded her understanding. 'In that case, you'd

better take the plunge and expand. It will keep your mind off him.'

Hannah nodded too as she finished her tea. She felt younger and full of enthusiasm. It must be seeing Vi, it was just like the old days at Faulkner Square.

Chapter Twenty-Seven

'I can't justify spending so much money when people are starving,' Hannah said firmly to Lily. The day's business had finished and Lily and Hannah were stacking the pennies, halfpennies and farthings into piles, ready to fill the little bags from the bank. Everyone in the bank knew her well now; on Mondays she always took food in with her and they in turn often sent the office boy to her with large orders. They were one of her biggest customers for it wasn't only the poor and starving who came to her door, there were men and lads from the coal merchant's, tram drivers and conductors, postmen and telegraph boys, even – since the incident with Jack Duggan – the bobbies on the beat who swore her pies were the best they'd ever tasted, better even than their wives and mothers made. She had a two-tier system of payment and everyone knew about it. All the men in steady employment paid her fourpence, the same price as was charged in the shops.

Lily was persistent. 'I know it seems extravagant, Hannah, but it wouldn't be much really and she *is* four, she's not a baby any more.'

Hannah shook her head. This birthday party was all Lily's idea, thank God she'd not mentioned it to Jessica.

She couldn't help but think back to the party Jessica had had at Y-Garn or the memory of Richard standing so close to her as they'd both looked down on the sleeping child. Oh, she could have murdered Lily, not just for the idea of the party but because of the memories she'd tried, and almost succeeded, in banishing from her mind. Memories of a warm summer evening, the sweet smells of the garden that had crept into the bedroom through the open door and window and the scent of Richard. That indefinable, impossible-to-describe scent and the words: 'There will always be a place in my heart for you.' It all tore at her heartstrings and made her ache for him as she lay in bed at night, listening to Jessica's quiet, regular breathing.

'No, Lily, and that's final. She has so much more than any other child I know.'

'Now what's she doin'?' Ada asked, coming in from the yard with beads of sweat on her forehead and an armful of clean dry clothes and table linen.

'She wants me to give Jessica a birthday party.'

'A what? 'Ave yer gone mad, Lily? There's kids droppin' like flies from 'unger, aye, an' women too, an' yer want Hannah ter go wastin' money on a flamin' party, ter go flyin' in the face of God, more like! Oh, yer've gorra very short memory, Lily Sweeney. Many's the time yer went barefoot an' 'ungry yerself.'

Lily was contrite. 'I know, Mam. It was a daft idea.'

'Too flamin' right it was. I would 'ave thought yer would be helpin' Hannah as much as yer can with this bakery if yer've nothing else ter occupy yer mind. Now give us an' and ter fold this lot.'

Hannah sighed. She'd promised Vi before she sailed for home that she would give it a try. She'd searched for the right premises until she'd found a half-falling-down old block of stables which, after she'd finished with it, was just right, not too big, not too small. It hadn't been hard to find good workmen either. It was pitiful to see proud men almost begging for work. Materials too were cheap: there were few buyers. Over the weeks as the bakery began to take shape she tried to go down once a day, usually at lunchtime with pies, bread, soup and tea.

'God, missus, yer're a saint, that's what yer are,' one of the men had said to her once.

'I'm far from that,' she'd replied, 'but I know what it's like to live on charity. I was brought up in a workhouse. If I could give work to every man in this city I would. It's a terrible thing to see men brought so low.'

Now the bakery was almost finished and she and Ada and Martha had chosen the women and girls who were to staff it carefully. For a week they'd crowded Hannah's kitchen and watched, then practised the baking skills Hannah passed on to them. Vi's idea of selling soup and bread and tea had taken hold too and she now had Lily in charge of another house, the kitchen, scullery and front room of which she rented in Watkinson Street, the next street along. She didn't feel as though she was exploiting the poor as one man from the Health and Sanitary Board had suggested. But he'd been unable to find anything wrong and had left with a flea in his ear, not only from herself but from Ada too. His words upset her for a few days, though.

'Take no flamin' notice of that feller. He just 'ad a cob on 'cos 'e couldn't find anything ter complain about. "The poor" don't mind bein' ex—ex—that word he said, norras long as they can get somethin' ter eat. That feller never went ter bed 'ungry, I'd stake me life on it,' Ada had said.

Her thoughts returned to the present. 'There's something I've been wanting to say to you for a while now.'

'Oh, aye, what's up with yer now?' Ada asked.

'Once I've got everything sorted out and running smoothly I'm thinking of moving.'

'Where to?' Lily demanded.

'Oh, not far, just to a better area. Somewhere where there's a bit of greenery and fresher air.'

'Fresher air in Liverpool? The birds don't sing around 'ere, they cough like the rest of us,' Ada said scathingly.

'I'd settle for just the greenery and a bigger house. Nothing too grand.'

'Well, there's Cairns Street an' Arundel Street off Granby Street, that leads up to the park,' Ada suggested.

'Yes, I used to push Jessica in there when she was very small. It was nice but the houses are too big.'

'I'm not talkin' about them on Princes Road an' Princes Avenue. Why don't yer take Jessica an' this daft ha'porth of mine up there on Sunday afternoon, if the weather 'olds. It's "'eadache" weather, we'll 'ave a storm before long, mark my words.'

The weather did hold and so on a very hot humid afternoon they took the tram to Princes Avenue and walked up to Cairns Street which wasn't far from Princes Park.

'It's dead posh, Hannah,' Lily said, overawed. She wouldn't like to live around here; there were no kids playing out, no women standing on their doorsteps, and it was very quiet.

'They're like the houses in the squares but smaller.'

'There's a feller cutting the hedge over there, ask him if there's any to rent, like.'

Hannah nodded and they all crossed the road.

'Excuse me, could you tell me if any of the houses around here are vacant? I'd like to rent something.'

He wiped the sweat from his brow with the back of his hand. 'There's none 'ere, luv, but there might be one in Cawdor Street.'

'Where's that?' she asked.

'Two streets away. Do you want me to make enquiries?'

'Would you? I'd be so grateful.'

'What's your name an' where can I get hold of you?'

'It's Mrs Hannah Duggan.' Oh, she hated that name so much. 'And I live in number fourteen Norfolk Street, or you can ask at number twenty Victoria Terrace. It's quite all right, I can afford it,' she added, seeing the look of suspicion cross his face at the mention of her present address. 'I own Peckham's Bakery.'

He nodded and they walked on.

'The nerve of him! Did you see his face?'

'I did, but there's no reason to be ashamed of living in either Norfolk Street or Victoria Terrace. I wonder if he will find out or will he not bother. Come on, let's go to the park, it'll be cool under the trees and there's bound to be ducks on the lake which will keep milady here quiet for half an hour.'

'Can I feed them, Mam?' the child asked.

'We've nothing to feed them with, but if we come here again we'll bring something.'

It was the following week when Ada informed her that a feller had been looking for her at the bakery, so young Eileen Hayes had said. Eileen nodded shyly.

'Did he say what his name was?'

'No, just that 'e's the gardener you spoke to last Sunday.'

'Well, did he say where I could get in touch with him, Eileen?'

'No. All he said was, "Tell her that number eight Cawdor Street is up for rent. It's Coburg and Watkinson's Estate Agents in Old Hall Street that have the key." Then he went off.'

'I'll go first thing on Monday morning and get the key and have a look around.'

'And don't let them rob yer, Hannah.'

'I won't,' she'd answered firmly. She now felt she had as good a business brain as any man. Sometimes she stopped and reflected on just how far she'd come in life. If someone had told her four years ago that she would have her own business and be employing people, she would never have believed them. In four short years she'd had a child, become a widow, gone back to work in service and now . . . it was only a short time but sometimes it felt like years.

On Monday morning it was still very hot. As she set off, although it was early she felt the sweat begin to trickle down the back of her neck and she wished she didn't have to wear a hat, even the very light straw she had on. But no one of any standing went out without a hat and she knew it finished off her smart outfit. She particularly liked the pale apple-green cotton dress whose hemline came to her calves because of the square neckline and the white sailor collar. She'd seen it in the window of Frisby Dykes in Lord Street and she'd gone straight in and bought it. 'It might have been made for Madam,' so the saleswoman had said. It was ages since she'd bought a dress. She always made her own and Jessica's and she helped Lily to make her clothes too, when she had time. Her life was terribly full but that was deliberate. She'd made it so to keep her mind from wandering down paths that were so painful. At the end of the day she was too exhausted to dredge up memories.

One look at her and the young man at Coburg and Watkinson's handed her a key and asked if she would like him to accompany her. She'd refused politely. She wanted to get the feel of the house. It was so important.

She wanted something of the atmosphere of Y-Garn. Oh, she knew that that was a big, rambling house, this was small by comparison, but she wanted somewhere where people had been happy. She didn't want somewhere soulless or cold.

She got off the tram and began to walk down Granby Street counting the side roads off as she passed them. Cawdor Street was the seventh on the right. Was it a lucky number, she wondered idly? She would be glad to get inside and out of the fierce heat.

The house didn't look in any way dilapidated or unkempt. She deliberately hadn't asked what the rent was, she wanted to see it first. It was a sort of yardstick on which she could gauge her success.

A long, narrow path led up to the front door. The small garden was a little overgrown but a riot of colour. The house was a red brick Victorian villa type. She looked upwards, judged it to have three storeys and then thought it probably had a cellar too. The bay windows both upstairs and downstairs were wide; it was quite a substantial house. There probably wouldn't be any furniture but that didn't bother her. She wanted to pick for herself the things that would make the house a 'home'. A decent home of her own at last.

The windows were all clean, the paint on the front door was glossy, the brass letter box and knocker were only slightly tarnished. She put the key into the lock and turned it.

'Hannah! Hannah!'

She turned quickly and her stomach turned over.

'Hannah, I thought it was you. I'd recognise you anywhere.' Richard Hughes was smiling with genuine pleasure as he came up the path.

'Mr Richard. I . . . I . . .' she stammered, thrown completely into shock at his sudden, unexpected appearance.

'Is this where you are living now, Hannah? Siân said you wouldn't go back with her.'

She nodded; she couldn't trust herself to speak. Things had been going so well lately, why did he have to keep turning up like the proverbial bad penny? Except that he wasn't bad, she thought. That was one of the things that had drawn her to him. He was a good man who had never changed and she still loved him so much.

'How long have you been here? I've just called on a patient. I was getting into the car when I caught a glimpse of you and came back.'

She swallowed hard. 'I don't live here, yet. I only came to view it.'

'Oh, and do you think you'll take it?'

'I don't know.' He was smiling down at her, his eyes full of interest and happiness. He was genuinely glad to see her, she thought.

'Have you been inside?'

'No, not yet.'

'Well then, open the door and we can both get out of this infernal sun.'

The hall was cool and shadowy. The sunlight coming through the stained-glass oriel window on the staircase wall threw coloured patterns on to the floor. She didn't

want it to be like this. She had wanted to wande
around alone. Hadn't she turned down the estat
agent's offer? Oh, why, why, why had he just bee
passing? 'If you don't mind, I'd ... I'd like to loo
around by myself.'

'Of course I don't mind. Oh, Hannah, I'm sorry t
force myself on you like this. I'll wait here, it's cool. I'
sit on the stairs, if that's all right?'

She nodded and made her way through the groun
floor rooms. They were all nicely decorated and clea
but she couldn't concentrate properly. She stood b
the french window looking at the back garden. Fo
once she wished he would go away.

'Well, how does the ground floor rate then?' he aske
as she came back into the hall. She seemed to hav
grown more beautiful, more poised and she was we
dressed now. She didn't look like anyone's servant an
more.

'It's ... it's fine. Would you ... mind?'

He got to his feet to let her pass.

When she reached the upstairs landing she caugh
hold of the banister rail tightly. She was going to fain
– but she couldn't let that happen. She *couldn't*! H
would have to come upstairs to revive her and he woul
have to hold her. The dizziness made her sway but sh
fought it down. No! No! That wasn't going to happen
She made her way around the bedrooms and bathroom
in a daze, then she retraced her steps.

He got up as she came down. 'Does it pas
inspection?'

He was smiling at her and she pulled herself together. She wasn't going to appear so young and awkward as she'd been when last she'd seen him.

'I think I'll take it. It depends on the rent.'

She made for the front door.

'Hannah, wait. Can I give you a lift in the car, back to . . .?'

'Thank you, but no!' She didn't want him to drop her off in Norfolk Street.

'Well then, it's a shame for us not to catch up on . . . things.' He sat down on the wide stair and indicated she should sit beside him.

She hesitated, then came back, folded her skirt and sat down. She tried to make sure there was no bodily contact between them.

'So, you look as though you're doing very well.'

'I am, thanks to Mrs Howard and Vi and some very hard work,' she said proudly. She *was* proud of her achievements.

He looked puzzled.

She looked at him, then forced herself to look away. 'I now own a bakery. I started my own canteen or cannie as it's called, not long after I came back to Liverpool. Mrs Howard taught me how to bake, so I made pies and sold them from my doorstep. People were desperate then, they're even more so these days but I don't charge much. Just a penny. I have two places now, I sell soup, bread and a mug of tea for a halfpenny too. It works very well so when Vi – Violet Rowan, you remember? – came home from Canada she persuaded me to open my own bakery.' She smiled at the memory.

'Yes, Rowan always seemed like a girl with good ideas and common sense.'

'She is, I think Canada suits her. Her husband's got a good job on the railways and they are about to buy their own house.'

'Really?'

She nodded.

'And what about Jessica? How old is she now?'

'Four and a little madam she is too. It's Ada . . . Mrs Sweeney who seems to be able to cope with her best. She's a bright child, she's ready for school now.'

Richard looked down at his hands, remembering how lovely the two-year-old Jessica had been. He and Maria had no children – yet.

'How is . . . your wife?' She couldn't say Maria. It was stupid, she knew, but she just couldn't do it.

'She's very well. She . . . We're having a baby, in a couple of weeks now, so please God all will be well this time.'

'Why?'

'Because she's lost three.'

She heard the note of sadness and regret in his voice. 'I'm sorry. I really do mean that.'

'I know you do, Hannah.' He paused. 'I don't suppose I have the right to know but I never really found out what happened to your husband. You left and then I didn't hear of you again until you went to Siân in Wales, but there was a suggestion that things hadn't gone very well for you.'

Now she looked down at her hands, twisting them together nervously. She didn't want to tell him, but she felt so tired: tired of keeping her feelings for him in check. There was no reason why he shouldn't know how much she'd suffered. It was all in the past now.

'He died of the cold. He froze to death. He was drunk – he was always drunk – and he gambled and he beat me. I . . . I'd had enough. He'd beaten me badly and then he tried to hurt Jessica. I fought as hard as I could and finally he left me alone, staggered down the lobby and fell, unconscious, on the front steps. I . . . I . . . left him there to die. It was Mr Donaldson who took me in and then sent me to Miss Siân.' She looked up at him, almost defiantly. 'So, now you know my secret.'

He remained silent. No one, not even his sister, had made any mention of all this. He was shocked and appalled.

She plunged on. He might as well know everything. 'So now I live in a house by the Queens Dock, a house in the slums, where I came from. I was born in Victoria Terrace. I'm as much a "slummy" as any shawlie. But I want the best for Jessica, that's why I've worked so hard and why I now want to rent this house, or one like it. It's for her, so she'll live in a nice neighbourhood, near the park, and go to school here too.' She stood up and smoothed down her skirt. 'I'd better take the key back. It was . . . nice to see you again and I hope everything goes well this time.'

He smiled at her wonderingly. She was such an enigma to him. She'd had a terrible life and yet she seemed to have the courage to rise above everything, the kind of courage he knew he didn't have. It made him feel humble. She'd had nothing in life except what she'd fought and worked for and now she seemed to have come out on top. But was she happy? He wasn't sure. Certainly he'd had everything he could have wished for in material terms but he couldn't swear that he was either happy or content. And she had the one thing he longed for: a child.

He followed her out and waved before getting into his car and driving off. She clung to the gate and then the tears began to fall. She could never forget him, no matter how hard she tried. But had fate played another cruel trick on her by this chance meeting so he could tell her that Maria was going to have their baby? Because of that he was even further out of her reach than ever.

Chapter Twenty-Eight

In the weeks that followed, Hannah tried so hard to forget that meeting and the knowledge that he would soon become a father. Often, though, at night, she would lie awake wondering whether it would be a son or a daughter. Would it be a boy with his stature and looks or a girl who resembled her pretty mother? Either way it would be showered with love, comforts, gifts, the best that money could buy. That child wouldn't be born in a hospital to a poverty-stricken mother and a drunken, violent father. They would bring someone to their house to look after it, not the other way around. That child would never be fed laudanum as Jessica had been, nor its cries met with annoyance or indifference. There would be a fancy and expensive crib, not a drawer lined with cotton. He would make a good father and his own father would be happy too; it would be Ellis Hughes's first grandchild. She knew that he would want a boy to carry on the family name.

During the day she seldom had time to think of him. She was choosing furniture and curtain fabrics, thick fluffy bath towels and all the other things that they'd never had. She still had five of the gold sovereigns Siân had given her; and these she was saving for Jessica for she couldn't now envisage a future filled with want and hardship. When the Depression was over, and surely it *must* be soon, she intended to open a proper café, maybe two or even three, selling simple meals in clean and bright premises at a price most ordinary working people could afford. 'Peckham's Pantries', they would be called, a name Vi had suggested in her last letter. They wrote frequently and in great detail to each other and some day, when Jessica was older, she intended to go and visit Vi. A long sea voyage would be too much for a child so young to undertake. Many children did go, but not to visit – to live.

Ada and Martha had come to help her move. She'd spent hours sewing curtains and cushion covers on the Singer treadle sewing machine she'd bought cheaply. There was so little money around these days that almost anything could be bought for half its original price. All the pawnbrokers and second-hand shops were bursting with things desperate people had taken to them. Many were not now buying or taking anything else. She'd got a good deal on the furniture and the curtain materials.

''Ow the 'ell are yer goin' ter put those curtains up? That winder's a terrible height,' Ada asked, frowning as she looked upwards.

'I'll get a step ladder and if I can't manage I'll get one of the men who are coming to deliver the furniture to put them up.'

'They'll take some cleanin', Hannah, will them winders,' Martha added. She'd never seen a house with so many rooms before.

'The two of yer will be rattlin' around the place, it's so big,' Ada had commented when she'd first come to see it.

'An' all that cream paint will show every dirty mark, yer'll spend yer time cleanin', Hannah,' Martha had added.

But Hannah loved the brightness of the house. She was sick of dark greens and browns which often disguised damp patches. The high ceilings, with their moulded ceiling roses, the light-coloured wallpapers and the cream paintwork all made it seem much bigger than it really was. She especially loved the room that opened on to the garden. It was such a pleasure not to have to look out on a back yard with a privy and it was somewhere where Jessica could play in safety. The flowers, shrubs and roses were her special delight and she was looking forward to sitting by the french windows on the warm summer nights.

'Hannah, them fellers with the furniture 'ave arrived,' Ada called and she went through into the hall. ''Ow much did yer buy, the whole shop?' Ada commented as the men began to unload the van.

'I didn't have much in Norfolk Street so I needed a lot of things and I've got two bedrooms that will have no furniture in them at all. I needed a new table and chairs for the kitchen, I'll probably spend most of my time in there.'

'So what do yer want that big posh one with the six chairs for?'

'It's for the dining room. I'll probably never need to

use it but, well . . .' she shrugged.

Ada exchanged looks with Martha. She knew where Hannah got these ideas from – Mr Ellis Hughes's houses. They were far too grand for the likes of herself although Lily was getting some fancy ideas lately. 'I'm nor 'avin' yer turning inter a snob, Lily Sweeney!' had been her final words in the last argument they'd had.

'Oh, I like this, Hannah. A good bit of material, this is.' Martha fingered the sofa cover. It was a heavy chintz printed with red and pink roses and peonies.

'Right, missus, if you'll tell us where to put the rest of the stuff we'll take it upstairs, then we wouldn't mind a cuppa, if you don't mind, like. Thirsty work this.'

'Don't be so 'ardfaced, youse. Yer should be glad of the "thirsty work" an' the wage at the end of it, never mind askin' fer tea,' Ada said cuttingly.

'It's all right,' Hannah said hurriedly. 'I'd intended to give you some beer. I got a jug from the pub on the corner of Granby Street, it's keeping cool in the larder.'

'God bless you, missus,' the workmen replied with a look of triumph directed at Ada.

'It's one of 'er failin's, she's a soft touch an' some people know it!' Ada said to Martha in a loud voice.

Later on Lily arrived bringing Jessica with her. Mrs Kelly had been minding the child, and Mary Kelly, her eldest daughter, had been put into the cannie in Norfolk Street to serve while Hannah, Ada and Martha were in Cawdor Street.

'God, isn't it big!' Lily exclaimed, wide-eyed.

'Don't you be takin' the Lord's name in vain, Lily Sweeney, an' yes it's big. Don't we know that, Martha, us havin' dragged furniture around all day?'

'Go and see the garden while I make everyone a cup of tea,' Ada instructed her astonished daughter.

'Is this where we're going to live now, Mam?'

Hannah smiled at Jessica. 'Yes it is, you can play in the garden all day and after we've had our tea I'll show you your room.'

'Is it a surprise, Mam?' Jessica asked, jumping up and down.

'Yes, it is. Go on now.' She gave the child a gentle push into the garden.

'Wouldn't yer think yer was in the country, Ada? Not that I've ever been ter the country but I've seen pictures, like. Yer wouldn't think yer were in Liverpool at all.'

The daylight was slowly fading as, tired and hot, they drank their tea sitting on the kitchen chairs Hannah had set outside on the paved area that led down to the gently sloping lawn. It was at least cooler outside now the fierce heat of August was passing. Hannah was looking forward to September and October. She loved the autumn.

'Yer don't intend ter see ter this garden yerself, do yer?' Ada questioned her.

'No, although I'd love to. I've no time, so I've got a gardener cum odd-job man.'

'We could 'ave done with that feller terday,' Ada said, rubbing the back of her neck. She was getting stiff. 'Still, we've managed. Yer mam and da would be dead proud of yer now, Hannah. No one from our street 'as ever come up in the world like youse 'ave.'

'It's more than I ever had in my life before. But I'll still be working, to pay for it all. It's taken almost every penny I had to buy all this and I'm going to save hard from now on.'

Both older women nodded their agreement. They had very little by comparison and yet their own homes had been improved, with Hannah's help, over the years. They had more comforts now than they'd ever had, they didn't have to worry about coal and light and food any more. Both were now able to be generous to their unfortunate neighbours.

Jessica came towards them, a huge bunch of flowers in her arms. She dropped them all on Hannah's knee. 'I picked them for you, Mam. Can I see my bedroom now?'

Hannah rose, gathering up the flowers. 'Lily, will you put these in some water for me? They're lovely. Flowers from my own garden. I'd never have believed it.' As she took her daughter's hand she remembered how much Siân had loved flowers in the house.

'Can I come and see too?' Lily asked.

'Of course you can, your mam and Martha have already seen it.'

Lily deposited the flowers in her mother's lap and Ada tutted and looked at Martha with raised eyebrows. Lily would probably be demanding that they have flowers in their house next. She tried to copy everything Hannah did.

'Close your eyes tightly and don't open them until I tell you to,' Hannah instructed and Jessica covered her face with her hands. 'And no peeping through your fingers.'

Hannah opened the door and took Jessica's hand and led her inside.

'Now you can look.'

Jessica silently picked up the small teddy bear that Hannah had placed on the chair beside the bed and gazed around her in wonderment.

'Oh, Hannah, it's ... it's ... gorgeous!' Lily exclaimed.

The whole room had been painted white, but there was a wide wallpaper border just above the dado line. It had pink roses rambling over the letters of the alphabet which were burgundy and crimson. The bedspread was white but patterned with rosebuds as were the curtains and the cover over the chair. The window seat was covered in pink brocade and there were pink mats on the floor. The window was open and the flimsy voile curtains were moving slightly, stirred by the breeze. There was a small kidney-shaped dressing table, its frilled cover pink and white as was the matching stool. On the walls were pictures of animals and on the dressing table was a comb and mirror set, the backs of which were decorated with rosebuds.

'Hannah, she'll have it filthy in no time,' Lily cried.

It was beautiful. She'd never seen anything like it and for a child! Well, it would be wasted.

'That's exactly what your mam said plus a lot of other things about being "spoilt rotten"!'

'It's true.'

'No, I think she'll take more care of it and she obviously likes it.'

'Who wouldn't like it?' Lily said with envy. It looked like something out of a story book.

Jessica was in bed and Hannah was sitting in the garden room as she had decided to called it. At the end of a long and tiring day it was such bliss to be able to sit in here with a cup of tea and relax for a bit before she too went to bed. September had arrived and there was that first smell of autumn in the air and the dew was already heavy on the grass. It had been cut that day and the smell still lingered.

She'd finished her tea and was sitting in a sort of contented trance when she heard someone knocking on the front door. She sighed, wondering who could be calling on her at this time of night. She'd seen both Ada and Lily today so there could be nothing wrong there. She deposited her cup and saucer in the kitchen and went to open the door.

Mrs Howard stood on the doorstep and as soon as Hannah saw the expression on her face she knew something was wrong.

'Mrs Howard! What's the matter? Come in.'

Edith Howard looked at Hannah and marvelled that

this girl had once stood in her kitchen, wearing that terrible dress and awful boots, and looking so brow-beaten, tired and half starved. It didn't seem all that long ago at all. But now she was a well-dressed, poised and beautiful young woman.

'Come in and sit with me, Jessica's in bed. Will you have a cup of tea?'

Edith Howard shook her head. 'No, Hannah, I won't stay long.'

'Well, sit down and have a glass of sherry. Lily bought it. She said living in a house like this I should be able to offer guests tea or a glass of sherry. She read it somewhere.' She smiled as she remembered Ada's words on the subject of Lily's latest suggestion, though she was still worried about the reason for Mrs Howard's visit.

She led the older woman to a chair and went to fetch the sherry and the glasses while her guest took off her hat and jacket. Hannah poured them a glass each and then sat down.

'I should be coming here full of praise, admiration and happiness. And you deserve it all, Hannah, you've worked so hard all your life, half the time under the most terrible conditions.' Mrs Howard took a sip of sherry and shook her head slowly. Life was very unfair to some people.

'So, tell me what's wrong. Is it Miss Siân? Is that why you're back in Liverpool?'

'No, I'm still with Miss Siân. I managed to find a good cook for them at Faulkner Square. Both she and her little boy are doing well.'

'Oh, she has a little boy? I never knew that. She must be so happy.'

'She is and David, as she's called him, is thriving. They all love living out there. *I* love living there.'

'Then what is it? What's wrong?' All of a sudden she went cold and goosebumps appeared on her arms. Richard! Oh, what was the matter with Richard? Only Mrs Howard and Mr Donaldson knew how she felt about him. Siân, her husband Henry, Maria, Elinore Stephenson, none of them knew. What had Mrs Howard come to tell her?

'It . . . it's Mrs Hughes, Maria.'

Hannah let her breath out slowly. Thank God it wasn't Richard.

'What is it?'

Edith Howard took a drink of sherry then rooted in her pocket for a handkerchief with which to wipe her eyes. 'She . . . she's dead, Hannah.'

'No! What . . . what . . . how. . .?' She was bewildered.

The older woman sniffed. 'She was having a baby and everything was going so well—'

'I knew that,' Hannah interrupted. 'I met him the day I came to look at this house. He told me she was nearly due.'

'She was. Everyone was so delighted, she'd lost all the others.'

'He told me that too.' She was feeling calmer now. She had felt sorry for Maria, it must have been ppalling for her to lose three babies.

'She died . . . having the baby. They all did everything ossible. Mr Richard and the doctor from Rodney treet. The baby died too.' Mrs Howard dabbed her es again.

'What was it?' Hannah asked quietly.

'A little girl.' Mrs Howard dissolved into tears and annah got up and put her arms around her.

'I'm sorry, so very sorry. She really was such a nice erson. How . . . how is he taking it?'

Mrs Howard wiped her eyes. 'Badly. He hasn't poken or eaten since the funeral over ten days ago ow.'

Hannah's heart went out to him. He'd loved his wife nd he'd wanted a child desperately. She'd known that as the case ever since the day he'd stood with her ooking down at Jessica sleeping. He'd asked about ssica the day she'd met him, too. He'd lost them oth. His wife and his daughter.

'Do you want me to see him? Try to talk to him?' he knew it would be difficult for her, but she'd do it if would help.

'He always had a soft spot for you, and I know . . . ell, I know—'

'How I've always felt about him,' Hannah finished. Mrs Howard nodded.

'Do you want me to go there or should he come ere?'

'I think it would be better if you saw him in Faulkner quare. It's where he's staying. The other house is shut

up. It's the memories, you see. He won't go to M
Siân either – for the same reason. Oh, Hannah, we'
all tried. Miss Siân, Mr Thomas, the Master. Or
Arnold knows I've come here to see you, to see if .
She was so upset that she didn't notice her use of t
butler's christian name.

Hannah nodded. 'I'll come tomorrow evening.'

'I don't know if it will do any good, Hannah, b
you can try. It's terrible to see him. Miss Siân did
want to go back to Wales but her father persuaded h
in the end. There's nothing we can *do*!'

'Then I'll come at seven o'clock,' she promised.

Edith Howard finished her drink and got slowly
her feet. Hannah placed an arm around her should
as they walked down the hall.

After seeing her out Hannah returned to her cha
The garden was in darkness now: the nights we
drawing in. She refilled her glass and drained it in or
gulp, then she covered her face with her hands. O
what would she say to him? What would comfort hi
at all? How could she offer words of condolen
without betraying her love for him? Was she mad? Sl
must be crazy to have promised to see him. It would l
the hardest thing she'd ever had to do in her life. To te
him how wonderful his wife had been and that tin
would soften the pain, when all the time she'd want
say that *she* loved him, that *she'd* care for him. At la
she got to her feet, feeling chilly. She shut the doo
and pulled the curtains. She was tired but she kne
she'd get little sleep tonight.

* * *

Hannah was glad that the weather was cooler, she was tired and nervous and had felt sick all day. So much so that Ada had remarked upon it, but now as she walked towards the house that faced the little park she felt even worse. Half the night and all day she'd tried to think what she would say to him and all day it had been useless. How could she say she was so sorry when she knew deep down that Maria's death had left him a free man again. Oh, how could she even think like that? How could she be such a hypocrite? But she would have to be. It wasn't the time to tell him of her feelings.

She knocked on the back door and Blandford opened it, looking surprised to see her.

'Is someone expecting you, Hannah?'

'Yes. I . . . I know about Mrs Hughes. I've come to offer my condolences.'

She followed him into the kitchen where Elinore looked at her with surprise but neither Mr Donaldson nor Mrs Howard raised an eyebrow.

'May I . . . can I . . .?' she faltered.

'Of course you can, Hannah. I'll take you along to the drawing room myself,' Arnold Donaldson said firmly, propelling her gently to the door.

'How is he tonight?' she asked when they were in the hall.

'Just the same. He goes to work, and I suppose other people's ills and ailments take his mind off . . . things here. But he's not eaten or spoken.'

Hannah nodded. 'Don't announce me formally, please. Just open the door.'

He nodded and did as she asked, then closed the door softly behind her.

Nothing in this room had changed. It looked the same as it had done since she was last here for Miss Siân's wedding. He was standing with his back to her, looking out over the garden. He leaned against the door-frame, one hand supporting him; in the other hand he held a cigarette. Oh, she longed to run to him, to throw her arms around him, to say everything was all right now that she was here. She would look after him, she loved him and from now on she would never leave his side. But she could never do that. She took a deep breath to steady herself and she walked quietly across the room, her footsteps deadened by the thickness of the carpet.

'Richard,' she said tentatively. It was the first time she had ever addressed him by his name without the formal 'Mr' before it.

He turned slowly and she had to fight to control herself when she looked into his eyes. The sorrow she saw there was like a knife going straight through her heart.

'Hannah?'

'Yes. Yes, it's me. I came to say how sorry I am about . . . about . . . them.'

From a world that was filled with darkness and despair she had suddenly appeared and he reached out for her.

She held him in her arms as he cried brokenly on
er shoulder, his tears soaking her dress, his whole
ody shaking. Oh, so often she'd dreamed that he
ould hold her in his arms but she had never thought
 would be like this. Never ever like this! The shadow
f Maria fell between them – maybe it always would.
he held him like a mother holds a child and stroked
is hair and tried to soothe and comfort him. Her own
ears fell unheeded on to his head, she could feel both
eir hearts beating, but she couldn't hold him as a
ver now. Maybe she never would.

e was calmer when she'd left him. He'd promised to
at and take care of himself for she pressed on him the
ct that Maria wouldn't want him to be like this. And
at had been the hardest thing of all to say. She'd said
othing to anyone when she went back into the kitchen,
he just nodded at Mrs Howard, let herself out and
alked through the heavy dusk to the back door. When
he had closed it behind her she leaned her face against
 and cried brokenly. She would never come here again.
 would break her heart into little pieces.

Chapter Twenty-Nine

'Mam, can we go to the park?' Jessica asked of Hannah who was trying to work out some form of costings for her new business venture. The top of the table was covered with lists of expenses and items of furniture and kitchen utensils.

'Do we really have to? Mam is busy.'

'But it's ages since we went there and I like feeding the ducks.'

Hannah sighed and looked at her daughter. In the dark eyes she saw a mirror image of herself at Jessica's age: mischief and mutiny mixed. Next month she would be five and in September she would start school. Hannah looked out on to the garden. As usual it had a calming effect on her. She'd spent a lot of time in it after she'd gone to Faulkner Square that terrible night. She'd pruned roses and shrubs, overseen by the gardener. She'd weeded and planted, again aided by the gardener for, as she said to Ada, 'Left to myself I wouldn't know a weed from a flower.' She'd even dug and planted a new border, all that and work every day. But it had been what she needed. She was always too exhausted to think of Richard Hughes. She'd kept in touch with Mrs Howard who passed on any news to her. Miss Siân was having another baby. Mr Thomas had at last found himself a wealthy wife, much to everyone's relief, and Richard, well, he too seemed to be throwing himself into his work.

'Oh, Mam, it's a nice sunny day and soon I won't be able to go anywhere, I'll be at school.'

Hannah pushed the clutter on the table away and stood up. Jessica was right, it was a beautiful June morning and once she did start school, outings like this would be confined to weekends and holidays. She shouldn't put work before her child.

'All right, go and get a slice of bread and break it up into little bits.'

'Just one slice?'

'Yes. It's a terrible waste when there are children still going hungry. I keep telling you how lucky you are. Go and put on your sun bonnet.'

'Do I have to?' Jessica complained. She hated wearing hats of any kind, but Mam always insisted.

'Yes you do. You'll get sunstroke and then you'll be sick.'

'Aunty Ada never makes me wear it.'

'Well, I'm your Mam, not Aunty Ada.' She made a mental note to ask Ada to make sure she wore it in future. Hannah put on her own hat, a pale, honey coloured Bankok straw with a wide brim and a pale blue ribbon trim. She wore a pale blue cotton dress, cool for summer, and beige shoes with her favourite T strap fastening.

The park was quite empty at this time in the morning, but it was the nicest part of the day, Hannah thought. Everything was fresh looking, the leaves on the trees and the grass still glistened with dew.

'Why didn't you bring that hoop I bought you? The one you made such a fuss about?'

Jessica shrugged. 'I'd sooner feed the ducks.'

Hannah pursed her lips. Maybe she was spoiling Jessica too much. They walked along the pathway down to the lake which shimmered in the morning sunlight; there were still a few wisps of mist drifting over it.

'Don't throw it all in at once. Go around to the other side too, that way they'll all get some. Not just the greedy ones.'

Hannah sat down on a bench and watched the child. Once again she reflected that everything she had, everything she'd worked so hard for was for Jessica. And she was growing up to be a beautiful child. Her light brown hair was worn in ringlets, her fair complexion would soon become a honey colour with the sun and her big brown eyes, fringed with dark lashes, were the first thing people noticed about her, often complimenting her on the fact. Everything Hannah had done in her life was for Jessica. Her thoughts returned once more to the plans for opening her first proper café. She'd managed to save quite a bit of money and Mr Donaldson had gone with her to see the bank manager to see if they would give her a loan to help her get started. The bank manager had seen his way clear to lend her the money and seemed impressed when she outlined her plans to open more of them. She was a good customer. There was another matter on her mind too. Vi had written pleading with her to go and visit. She'd written back saying she'd love to but she was very busy.

'Yer're not *that* busy. Yer employ people to run things for yer. Why don't yer go? 'Ave a bit of an 'oliday, like,' Ada had encouraged her.

'It's a long way to go for a holiday.'

'Yer've never had an 'oliday of any kind.'

'Neither have you,' she countered.

'Well, that's different. I don't want an 'oliday. No, a day trip out to Llandudno or the Isle of Man is as far as I'd go.'

'But what about my new idea? I've done a lot of work on it, you know that.'

'Well, it'll wait. It's waited this long,' had been the final word on the subject.

Now she sat in the shade of a huge willow. She turned the matter over in her mind. Should she go? Would her new plans wait? She'd love to see Vi again. To see her house and her little boy, and Vi was expecting again. She would never forget the sight of Vi in her wedding dress, still clutching her bouquet, going up the gangway to a rousing cheer from the crowd. Oh, how desperate she'd been that day, clutching her sick daughter, struggling with her alone. Things were so much better now. Maybe she would go, later in the year when she'd got her new venture off the ground. Yes, she'd write and tell Vi she'd go over in October or November. She obviously wouldn't see the countryside at its best, but she would be going to see Vi.

She watched Jessica run around to the side of the lake followed by a line of ducks. She smiled; it was comical to watch, rather like the Pied Piper of Hamelin from one of Jessica's story books. As she continued to watch she noticed a man standing on the grass verge, watching her daughter. At this distance she couldn't see his face. She got to her feet. There were so few people in the park at this time of day and she was suspicious of strangers, something she'd tried to instil into her daughter. 'Never take any sweets from a man or boy you don't know and don't speak or go off with them, no matter what they tell you. Remember that, Jessica. It's very important.' She had never quite got over her fear of the Duggan family even though Ada had said they'd cause no more trouble. After all, Jessica had a lot of Duggan aunts and uncles and cousins. There was a whole tribe of them and if they knew she had money they'd demand some of it, or else – what?

He was still watching Jessica as she drew closer, her brow furrowed in a frown, a demand for an explanation on the end of her tongue. Then she stopped dead, her hand going to her throat. It was Richard Hughes. She didn't know what to do. Should she turn and walk away? He obviously wouldn't hurt her child. Maybe she should go and confront him? Before she could make a decision he turned and caught sight of her. It was too late to walk away now.

'Hannah? I thought you must be here somewhere. There's only one person she could be. She has the most beautiful eyes.'

She smiled. 'Thank you, but I'm afraid she knows it.' She clasped her hands behind her back so he wouldn't see them trembling – he always had this effect on her. 'How . . . how are you?'

'Much better now. I never thanked you for coming to the house to see me.' Strangely he wasn't embarrassed, although he felt he should have been, a grown man sobbing in her arms like a child.

'Oh, that was nothing. Mrs Howard came for me, they were all so worried about you and we've . . . well, we've been . . . friends. We have for a long time.'

He was remembering how she'd looked the first time he'd seen her, and after that bit of trouble with Tom; how she'd become so upset when she'd heard of his engagement; and the time he'd kissed her. How much pain and anguish he'd caused, he thought. Yet here she was, grown-up now and beautiful and talking with easy confidence, as though she'd lived in Cawdor Street all her life.

'Do you remember me once saying to you that there would always be—'

'A place in your heart for me,' she interrupted. 'I never forgot that. Yes, we're friends.' Why did she keep saying that word? They were more than 'friends', at least she hoped they were. She had always loved him and he knew it, or had he simply chosen to forget that? The class divide still separated them and she didn't want to continue along this hopeless road. It could lead nowhere.

She changed the subject. 'So, what have you been doing?'

'Working. I wasn't cut out for general practice. I'm a surgeon. An orthopaedic surgeon.'

'What is that exactly?'

'I mend or try to mend the bones that people break or correct the deformities they are born with.'

'Like Jessie? You were good to her.'

'Poor little Jessie. Life hadn't been very good for her, had it?'

'No.' Her gaze strayed to her daughter who was now surrounded by ducks. 'I called Jessica after her.'

'Vi, Vi Rowan is doing very well in Canada. She has a little boy and is pregnant again.' As soon as she'd said it she could have bitten her tongue. 'Oh, I'm sorry. I'm so sorry. I'm a complete fool!'

He shook his head. 'It's all right, Hannah. I've more or less come to terms with it all now, but I know that Siân feels awkward. My brother's wife seems hell bent on producing an heir which of course will put little David at a disadvantage, he not having the name Hughes. I know they all assume that I'll never have—'

'Don't say it!' she interrupted. 'Don't let them feel sorry for you.'

'I don't. But never mind me, what are you doing now?'

She smiled at him. 'Deciding whether or not to go to Canada for a visit or open the first of my new cafés.'

'Indeed? You seem to have a good business head on your shoulders, Hannah.'

'I work hard and anyway I find it better to keep myself occupied. It's all for Jessica, so she will never know the misery that I grew up with.'

They both turned to watch the child.

'She'll break many a heart when she's older, Hannah. You'll be inundated with prospective husbands.'

She laughed. 'Not if I can help it. She'll have a strict upbringing although I have to admit I do sometimes spoil her.'

'And why not? All your life you've struggled and it's only natural that you want the best for her.'

Hannah nodded. 'She . . . she is all I have. The only thing that's precious. All my business ventures could disappear and I really wouldn't care. Not as long as I have her.'

'I know what you mean, Hannah.'

'Do you?' she challenged softly.

He looked thoughtful. 'No, I don't suppose I do. Compared with you I've had everything on a plate and now, well, I . . . I have my work.'

She heard the note of loneliness in his voice.

'All I ever wanted in life was a family. A real family,' she said.

'Didn't you have it for a short time?'

She nodded. 'Yes, but it *was* only for a short while. The good part only lasted a matter of months. I should never have married Alfie, everyone tried to talk me out of it, even Mrs Howard, but I wouldn't listen. I never loved him. I just thought I did.'

'Then why did you marry him?'

She looked up at him and then glanced away. She couldn't tell him. She doubted that she ever would.

416

'Because I wanted to get . . . away. To have more freedom.'

He thought he knew the real reason: she'd married to get away from him. She'd told him she loved him and he realised she'd meant it even though he'd told her it was just infatuation. Because of that she'd married a drunk, a gambler and a wife-beater. Did she still love him? She had never remarried. Had infatuation changed into something more lasting? Something much stronger and deeper? She was a woman now, not an impressionable girl. And when she'd comforted him that evening her tenderness had meant more than all the kind words others had heaped on him.

'I know I've no right to ask, Hannah, but perhaps we could see each other?' he said tentatively.

'See each other?'

'Yes, come here to feed the ducks with Jessica, until she goes to school.'

'I don't bring her down every day.'

'I know that, it's the first time I've seen you both here and I do come often, very early in the morning. Will you come and bring her with you?'

'Yes.'

'Then should we say . . . on Tuesdays?'

She nodded her agreement. She refused to get her hopes up. He thought of her as a friend and probably always would. Once she would have been so excited, ecstatic even, but now . . . now she'd grown up. She still loved him but her love was tempered with a caution born of bitter experience.

'Then I'll see you next week?'

'Next Tuesday then. Jessica, come here. We're going to have to go home now. I've a lot of things to do.' Reluctantly the child joined them.

'This is Mr Richard Hughes. A . . . a friend of mine.'

Richard looked down into the eyes that were just like Hannah's.

'Hello, Jessica. I've made your mother promise to bring you here to feed the ducks every Tuesday until you go to school.'

'Really? Honestly?'

He laughed. 'Really and honestly and I'll bring some bread too.'

The child clasped Hannah's hand and started to skip.

'Jessica, stop that, Mam is too old now to play skipping with you.'

'I don't think "Mam" will ever be old,' Richard said to the child, laughingly. Hannah's heart started to beat in a jerky sort of way.

Hannah told Ada about it when she went down to see her in the afternoon.

'Go, Hannah! Yer go, yer've loved him all yer life. Oh, I know I said it was useless, what with 'im bein' so rich an' all, but now yer've got money of yer own and don't forget yer businesses. I'd say 'e would be gettin' a bargain if—'

'That's just it, Ada. If! If! If!'

'Well, you go just the same. Yer never know.'

Hannah smiled. 'When I first went to work for them, Vi told me about a parlourmaid from a house further down. She'd married one of the sons and there had been such a fuss that they'd emigrated.'

'So? That was then, this is now and yer're not a parlourmaid.'

'No I'm not, but I'm still working class.'

Ada shook her head. 'If the chance arises, Hannah, take it. I know I said in the past to stay well clear but things are different now.'

Hannah smiled at her. 'We'll see!'

Chapter Thirty

The Tuesdays had increased to include Thursdays as well, but still Hannah wouldn't lower her guard to let him see just how much she loved him. And she did. Far more now than she'd ever done. She found he was easy to talk to and he answered all her questions with patience. He also had unlimited time for Jessica and as she watched them together she thought once more what a shame it was that he had no children of his own. He would make a wonderful father.

'Are you still debating what to do in the near future?' he asked one Tuesday towards the end of August.

It wasn't a bit like a summer's day, she'd thought that morning, looking up at the grey sky and watching the bushes in the garden bend before the wind. She'd secured her hat with two hatpins and had made Jessica wear a coat, albeit a lightweight one.

'Yes, and I'll have to make my mind up soon because not only will Jessica be going to school, but Mr Parks, the bank manager, keeps asking me do I want the loan or not.'

'So, what have you decided?' They'd discussed both options frequently – and they'd disagreed. Once they'd even argued over it.

'I keep thinking that it won't be fair to keep Jessica

off school for that length of time when she's only just started and if I went in October or November she'll miss a lot of lessons. But I *do* want to go to see Vi so much.'

'But you'll open your cafés instead, as planned?'

'Yes, I suppose I will, but somehow I don't seem to have as much enthusiasm for it all now. I should be planning, looking for suitable premises, but some- how . . .' She shrugged.

He got to his feet. 'Let's walk for a bit, I've always found that walking helps concentration.' He reached out and took her hand to help her up and she gritted her teeth. Her emotions were getting the better of her again. She knew just why she had so little enthusiasm for her new venture: all her free time was spent thinking about him. She would go over and over in her mind every single thing he said. The way he gently teased her about something he called her 'business acumen'. The way he threw back his head when he laughed. The way he smiled at both herself and Jessica. Was she imagining the particular way he looked at her daughter?

She was surprised when he continued to hold her hand and not even start to walk. She looked up at him almost fearfully. Oh, what was the matter? What was he going to say? That when Jessica went to school there would be no more of these meetings? She couldn't bear to think of being rejected again.

He looked down into the dark depths of her eyes and, as once before, he was mesmerised. He loved her. He'd thought he'd never love again after Maria had died. In fact he'd sworn he never would. But there was something about Hannah that was different. Special. He'd always known it, felt it, and his feelings had grown over the last weeks. But she had given him no sign at all that she considered there to be anything between them except friendship. Perhaps what she'd felt for him had indeed been infatuation, which had died over the years. She seemed content with her life. She'd told him that Jessica was the most precious thing she had. Did she never think about marrying again? Did she not want more children? Marriage for her had been a disaster, so would she reject him? Oh, she'd be as kind and gentle as possible, but would she say 'No' and mean it? There was only one way to find out, yet he was hesitant and nervous. She was strong, she'd fought for everything she had and he admired that, but was she so strong that she now needed no one?

'Hannah, I . . . I'll take you out to Canada,' he said quietly, searching her face for some sign.

She looked puzzled. What did he mean?

'Richard, what are you saying?'

'I'm . . . asking you to . . . marry me, Hannah.'

She swayed and he put his arm around her waist to steady her. He thought she was going to faint, she'd gone so pale.

'Hannah! Are you all right? I'm sorry, it must be a surprise.'

'No, no, I'm fine. I . . . I'm just so confused.'

'I love you, Hannah, I think I always have but other things . . . circumstances . . .' He fell silent as the tears

423

filled her eyes and slid down her cheeks.

He was not to know that they were tears of pure joy. This was what she'd yearned for for so many years: to hear him say the words that she thought he'd never utter. She dashed the tears away with the back of her hand.

'Oh, I'm such a fool.'

'Does that mean . . . no?' He was as tense as the day he'd first walked through the doors of the hospital.

'No! It means I love you. I've never loved anyone but you. I married Alfie on the rebound because . . . because . . .'

He gathered her in his arms and gently kissed her tear-stained cheeks. 'Hannah! Hannah! Will you marry me?'

'Yes. Oh, yes please, Richard!' She closed her eyes as her lips opened beneath his and the world seemed to spin around.

'I'll take you to Canada for our honeymoon,' he promised, gently stroking her cheek with his index finger.

She opened her eyes. It wasn't a dream. 'I don't care where we go, I'll go to hell and back as long as I'm with you.' Her eyes were sparkling as she looked up at him.

'Mam! Mam! Look!' Jessica tugged at her skirt and they drew apart.

'What have you got?' Richard asked her, bending down, intending to tell her the news that she was to have a stepfather.

'It's a bird. A little bird. It was lying on the path.'

Hannah too bent down.

'Let me look at it.' Richard turned the young blackbird in his hand. 'It's just stunned. It's only young, it's probably flown into something.'

Jessica looked up at Hannah with concern. 'Will it die, Mam?'

The words echoed across the years and Hannah was a child again. She was looking into her da's eyes and asking him the same question. She could hear his voice, feel the roughness of his uniform, the gentleness of his hands. She smiled at her daughter and then Richard.

'No, it won't die, Jessica, not this time. We'll take care of it.'

Headline hopes you have enjoyed reading TAKE THESE BROKEN WINGS and invites you to sample the beginning of Lyn Andrews' heart-warming new saga, MY SISTER'S CHILD, out soon in Headline hardback . . .

Chapter One

1909

'Mam! Mam! Come quick! Come *now*!' Tom Ryan's young face was flushed and his breath was coming in short, painful gasps. He caught and held his mother's arm tightly, his fingers pincer-like around the firm, bare flesh below her rolled up sleeves.

'In the name of God what is it?' Molly cried out in pain. 'What's wrong? What's the matter with you?' She prised her arm from her fourteen-year-old son's vice-like grip, anxiety filling her dark brown eyes, the muscles in her stomach contracting with fear. He was in a terrible state. Whatever could have reduced her normally stoic son to a gabbling, shaking wreck?

Tom had regained some of his breath and his face had lost the ruddy flush of exertion and was now unnaturally pale. 'It's what . . . what Da was afraid would happen. Come *on*, Mam,' he pleaded, once more grasping her arm.

Molly suddenly realised what he was talking about and, pushing Tom aside tore off her apron, flinging it across the kitchen table on which the dirty dishes from teatime still remained. She turned distractedly to her daughter.

'Ellen, go up the street and see how many men and lads you can get and then follow us down. Go on, girl, don't stand there with your mouth open like a cod on a fishmonger's slab!' Molly was already reaching for her heavy black shawl but didn't bother to wrap it around her dark, neatly coiled hair as she always did when she went out of the house.

Her daughter stood for a few seconds, totally transfixed and mesmerised by the scene unfolding before her eyes. At sixteen she was taller than her petite mother, her hair was lighter than Molly's, more of a chestnut colour, but she had her father's clear grey eyes which were now wide with fear. What they'd all dreaded seemed now to have happened and she could see all their recently acquired financial security evaporating. These days they had far more than any of their neighbours in Milton Street possessed in the way of money, food, coal and decent clothes, but they'd been just as poor and desperate to keep a roof over their heads until at least six months ago. Now it seemed that their good luck had deserted them and their former misery was about to return. 'One step forward, two steps back,' she muttered before gathering her senses and galvanising herself.

'Mam, shall I go and get the brigade too?'

Molly turned back, her thoughts racing distractedly around in her head. 'No! Get one of the young lads to go, better still, if you or anyone else knows where that young hooligan of a brother of yours is, send him.'

'Our Bernie's at Cooney's. When I ran up the street I saw him swinging on the street lamp with Teddy Cooney outside their house,' Tom supplied, his eyes filled with fear and impatience.

'I'll swing for *him*!' Molly said grimly. 'Ellen go and get him and then for God's sake get on with finding help before your Da loses everything and we all have to go on the parish!'

Ellen needed no second telling. Without even waiting to grab her own shawl, she followed her mother and brother out into the bitterly cold, frosty night. She didn't even pause to watch her mother and brother start to run down the street, instead she went immediately up the steps of number sixteen and hammered on the door until it was opened.

'Is our Bernie here? Is he? It's terrible! Something terrible has happened and we need him, now!'

Gussie Cooney turned and yelled down her dark, damp lobby, 'Bernie Ryan! Yer sister wants yer! Now! Gerrout 'ere!'

Mrs Cooney took in Ellen's white face and fear filled eyes. The girl looked half demented. It had to be something very bad.

'Is it yer Mam, Ellen?'

'No, Mam's all right.'

'Then what's up with yer, luv? Yer look as though yer've seen auld Nick 'imself.'

'Oh, please, please Mrs Cooney, can Mr Cooney and the lads go down to the yard. Our Bernie's got to go and get the brigade and I've got to get as many men as I can to help.'

'Holy Mother of God! Is the yard on fire? Is that why yer need the fire bobbies?' Alarm now replaced curiosity in the older woman's eyes and her hand went to her throat.

Ellen nodded. 'Oh, please hurry them up!' she begged before turning away as her neighbour gave young Bernie a shove and told him to run like hell to the nearest police station. She muttered a sincere prayer that no one would be killed and the damage would be light. She had a lot of reasons to thank Molly Ryan these days, the food on the table and the fire in the range, just to start with.

Ellen went from house to house pleading desperately for help. Soon men and boys were rushing out from the decrepit old houses, some in shirt sleeves, some pulling on greasy, threadbare, often torn jackets. Crisscrossing the street, she finally reached the bottom. Thank God this was the last house, she thought as she hammered with what strength she had left on number thirty-six.

Number thirty-six was the home of John Meakin and his family. The Meakins were not popular. They kept themselves to themselves, John Meakin saw to that. He ruled them all with a rod of iron and Mrs Meakin was terrified of her husband. Ellen had often heard her mam and Mrs Cooney discussing the woman's plight.

When the door was opened by Mr Meakin himself

Ellen instinctively backed down to the second step.

'Oh, Mr Meakin! Please help! Please come quickly, there's a fire at the yard, everyone else is going up there! Look all the men are going.'

John Meakin glanced briefly up the street then turned to stare at her. He was a small, dark wiry man. 'Ferret Face', Tom and Bernie called him and she thought the description fitted him well. But this was hardly the time for such deliberations.

'Then you won't need my help, will you, girl, if half the street's gone already? It's nothing to do with me what goes on at that yard. I've heard it's not up to much anyway. I think he's got a nerve to call it a "business". Now he thinks he's better than anyone else, *all* you Ryans think you're a cut above. I remember a time not long ago when you used to come knocking here in rags, asking to borrow a bit of this, a bit of that, as if we were made of money. "The Cadging Ryans" I used to call you – still do. So clear off and let a decent man have some peace and quiet after a proper day's work.'

The door slammed in Ellen's face, leaving her stunned. Why was he taking that attitude? What he'd said about them having to 'borrow' bits of food was true but he didn't have to be so rude and nasty. It was as if he hated Da, and as far as she knew he had no reason to. She'd only asked for help. Suddenly tired, she leaned against the corner of the soot-encrusted wall of the next house where it joined the narrow alleyway that led into the darkness of Number three

Court. The property there was in an even worse state than the rest of the street. One standpipe and a single deep gutter ran down the middle, always clogged up with rubbish. The two privies that served nearly thirty people stank even in the depths of winter.

She caught her breath and, putting John Meakin's malicious words out of her mind, began to run up the street again. She didn't stop, not even before crossing Marybone, a main road. Then, when she reached Freemason's Row, she saw the flames shooting upwards, piercing the blackness of the night sky and the column of smoke so thick, it was smothering the stars. Thankfully, in the distance, shattering the stillness of the night, she heard the clanging of a bell. At least Bernie had been quick.

'Oh, God! Please don't let it be too late, please don't let *everything* have gone! Please let it only be a small fire.' Her prayer, uttered with her eyes cast to the heavens, was fervent but she knew by the flames and smoke that it wasn't a small blaze. The furious clanging of the bell grew louder and louder and an engine passed her, the men clinging on for dear life, still struggling to button up their jackets.

She broke into a run again and then stopped dead at the corner of Freemason's Row and the wide entry that led off it. She bit into the back of her hand to stifle the scream that rose in her throat. Ahead of her was a scene that filled her with terror. It was like a picture of Hell. Against a lurid background of orange, red and

llow flames, figures, dark and unrecognisable, seemed
flit in and out of the dense clouds of acrid smoke.
ne minute they were visible, the next they'd disap-
ared. Then sheer panic galvanised her. Her da,
r mam, and her brother were somewhere in that
ghtmarish inferno!

'Mam! Mam!' she screamed, pushing her way
rward, tripping over the coiled hoses the firemen
ere rapidly unrolling.

'Don't go any further girl! There's nothing you can
!' one yelled at her, but she ignored him and ran
rward.

The smoke and heat hit her and brought her to a
lt. It scorched the back of her throat, half blinded
r, seared her face and hair, but she stumbled on, her
nd across her nose and mouth, her eyes watering
d smarting. The roar of the flames beat loudly against
r ears, as did the yells and shouts of the fire fighters,
d of the men and boys who were making a chain to
ss buckets of water filled from the standpipe as near
they could get to the fire. Behind them she could
ar the terrified, high-pitched cries of panic-stricken
rses.

She tried again, screaming out for her da, Molly and
ung Tom, but it was useless.

'Get back, girl! Get out of the bloody way!' someone
lled, and she was suddenly lifted off her feet and
ung around. She struggled violently but could do
thing to break the grip of the strong arms that held
r prisoner. Then, despite the cacophony, she heard

the sound, not as loud as any of the others but it m
her renew her struggles. She could hear it. She *coula*
was as if someone was striking an anvil with an i
bar, repeatedly and quickly. She *knew* it was some
trying to break the bolts on the stable door.

'Let me go!' she screamed. 'Let me go! It's my
That noise . . . can't you hear it? He's trying to o
the door!'

The grip didn't loosen. 'I know, luv, but there's
much he can do, the heat will have twisted the me
One of the lads has his hose trained on the door a
your da, but he'd better get out of there soon bef
the roof collapses, it could go any minute!'

She realised he was right. The whole ramshac
building was ablaze, the flames leaping skywards fr
the roof. The horses' screams of terror, almost hum
in their pitch and intensity, became louder as did
sound of the pounding of hooves against wood.

Tears were running unchecked down Ellen's chee
'You've got to go and get him out! Get him out fr
there, please? And my mam, don't forget my mam!'

'God Almighty! Your mam's not in there, luv.'

'Where is she?'

He set her down on her feet. 'At the gate. Look,
of the lads is holding her and your brother. Go on o
to them.'

Before Ellen could move they heard the panels
the heavy wooden door splintering, followed by the
splitting crash as the door fell outwards and downwa
sending a shower of sparks shooting upwards. She

erself being caught up and swung around again as
ae fireman pressed her against the wall, his body
rotecting her. Over his shoulder she saw an enormous
lack shape, eyes rolling white with terror, huge white
athered hooves thundering on the wet cobbles, the
nick black mane on fire. It filled the entire field of her
sion and passed so close she could smell the burning
orsehair. Then a figure, bent double, appeared from
ae wall of smoke and flames, and Ellen recognised her
ather.

'It's Da! It's my da!' she screamed and was instantly
eleased as her protector ran forward and half carried,
alf dragged her father to the gate and away from
anger.

Jack Ryan was in a state of collapse. Heedless of his
wn safety he'd plunged in, desperately trying to save
ae small business in which lay all his dreams. It had
een the means of escaping the grinding poverty of the
ast and making a secure future for his family. It was
l he'd thought about. It was all he'd cared about.

Molly cast off the grip of Tom and Bernie and fell to
er knees beside her husband, not even feeling the
rring of the hard cobbles.

'Jack! Jack! Speak to me for the love of God, Jack?'
Iolly pleaded, placing her arm around his shoulders,
eling the warm, wet charred cloth of his jacket
isintegrating beneath her fingers.

The fireman helped him sit up.

'I'm all right,' he croaked. 'I'll live, Moll, but
verything . . . everything I've worked for . . .' He

couldn't go on. He began to cough and he was shakin

Ellen put her arms around her brothers and dre
them close, they too were shaking and crying and sl
herself was fighting back the tears. Da looked so . . . s
beaten. 'It's all right. Da's not hurt and neither is Man
she comforted, trying to keep her own voice steady.

'What about Eddie?' Tom suddenly asked.

In all the terror and confusion their step-brothe
Eddie had been forgotten, as had Annie, their ste
sister, for Molly was Jack Ryan's second wife.

'I don't know where . . . where he is,' Ellen replie

'Well, he's not where he should be and neither
that little madam. They should be here helping your
and me.' Molly's voice was shrill with fright.

A shot rang out and Jack Ryan covered his face wit
hands that were badly burned.

Molly crossed herself. 'Oh, Holy Mother of Go
the poor beast.' Then she looked up to see a policema
towering above her. Another one was coming over
join him and was holding a revolver. Only the poli
and vets were allowed to put down horses and rab
dogs.

'I'm sorry about that, luv, you've got to be cruel
be kind. It was too badly . . . hurt. In a terrible sta
really. The only thing we could do was put it down b
the other one doesn't seem too bad. In a real state
shock, but gradually calming down. There's a lad wh
is going to lead it away from all the noise and confusio
We'll call an ambulance to take yourself and yo
husband to hospital. Are the kids all right?'

'Yes! But we don't need an ambulance. We're not at bad and I . . . I'll tend to my husband.'

'Well, if you're sure, but I'd get someone to look at ose burns. It'll take a while yet to get that out.' He rked his head towards the fire and the still-burning ildings. 'They'll have to move all the coal bit by bit st to make sure it's not left smouldering, then restack It's bad luck it being a coal yard.'

Jack just nodded. It would probably take the best rt of twenty-four hours to sort out what was left.

Ellen helped her mother to her feet. The crowd was elting away and, as the constable had said, a lad was lping to hold and calm the other shire horse. It was ntinuing to rear and plunge, its eyes wild, there were cks of white foam around its nostrils. Narrowing her es in the dark and the smoke, she realised the lad as Eddie. Ellen glared at him. Trust him, always too ming late to be of any use, and there was no sign at of Annie. She was probably still in town with her ends.

Molly tried to compose herself. 'Let's get you home, ck.' She began examining his injuries as gently as one uld. 'I've got some goose grease, that'll help ease the rns, but we'll get the doctor. You're sure nothing's oken?'

Jack Ryan shook his head slowly. 'Only my heart, oll. Only my heart.'

The Ties That Bind

Lyn Andrews

Tessa O'Leary – the only daughter in a family (fatherless boys, when her mother dies she's he brothers' lifeline to survival. So for Tessa the priva tions of war are just another battle to be fought for young woman who was born fighting . . .

Elizabeth Harrison – oppressed by her shopkeepe mother's snobbish expectations, it seems the comin war offers an escape from her family's emotional tie – but at what cost?

The Ties That Bind – the unputdownable story (two young girls in the slumlands of war-wracke Liverpool, bound together by a friendship that su mounts disaster, poverty and heartbreak . . .

'A great saga' *Woman's Realm*

'A compelling read' *Woman's Own*

'Gutsy . . . a vivid picture of a hard-up, hard-workin community' *Express*

'Spellbinding . . . the Catherine Cookson of Liverpoo *Northern Echo*

0 7472 5808 2

HEADLINE

Angels of Mercy

Lyn Andrews

Blue-eyed, blonde-haired, full of smiles and sweetness, even as babies twins Kate and Evvie Greenway captured the hearts of Liverpool's Scotland Road slumlands. But now they are almost adults the two girls find that being pleasant, popular and blessed with a loving family isn't quite enough. For they've both fallen for men who will break their youthful hearts . . .

But these sorrows are nothing to the tragedies that await them and so many others when the Great War breaks out. Determined to do their part, Kate and Evvie sign up for nursing training and are despatched to the Front, a terrible world far from the life-affirming energy of their homes. Can anything, hope, love or the bond that has always united the sisters, survive all that lies in store for them?

An unforgettably moving triumph from a masterful storyteller . . .

'A vivid portrayal of life' *Best*

'Gutsy . . . Andrews paints a vivid picture of a hard-up, hard-working community . . . will keep the pages turning' *Express*

'Lyn Andrews presents her readers with more than just another saga . . . She has a realism that is almost palpable' *Liverpool Echo*

0 7472 5807 4

HEADLINE